The
NERO
DECREE

GREGORY LEE

The NERO DECREE

THOMAS & MERCER

Printed in the United States of America.

Published by Thomas & Mercer, Seattle
www.apub.com

ISBN-13: 9781477808719
ISBN-10: 147780871X
Library of Congress Control Number: 2013906100

For my girls.

Prologue

NUREMBERG TRIAL
JUNE 20, 1946

Testimony of Albert Speer, the former Reich minister of armaments, when questioned by his lawyer, Hans Flächsner:

Flächsner: Herr Speer, were orders given to destroy industry in Belgium, Holland, and France?

Speer: Yes . . . Hitler had ordered [at the beginning of July 1944] a far-reaching system of destruction of war industries in all these countries. . . . Army Command West was responsible for carrying out these orders. . . . I informed [the commanding general] that, as far as I was concerned, this destruction was senseless . . . and that I, in my capacity as armaments minister, did not consider [it] necessary. Thereupon no order to destroy these installations was given. By this, of course, I made myself responsible to Hitler for the fact that no destruction took place.

Flächsner: With regard to the other occupied countries . . . did you use your influence to prevent destruction?

Speer: From August 1944, in the industrial installations in the Government General, the ore mines in the Balkans, the nickel works in Finland; from September 1944, industrial installations in northern Italy; beginning in February 1944, the oil fields in Hungary and industries in Czechoslovakia.

Flächsner: At the beginning of September 1944 when enemy troops approached the German boundaries from all sides, what were Hitler's intentions . . . for the preservation of the means of existence for the . . . population?

Speer: He had absolutely no [such] intention. On the contrary, he ordered the "scorched-earth" policy with special application to Germany. . . .

1

CHARLOTTENBURG, BERLIN
JUNE 1934

The metronome that rested on the piano always made Thomas think of his father, Nicolas. When Thomas was a boy, Nicolas would reach over to the small wooden box with a curved top and pull the metal arm from the catch before releasing it on its short journeys from one pole to another. Thomas had not used the metronome for years—he was an accomplished pianist now—but he liked the idea of its reliability.

"So, Thomas," Nicolas said to his son with a half smile as he passed from the kitchen into the parlor. He pulled at one end of his thick mustache, which curled upward. "What are we to have?"

"What would you like, Father?"

It was a game they played, a ritual that offered familiarity and comfort when so much about them was changing. Nicolas settled into his high-backed chair, his slender hands resting on its worn arms.

"Oh, I don't know," he said after a while. "You're eighteen now, old enough to know your own mind. Why don't you choose something?"

Thomas smiled. Usually if Nicolas came into the parlor to listen to him practicing, then he wanted to hear Bach. Thomas thought for a moment, his eyes casting outside the high windows that he had cleaned that morning. Outside, an aging gray mare, its mane matted and grisly, was pulling a coal cart. A flatbed truck with wooden sidings pulled up behind the cart and the driver honked his horn. When the truck was eventually able to pull past, the two men in Party uniforms in the front shouted and made gestures at the man in the cart, who sat holding leather reins. He turned his tired face the other way, as if he hadn't heard them.

Thomas moved his hands to the piano keys, rested them momentarily, and then began to play. The music flowing through him was familiar and golden, pulling him onward. He had no choice but to follow it. He watched, examining his father, as Nicolas lowered his head to concentrate. There were deep lines on his face now and a stooping manner of a man in decline.

Thomas knew that his father had watched as members of his history department—mainly those who were unwilling to teach a revised version of the subject or had "un-German" political beliefs—had been taken away. The prison on Prinz-Albrecht-Straße was full, so some were incarcerated in the old military prison in Tempelhof, which was now run by the Gestapo. Thomas had passed by this place, Columbia-Haus—which was near the barracks—on his bicycle only last week. Slowing to examine its mean stone walls on Friesenstraße, he had experienced an involuntary shudder: It was said that the place possessed dungeons and 156 cells in which there were hundreds of prisoners. Most were on their way to the new camp in Oranienburg, near the Hohenzollern Canal, where an old factory had been repurposed.

Thomas had tried to put it out of his mind and had headed onward to the swimming pool, where he had competed in the youth games, winning the hundred-meter butterfly as he always did. On his way out, as he squeezed through the bronzed and uniformed teenagers who smelled of chlorine, a tanned girl with tight blond plaits had smiled at him in a shy way that was, he thought, an invitation of a sort. He had seen the badge of the Bund Deutscher Mädel—the League of German Girls—on her shirt. It made him wonder what was really in her heart. He had arrived late and left early, slipping away before the parade with its triangular flags, songs, and spontaneous cheers for the Führer.

Thomas had been playing the piano for perhaps five minutes when the banging started. He heard a thump on the ceiling above them, as if a large object had been dropped. A few minutes later there was a thudding of footsteps. Thomas continued to play and looked over at his father. Nicolas's face was creased with effort, the lines around his eyes and mouth betraying tension as he tried to focus on the music.

Slam!

A door upstairs crashed into its frame.

Bang! Bang! Bang! Bang!

The noise of boots on the staircase blotted out all trace of the music. Nicolas could no longer make a pretense of listening—he slammed his pipe down, spilling its contents onto the crocheted cover of a side table.

Bang! Bang! Bang! Bang!

The noise was heading toward them now, down the creaking staircase. It sounded like someone was rolling a boulder that was hitting every step on its way down. Nicolas hauled himself from his chair. His back stooped, he walked toward the hallway, his footsteps uneven and shallow. Thomas stopped playing. His father was in the hallway. No one was listening to him now.

"Dieter!" Nicolas shouted to his stepson. "What on earth are you doing?"

"I have a meeting to attend," Dieter said. His voice was low and confident. The noisy provocation was now matched by undisguised insolence. Dieter no longer used a deferential tone toward Nicolas. His manner was one of barely concealed contempt.

"Look at yourself, Dieter. What do you think you look like?"

"Like a patriot, of course."

Nicolas didn't answer.

As he approached the hallway, Thomas watched his father's liver-spotted hand reach out and clasp the doorframe to steady himself. The sinews were raised, pressed hard against the skin.

"Ah, of course," Dieter continued. "I forgot that you might not recognize a uniform, seeing as you've never worn one. Two million Germans died on the western front, including my father, but you never managed to take up arms to defend our country."

Thomas turned the corner into the hallway and laid eyes on his half brother. Dieter was heavyset, awkward, and pallid. The uniform offered Dieter poise, as if it organized a body that was inherently muddled. He had never been particularly academic or athletic, but there was a raw energy to Dieter, an unapologetic aggression that had made Thomas wary of him. His friends' big brothers would playfight with them, holding back from using the full extent of their force, but Dieter would never pull his punches. If Thomas found himself in a physical confrontation with his half brother, he knew that there would be no restrictions to the elder's behavior.

Which is why it was no surprise to Thomas to see his half brother standing in the hallway in the brown shirt and office jacket of an *Oberscharführer* in the *Sturmabteilung,* the Nazis' paramilitary thugs. This was a uniform of a brawler, a playground bully, a willing facilitator. Thomas could smell the polish on Dieter's boots, could see the slight bulge of his belly above his belt and the blue diamond insignia denoting rank on his collar. The brown strap on his kepi bit into the fat beneath his chin, which was raw and freshly shaved. Thomas had learned that the color on the top of the kepi signified the wearer's *Gruppe:* Dieter's was black, denoting his allegiance to Berlin-Brandenburg. Thomas had seen them in the streets, waving flags, smashing windows, sticking their boots in innocents' groins.

He thought: If the SA didn't exist, then Dieter would have willed it into being.

"Dieter, I implore you," Nicolas said. "I know that you have friends in this . . . this . . . organization, but you need to think about what you're doing. The consequences. The future. Your responsibilities."

"You're right," Dieter said, exhaling. "That is *exactly* what I am doing."

"No good will come of this folly," Nicolas replied.

Dieter raised his chin defiantly. There was something more than fire in his eyes, Thomas thought. He had seen it in a priest before: devoutness.

"Please, Father," Thomas said, taking Nicolas's arm. He could see that his father was trembling. He had never been a strong man; his absence from the Great War was due to chronic asthma, a condition that had caused him to retire to his books, to study Greek and Latin. A diktat had recently been handed down that his course was to be given a Germanic slant—now the warriors of Greece were ancestors of the Aryan race. Nicolas had yet to agree to teach it.

The old man shook Thomas's hand away.

"You and your friends can march all you like," Nicolas said, "and yes, you can torment decent people"—he jabbed a bony finger at Dieter—"but we know that, at heart, you are weak unless you are in your destructive herd."

Dieter set his jaw hard, his eyes dead as he stared at his stepfather.

"You call eighty thousand Party members at the Lustgarten a herd?" Dieter clapped his right hand on the red armband on his left arm. "You know, sometimes, old man, I wonder where your loyalties lie. Remember, we are on the watch for defeatists and traitors."

Nicolas ignored the comment. Instead he grasped his step-son's upper arm.

"Don't go, Dieter," he said. The anger that had risen in him moments before had subsided. This was a request from the heart. Dieter turned away briefly before returning his eyes to his stepfather. His gaze was unwavering.

"I have to," he said. "My unit is waiting for me." Dieter opened the door. Outside three of his uniformed friends were standing in the street, their bodies angular and tense. They peered into the hallway.

"Damn your unit!" Nicolas shouted. Dieter glanced from the members of the SA outside—one of them was not much older than Thomas—back to his stepfather, who was breathing heavily.

"No, Nicolas," he said eventually. "You are the one who is damned."

Dieter slammed the thick wooden door behind him. His boots clattered on the steps outside. Thomas heard his half brother giving what they called the "German greeting" to the men outside. Nicolas shuffled back into the parlor. Thomas went to the kitchen to make some coffee, which his father liked to drink before bed to prevent him from falling asleep while reading.

He came back into the parlor to discover that his father had poured them both a large glass of whisky—a drink Nicolas had developed a taste for when teaching at the University of Edinburgh.

"*Auf uns*," his father said: to us. Thomas walked over and knocked his glass against his father's.

"Shall I play again, Father?"

"Not tonight," Nicolas said. "Tonight we shall talk, Thomas. . . ."

His voice was dry, cracked. Thomas straightened his back—his father had never spoken to him like this before—and put his index finger to his lips. Talking frankly was dangerous: The walls of the house were not impervious to voices, and the Gestapo relied on denunciation to maintain an undercurrent of continual surveillance. Who knew who was listening and what trouble it might bring them? Thomas pulled an ottoman next to his father's chair.

"This is the beginning, Thomas, make no mistake," Nicolas said, his voice quiet now. "Darkness is descending."

"Hush, Papa," Thomas said. "Don't upset yourself."

"I am sorry to have brought you into such a time," Nicolas sighed.

"It will be all right," Thomas said, immediately regretting the banal sentiment. It wasn't going to be okay. Yesterday he had seen a worker whitewashing a curb. Thomas had asked the man what he was doing, and the man, a Pole, explained that it was preparation for an air-raid blackout exercise. *Why?* Thomas had asked. The man had shrugged. None of his business—he was just doing his job. And Thomas realized—right there, right then, standing on that street corner in Prenzlauer Berg—that these men, they wanted a war. They were *willing* it to happen.

Nicolas got up and poured himself another measure. On his way back to his seat he paused by his battered, ancient Seidel und Naumann typewriter and ran his hands over the keys fondly.

"What a mess . . . what a mess . . . ," Nicolas said. "You know, I miss your mother so very much."

Thomas had never met his mother, Hannah. He knew nothing about her or her family other than that she had died while bringing him into the world. There was one photo of her on the dresser, a portrait taken in 1910 when she was in her early twenties: a young woman with a small, mischievous smile; quick, intelligent eyes; and thick black hair pulled back and arranged in a bun. The thought of this woman bleeding to death in a delivery room was the reason Thomas had long nurtured a desire to make a career in medicine.

"She was a strong woman," Nicolas said. "She dealt with a lot from her previous husband, Wilhelm."

"He died in the Great War, didn't he, Father?"

"During the war, yes . . . ," Nicolas said, his voice trailing off.

"I wish I had met her," Thomas said.

"You must not feel any sadness about your mother," Nicolas said sternly. "She would not have wanted that. I know that she would willingly have given her life to make sure that you arrived among us. That was the kind of person she was. I have never met anyone like her."

Thomas finished his drink, despite his distaste for scotch.

"I am sorry, Thomas," Nicolas said. "I know that it must be hard for you to think about your mother."

"It is," Thomas said. "I can only imagine her from what you tell me."

"No, no . . . ," Nicolas replied. "You need not only imagine. You can feel her, no? In your veins. Her blood running through your heart. That is her legacy, Thomas. I can see her in you, even now."

The two of them brought their glasses together again.

"Now, Thomas," Nicolas said. "Now that we are talking like men, it is a good time for me to tell you something important."

"Yes, Father," said Thomas, watching as his father got up again. Tonight he was like a young man at a dance, unable to contain himself and desperate to do what he needed to do before the evening passed.

Nicolas walked to the fireplace, then reached up and pulled a brick from inside the chimney. He felt inside a hole, retrieved something, and held it up for his son's inspection. Thomas looked carefully and recognized a key about the length of his father's thumb. At one end of the shaft was a loop of metal, presumably so that it could be strung on a belt or chain. Nicolas approached his son and handed him the key ceremonially. His face had lost the false bonhomie of the whisky; it betrayed only resolution.

"It's time that I gave you this," Nicolas said. He didn't return to his seat but instead crouched down on one knee to address his son. Thomas cupped his hands and held the key as if he had scooped water from a stream.

"You know the Danat-Bank on Behrenstraße, on the corner of Glinkastraße?" Nicolas asked. Thomas nodded. He and his father had been there together when he was younger. It was a grand place with marble floors and long wooden counters where bespectacled men and starchy women would count money and conduct transactions in hushed tones. He liked being taken there: It was as if his father was sharing some of the secrets of adulthood with him.

"If you go downstairs there is a room where they store people's valuables," Nicolas continued. "I have a box down there that contains something important to me. Something important for us. We must do everything we can to keep it from these people that surround us now. I fear for my future, Thomas, so I pass this key to you, my son."

"But, Father," Thomas interrupted, breaking the solemnity of the moment. "Time will pass; things will change. We just need to keep our spirits up and our heads down, you'll see."

Nicolas shook his head gravely. He pulled himself up to sit beside Thomas, and leaned in to his son.

"I admire your optimism, Thomas," he whispered. "But for now, this key is yours, yours to protect. We have no other choice." Nicolas sighed. "I do not mean to burden you—you have been everything a father might want from a son—but I need to pass this on to you in case . . ."

Nicolas did not finish the sentence.

"The box number is 1518. Do you understand the significance?" Nicolas raised his eyebrows to show that he was waiting for a response.

Thomas nodded. It was Dieter's year of birth followed by his own.

"What's inside the box is crucial for your future, for the man you will be once we are through this terrible mess."

"I understand, Father." Thomas clasped the key momentarily before slipping it inside his jacket pocket.

Nicolas leaned forward and hissed urgently, glancing toward the front door as if time were running out. "There is one other thing, Thomas." Nicolas bared his yellowing teeth. "You must never, ever, tell Dieter. If you do, what's in there will be lost forever. Dieter must be kept away from that box at all costs. It will be dangerous for all of us—especially you—if he finds it. Do you promise me?"

Thomas nodded. He knew they lived in dangerous times, but was his father exaggerating the degree of peril?

"Promise me this," Nicolas pressed him.

"I promise you, Father," Thomas said.

"Good," Nicolas said, standing up. It was clear the conversation was over.

"Good night, Father," Thomas said, rising. "I hope you manage to rest."

"You too," Nicolas said. Then, as Thomas turned to leave the room, he grasped his son's arm briefly. "I'm sorry, Thomas, truly I am," he said. "One so young as you should not face such dark times."

Thomas looked at Nicolas and saw his father as he had pretended not to see him over recent months: sick, worn-out, scared.

"Good night, Father," he said, and walked upstairs to his bedroom.

Thomas struggled with raised voices in his dreams—two men shouting at each other in the night.

He turned over and the noise continued, the protagonists ever more voluble and quarrelsome. Then he realized: These weren't voices of an uneasy dream; this was his father and Dieter, angry and set against each other as he had never heard them before.

Thomas rolled out of bed and walked out onto the landing, his feet warm against the floorboards. He crept down the stairs until he could see his father and his half brother, who were squared up to each other in the living room. While Dieter might have been smaller than Nicolas, he stood tall, his chest much wider than his stepfather's. Nicolas's face was purple with exertion; his hair hung loosely over his face.

"Look at you," Nicolas said. "You're nothing but a thug. I can only imagine what your mother would have thought."

"And I can only imagine what was going through her head when she married you," Dieter said. "A weak, old coward who spends his days reading dusty books."

"Books I imagine you and your type would like to burn," Nicolas said. "'Action Against the Un-German Spirit' indeed." His voice rose. "God give me strength to face down such foolishness!"

"Be very careful," Dieter said. It was the first time he had lowered his voice. His tone scared Thomas more than the shouting. "I am running out of patience with you."

"*You're* running out of patience?" Nicolas said. "I think that we are in agreement on something at last—you must leave this house tonight, Dieter. I no longer want you living under this roof. Out!"

Nicolas moved to usher Dieter from the room. Dieter looked at Nicolas for a moment and began walking very slowly toward the doorway, a thin smile on his lips.

"You think that you can give me orders? You think that you and your type—intellectuals, the metropolitan elite—are still in charge?" Dieter said. There was a spiteful carelessness to his words. The confrontation had built momentum and, instead of waning, it had spun out of control.

Thomas felt the ground beneath him shift—there was no way back now.

"I order you out of my house!" shouted Nicolas, following Dieter to the hallway, where he flung open the front door. By this time Thomas was in the hallway too. He saw that Dieter was absently rubbing his fists as he stood before his stepfather. His knuckles were raw. Thomas noticed the smell of smoke coming from his half brother's clothes, which were streaked with soot.

"So the weakling's spawn emerges from his crib," Dieter said, examining Thomas with a derisory glare. "I notice that you haven't been attending youth group meetings. Perhaps the influence of your father has proved decisive. The apple doesn't fall too far from the tree, after all."

Thomas peered outside. Dieter's SA friends were waiting for him by a truck. They were looking into the house expectantly, as if deciding whether to move from being observers to participants.

"It's time that you met some of the people who you have been slandering with your weasel words," Dieter said. He pushed his father toward the door. Thomas watched as two of the SA men perked up, watching Nicolas grasping the doorframe.

"Stop this!" Nicolas ordered. With his bruised hands, Dieter shoved his stepfather forward until he teetered at the top of the short stoop down to the street. At the bottom of the steps the SA men waited for the old man to tumble. Dieter stepped toward Nicolas and shoved him down the stairs. Nicolas's arms flailed as he grabbed hold of one of the handrails on his way down: There was a hollow ring from one of the metal stanchions as Nicolas's knees crashed into it.

The SA men gathered around the sprawling figure as he moaned in pain on the pavement. He was doubled up, howling quietly to himself.

"Dieter!" Thomas shouted. "Please! What are you doing?"

Dieter, his face softened by the gaslight from the street lamps, looked up at his half brother, who stood in the doorway.

"It's only what I have to do," Dieter said.

Thomas looked at his father, his body hanging weakly between the thick uniformed arms of Dieter's collaborators.

"Don't, Dieter," Thomas said. "I beg you."

Nicolas raised his head to Thomas. Drops of blood from a gash above his eye were staining the front of his shirt. He stared weakly at his son. The boy was all he had and his view was dimming. Then, from deep within, as if summoning the last essence of himself: "Thomas."

Nicolas raised his hand and reached toward him.

"Help me, son. . . ."

Thomas stepped toward his father. As he did so another two SA men emerged from the shadows. Dieter commanded them to wait.

"Go ahead," he goaded Thomas.

Thomas looked at Nicolas, but remained still.

"Can you hear me?" Dieter asked his half brother, before pushing him backward. Thomas stared blankly down at his father, petrified by what he was witnessing.

"Still nothing?" Dieter demanded.

Thomas hung back. He felt like his body had shut down, as if he were not even there but rather floating above the scene, a numb observer.

"I thought not," Dieter said. "You're weak just like your father."

Nicolas was dragged, moaning, onto the back of the truck, the SA accomplices laughing and joking as they dumped their human cargo onto the wooden struts in the bed of the vehicle.

Dieter stepped closer to his half brother, his gaze level and all-consuming. Thomas saw Dieter's arm cock, and readied himself for a blow. Instead, his half brother clapped him on the shoulder, as if sharing a joke. Then he leaned in close, his teeth bared and his lips tensed.

"You can't even save what you love most," he said. He raised his palm and patted Thomas on the cheek. Thomas could smell the nicotine on his fingers. "Remember: You are either with us, or you are against us, *brother*."

Dieter walked to the side of the truck and grabbed a handrail before slapping the side of the vehicle. As the truck began to peel away from the curb, Dieter shouted, "Do not make the same mistake as your father."

Thomas breathed in the diesel fumes as the vehicle sped away. He waited for a few moments until he could no longer hear the engine in the still of the night.

Thomas walked up the steps into the house alone.

The next day, Thomas rose and went to school for the last time. As the other pupils celebrated the end of their schooling and discussed their summer plans, Thomas barely registered the occasion, skipping the celebrations when the bell rang after the final lesson. He wandered home through the quiet streets until he arrived at his house. It was the only place he had ever lived: a Wilhelmine single-family home in a neighborhood of doctors, academics, and accountants. He gazed at the wooden front door with its etched-glass panels. He was sure that he had closed it this morning when he had left, but it was now slightly ajar. He pushed it open and walked inside. They had been robbed: The parlor had been turned upside down. Books and papers were scattered everywhere, drawers had been pulled out, and furniture overturned. Even the pictures had been taken from the walls, and their backs slashed open.

Thomas surveyed the scene of devastation. Suddenly he heard footsteps upstairs. There was a familiarity to the sound. He recognized the sound of those boots: It was Dieter.

Thomas edged slowly up the stairs to his father's bedroom. Through the crack in the door he could make out his half brother, agitated and exasperated, systematically pulling apart the room. Thomas pushed the door. Its creaking made his half brother look up, as if he were in danger. Dieter was red-faced and wild-eyed; the parts of his hair that met his face were soaked with sweat. He had not undressed from the night before—his uniform was soiled and disheveled. Dieter launched himself across the room at Thomas and grasped his shoulders.

"Where is it?" he demanded.

Thomas looked at him, dumbstruck. So much had happened in the past few hours, and now he was being asked a question about which he knew nothing.

"Don't you try and play dumb with me," Dieter said, shaking his half brother.

"What are you doing, Dieter?" Thomas asked. "Where is Father?"

Dieter wiped the sweat below his nose with the sleeve of his shirt.

"Father? Father? My father is long gone."

"You know who I mean—my father."

"Oh, you mean the traitor Nicolas Meier? At this moment he is at Prinz-Albrecht-Straße, but I don't think that he will be there long."

Thomas swallowed hard. The name of the Gestapo headquarters evoked terror.

"So he will be home soon?"

Dieter gave Thomas a look of disbelief. Did the boy not understand what had happened to Nicolas? Did he not know that the next stop for people who had been apprehended by the security services was a stay at Oranienburg, a new kind of camp where the enemies of National Socialism would be reeducated? Was Thomas demonstrating denial or stupidity?

"Forget your father, Thomas, forget him. Thinking that way will do you no good."

Dieter released his half brother.

"It's you and me now, *Bruder*. Just you and me."

"But what about father?"

Dieter shook his head.

"Dieter, I don't understand," Thomas said. He was tired. Confused. His half brother's mania wasn't unusual, but he was more used to it being directed toward his father. He sensed that something even more awful than the violence of last night had happened, but he wasn't able to fathom it.

"You really don't understand?" Dieter said slowly. "Come on." He led Thomas downstairs and into the parlor. As they entered the room, small white feathers spun up into the air.

"Show me where it is and it won't be so bad for you," Dieter said.

Thomas examined Dieter. Whatever he believed, he believed profoundly. This wasn't a game: Whatever it was that Dieter thought Thomas possessed, he was convinced of it.

"I am tired of this now, Thomas," Dieter said, an irritated calmness in his voice. It was as if he were trying to hold back every part of his body so as not to lose his mind.

Thomas's expression remained impassive.

"Tell me. Now."

Thomas looked back at Dieter. There was nothing in his eyes to betray his knowledge.

"Where is the key?" Dieter snapped.

Of course. The key.

"Everyone knows that Father had a safety deposit box in which he stored his valuables. I heard him talking about it many times. I know you accompanied him to the bank when you were little."

"What's in it?" Thomas asked.

"Riches," Dieter said. "Money, jewels, gold . . . who knows?"

Thomas nodded.

"I think you're playing a clever game: You ask questions and keep me talking while planning to steal it all for yourself."

"I'm not going to take anything," Thomas replied.

"You lie," Dieter said, moving toward Thomas, his body stiff, uncompromising. His arm was extended in front of him, and he pushed his half brother until Thomas backed into the wall. There was nowhere to go.

"You and him were thick as thieves," Dieter spat. "A proper couple of old women in each other's business. Don't pretend he didn't give you a nod and a wink. I know that you know where it is."

Dieter began reaching inside Thomas's pockets, turning each inside out before pulling his half brother's jacket from him and searching the lining.

"I know you have it, Thomas, I know you do."

"Dieter, I have no idea what you're talking about," Thomas said. It was the first time that he had lied, but his father's instructions had given him courage. He had failed his father the night before; he would not fail him again by giving up the key.

Dieter gritted his teeth and put his right hand across his half brother's throat. "I swear that I will not hesitate to finish you."

Dieter let his hand drop. He looked around the messy room. Thomas reached up and rubbed his throat where Dieter had left thick welts that matched the width of his fingers.

"There *must* be another way," said Dieter angrily. "I will go to the bank and explain to them that the holder of the key is incapacitated. There will be a master key that will allow us access. Which bank did you go to with your father?"

"I can't remember," Thomas said. "I was very young. I—"

Dieter stepped forward, grabbed Thomas's hair, and banged his head against the wall.

"Danat-Bank," Thomas said timidly. "The one at Schinkelplatz."

Dieter nodded, satisfied and unsuspecting of the lie— Thomas had only ever accompanied his father to the branch on Behrenstraße.

"While I'm out, you must hunt for the key," he instructed. "Every cushion, every picture frame, every cupboard must be thoroughly searched. You hear me? And for your sake, I hope that you find it."

Dieter's meaning was clear: At his whim, Thomas would follow his father onto the back of an SA truck.

"I'll start looking now," said Thomas, starting to lever up a floorboard as his half brother stomped from the house. But, when he was sure Dieter was gone, Thomas stood up and looked around the parlor. He didn't recognize it. The world that he had known had shifted, distorted into grotesque shapes, as if by a fairground mirror. This wasn't his home any longer.

He went upstairs and pulled his father's worn leather suitcase from under the metal-framed bed and took it to his room. There he neatly folded his clothes and laid them inside the case, then took it downstairs and left it by the front door. He found the portrait of his mother and one of his father amid the debris in the parlor and placed them inside the winter coat he had packed to protect the glass. He looked around the room. There, in the corner by the window, was the piano. He walked over and began to play. Bach: the *Goldberg Variations*. When he had finished, he folded down the cover to protect the keys, picked up the suitcase, and closed the front door behind him.

He would never return.

2

JUST WEST OF THE RIVER ODER, BRANDENBURG
MARCH 31, 1945

The two stick-thin, scabrous men carrying the wounded soldier on the stretcher muttered to each other in Russian. Doctor Johann Schultz assumed the prisoners, who were forced laborers, hadn't eaten for several days. That wouldn't make them that different from him, or from any of the other staff at the field hospital. The Soviet cadavers delivered their cargo to the trauma room and limped out, bedraggled and infested. Johann examined the patient lying motionless on the oilskin before him and tried to assess whether he was able to do anything for the man. He blinked several times as if trying to alert his eyes that they were required to function: He was almost seeing double with tiredness.

The man was in his midforties. About a decade and a half older than Johann. The patient was typical of those he was treating now: mostly old men, young boys, and grizzled veterans of the eastern front who had somehow managed to survive long enough for this, the endgame. They marched on, and fought on under pain of death, but none of them was under any illusions: They were playing out the finale. The war was over, and all they could hope was that they might survive the coming offensive from the east. The whispers of intelligence floating around the front were that the Soviets were preparing a final, devastating attack. There were, literally, millions of battle-hardened Ivans waiting for orders to advance.

Word was that some German units had had white handkerchiefs confiscated from them to prevent surrender. They peered through the mist knowing that the Bolshevik tempest would hit them soon. Perhaps within days. The Soviets were waiting for the first real signs of spring to move their ragtag might forward. Resistance in Poland and West Prussia had been smashed, troops and civilians alike murdered, mutilated, and raped. It was to be expected. When the Wehrmacht had moved east nearly four years before it had been equally unforgiving.

So this is what it had come to: Johann attempting to save the life of a malnourished, exhausted *Unteroffizier* of the Eleventh Army, who appeared to have scurvy. As the orderlies cut through the corporal's uniform they could see the lice scurrying from the light, searching for a warm host. Johann examined the wound. A single shot. Most likely a sniper: There was little combat underway. The man moaned. Johann hoped he wouldn't lapse back into consciousness: He would then have to use some of his precious supplies of tranquilizers. They had received some from Berlin last week, but had been told not to expect any more.

Johann tried to remember what time of day it was and realized that he didn't know whether it was night or day. Few of the medical staff could remember days of the week any longer, but not knowing whether it was night or day outside the fetid, stinking canvas shelter that served as the triage unit was another tangled level of disorientation. All of the doctors were like Johann, men who had been taken from the hospitals and surgeries throughout the Reich and asked to patch up the bodies of those who remained to fight; specially detailed officers prowled the unit, searching for men who could be ordered back to the front. The women—both nurses and doctors—had all been evacuated, many to Berlin to remove them from the immediate clutches of the Red Army, just as they had been at Stalingrad. There was plenty to do in the city as the RAF and USAF continued to unload their terrible cargoes almost completely unchallenged.

The man moaned again.

"Hold his shoulders," Johann instructed an orderly. "Press down." The drab light was so weak that he often relied on his sense of touch and his instincts in order to work. He knew, of course, that the exercise was as futile as the presence of the Ninth Army—strengthened the previous summer by units redeployed from Italy—across the river from the Soviets: It was likely that the soldier's wounds were already teeming with bacteria. Even if they weren't, the chances of his surviving the poorly equipped, infection-rich field hospital were slim.

He put his hands on the left side of the soldier's stomach and felt just below the ribcage. It was rigid, filled with blood hemorrhaging from the spleen. He could attempt a splenectomy—he had done it before in the field, sometimes without anesthetic—but the man had lost too much blood. He couldn't conduct a transfusion because he had no plasma.

"Make him comfortable," Johann said to the orderly, who knew what this meant: They would leave him on a canvas cot, which was probably still warm from its previous occupant, until he died. Until recently Johann had been able to ship most of the wounded back to hospitals behind the lines, but the system had collapsed over the past few weeks. If the soldier was lucky, he wouldn't regain consciousness.

The orderlies shuffled away with the corporal, and Johann decided it was time to discover what time it was. He pushed a canvas flap aside and stepped outside into early-morning mist. He couldn't see more than twenty yards in front of him. In the gloom he could make out silhouettes of people moving in the distance.

Voices—flat, muted by the heavy air—rang out occasionally. He rolled a thin cigarette and lit it, feeling the stubble on his chin as the back of his hand brushed against it.

At that moment Kommandant Henke, the commanding officer, appeared around the corner, a steaming mug of ersatz coffee in his hand. Johann saluted.

"Ah, Johann," he said. "Morning. How are you?"

Johann started to speak, but Henke, who was small with a shaved head and deep olive skin, raised his hand.

"Apologies, stupid question," he said. Henke stared into the distance and took a sip of his drink. "They'll be here soon." He started on his way before halting and swiveling around.

"Look, I probably shouldn't tell you this, but I got a communiqué asking that you attend some ceremony in Berlin later this week. Some nonsense from the propaganda ministry. Even now Goebbels likes to hand out his medals. They want to give you one."

Johann saw Henke flick his eyes to the floor. He looked back up at Johann. "I know you'd like to go—your family are still there, aren't they? But I can't afford to lose you. Not now," he said. "I'm sorry, I really am."

Johann nodded. He felt his bottom lip stiffen, an unconscious expression of anger. He wished that Henke had never told him. Being so close to returning to Berlin was more painful than filing away his yearning, boxing it up and placing it, undisturbed, in a far corner of his mind.

When Henke had gone, Johann punched the air angrily before throwing up the canvas entrance to triage and marching in. It crossed his mind that, if he had gone to the ceremony, he would not have come back.

But here he was in what passed for an operating theater full of people waiting for his orders. *Back to work*, he thought to himself. *Blot it all out.*

✹

The patient was freezing: He had clearly been outside for most of the night. His face was completely white from shock—circulatory, not nervous. The man's leg was smashed. There would be bone fragments throughout the wound. The only way to save his life was a transtibial—below the knee—amputation.

"Do we know what happened?" Johann asked, rubbing his hands with alcohol as an orderly tied the strings of his apron.

"The poor bastard had his leg run over by a cart drawn by a horse," the orderly said, chuckling. Johann raised his eyebrows in surprise. He couldn't believe that the horse hadn't been eaten already. He started to salivate at the very thought of meat—rich, fatty, delicious meat.

He thought about the meal that his wife, Anja, and he had had before he left for the war: the most delicious roast goose, potato dumplings, and red cabbage that he had ever eaten. He wondered if anyone ate like that any longer, beyond the Party grandees. He worried for Anja—there had been no mail for three weeks. The explosives that rained death from the sky were terrifying enough, but how was she living even if she survived the bombing? There was surely very little food in the city now.

The world had turned upside down in seven short years. The two of them had been a young, hopeful couple back in thirty-eight. They had met through a friend of Anja's who worked at Charité Hospital, where Johann was interning. Two months later he had taken her boating on Lake Müggelsee and produced a small box with a ring that he had used the last of his modest savings to buy. The bank employee on Leipziger Straße had looked at him sternly as he passed the money across the counter, as if Johann were doing something frivolous and unfathomable.

They had married quickly, a small ceremony in Mannheim, where Anja had grown up. Johann had no relatives and Anja's parents were both dead, so the wedding party consisted of her sister and her family and a few friends. There had been dancing late into the night. Johann continued to build his reputation and Anja was promoted to a senior teaching position at a school in Schöneberg, a few stops on the S-Bahn from where they lived. They had wanted a family so badly, had never imagined the possibility of *not* being parents, but after a couple of years of trying had been informed by a pompous doctor near Potsdamer Platz that it wouldn't be possible. The way that the man had informed them was meant to convey to Anja that she had not only failed to fulfill a biological imperative: She was letting the nation down. It was a woman's duty to deliver babies for the Führer. If she failed in this responsibility was she any use to the Party at all?

By the beginning of the war, however, Johann and Anja found themselves looking after—and loving—a child. It wasn't in the circumstances that they had hoped. Anja's sister and her husband had been arrested and taken away for daring to speak out against the regime. The Party had, in its beneficence, allowed their then ten-year-old daughter, Nadine, to be allowed to live with Johann and Anja after the couple had pleaded with two functionaries in a smoky office on Wilhelmstraße. By that point, doctors with surgical experience were in demand, and Johann had managed to position himself as a patriotic soldier who wanted only to save the girl from his Bolshevik sister-in-law. It ran counter to everything within him—sticking his head above the ground, lying about his loyalty to the war effort—but it was enough to win Nadine her freedom. For Johann, this was justification enough.

The injured man groaned.

Johann shook his head. He had been daydreaming. He needed to be Oberstabsarzt Schultz again, the military surgeon. He got to work, clamping the blood vessels with hemostats before tying sutures around the artery and the vein. Then he transected the muscle around the bone, before beginning the part that he loathed the most—the brutal, visceral work of cutting through human bone. He loathed the sound more than any other. Johann worked quickly, wiping the sweat from his brow on his own greasy shoulder. Once the bone was severed he grabbed a file and smoothed down the rough edges of the remaining tibia before pulling down the muscle flaps and sewing up the skin. He doused the stitches with iodine and called for orderlies to dress the wound.

The patient was carried, asleep, from the makeshift theater. Johann looked at the bandaged stump and hoped that he didn't bleed through it—there weren't any dressings to spare.

He was thirsty. He wanted coffee. He needed rest.

He staggered toward his quarters and nearly bumped into the burly figure of Otto Deitch sucking on his empty pipe.

"I've been looking for you," Otto said urgently in his baritone. "I have news, Johann." Otto possessed a broad jaw that had a permanent gray shadow. He looked happy, but there was an awkward bearing to him, like he had been caught doing something he shouldn't.

"You've got some tobacco for that damn pipe?" Johann said, playfully punching his friend on the arm. The two of them had been together since forty-one—a lifetime in eastern-front terms. Otto was the only doctor with whom Johann felt comfortable talking freely.

Otto looked around and lowered his voice.

"Look, I know that you might not like to hear this, and believe me, I suggested you should go before me, seeing as you have a family," he said and paused. "I have orders to go back to Berlin. I'll be at Moabit Hospital. They're expecting civilian casualties. They're short of surgeons. Look . . ." Otto produced a communiqué, which he handed to Johann, who read the document. He passed it back to Otto and pinched the bridge of his nose. Clearly Henke had no authority over this decision.

Johann swallowed. He thought of Berlin. He thought of Anja and Nadine.

"When?"

"Tomorrow." Johann tried not to reveal disappointment, but Otto could tell his friend wished it were him heading west. "I know. It's insane. We can't get patients out but they can get me back. I'm sorry, Johann."

Johann nodded. "It's not your fault."

"I was thinking that maybe you should put in a request to Henke—they might be looking for others."

Johann nodded. "I'll try that," he said halfheartedly.

"I will check in on Anja and Nadine for you," Otto promised. "I have the address. I'll do what I can. And here's my address." He slipped a piece of notepaper into Johann's pocket.

"Thanks," Johann said.

The men stood awkwardly for a moment, knowing that this was likely to be the last time they would see each other. Then, simultaneously, they moved forward and shared an embrace.

"Good luck," Johann said.

"You too, my friend," Otto said. "You too. I will see you in Berlin."

Johann continued on his way, a thick lump of sadness sitting, like a stone, in his heart. How he wanted to go home. Henke should have kept his fat mouth shut. Johann wanted only to be with his Anja and Nadine. He would do the next best thing; he would go back to his quarters and write to her. He would engross himself, as he often did, in what they would do after the war. He would imagine himself away from this place. He fell onto his cot and started to write: "My dearest Anja . . ." In the distance he heard a screech of brakes as another casualty was brought for treatment. Someone else could deal with this one.

"Sir! Sir!"

Johann pushed his eyes open with almost superhuman effort. Had it started? Were the Reds attacking? He needed to be better prepared than he was. They were only three miles from the Soviet Third Shock Army and Eighth Guards Army—the place would soon be flooded with the injured. They would need to start evacuating patients soon, get them to safety. He fumbled his way to his feet and grabbed a tin cup he had left on the floor containing some phony coffee and downed it, wiping his mouth with his sleeve. He paused. He couldn't hear artillery. Had they been overrun already?

It was only then that he saw them: two men in earth-gray tunics. Brass, by the look of them. But then, as his eyes began to adjust, Johann read their collar patches, shoulder boards, and cuff patches and realized that these men weren't army—they were SS. The three diamonds and silver bar were those of an *Obersturmführer*, a first lieutenant. The other man had only two diamonds, marking him as an *Oberscharführer*, a staff sergeant. Just the sight of the peaked caps made Johann want to vomit.

"Heil Hitler!" the *Obersturmführer* barked, snapping out a German greeting. Johann hadn't heard one of these for a while and was mildly surprised. He replied with a groggy salute and a mumbled greeting. Even now it was not safe to ignore Nazi formalities.

"We are not disturbing you, *Oberstabsarzt?*" asked the *Obersturmführer*. "The *Kommandant* recommended that we should come to you, as we have a matter of extreme urgency to attend to." Johann examined the SS officer. The man looked hungry and his attention to SS grooming standards didn't conceal his bedraggled state. He was trying to present himself as a figure of authority, but he seemed alarmed.

"How can I help you, *Obersturmführer?*" Johann asked deferentially. He picked up a stethoscope that was lying next to his bed as if it were a talisman.

The man stepped forward. He was lean, with clear blue eyes and a thin triangular face that looked almost like it had been polished, such was its smoothness. Johann held his hand out.

"Ostermann," the *Obersturmführer* announced. "And this is Lehman." The *Oberscharführer* saluted Johann, who returned the compliment.

"I am very pleased to make the acquaintance of the *Oberstabsarzt*," Lehman said. "And may I offer my thanks for the work you have done for our valiant soldiers." Johann made him in a moment: a toad who joined the Party on day one. A follower with enough street smarts to decipher which way the wind was blowing and to cozy up to those in power. Men like Lehman were the backbone of the entire toxic enterprise.

"Let us not delay," Ostermann announced. "Come with us."

It was an order, not a request.

Johann reluctantly followed the SS officers back through the mud and mist to the triage area. He wanted only to sleep. Was there no one else that they could have gotten to do this?

He found himself falling in behind Ostermann and Lehman, who were walking at a hasty clip, their britches rubbing together. He skidded through the slippery ground after them and inside the tent, which reeked of dirt and bodies.

On an examination table in the corner he saw the body of a third SS man. For the first time he realized the significance of the insignia on their uniforms: They were *SS-Reichssicherheitshauptamt*.

The Reich Main Security Office.

He felt a wave of tension pass up his neck and into the lower part of his head.

These men were intelligence officers of state security. Johann's state of alert lurched from a sensation of constant, monotonous anxiety to high-pitched fear.

The man on the examination table was lying still and silent. The room smelled as if something had been cauterized. An orderly cupped his hand over his nose as if trying to minimize the stench. Johann noticed that much of the officer's clothing on his upper body was burned. One of his arms was hanging over the side of the table. In the gloom it looked like he was wearing a silver bracelet. Johann looked closer: No SS man would be permitted to wear jewelry. He realized that the object was, in fact, a manacle that was attached to a chain. Johann followed the chain downward. The other end was attached to something else that was resting on the floor—a large, battered brown briefcase that looked to be stuffed to bursting.

Ostermann followed Johann's gaze, flinched, and quickly walked over to the side of the table and unlocked the chain. He picked up the briefcase, carried it back to his position, and placed it between his feet.

Johann's skin burned as he sterilized his hands with alcohol.

"What happened?" he asked the officers who were waiting stiffly behind him.

"A phosphorous grenade," said Ostermann.

"I didn't know that any of our units were close enough to Russian lines to get hit with a phosphorous grenade," Johann said, immediately regretting his words. Medical staff were not supposed to talk this way to officers of the Wehrmacht, let alone the SS. They were supposed to mind their own business and get on with repairing bodies to be sent back to the front.

Johann felt Lehman shoot a glance at his senior.

"It was not the enemy," Ostermann replied. "There was an accident."

Johann said nothing.

He turned and dried his hands and, while he was doing so, took a look at the patient.

At that moment, he found himself unable to breathe.

Johann reached out and held onto the examination table, steadying himself. His legs buckled slightly before catching himself.

"Is Herr Doktor all right?" Lehman asked, although Johann was oblivious to anything around him. There was nothing in the world at that moment that could have dragged his attention away from the burned face in front of him.

"Sturmbannführer Dieter Schnell," said the orderly, examining the man's dog tags and writing the name on a clipboard.

Johann's head spun at the very mention of the name. He had run so far and for so long. . . .

He reached forward and began examining the wounds, but he found himself trembling. His hands were no longer doing what he wanted of them.

He needed to get a grip.

"Is there something wrong?" hissed Ostermann into his ear.

Johann took a deep breath and forced his eyes wide. He had to focus. He needed to pretend that this was just another patient, just another *Sturmbannführer* with bad injuries—burns that, should they become infected, could be the end of him. Ostermann was next to him, suspicious and predatory.

"This man is a hero of the Reich," he said menacingly. "A recipient of the Iron Cross and a Black Badge for the Wounded." Johann checked the second buttonhole of the officer's tunic. There was a red, white, and black ribbon and below it a black oval badge embossed with a helmet marked with a swastika.

Of course. This had been Dieter's destiny.

"If he doesn't survive there will be questions raised about your competence," Ostermann continued.

Johann turned and glared at the *Obersturmführer.*

"Let me do my work," Johann said.

And while Johann had barely slept for days, had not eaten a proper meal in months, had not voiced a cross word or stuck his head above the parapet for years, his dread had nothing to do with his physical degeneration: His alarm stemmed from a night in June 1934 when he watched as SA thugs dragged his father from the family home.

Johann Schultz was a name of convenience, the one that he'd used to gain a scholarship during the entrance exam to the Berlin University medical school a decade before.

Dieter might have come a long way since his days as a street brawler, but eleven years after consigning his stepfather to Oranienburg concentration camp, the *Sturmbannführer*'s tenuous hold on life was dependent on his surgeon half brother, formerly known as Thomas Meier.

3

"So, *Oberstabsarzst,*" Ostermann inquired, edging nearer Johann, "what is your prognosis?"

Johann kept his hands moving, trying to disregard the identity of the person he was treating.

"Speak up, Meier," Ostermann persisted.

Johann felt like he had been dealt a heavy blow to the solar plexus. He wheeled around and stared, wide-eyed, at Ostermann.

"What did you say?" he asked.

"I merely want to know . . . ," Ostermann said impatiently.

"No, *what* did you say?" Johann repeated.

"I said, 'Speak up, Schultz.'" The SS man's voice was terse, his eyes hard. He was trying to control Johann, but Johann could sense that Ostermann was as full of dread as he was. This was no routine treatment. Two officers accompanying another into triage was virtually unheard of.

"Oh . . . ," Johann said, looking away. In his exhausted, paranoid state, his mind was playing tricks on him. He paused momentarily before nodding an apology to Ostermann, who remained motionless. "I'm sorry, I . . ."

"The *Oberstabsarzt* forgets himself," Ostermann said, bristling with tension.

Johann continued to work on Dieter. He told himself to drive fear from his mind. He had to think of his half brother as just another patient. Johann needed to do what he had done for years and switch off the part of his mind in which Dieter constantly lurked, the section of his brain where he would always be seventeen-year-old Thomas Meier.

Eleven years of flight. Over a decade of reinvention, holding down dark fears and shouldering the formidable burden of guilt for what had happened to his father. Johann had done everything he could to leave his identity as Thomas behind. He had not breathed a word of it to anyone—not even Anja. Yet his unconscious had never allowed him respite—he saw his father's pleading face in his dreams almost every night. During hours of daylight he went about his business with his memories buttoned down as tightly as he could manage. Johann knew that Dieter would be out there searching for him, and should his half brother find him he would bring harm upon him. He would be in a camp within hours. So he carried on with his life as best he could, hoping to be left alone to work and to love. He would not betray himself.

Johann pushed other thoughts from his mind and fulfilled his role as a doctor. He wouldn't let his half brother's barbarism affect that which Johann held dear: his ability to heal. After treatment Dieter was stretchered to a private area that had been commandeered by Ostermann. The SS had no jurisdiction, but everybody did as they were told.

Johann returned to his billet once he had signed Dieter's paperwork. But exhausted as he was, he couldn't find it within himself to rest. Images of his father continually flashed through his mind. Johann had worked tirelessly to bury the memories of his former life, had done all he could to build an existence from the darkness of Dieter's hateful dogma.

He had become Johann Schultz not out of choice, but from necessity. To continue with the burden of what had happened— how he had just watched as they took away his father—had seemed impossible. He needed to change skin. And as Johann, he had met Anja, the woman who had shown him that there was indeed beauty and kindness in the world.

Johann paced around the doctors' quarters, drawing irritated glances from those off-duty officers who were trying to sleep. He smoked furiously, lighting each cigarette from the butt of another. It had come as no surprise to Johann to see the repellent uniform upon his half brother. The SS was, after all, the height to which those of Dieter's disposition aspired. But fearful as he was, Johann was nevertheless fascinated and intrigued that someone who shared his own blood could search out such darkness.

Why was he here? Intelligence officers surely had no business being so near the front line at this point in the war. He could imagine what Dieter had done over the past decade, but Johann wanted to know more—as if, by immersing himself in his half brother's black-hearted ways, he could fully understand the horrifying times he found himself living in.

Johann burst outside and walked toward the checkpoint that served as the entrance to camp. He had stopped for a moment to light a cigarette when he heard the squelching of boots behind him.

"*Oberstabsarzt!*" came a voice. "*Oberstabsarzt!*"

He recognized the voice. That creep Lehman was waddling through the mud toward him. There was nowhere Johann could run. As much as he needed to clear his mind, to try and process what had happened, he would have to be as civil as he could manage.

"*Oberstabsarzt,* I need a moment of your time," he said, straightening his back.

Lehman's bonhomie had vanished. A terrible fear swept through Johann: *They know.*

Dieter has communicated who I am. At the very best I will be taken somewhere and worked to death. More likely I will be executed here and now, my body smothered with the lime and buried in a pit beyond the outhouse.

"I see," Johann said. He was defenseless. He rarely carried his P38 pistol with him. He weighed up Lehman. The man looked strong, but maybe Johann could wrestle the *Oberscharführer*'s gun from him and escape into the fog before he could summon help. Lehman leaned into him, his sweaty upper lip trembling slightly.

"My leader, Sturmbannführer Schnell," Lehman said. "What are your thoughts?"

Johann was overcome with nausea. He didn't want to think about Dieter.

"I did what I can," Johann said.

"So he will live?"

Johann shrugged. "Perhaps."

Lehman pointed at Johann accusingly. "Then we must get him to Berlin," he said. Johann detected a fevered tone to Lehman's words. He sounded frantic. Both he and Ostermann seemed much more anxious than was usual for soldiers pondering the fate of a fallen comrade.

"We haven't been able to move any patients for a few days," Johann explained. "Air travel isn't safe and we don't have enough trucks."

Lehman continued to stand with him, staring off into the distance. It dawned on Johann that the SS man was looking for companionship.

"You will wait for Sturmbannführer Schnell?" Johann asked.

"We shall see," he said. "The *Obersturmführer* is awaiting further orders."

Even the communications systems are failing, Johann thought.

"Yes, I understand," Johann said, lighting another cigarette, hoping that it would calm him.

Lehman cast his eyes around and drew a small circle in the mud with the toe of his boot.

"We have strict orders," he said quietly. "We must be gone tomorrow. We are supposed to rendezvous with another unit tomorrow night. At a farm between here and Berlin."

An alarm went off inside Johann's head.

"Part of your mission, eh?" Johann said, as charmingly as he could muster. He would discover Dieter's role if he kept flattering this pudgy little man. He had just opened his mouth to ask another question when Ostermann popped out of a nearby tent.

"*Oberscharführer!*" he shouted. Lehman flinched like a dog caught in the act of defecating on a carpet.

"Yes, sir!"

"We must stay here tonight," he said, his voice diminished by the moisture in the air as he approached Johann and Lehman. "We leave tomorrow."

"Yes, sir," Lehman answered. "I will make all necessary arrangements."

Ostermann approached the pair of them and raised himself up on his toes. Johann found himself stepping back.

"Well, well," Ostermann said. "We have a nice little kaffeeklatsch here."

Lehman, a successful survivor of the system, sensed the potential danger.

"We were just discussing the status of the *Sturmbannführer,* sir," Lehman said, glancing at Johann to let him know that it was his turn.

"Yes," Johann said. "I'm afraid that it's touch and go. We can only hope."

"The *Oberstabsarzt* would do well to remember, as we face our nation's gravest hour, that there is always hope," said Ostermann as if he could read Johann's mind. "Hope is named the Führer."

"Yes," Johann said, "I am full of hope."

But, he thought, *hope isn't always enough.*

Dieter might die.

But he might not.

There was no harm in helping his half brother on his way, once he had learned Dieter's secrets.

That night, although he was on duty, Johann watched the officers' mess closely. He noticed that Ostermann and Lehman had a bottle of schnapps with them. Johann kept watch on the two SS officers as they drained the bottle and grew louder. Around midnight, Ostermann stumbled to bed. Johann immediately ran to his billet and pulled his last bottle of schnapps from beneath his cot and hurried back to the mess. Lehman, his face red, his eyes glassy, his hair plastered to his head with sweat, and his tunic unbuttoned, was rousing his body from the bench.

"Oh, no," Johann said to him as he approached the table. "Surely you're not turning in for the night?"

"Ah, *Oberstabsarzt*, a pleasant surprise," Lehman replied. "Yes, I have no choice. Ostermann will skin me alive if I stay out late."

"He'll never know," Johann said. "I just saw him stumbling off somewhere. Probably trying to find some more to drink."

"Or a girl!" Lehman said, clapping his hand on Johann's shoulder.

"No need to stay out late," Johann said. "Come on, I've just finished my shift. Let us have a drink to Sturmbannführer Schnell."

"What have you got there?" Lehman said, pawing the bottle. "My, my . . . this looks good."

"The finest peach schnapps," Johann said.

"Then it would be churlish not to toast the *Sturmbannführer*," Lehman said, flopping back onto the bench.

Johann sat opposite him and poured two large measures.

"Krieg ist Krieg und Schnaps ist Schnaps," Lehman announced, holding up a chipped glass. The men drank. Johann was mindful of being seen in the mess. If Henke caught him drinking on duty there was every chance that he would be put on a charge, Soviet attack or no Soviet attack.

"The *Sturmbannführer* must be a very brave man," Johann said, pouring Lehman another measure and playing on the SS man's hero worship.

"Oh, yes, he's brave, all right," Lehman said. "And hard. Ruthless. He's what you might call an ideal SS man. He'll see this thing through to the end."

Lehman took another drink. Johann noticed that the *Oberscharführer* wasn't wearing his service pistol. He probably imagined it was unnecessary in a field hospital.

"I apologize, doctor," he said. "I didn't mean the end, you know, in that way. We will never give in. We will be victorious despite the current . . ."

"Relax, Lehman," Johann said, playfully punching him on the arm. "We're all friends here. I know what you mean."

Johann watched the portly man. There was opportunity here— as he had hoped, Lehman's tongue had loosened. He decided to take a gamble.

"So Ostermann told me about the briefcase," he said.

Lehman's bonhomie withered and his face turned thunderous. Johann had blown it. In trying to call Lehman's bluff, he had miscalculated and exposed himself. The SS man took another gulp of schnapps and then attempted a refill. He slopped as much on the table as in his glass. After taking a breath he placed his hands on the rough wooden bench and pushed himself so that he was standing. Johann braced himself. Lehman swiveled his head around to see who was nearby, his face troubled.

"Come with me," he said, and stepped outside. They walked for some time, until they reached a line of trees. There was nothing here. Just darkness.

"You're from Berlin?" Lehman asked.

"Yes," Johann replied.

"You still have family in the city?"

Johann hesitated. Would his mistake cost Anja and Nadine too? He reasoned that, even if he didn't reveal the information, the Gestapo would be able to track them down within hours.

"Yes," he replied.

"I thought so," Lehman said. "I can tell a Berlin accent." He trembled with the chill and fastened a couple of buttons. "Look, I think that you're a good sort."

Lehman paused—perhaps he had already exposed himself too much. "I can trust you, Schultz, can't I?"

"Of course," Johann said. "Anyway, who is going to listen to the word of a doctor over an SS officer?"

This seemed to embolden Lehman.

"Yes," he said. Johann couldn't see him in the darkness, but he knew that he had assuaged Lehman's fears. "You see, Schultz, the people are scared of the Soviets. And rightly so—they are beasts. But what they don't know about are plans from within."

"You mean the Führer's miracle weapons?" Johann said, playing the fool.

"No, no," Lehman said. Johann could just about make out Lehman stepping nervously from foot to foot. "Where's that schnapps, eh?"

Johann thrust the bottle into the darkness. Eventually Lehman's outstretched hand made contact with the vessel, and Johann heard the clink of the bottleneck on the rim of the SS man's glass.

"Where does your family shelter from the air raids?"

"In the tunnels of the U-Bahn at Friedrichstraße station and the bunker on Reinhardstraße," Johann said. He thought about Anja and Nadine huddling in the squalid darkness, the condensation on the ceiling being shaken from the roof by the aftershocks.

"I visited Berlin once," Lehman said. "We came as a group. Our local SS unit—this was back in the old days, you know. We were part of a parade and then we took in the sights. The museums, the river, the cathedral, the zoo, Schloss Charlottenburg . . . It was beautiful. Of course, they wanted to show us all the new buildings, but it was the old Berlin that I liked, the Berlin of the German Empire."

Lehman sighed. Johann didn't know where this reminiscence was going. Why had Lehman asked about his family? And why on earth had Johann told him about Anja and Nadine and where they sheltered? He must be more drunk than Johann thought.

Johann heard Lehman coughing. He wondered if he might be vomiting from all the booze, but he realized that the SS man was sobbing quietly. He snorted a couple of times, then spat, clearing the mucus from his nose. There was absolute stillness. Johann couldn't recall such quiet.

"I think that it's over," Lehman said.

"The war?" Johann said gently. He felt Lehman slowly giving in.

"Not just the war," Lehman said eventually. "Everything." He sighed. "This country. Us."

"Come, come . . . ," Johann said. "We will rebuild. We will reestablish what is great about this country, we will—"

"You just don't understand, do you?" Lehman interrupted him. "Why would you? After all, I only heard about it twelve days ago. What we were doing—it wasn't just our main mission. There was something extra they had us do. An executive order. Right from the top."

Lehman stopped talking. Johann held his breath. Surely this was it.

"I should be getting back . . . ," the *Oberscharführer* insisted.

Lehman made to move, but Johann put his hand out and pushed it against the SS officer's chest. He would not be denied after coming so close.

"What don't I understand, Lehman?"

"I've had too much to drink," Lehman snapped.

"Come on, Lehman," Johann whispered. "It's just you and me, two soldiers talking."

It was hard to discern Lehman's face in the dark, but Johann thought he could make out the man's resolve melting a little.

"We have orders to ensure that all units on the front and behind it comply with an executive directive from the Führer himself."

"But what is it?" Johann demanded more firmly than he should have. "And what has it got to do with Sturmbannführer Schnell and you being here?"

"Enough!" Lehman said, and broke away from Johann. He started to stumble back toward the mess, which seemed a long way away now.

"We were surprised to see officers from the Reich Main Security Office arrive," Johann said, trying to calm him. "That's all."

Lehman stopped.

"And we were surprised to come here," Lehman said. "It wasn't part of the plan, but Ostermann and I thought it in the best interests of Sturmbannführer Schnell."

"You did well, Lehman, you did well," Johann said. "Without your bringing him here he would already be dead."

Johann could sense Lehman's fear. He and Ostermann were afraid that they had compromised the mission, whatever it was. Lehman had said that the directive was an addition to another, central task. And earlier in the day he had talked about a rendezvous tomorrow night. What was so important about it? Why was Lehman so concerned?

"Surely you can wait another day or so to see if the *Sturmbannführer*'s condition improves?" Johann said, testing Lehman.

"We have to leave tomorrow night," Lehman hissed. "With or without him."

Silence.

Johann waited. He could sense Lehman had more to say.

"We have a rendezvous."

"The farm?" Johann ventured. He was sure the meeting would explain Dieter's presence—it was surely why Dieter was here.

"I have been thinking about the route and the quality of the roads and how we will fit the *Sturmbannführer* in the *Kübelwagen*."

Lehman was rambling now. Drunk beyond reason. There were no restrictions, no editing of his thoughts.

"The Wenck farm on the Zossen Road, just near a crossroads two miles south of Müncheberg," Lehman said to himself quietly. "Ostermann made me remember it. We're not allowed to write it down."

"But the *Sturmbannführer*," Johann interrupted, "what is his role in this?"

"There is a handover," Lehman said quietly.

Johann's mind flashed back to the briefcase chained to Dieter's wrist.

"Tell me what he—"

"You will not hear anything else from me," Lehman slurred, pulling away from Johann. "You will only find out by going to the farmhouse."

"What is happening there?"

"Go there yourself if you want to find out," Lehman shouted in the darkness.

"Tell me," Johann insisted.

There was silence. Johann could tell that Lehman had stopped moving.

"What is happening there?" Johann pressed. He was getting closer to Dieter's secret. He could sense it.

More silence.

"Tell me, Lehman."

Finally the SS man spoke.

"You ask a lot of questions," Lehman said coldly. "None of it your business."

"Maybe we should hit the sack, eh?" Johann said, suddenly scared. He had ventured well beyond safety. He heard the movement of tree branches above him.

There was a rustle of clothing and suddenly Johann wasn't able to breathe: Lehman's wurst-thick fingers were around this throat, his chunky thumbs pressing into Johann's windpipe. Johann tried to beat away Lehman's hands, pulling on his arms, but the SS man was too strong.

"You shouldn't have asked," Lehman hissed. "You shouldn't have asked."

4

The suffocating pressure on Johann's throat was softened only by the whirling dizziness of his mind.

"You traitorous bastard," Lehman hissed, flecks of spittle flying from his mouth and hitting Johann in the face.

Johann's head spun as his brain began to crave oxygen. Standing in a field in Frankfurt an der Oder, his life being ended by a drunken sociopath, Johann wondered how long it would be before he lost consciousness. Thirty seconds? Maybe forty-five?

"I knew there was something suspect about you," Lehman said. "I *knew* it."

Johann pulled on Lehman's wrists, but his efforts were having no effect—the SS man was stronger than him and his grip was showing no sign of weakening. Johann could feel his energy ebbing. He sensed the opportunity to relax into a delicious sleep. How he deserved it. . . .

"That's it," Lehman said, sensing Johann weakening. "Very soon you will feel nothing. Just relax. . . ."

Johann was galvanized by the executioner's words. He lashed out with his right foot and drove it into Lehman's knee. There was a crunch. The SS man stumbled and lost his grip. Johann gulped down air, his throat burning. His breaths were coming like sobs: deep, pained, body-rocking like those of an alcoholic with the DTs. He heard Lehman coming for him and stepped to the side. There was a whoosh of energy and the big man fell in a heap. Lehman had lost the advantage of his strength. Johann had the upper hand, dodging the *Oberscharführer*, who was stumbling around, crashing into trees.

As Johann backed away from Lehman's lunges a horrifying thought struck him: Only one of them would walk out of the woods. Lehman couldn't allow him to escape; his revelation about the rendezvous would end with a bullet to the head. And Johann couldn't allow Lehman to get back to the hospital. The allegations of an SS man—no matter how drunk—would be the end of him.

One of them would die in the next few minutes.

Johann felt a rush of air past his face: Lehman throwing a hay-maker. If it had connected he would not be conscious. He needed to think. He couldn't keep dodging the SS man indefinitely. He was tiring—if Lehman were to grab him again he would surely squeeze the life out of him. Being able to avoid Lehman wasn't enough; he needed to kill the man. Even in his state of panic he considered the irony—after six years of doing everything he could to save lives, he was now desperate to end one. He had to if he was to survive.

"You're pathetic," Lehman goaded Johann. "I'll cut out your traitor's heart!"

Lehman bellowed and came at him. Johann could see his silhouette against the bluish darkness. Just as the SS man closed in on him he jumped to the side. Lehman stopped and turned.

"Give up, doctor," he said. "You're already dead."

Lehman was close enough now to be able to see Johann, who started to move through the woods as quickly as he could. Branches tore at his clothes and whipped his face. He could hear Lehman crashing after him like a bear as the two of them plunged deeper into the woods.

After a few minutes they came to a clearing. Johann bent forward, hands on knees, exhausted. He would not be able to keep this up for long. He needed to do something decisive. Then it came to him—a single chance to end their fight. He gathered himself and set off again, accelerating across a meadow. His legs were soaking now from the rainwater and dew on the grass. He could see the silhouette of the tree line ahead of him. He slowed a little to let Lehman catch him: Johann wanted the SS man to be as close to him as possible without being able to grab him. Lehman would surely think Johann was done for now—that, with a little more exertion, he would fall upon his prey and finish him. There were no more than ten meters between them.

My God.

Johann was down. His boot had snagged on something—a branch or a root maybe—and all he knew was that he could smell the rich, damp earth clinging to his face. He forced himself up as quickly as possible but felt Lehman's hand around his ankle.

He was caught.

Johann smashed his other foot backward as hard as he could into Lehman's face. The SS man screeched and let go, and Johann was on his way again. He looked around in the moonlight to see Lehman doggedly stumbling after him. Johann couldn't go on much farther. He needed to rest. His lungs and heart were at capacity. But he had to hold on. Had to push ahead. He was almost there. He pulled back a little to let Lehman get close. He could hear the man coughing and spluttering behind him, but his footsteps remained constant.

Lehman thought that the chase was over.

Twenty meters.

He could feel Lehman was there now.

Ten meters.

Lehman's moonlit shadow was upon his.

Five meters.

Keep going, keep going, and—Johann threw himself sideways.

Lehman fell into the darkness with a roar, his limbs flailing. Johann lay there in the night trying to catch his breath. There was utter stillness around him. The edges of a ravine gave off an almost otherworldly glow, as if they were being lit for a theatrical production at the Schillertheater on Bismarckstraße. Johann pushed himself to his knees and peered downward.

Dead air.

If Lehman was injured surely he would be moaning. Maybe the booze had softened the blow for him. No, he was dead. There was no way a man could fall onto the rocks below and live. Johann had discovered the place a few days before during one of his head-clearing walks. It had seemed incongruous compared to the rest of the landscape—a steep, rocky ravine seemingly scooped out by a giant hand. Now a dead SS man lay at the bottom of it. They were only about ten minutes from the field hospital, but they might as well have been deep in the Bavarian forest.

He felt his hand trembling. He knelt down and started to vomit. The spoils of the victor.

Only one of them was walking out of the woods tonight.

Both he and Dieter were murderers now.

He had killed a man.

This was what he thought as he shivered through the woods on his way back to the field hospital. He might not have shot or stabbed or strangled Lehman, but the SS man was lying dead, his head smashed on rocks at the bottom of a ravine, because of Johann. He wasn't the executioner, but he was certainly the engineer of Lehman's demise.

And while he felt fearful about what he had done, Johann didn't feel any guilt. He was beyond that now. In the past he might have been inclined to keep his head down and hope to avoid the attention of the Party; now he knew that he was willing to do whatever he could to bring them and their ways to an early end. He had seen too much death to care when the murderous and ruthless departed the fray.

Lehman's words had only served to confuse Johann. The SS man had talked about something the Nazis were planning in Berlin—an event Lehman was too scared to tell him about. He had said that the explanation for the mission would be found at the farmhouse tomorrow. What was it that Dieter and his fellow SS officers had been doing?

His mind was made up. He would return home to Berlin for Anja and Nadine. But first he would extinguish Dieter's mission—and avenge his father.

He would kill Dieter.

The risks were terrible, but as the ice grew thinner, Johann thought, he would have to skate all the more furiously.

Still soaked from the woods, Johann crept carefully into the room where Dieter and Ostermann were quartered. Part of an abandoned farmhouse where patients awaiting evacuation were being held, it was quiet except for the sounds of moaning and breathing. Dieter had been put in a screened-off area, and before it there was an improvised antechamber where Ostermann lay rigidly in a cot, his body straight and still. Johann walked slowly past the *Obersturmführer,* watching him carefully for signs of wakefulness.

Johann pulled back the tarpaulin that had been hung to create the private area for Dieter. His half brother was wheezing, his breath jagged. Someone—probably Ostermann—had left a lantern burning. Its glow cast deep shadows throughout the room, giving the space a jaundiced warmth. It reminded Johann of a painting he had seen once—a Dutch master, he thought. All was dark except for one burnished light.

Johann looked down at his half brother's face. It had been worn by time. There were lines across his forehead and down both sides of his mouth that were deep enough for Johann to lay a thermometer in. His eyes were similarly damaged. His wrinkles—starbursts emanating from his eyes—were those of a man who had spent much of his life subjected to the elements. Johann felt no flicker of sibling warmth: There was nothing in his heart but hatred for Dieter, his father's killer.

Johann hadn't expected him to still be alive. But then, he reasoned, he was just judging the injuries, not the man who bore them. Dieter was an opportunist, a passenger of history, like Lehman. His identity was determined by his loyalty to the Party—his biology and physical presence were almost irrelevant. He had been part of this movement from the very beginning; now he must ride out the rest of it.

There was an abrupt creak. Johann froze. He listened and realized it was just Ostermann turning over. He needed to hurry; the *Obersturmführer* appeared restless.

Johann had to find the briefcase. He was sure that its contents would offer a clue about the farmhouse meeting the following night. He looked about the room and noticed a stack of Dieter's personal effects, and what looked to be a spare uniform piled on a wooden box. Johann rifled through it and searched around the edges of the room in case he'd missed something in the darkness. Maybe they had left the briefcase in the SS *Kübelwagen,* which they had parked on a grassy embankment just behind one of the temporary patients, rooms. Johann crouched down and reached under Dieter's cot. He moved his hand around until it hit an object.

He felt it: leather. Surely Ostermann could have thought of a better hiding place than this? Or maybe he wasn't trying to conceal it; the notion of SS property being stolen was so alien that the *Obersturmführer* hadn't thought about secreting the briefcase anywhere other than close to its envoy. Johann slid the case along the ground and into what little light there was. It was heavy, packed to bursting. He examined the case in the half-light: battered brown leather with a handle that was worn smooth, except where the stitching had frayed. A steel hoop passed through it—the fixture for Dieter's chain. There were no official markings. The carryall could have been the property of a provincial doctor or accountant.

Johann pushed down the brass clasp. The mechanism clicked—but it wouldn't open. He pulled at it, but it remained fixed. Maybe it was just stiff. He tried again but the lock stuck fast. He would need a knife to wrench it open.

He stared at the case and was suddenly overwhelmed with anxiety. He was in way above his head; he should just leave. He might be better off not knowing the world that Dieter had embraced. He should just disappear now, in the dead of the night, and return to the city. Surely he and Anja and Nadine would be able to escape west in the chaos that grew greater every day. . . .

He stood fast.

Lehman had been desperate enough to try to kill him rather than reveal the full extent of their task. Why would three intelligence officers be heading west with the Red Army at their heels? Was the briefcase related to the order from the Führer that Lehman had refused to tell him about, or was it related to the "main mission" that Dieter had been leading? Johann knew the case might contain the answer—why else would it have been chained to his half brother's body? Now that Lehman was dead, the meeting at the farmhouse was his only means of finding out.

Johann froze. He heard Ostermann shift his body and let out another sigh. There was no other movement. The *Obersturm-führer* was still asleep, but he must make haste. He put down the briefcase and pulled a brown bottle from his pocket and examined it briefly: sodium thiopental, a barbiturate used in anesthetics. In the field its contents were as precious as any commodity. Over the previous few months Johann had spirited several bottles from the pharmacy for use on patients when supplies had dried up. It was not unusual for doctors to do this—but most of them were planning on saving it for personal use. When the time came they would load their syringes, find a vein, and push the liquid into their bodies, slipping away beyond the reach of the Nazis and the Red Army.

He pulled a syringe from another pocket and drew the liquid into the barrel. Usually he was precise with measurements. Tonight, however, he drew back the plunger as far as he could: He wanted to ensure that he would administer the most powerful dose the device would allow.

He placed the syringe on top of Dieter's bedcover. He would end it now. He would do it for Nicolas. And for Thomas.

Johann slapped his half brother lightly on the cheek—he didn't want to risk waking Ostermann. There was no response. He tried again, but Dieter slept on. He felt angry: He wanted Dieter to know what he was doing and why. He wanted his half brother to watch while Johann administered the fatal dose, to know that Nicolas had been revenged.

Johann slapped his half brother hard. Dieter's eyes flickered to life for a moment before settling closed again. Johann hit him again. Dieter's eyes opened and searched the room, adjusting to what was before him. Johann perched on the edge of the cot next to Dieter and held up the lantern. His half brother registered the movement and focused his eyes to determine its origin.

It took a moment for the information to register: Dieter's body, even in its injured state, buckled as if it had received an electrical charge. His eyes were wide open, the irises alert and questioning. Johann couldn't tell whether his half brother was disbelieving or fearful. Johann leaned in close and whispered to Dieter as quietly as he could, his voice halting and broken from the excitement of the moment.

"You're not hallucinating," Johann said. "It's me."

Dieter flinched, as if witnessing an apparition.

"Ha!" Johann couldn't help a brief moment of . . . what? Victory?

"The great defender of the fatherland reduced to this."

Dieter tried to move, to push Johann from the cot, but he was too weak. He opened his mouth to call out, but there was only a low gargle. Johann watched as his half brother came to the realization that he no longer had the power to determine life and death—that he was subject to the whim of the younger sibling he had dismissed as weak and worthless.

"You arrived seriously injured yesterday at the field hospital and I performed my duty as a doctor," Johann whispered. "But now, Dieter, I will end things for you. Your war is over."

His half brother's breathing became more pronounced. He opened his mouth again, but there were no words.

"There's no need to speak," Johann said. "Nothing you can tell me, nothing you can do, will stop what's about to happen."

He fumbled inside his shirt before finding a metallic object, which he held in front of his half brother: the key.

"This ring any bells, Dieter?" he asked. "Huh? You remember this? You wanted it so badly that you would destroy my father. . . . I had it all along. Why? Because if I had it I knew that you never would."

Johann swung it so that the metal brushed Dieter's cheek.

"There—you touched it," he said. "But you will never hold it, never know what secrets it has. But I have something else for you."

Johann pulled the syringe from the bedclothes. A clear drop of liquid had collected at the tip of the needle. He held it up to Dieter's face. His half bother's eyes narrowed and his body heaved before slumping back into the cot. Dieter's bandaged arms rose slightly and fell back, as useless as those of an infant. Dieter tried to turn, to make some noise. Johann leaned forward quickly and pressed on his half brother's chest to prevent him from shifting.

With his other hand, Johann raised the syringe to Dieter's bicep.

The needle was hovering an inch above his skin when the silence was shattered. It felt, to Johann, like the crash of thunder.

"What are you doing, *Oberstabsarzt?*" came a booming voice.

Johann paused and turned to look at Ostermann, before returning his gaze to Dieter as if nothing was amiss.

"It's a painkiller," Johann explained matter-of-factly.

He could still do it. Ostermann would think that Dieter was merely sleeping. By the time he discovered otherwise, Johann would be on his way to Berlin. He was about to push the needle into Dieter's flesh when he felt Ostermann's hand upon his wrist.

"Put it down," Ostermann told Johann.

Johann saw Ostermann's moist eyes in the darkness, rimmed with red but determined. Johann had only a moment to decide what to do. The briefcase was on the floor—should Ostermann see that he had dragged it from under Dieter's bed he was finished.

"All right," Johann said. "What's your concern?"

"Is this the usual amount of painkiller?" Ostermann said.

Johann nodded. His hand was beginning to shake a little now from the tension of Ostermann's grip. He glanced at the tip of the needle, no more than an inch from Dieter's arm. He could kill Dieter in a second if he tried.

"An orderly came and gave the *Sturmbannführer* his medication but an hour ago," Ostermann said.

"Really?" Johann said, his brow furrowed with phony concern. "I saw no mention of it on his chart. The nurse must have forgotten to write it down."

Ostermann nodded, although he didn't appear entirely convinced by Johann's words. He stood his ground, suspicious, like a wild animal facing a human offering food.

"I will make sure that he's punished," Johann said. He wondered whether he could wait to kill Dieter until the morning, once Ostermann was distracted by his preparations to leave. He felt Ostermann's grip loosen. Johann held the syringe close to his half brother. *Do it! Do it!* he told himself.

He pulled it back.

"I suppose that these things happen," Ostermann said.

"We are all very tired," Johann replied.

Ostermann examined him for a moment, shifting his head to the side.

"What happened to your face?" he asked.

Johann reached up and touched his right cheek. He looked at Ostermann and realized that the SS man was now staring down. His eyes were upon the briefcase. . . .

Both men made to grab each other at the same time, but Ostermann had the advantage of height. He fell upon Johann and the two men tumbled down on Dieter, who sat up violently from the pain.

Johann held on to the syringe with his right hand, punching Ostermann in the side of the head with his left. He felt the SS man's hands reaching for his eyes. He needed to end this situation quickly—other medical staff might be drawn to the disturbance. He plunged the needle into Ostermann's neck and rammed the sodium thiopental home with the heel of his hand.

Ostermann shook as if a tremor was passing through his body. He lurched backward, staggering as he lost all sensation, and pulled the device from his neck.

But it was too late. Johann watched as the man's knees buckled. He read the signs: Ostermann's heart was suffering arrhythmia, his brain was lapsing into unconsciousness, his nervous system was demonstrating signs of dizziness, confusion, blurred vision. . . . Finally Ostermann succumbed to complete cardiovascular collapse. He fell as if he had been hit on the head with a rock.

Johann turned to see Dieter staring hard into his eyes. His half brother knew that Johann had intended to kill him this way. Ostermann had saved him from the deadly dose.

Panicked, Johann leapt up. He had planned to steal in and kill Dieter unnoticed. No one would have suspected foul play. He could have slipped away to the farmhouse rendezvous quietly. Now there was a dead SS man on the floor and a witness to that homicide. What to do first? He needed to kill Dieter—should his half brother regain his power of speech Johann was sunk. His eyes met those of the *Sturmbannführer* again. Johann could see Dieter burning with frustration—the man wanted nothing more than to lash out and scream at the top of his lungs, but his body had failed him.

Johann tried to think clearly. Time was on his side. Dieter was trapped. He needed to deal with his most pressing problem first: Ostermann.

Johann walked from the screened-off area and looked around. There was no one outside the room or in the entranceway to the makeshift ward. He dragged a coarse gray wool blanket from Ostermann's bed and wrapped the dead man in it before placing the body on his shoulder.

Johann lolloped quickly outside, imagining what he might say should anyone confront him. He cast glances around to see if he was being observed, but the darkness meant that he was concealed except at close quarters. The night was still and quiet except for the noise of his breathing. He moved quickly, knowing that should he drop Ostermann, he might not have the strength to pull the corpse up again. His neck ached and his right shoulder burned. Ostermann became heavier the farther he went. He passed down a narrow lane and reached the latrine, pausing momentarily to listen—no one appeared to be using it. He dumped the body inside and dragged Ostermann to a spot inside the old farm building, where there was a beam about seven feet off the floor. He removed the man's belt and slung it over the beam, before using all his might to lift the corpse and push its head through the loop that he had created with the black leather. Shattered by the effort of lifting, Johann collapsed on the fetid floor. Looking up, he saw Ostermann swinging from side to side above him. *Just like the arm of a metronome*, Johann thought.

There, for the entire world to see, was a man who could take no more. It was not uncommon—suicides were increasing as the prospect of an encounter with the Red Army became imminent. Better to get drunk and hang yourself than wind up on the end of a bayonet or in a gulag. They would find Ostermann tomorrow and not think beyond the story in front of them—Dieter's silence would see to that.

As he walked back from the latrine, panting with exertion, Johann paused for a moment. He watched the vapor from his breath disperse in the night air, and wondered how, in the space of two hours, he had come to be responsible for the deaths of two men. He had always thought that he was no more a killer than he was a porpoise. Now Lehman and Ostermann both lay dead— their demise the result of his desperation. He was not proud to be a killer, but he had little regret about his choice of victims. Two fewer SS men was a good thing.

He snapped out of his momentary reverie. He needed to deal with Dieter immediately.

He had to get the briefcase—even if Dieter could talk, Johann knew that his half brother would never reveal his secrets. Trudging back to the facility in the freezing night, terrified and fatigued, Johann had a realization: With Lehman and Ostermann dead— and Dieter soon to join them—the only way to discover the threat to Berlin and the significance of the mission was to attend the rendezvous at the farmhouse as Dieter himself.

He stopped. Had he lost his mind? He reasoned that it was no more an unimaginable act than his having killed two members of the SS.

He started to walk again. He tempered his fear of the farmhouse by insisting to himself that, after he had discovered the mystery of Dieter's mission, he would find Anja and Nadine in the dark, ruined city. They would reach the American lines. They would rediscover life.

It was what he had always vowed to his wife. He and Anja had discussed the arrangement the last time he had visited Berlin, at Christmas: When it seemed that the end was near, they would find a way out of the city to the west and head for the American or British lines. Rumors had been circulating that the closer the Soviets got to Berlin, the more likely it was that Wehrmacht forces in the west would put down their arms to allow the GIs and Tommies to liberate the capital. There had been fevered speculation about what would happen should the Soviets get to the city first. There had even been chatter that senior military figures were willing to negotiate with Eisenhower behind the Führer's back.

He hurried through the mud to where he knew that Dieter was lying paralyzed, waiting for him. He stepped inside the tent, walked into the antechamber, and rifled through Ostermann's belongings, taking only the keys for the *Kübelwagen*. He pushed back the flap to Dieter's room—he needed to fetch the briefcase and his half brother's uniform.

Johann didn't need his eyes to adjust to see that there was another doctor in the room—Andreas Karl, a small, twitchy man in his fifties who had only recently been called up. Johann barely knew him, but he was a type: the anxious man who had hoped to escape the war. But right at the end he finds himself in the thick of the horror.

"I thought you finished at four," he said, not unkindly.

"That's right," Johann said.

"It's nearly four-thirty," Karl told him. "Go and get some sleep. You look dreadful."

Johann glanced over at Dieter. His eyes were closed.

"He was hallucinating," Karl said. "Going on about someone called Thomas killing a man. He was out of his mind. I knocked him out."

"Four-thirty already?" Johann said, rubbing his chin thoughtfully.

"The Soviet advance will start soon," Karl said. "We need to be ready."

"I know, I know . . . ," Johann said. "But this patient. I saw him when he first arrived. You know how it is—Sometimes they get under your skin."

Karl nodded wistfully.

"I know that feeling," he said. "I heard he was a mess when he came in, but it looks like you saved him."

Johann flinched at Karl's final words.

"Do you have a pen?" Karl asked, patting his pockets. "I left mine next door."

"Sorry," Johann answered.

"Oh, well . . . ," Karl said, pushing back the flap. "It's only next door, I suppose."

The second Karl was out of view, Johann quickly reached under Dieter's bed and grabbed the briefcase and an SS uniform that Ostermann had brought from the vehicle—the one Dieter had been wearing when he arrived had been ruined. Hastily he pushed them into the bottom corner of the side of the tarpaulin that was being used to come in and out of the room. As soon as he had finished, Karl came back in.

"Come back tomorrow," Karl said. "You won't miss anything."

"Okay," said Johann. "I'll do that."

He needed to calm himself. The situation was under control. He would deal with Dieter tomorrow when there was an opportunity to be alone. Then he would escape to Berlin. He took one more look at his half brother and edged from the room, watching as Karl updated Dieter's chart. As Karl hummed to himself, Johann dragged the briefcase and uniform from beneath the tarp.

What Johann missed as he disappeared outside was Dieter's eyes opening.

Their silent pleas to Karl remained unheeded.

5

His dreams were of his father. Chopping wood together at a cottage in the Rhineland. A Bach concert at the Steinway-Haus on Hardenbergstraße. Eating black bread and fried eggs for breakfast on a Sunday, a roaring fire in the grate . . .

Johann opened his eyes and, above him, he saw green army canvas. He took a sip of water from a tin mug by the side of his bed and ran through the many reasons he had to feel fearful.

He checked his watch. He was on duty in twenty minutes. He felt the stubble on his chin. If his plan was to come together and Johann was to make the meeting at the farmhouse that evening, he would need to shave. Ten minutes later he patted his pocket as he walked from the mess back to Dieter's makeshift quarters. It was there—his last ampoule of sodium thiopental.

Johann passed into the anteroom. It was as if Ostermann had never been there. His possessions had been removed and another patient, his face entirely covered in bandages, was asleep on the cot. This time, Johann thought there would be no waking his half brother, no grandstanding. Johann would get into the room, administer the medication, and get out. The orderly would find Dieter dead on his next round—and Johann would be gone.

He pushed back the canvas and slipped into the room. It was dark inside. There was the sound of irregular breathing as Johann crept forward toward the mound of blankets. He pulled the ampoule from his pocket and filled the syringe. Now was his chance. Johann pulled back the cover and readied his thumb to deliver the fatal dose. Goodbye, Dieter, and good riddance. He grabbed an arm, his eyes searching for a vein. A final glance at his half brother . . .

Nausea flowered in his stomach.

The man in the bed wasn't Dieter.

Johann burst into the doctors' quarters, looking for Karl. The room was as gloomy as any of the wards, lit as it was by lanterns. There were no windows—any chink of light would bring a volley from Soviet Katyusha missiles. Karl was sitting on his bed writing a letter. Johann noticed that, even in the chaos of a military hospital, Karl was writing on beautiful stationery using a fountain pen.

"The patient Schnell," Johann said loudly. "What happened?"

"Quiet!" came a voice from the other side of the room.

"Where is he?" Johann asked, aware that he didn't want the entire room to know the extent of his panic.

"He's fine," Karl said, smiling. "Soon after you came in last night a truck arrived to collect the most seriously wounded and transport them to Berlin."

Dieter would be in Berlin within two days. Three at the latest.

"I thought it best to ensure that Schnell was on the truck," Karl said. "The injuries aren't as significant as we first thought, and he's responding well to treatment. He'll make it."

Johann nodded as if expressing medical agreement. He felt a terrible darkness pass over him. A bead of sweat hung from his nose.

"Are you all right, Schultz?" Karl asked. "You appear to have a fever."

"I'm fine, I'm fine . . . ," Johann bluffed. The news had sent him into a state of high panic. He needed to act. He needed to return to Berlin—when Dieter recovered consciousness his first act would be to denounce Johann.

Anja and Nadine would be picked up by the Gestapo within hours.

Karl continued to examine Johann.

"Look, I'm sorry to ask," Johann said, "but can I have a sheet of writing paper and an envelope? I've run out."

"Of course," said Karl, reaching beneath his bed.

Karl nodded courteously and handed Johann the stationery.

"I'm sorry to bother you," Johann said, aware that there were now other eyes upon him. "I was just concerned about the patient because I worked on him yesterday. I wanted to know if there had been any further developments."

"Would you like some water, Johann?" Karl asked.

"No, no." He was aware that his body was almost vibrating with anxiety. He was certain that those in the room could smell it above the stale sweat, dirty clothes, and troubled sleep. "I should get moving; my shift has already started." With that, Johann walked from the room, aware that several of its occupants were now watching him curiously.

He felt the shape of Ostermann's car keys in his pocket and knew that this was his best—no, only—chance of escape.

Otto was inspecting a panzer gunner with a shoulder wound—the smell alone told him that gangrene had set in—when he felt an urgent tapping on his back. Before he could spin around, he heard a familiar voice.

"Otto!"

He turned to see his friend. Johann was sweating, agitated. This wasn't the man Otto knew. Johann was usually a calm, solid, dependable presence—the last to crack.

"Is everything okay?" Otto asked. He held his soiled hands in the air between them.

"I need you to take something to Berlin for me," Johann said rapidly.

Otto examined his friend, trying to read the anxiety. "Of course," he said, turning back to his work. "I'll come and see you before I leave this afternoon."

Johann grabbed his arm and looked deep into Otto's eyes before looking around to see if anyone could overhear them.

"Don't worry," Otto whispered. "I'll find you."

"There's no time for that," Johann said. He slipped a letter into the pocket of Otto's olive-colored examination gown.

"Johann, are you all right?" Otto asked. His tone was one of concern. He had never seen Johann this agitated and furtive.

"See that it gets there safely," Johann insisted.

Otto recognized the need in his friend's eyes. He nodded.

"Do you *promise* me?" Johann demanded.

"I do," Otto replied. "Have no fear of that."

Johann nodded in thanks. "I will see you in Berlin," he said before leaving.

Otto listened to the wind playing on the walls of the tent and hoped that Johann was right.

Somehow he doubted they would ever meet again.

In an empty storage room, Johann quickly changed from his doctor's scrubs into Dieter's uniform, which he had stolen from beneath the bed. Beside him was the battered SS briefcase and a bag of belongings with some meager supplies—stale bread, a little salami, and a bottle of water. It would have to be enough to get him home, if home even existed any longer. The RAF and USAF might be flattening the place at this very moment, with his wife and niece inside. He must hurry; he was already late for his shift. It would not be long until they would start looking for him.

He steeled himself, knowing that this was just the beginning. He thought about Anja and Nadine. He thought about his father. That was enough.

He pushed open the door and walked to where the SS *Kübelwagen* was parked. He noticed the effect that the uniform had on those around him. They no longer saw his face; they just saw the field-gray tunic, the black boots, the peaked cap with the death's-head. How very odd to be perceived as that which you despise. The door of the jeep was unlocked. Inside, the vehicle was a wreck. The floor was caked with dirt and the interior bore evidence that it had been home to three men. Johann wondered how long they had been living like this. Clearly they had not been expecting an inspection at any point.

He turned the key in the ignition and the engine started. He sat for a moment. There was no going back now. Deserting meant almost certain death: The *Feldgendarmerie*, the unforgiving military police, were summarily executing all soldiers discovered separate from their units. If they found him, he would be killed immediately.

He made to put the car in gear.

Just then there was a rapping on the window. Through the condensation, Johann saw that it was one of the guards who watched the visitors' vehicles and the perimeter of the facility. The *Kübelwagen* was in gear—he could just put his foot down and go, but Johann wanted to slip away with as little fuss as possible. He needed to get a head start on the inevitable pursuers who would come after him to regain the briefcase. He wound down the window.

"Yes, *Gefreiter*," Johann said, with the haughtiness he knew an SS officer would use to address a common soldier. The man made a German salute. Johann noticed that the cuff of his coat was frayed and filthy.

"Good morning, sir," the soldier said. "I am very sorry to have to make this request, but we have strict instructions—I need to see your papers."

"My papers?" Johann said severely. "Surely not."

"I'm sorry, sir."

"This can't be necessary," Johann said sternly.

"I have my instructions, sir," the *Gefreiter* said, holding his ground. He was scared of Johann's uniform, but was now casting his eyes around the car. "Were there not two other SS men with you when you arrived?"

"That is no concern of yours," Johann said. "The operations of the Reich Main Security Office are not to be questioned."

"I understand that, sir," said the soldier. Johann hoped that the man would give up. Surely he didn't want to push this confrontation any further. But the soldier stood there stubbornly, examining the *Kübelwagen*. Johann reached around and felt for the Walther P38 pistol on his hip and pulled back the hammer in anticipation. He stared at the soldier evenly.

"I am sorry to have troubled you, sir," the soldier said eventually.

Johann nodded and began to wind up the window. He was free to go.

Just then he saw another man walk around the front of the car and begin to berate the *Gefreiter*. Johann couldn't move the car because the two men were arguing in front of it. He saw that the other man was an *Obergefreiter*, the *Gefreiter*'s ranking officer. Maybe he had seen that the soldier hadn't examined any of Johann's documents. The *Obergefreiter* was angry—his face was flushed and flecks of spittle were coming from his mouth. He marched around to the driver's window and rapped on the door.

Johann had to leave.

He put his foot down. The *Gefreiter* dived out of the way as the car skidded forward, with Johann praying that it would find enough traction on the sodden earth to move him forward. The wheels spun momentarily and then the car lurched ahead, before fishtailing wildly, as if it were being driven on ice. Johann heard small-arms fire behind him as he skidded up the lane toward the exit. He thought: The guard post on the road will have heard the gunfire. As he rounded a corner he saw the two guards running toward the car, their weapons raised. Johann pulled the car to a halt and jumped out.

"Quick!" he said to the guards. "There were shots near the perimeter!"

The guards looked at him, their chests heaving from the exertion of running in greatcoats. They saw only the uniform of the Reich Main Security Office, not the terrified human being wearing it.

"Very good, *Sturmbannführer*," one of them said, and they ran down the lane toward the hospital. The guards were so absorbed with getting to the sound of the shots that they didn't notice the car race toward the exit of the complex. Within a few moments, the *Kübelwagen* was no longer visible on the country road that led from camp.

Johann was gone, driving westward, the battered briefcase and a map next to him on the passenger seat, hope and fear filling his heart in equal measures.

6

Anja had woken up late. Recently her nights had been so troubled, so incomplete, because of the bombing, that she had broken her lifetime practice of early rising and could now be found in bed past nine on the weekend. Thankfully, this morning, Nadine had come in to wake her with a cup of warm water. How Anja longed for a proper mug of coffee. She hadn't had one for—what?—over four years. The damned rationing had killed her taste buds. She wondered if she would ever taste fresh fruit again. She pined for a peach or a strawberry. My goodness, even an apple, like the ones that used to be shipped from Bodensee, would be a delight.

Nadine had sat on Anja's bed for a few moments. The girl was used to spending time with her aunt in the morning, and Anja's late rising disrupted their routine. Anja had kissed Nadine, as she always did, before encouraging the girl—tall, pale, blond, the Aryan ideal—out the door. How funny that the people who produced such a specimen of Nazi approval should be victims of the state's unremitting unraveling of families.

"I'm not sure if the streetcar will be running," Nadine said, wrapping a purple woolen scarf around her neck. "I might have to walk."

"Then you'd better get moving," Anja said, pulling on a sweater. She heard her niece fussing in the hallway with the family dog, a Jack Russell named Flöhchen, who snapped playfully. Flöhchen had arrived with Nadine when her parents had been taken away. Anja and Johann hadn't had to plead with the authorities for the dog's life, unlike that of their niece.

"Come on, you'll be late," Anja said, moving from the bedroom down the corridor in her slippers. The floor had been too cold for bare feet for months.

"I've got plenty of time," Nadine said. "I'm a fast walker, when it's cold."

"I'll see you this evening, sweetheart," Anja said.

"Boiled ham for dinner perhaps?" Nadine joked.

"I'll see what I can do," Anja said with a smile, closing the apartment door. She listened as Nadine's footsteps disappeared down the staircase. Anja cursed herself for sending the girl out of their apartment, but she reasoned that she was as likely to find herself on the end of an incendiary device from a British Lancaster at home as she was at school, and there was an excellent shelter at the girl's school. Nadine had refused to be shipped to the countryside as part of the *Kinderlandverschickung* program. Children from the neighborhood had been relocated to the Sudetenland, or Saxony or Silesia. Nadine wasn't alone—the majority of Berliner children were still in the city. Many had gone away but became homesick and returned. Some, like Nadine, were even able to continue their schooling.

Anja was heading to her job as a teacher every day herself. She reasoned that carrying on a normal life was the only way that the two of them could remain sane. She knew, though, that the time was coming soon when it wouldn't be possible to walk the streets. Within weeks—maybe even days—she would have to take Nadine and escape west, as she had agreed with Johann.

They said the roads west were guarded to prevent mass escape. Yet, according to what was being broadcast, and what she saw on the newspapers read by those on the streetcars and buses that were still running, there was every chance that the Wehrmacht would manage to triumph against the Red Army.

The rumors were different. According to whom you spoke, the Americans were due to take Berlin within days. Or the

Americans had stopped their advance at the Ruhr. Or the Soviets were already across the Oder. Or Hitler had developed a miracle weapon that would vanquish the enemy armies on both fronts. Or Hitler was dead. The only consensus that Anja could detect was simple: Make it stop. The bombing, the killing, the heartbreaking letters from the front, the decimation of the city. Berliners were exhausted. More than five years of rationing, denouncements, air raids, darkness, and crushing loss had wrecked the physical and mental strength of those who were left to face the final days of the Third Reich.

Anja went to the kitchen and turned on the stove. She waited for a moment until the blue flame burst alive. She could hardly believe it. They might live in the last apartment building in the city to have gas. They hadn't had heat for the past two winters, so—although it was strictly forbidden—Anja had used the oven to warm the apartment. Coal was now as rare as gold.

She heated some water in a pan and washed her face, enjoying the warmth on her skin. Anja fixed her hair and made some porridge—she had waited in line for over an hour and a half yesterday after hearing that Michelson's grocers had oatmeal. How she yearned for a little honey to sweeten it.

On her way out of the building she checked the mailbox for a letter from Johann, unlocking it with a small brass key she kept in her purse. Anja closed her eyes and reached into the metal box, her hand feeling the sides before reaching the bottom.

Nothing.

Another pleasure deferred. Anja had almost given up on hearing from him; such was the irregularity of letters from the front. She moved into the vestibule and examined herself in a mirror before stepping onto the street. She had seen Johann three months ago, but she wondered if he would recognize her now—she had aged so much this winter. She was frazzled. Spent. Burned out.

But she continued to fix her hair and turn up for work as neatly dressed as she could manage because she couldn't think what else to do.

For the time being she would continue getting up in the morning, cleaning the apartment, and making improvised meals for Nadine, and she would not think too hard about Johann—if she didn't think too hard, she reasoned, the time apart would pass sooner. She prayed that she would answer the door one day and there he would be. But she now considered that unlikely. She thought it more probable now that if Johann came home at all, she and Nadine would be long gone to the west.

That day the school was visited—as it had been before—by officers of the *Staatspolizei*, who ordered a boy in Anja's class, Lars Ziegler, to report for *Volkssturm* duty at a depot near Schönfeld the next morning. Anja had contained her anger at the men, but had left them in no doubt about her feelings. The boy had come to say goodbye to Anja at the end of the day. He had offered his hand, but she had stepped forward and embraced him instead. She wanted to tell him to go and hide.

When lessons were over, she hurried to the grocer's. In the queue she befriended the woman behind her. The two of them made a pact. Anja would go to the baker to see if there was any bread while the woman waited at the grocer's for lentils. They swapped ration cards—this way each of them would only have to wait in line once.

By the time Anja got home it was dark outside. She went directly to the kitchen and breathed a sigh of relief after turning the tap and lighting the oven: They still had water and gas. Every day it seemed more extraordinary—half of the people she knew had neither and were relying on hand pumps. In Berlin! Even three years ago this was unimaginable. Now people were overwhelmed by happiness if they managed to find a lump of coal that had fallen from a passing train.

She looked to see if Nadine had put a letter from Johann on the dresser, even though she didn't really expect one. Old habits die hard. Flöhchen fussed around her, occasionally yapping with excitement.

Anja had a couple of old potatoes and an onion she had bought on the black market. She had been saving it, but today, after seeing Lars taken by the Gestapo, she needed to eat well. And Nadine needed it. The girl had the appetite of an adult. Anja fried the onion in the glutinous margarine that she had still not adapted to eating, despite years of enduring the stuff, and then added the lentils and potato. If she topped up the water there should be enough to keep them going for a few days. Beyond that, who knew? Anja couldn't believe that she would ever find herself in a position where she would be pining for *Eintopf*—the mysterious Nazi concoction of vegetables, broth, and mystery meat that the whole nation, from the Führer to the street sweeper, was supposed to eat once a week.

Nadine appeared at the kitchen door, stretching.

"That smells nice," she said, petting Flöhchen.

"Have you been sleeping?" Anja asked.

"Yes," Nadine replied. "I dozed off doing my Latin homework. The smell of the onions cooking woke me up. I thought I was dreaming."

"And it's not just onions," Anja said proudly. "We have lentils and potatoes as well."

"Tonight we eat like kings." Nadine smiled, stooping to pick up Flöhchen.

"Did you finish your homework before you fell asleep?"

"I have a little more to do. Vocabulary," Nadine explained. "I will do it after supper."

"Good. I have some sewing to do. We can sit and listen to the radio together."

"If there isn't an air raid," Nadine said.

How tired Anja was of spending her nights at the shelter, or packed into Friedrichstraße U-Bahn station. She almost wished the RAF would just drop a bomb directly on their building so she wouldn't have to climb from her warm bed, get dressed, and shuffle down the street in the darkness, apologizing to people she bumped into in the dark.

"Set the table, will you, please?" Anja called to her niece.

Nadine put down Flöhchen then stretched up into the cupboard and pulled down two bowls and plates and placed them on the table.

"No bread," Anja said, prompting Nadine to put the plates back.

"Tante, what will happen when the Soviets come?" Nadine asked.

"I don't know," Anja replied. This was the truth.

"What do you think will happen?"

"No one really knows, sweetheart."

"What do you imagine?"

"I imagine that they will kill all the Nazis and that we will have a new government and judges and that the city will be rebuilt. We will have shops, and cinemas, and parks again. It will take time, though. Or maybe the Americans will come. Things might not get much better for a long time. But then Onkel Johann will be home. And we will be together again. As long as we have that we can look after each other."

Nadine put a couple of glasses down on the table and folded her arms.

"Do you think we should leave?"

There was a pause while Anja considered what to tell Nadine. She decided that the girl was old enough to be told the truth.

"Your *Onkel* and I talked about it," Anja said carefully. "I hear that it is still possible."

"I think we should try," Nadine said quickly.

"Nadine," Anja said, "it might not be . . ."

"I know . . . ," Nadine said. "But the girls at school—there are all kinds of rumors going round about the Soviets. . . ."

Anja swallowed hard. She too had heard the stories coming from the east of mass rapes and sadistic violence. The reports traveled among the women in the ration queues. The Red Army was having its revenge for what had been done in the east by the Nazis.

"There are all sorts of *rumors* going round, my dear," Anja said, stirring the soup. The potato had almost broken down. She blocked out a mad rush of hunger—if she could only wait a few minutes longer, the meal would be all the more delicious.

"Tante, you know what I'm talking about," Nadine said.

Anja turned and approached the girl, laying her hand on her shoulder.

"If they come, we will outwit them. We will escape or we will hide," she said resolutely. "You don't need to worry—that's my job. You're too young for such concerns."

Nadine had finished laying out the cutlery but returned to its drawer and pulled out another item. Anja saw the glint of a large chopping knife in the candlelight. Nadine leaned her hips against the table and examined the stainless steel. The sharpener had come last week and Anja had had no money to pay him, but it was sharp enough.

"My parents didn't see it coming when the truck came for them," Nadine said firmly. "It was in the night. We left the house in our nightclothes." She sounded pensive, lost in her recollection. Then she looked up at Anja and stared directly into her eyes, sending a shiver through the woman. "But I will be ready for them this time. Any Ivan who comes near me . . ." Nadine brandished the knife. "And if I can't get them first, then I will make sure that they will not get their pleasure."

Anja saw that the girl was serious: She would rather take her own life than live with pain and humiliation.

"Nadine," Anja said. "I swear that you will never be in that situation."

"How can you know?" Nadine asked dismissively.

"Because I will never allow it to happen," Anja told her. The girl nodded gently. She might not have believed that it was the truth, but she knew that the sentiment was well meant. Anja turned to stir the soup. Flöhchen watched her patiently.

With her aunt's back turned, Nadine removed the knife from the drawer, went to the hallway, and placed it in the pocket of her coat.

She would leave nothing to chance.

7

The ambulance carrying Dieter crawled up Wilhelmstraße past the ruined buildings of the government district. The driver negotiated a fresh pile of rubble on the corner of Zimmerstraße, near the headquarters of the Air Ministry. He remembered the fanfare when it had opened in 1936—the Nazis claimed it was the biggest office building in Europe. It had been hit by the RAF, but was in far better condition than most of the structures in the area.

The driver had refused to look left out of superstition as he had passed the Reich Main Security Office on Prinz-Albrecht-Straße: Too many people had ended up shackled in its basement. Little did he know that the man in the back of his ambulance had spent the better part of a decade doing its work. He rounded a motionless streetcar (the vehicle was stationary because of an electricity outage), passed the long-abandoned British embassy, and headed over Unter den Linden—bomb damaged, like an aristocrat who had taken a life-threatening beating—and through the entrance to Charité Hospital, its red brick buildings and timbered gatehouse still, miraculously, untouched by the bombing. The driver had heard that some of the hospitals in Berlin had had vast red crosses painted on their roofs—a plea to the Allied bombers.

As Dieter was carried from the back of the vehicle he felt a cool breeze on his face and saw the familiar building looming above his stretcher. The air in the ambulance had been fetid but, strangely, he could smell blossoms in the air now. Could he possibly be in Berlin? And was that rustling noise leaves blowing in the wind? The legions of civilians desperate for firewood last winter hadn't killed off every bit of flora in the city. Even in 1945 there would be a spring.

He remembered back to when he had last been in a vehicle. They had been driving west for what felt like days. The three of them. Lehman, with his terrible flatulence, was at the wheel. Ostermann sat in the back, being obsequious. Dieter had had the orders only a month before, once the Russians had rolled across the Baltic states. After Bucharest fell in mid-February, rumors were rife that Vienna was next. Cities and regions began to crumble, and with them the state's darkest secrets.

Dieter had been given a *Kübelwagen* and a couple of flunkeys and told that no one was to know their mission. Officially they didn't exist. They drove clear across Poland in one mad dash, before zigzagging back through that cursed country from Majdanek to Auschwitz. The Ivans were never that far behind; he would look in the rearview mirror some nights and see the sky behind him illuminated with flares.

After they had collected the information from each camp they would leave their windows open to drive the stench from the vehicle as it strained along the buckled back roads. The noise from the air-cooled engine in the back meant that their ears rang for hours even after they'd come to a halt. They kept moving at night, taking turns to drive.

The briefcase rested on his lap at all times. He had locked and chained it to his wrist. He would return the microfilm to the propaganda ministry for "management," as his orders had been phrased, at the earliest opportunity, or he would die in the attempt. They rarely stopped, but one night, as they were driving through dense forest toward Frankfurt an der Oder, he had opened a window and smelled the freshness of the vegetation. He was worn-out and even the fresh air pouring through the window wasn't enough to rouse him. He needed to rest, even if it was for a few hours.

Then he saw it: a small farmhouse nestled at the top of a lane in a clearing. In the next three minutes there would be a frantic encounter with a farmer that Dieter barely recalled. He had noticed that the man was holding something in his right hand. It was hard and metallic. The farmer had thrown down his pitchfork in anger. Dieter began to raise his pistol, but he knew that he had seen the danger too late.

Everything went white. It was like the sun had exploded.

He was inside now—voices all around him. Orderlies, doctors, nurses, patients babbling. He was catching fragments of conversation, a different tempo and kinds of words to the military imperatives and banter he had delivered and been subject to for the last decade. Ten years of service. Of rank climbing and order following, of score settling, ass licking, and backstabbing. He had been a good soldier. He believed in the cause. He believed in the Führer. He believed in wronging Versailles's injustices to the fatherland. He loathed communism. The Soviets could do what they liked when they arrived; his heart would always beat with a burning belief in the rightness of the cause and what he had done to further it.

He was wheeled to a large ward with high windows covered in protective tape that contained dozens of beds. The room housed injured military personnel as well as civilians. The difference between the patients was age—the military were the sons of the civilians. There were a couple of quizzical looks in his direction, but most of the men just lay still, silently contemplating their injuries.

He was rolled into a bed—Christ, it hurt—and left to stare at the ceiling. He shifted himself so that he could at least get a view of the nurses as they passed. Moments later he fell asleep.

He was woken by two men standing above him. Wolfgang Pfeiffer and Ulrich Vogt. His friends! Both of them *Sturmbannführer*. They had not abandoned him. They would see this thing through together.

"The doctor said that he's doing well," Pfeiffer said.

"He's a tough old bastard," replied Vogt. "It will take more than a few burns to stop him."

Yes, yes, Dieter thought. *I am a tough old bastard.*

Suddenly it was as if thunder had boomed overhead, shocking him with its power.

Thomas! Or Johann, as he now called himself.

Good God! Why hadn't this occurred to him sooner? When they were bringing him to the bed why had he not recalled that Johann had intended to inject him with some poison? Was it lost to him that his half brother had whispered in the darkness in that disgusting field hospital that he was revenging Nicolas? That he had killed Ostermann?

He tried to sit up and signal for help.

"Look!" Pfeiffer said. "He's moving!"

The two men leaned over Dieter.

"Hello, old friend," Vogt said. "Glad to have you back in Berlin."

"Welcome home, Dieter," Pfeiffer said, striking the bed with excitement. "We knew you'd make it back safely."

"I'd better let a nurse know," Vogt said, disappearing.

Dieter beckoned Pfeiffer with his head. Pfeiffer moved in close, examining Dieter's face for clues. The injured man moved his lips—they were trembling. Opening his jaw was acutely painful.

"What is it, Dieter?" Pfeiffer asked, realizing that he was being told something. Dieter made a slight gurgling sound before finding that he was able to produce a noise that was closer to speech.

"You should rest, Dieter," Pfeiffer said.

Dieter opened his mouth again.

"Jo . . . ," he said, his voice fragile and faint.

"Try again," Pfeiffer said, realizing the urgency of what Dieter was trying to communicate.

"Johann . . ."

"Johann," Pfeiffer repeated.

Dieter nodded, exhausted but pleased.

"Who is Johann?" Pfeiffer asked. "Someone in your unit?"

Dieter shook his head. He tried to speak again, but his mouth was dry. He couldn't form the words. Dieter rested for a moment. He would try again.

"Sch . . . ," he started, but Pfeiffer hadn't heard. Vogt had returned with a nurse.

"Gentlemen, please," the middle-aged woman said, pushing past Pfeiffer. "The patient needs to rest."

Dieter summoned all his energy, and opened his mouth again. He would spit it out this time. He would make "Johann" pay.

"Uuuugh . . ."

"He's in a lot of pain," the nurse said, examining Dieter's file, which was attached to a clipboard. She wasn't even looking at Dieter.

"Schhhhuuu . . . ," Dieter slurred.

"What did he say?" Pfeiffer asked.

"I'm not sure," Vogt replied.

Dieter closed his eyes, trying to regain his strength. He thought about his half brother. Where had he been all this time?

A couple of years after Johann's disappearance, once Dieter had developed more influence he had friends in the Party investigate the archives and the public records. Nothing. The trail stopped in June 1934. There were records for the dead and those packed away to camps, so why nothing for Thomas Meier? It made absolutely no sense. He had not withdrawn a library book since 1934, had finished school the day after Nicolas was taken away, and had no military records.

The state was fastidious about recording every aspect of an individual's life. It was unthinkable that a person could just remove himself from the bureaucratic apparatus. There was no record of Thomas's death or his whereabouts. And not knowing was what drove Dieter over the next decade, for he knew that Thomas had the key, and with it the riches.

He could hear Pfeiffer and Vogt talking. He tried, once again, to tell them about Johann. They must hunt him down at the field hospital and bring him to Prinz-Albrecht-Straße.

He tried to move his mouth, but his lips weren't doing what he asked.

"His war is over, anyway," Pfeiffer said. "He won't be going back to the front."

"The front is coming to him," Vogt replied. "He doesn't need to leave his bed. What was he doing with only a couple of junior officers near the Oder, anyway?"

"You didn't hear?" Pfeiffer said. "A major operation. Clandestine. Huge problem. Everyone's scrambling to fix it. Someone has taken . . ."

Dieter kept running over the details as best as he could remember them. Their mission had been to collect the film and enforce the Führer's executive order. It had gone wrong. . . . It had gone so terribly wrong. . . . There was to be a meeting at a farmhouse with another group from the Reich Main Security Office. . . . *My God* . . . Where was the briefcase? Who had the briefcase? His heart skipped, as if it had received a jolt. If central command had discovered it was missing he would surely be shot. Thousands and thousands of records . . . The whole business . . . If it were to fall into enemy hands . . .

He had heard Ostermann saying that he was placing the briefcase under his bed. But Ostermann was dead. And that dolt Lehman couldn't be trusted to tie up his own bootlaces. There had been someone else in the room that night who could have come across it. . . . Dieter began to lose consciousness as the figures above him began to blur and turn to shadows. Before his mind went into neutral he had a singular realization: To find the briefcase he must find the man who was most likely to have it. The man who had attempted to kill him and had murdered Ostermann: He would hunt down his half brother, the traitor Thomas Meier.

Dieter forced himself to sit up, rising so dramatically that the nurse dropped the clipboard on his chest.

Of course.

Through a narcotic haze, Dieter grabbed the clipboard and rifled through the pages, fighting the pain of his injuries.

There it was in black ink—a doctor's notes in a careful hand that he recognized.

Dieter slammed his index finger onto the paperwork, prompting Pfeiffer and Vogt to lean forward and examine what Dieter was gesturing to. There, before them, was the name "Johann Schultz."

"Murder," Dieter croaked, his finger still resting on his half brother's name.

8

Anja, like many Berliners, went to bed with the radio semiaudible: The broadcast would be interrupted with news of an impending attack. It came an hour after she had fallen into an uneasy slumber. The music faded and a staccato voice snapped at her. The British planes were over Hanover: They had no more than twenty minutes to reach the shelter.

For the first time that day she had felt warm, and now she was pulling her clothes over her nightdress in the freezing room, her breath visible as her eyes adjusted to the darkness. She called to Nadine to ready herself. The wail of the sirens would begin soon.

Nadine was already at the front door of the apartment when Anja came out of her room. Their routine was well practiced: They left a bag with basic provisions—a flashlight, some food, their *Volksgasmasken* (she had found the money for the more expensive VM40 version), a flask of water, some candles and matches—by the front door and collected it on their way out. Nadine hugged Flöhchen and instructed him to hide. The last thing Anja did before they left—even in winter—was to open all the windows to protect them from the blasts.

In the early days of the war there had been a sort of novelty about the city being in total darkness at night. Luminous arrows had been painted on the walls, directing people to the nearest air-raid shelters. Anja remembered looking up and wondering at the stars: She had never seen the night sky above the city in such a way, masked as it usually was by the dirty haze of streetlights.

Early on she had detected a we're-all-in-this-together spirit— even from those who, like her, had dreaded being at war ever since she had first heard the ominous news of the German attack on Poland in September 1939. She remembered trying hard to imagine that it wasn't true, that somehow the conflict would be resolved and quickly forgotten. But then, two days later, she had been doing some sewing and listening to Liszt's Hungarian Rhapsody no. 1 on the radio when the broadcast had been interrupted with an announcement that Germany was at war with England. The news was being blared over loudspeakers in the street. Suddenly a deep dread, worse than anything she had felt before, filled every part of Anja's being. The air-raid sirens that she had heard on September 1, the ration cards, the piles of sand that had suddenly appeared on the street with burlap sacks that were to be filled by local residents, the appointment of a detested *Blockwart*—a functionary who served as the eyes and ears of the Party on every block.

In the years of darkness—literal and figurative—since then, the bombing raids from the west had become incessant. It now felt inconceivable that, fewer than five years before, Hitler had returned from Paris and was driven from Anhalter station to the Reich Chancellery on a carpet of flowers. Anja had seen it with her own eyes, one of many to skulk, uncheering, at the back of the crowd. They were there just to bear witness. Nowadays it was more likely that those Berliners would scoop up the flowers from the road and make soup from them.

As Anja and Nadine hurried through the darkness, they were directed by wardens toward what they called the "railway bunker" on the corner of Albrechtstraße and Reinhardtstraße. It was a *Hochbunker*, a five-story structure of thick concrete built aboveground—a testament to Berlin's sandy soil, which made deep excavation difficult. Sometimes they would head for the U-Bahn station at Friedrichstraße.

Nadine hugged Anja's elbow as the two of them progressed through the darkness, aware that other people were close by but not entirely sure of their whereabouts. Anja had made this journey so many times that she knew every inch of the pavement, every broken curbstone, the edge of each building wall. She could make this journey in daytime with her eyes closed, if she needed to.

They heard the first boom of explosions above the sound of the sirens and the flak coming from the antiaircraft towers—one at the Zoo, the other on Friedenstraße—as they filed through the doorway, which had been widened to allow a greater flow of people. The flak towers were supposed to be manned by girls not much older than Nadine now. Anja glanced up at the formidable building that had been constructed to much fanfare at the beginning of the war. What a tomb it would make: a poured-concrete sarcophagus. The building famously had walls that were more than two meters thick and a reinforced concrete roof, which was designed to survive—and had survived—a direct hit. There were a series of rooms, perhaps forty of them, each about ten meters square equipped with wooden benches for people to sit. Many were already lying on the floor in makeshift beds; others were squatting on suitcases that had been filled with essentials and mementos in case they were unable to return home.

There were lamps on the walls of each room that had been fitted with blue bulbs. The light was eerie: The inhabitants—elderly people, women with young children, soldiers on leave, guest workers from France, Holland, Italy, and Yugoslavia—were made to look spectral. Anja and Nadine walked through several rooms before finding a place to sit next to a woman with two young children, who, exhausted, were curled up on the bench beside her. The place was stifling. There were no windows—instead, overhead fans were supposed to extract the humid air. Condensation dripped from the ceiling onto those below.

"Are you hungry?" Anja asked Nadine once they were settled, raising her voice above the droning of the ventilation system. The girl shook her head.

"I'm worried about Flöhchen."

"He's underneath the sofa," Anja said. "He'll be fine."

Nadine looked around—even children were self-conscious enough to know that they must watch their words—and whispered, "Do you think Onkel Johann will come?"

Anja smiled in the gloom and moved a strand of hair that had fallen over the girl's face.

"When can we leave?" Nadine persisted.

"When Onkel comes."

Nadine's face lit up.

"When, Auntie, when?"

"Soon, I hope. He will try. Now shush. Let's talk about this later."

Anja knew that Johann would do his best to reach them, but she wondered if it was really possible for him to travel—what was it?—the eighty or one hundred kilometers to Berlin from where she had last known he was.

All the same, she had made it her business to find out if the trains were still running from the main stations. Some were too badly damaged by the bombing to be safe to operate. She had heard that there were trains running from the central station, Lehrter Bahnhof. For the time being it was still operating, but in order to prevent mass flight from the city only those with the proper documentation were allowed to travel. Anja had no idea how she might get the right papers; they were only available to those with Party connections.

An incendiary device exploded only a few streets away, shaking the building. The woman next to them on the bench was hugging her children tight as if by her own strength of will she could prevent them from being harmed.

Anja looked at Nadine and realized that if she had to, she would carry the girl to the American lines.

"We will leave when the time is right," Anja said to her niece quietly.

Johann had made her promise that she would flee the city even if he was unable to reach her. As much as it pained her, she would do what she needed to get Nadine away from Berlin once the final battle had begun. They would not be trapped amid the inevitable horror.

That night, with death falling again from the sky, Anja knew what it was like to be utterly powerless. But she determined one thing: She would protect her niece with every ounce of strength and cunning she had left—she would find meaning and purpose amid the chaos.

They could remain here no longer. They would break out of Berlin.

9

Johann jammed on the brakes, bringing the *Kübelwagen* to a skidding halt. The briefcase slid from the seat and fell to the floor. He jumped from the jeep and searched in the trunk for some tools. He found a screwdriver inside an empty ammunition container, returned to the front of the vehicle, and looked around to make sure he was not being followed. Ever since he had escaped from the hospital, Johann had been desperate to know the contents of the briefcase.

Lehman had told him that he would only discover Dieter's mission if he went to the farmhouse, but surely the case would offer clues.

He forced the screwdriver into the keyhole of the briefcase and twisted it hard. Eventually the lock snapped. Johann pulled at the brass clasp—but it wouldn't shift. The mechanism rotated when he turned the screwdriver, but breaking it had made no impact on the effectiveness of the lock. He pushed the tool into the clasp and levered it, twisting the screwdriver forcefully. Finally, with a loud crack, the clasp came apart.

Johann pulled the case open wide and looked inside. It was packed tightly with a jumble of taupe envelopes of different sizes and shapes. He pulled one out and saw a series of numbers and letters written, in pencil, on the front. He reread the code, but it made no sense to him.

The envelope was sealed. He hesitated opening it for a second before inserting his thumb into the flap that had been glued shut. The gum parted in thin strands before pulling apart. Johann reached inside, his hand trembling, and pulled out a small box about four inches square and an inch deep and put it on the hood of the *Kübelwagen*. The code had been written on the box by the same hand that had written on the envelope—the same two letters began the progression. He pulled open the box. Inside was a dark metal spool. Johann pulled it from the box and saw that, wrapped around the spool, was a thin strip of celluloid.

Microfilm.

He had used it when he had been interning at the hospital years ago for research purposes. Johann pulled at the loose end of the strip and held it to the sky. In the weak light it looked to be black with vertical gray patches. Johann's eyes were beginning to ache now: The strain of the events of the past hours and concentrating on the road were taking their toll. The images were much too small for him to read anything, but Johann could tell that each of them was a negative of a photograph of a document.

He placed the spool back in the envelope and stuffed it into the case. He prized out another couple of envelopes—both of them had handwritten code on the outside—and felt them. Inside each was a square container the same size as the one in the first envelope. He knew now what was in the case—dozens of envelopes containing microfilm. But he could still only guess at the significance of this information. All he knew for sure was that Dieter and the men in his unit were willing to die to protect it.

He hunted through the case to see if there was anything that might enlighten him about the Berlin mission that Lehman had talked about.

Nothing.

He sighed. Had he imagined something of great portent that didn't exist? Had the SS unit just been fulfilling a simple mission? He thought not, but he was no closer to discovering the truth—or Dieter's part in it.

He packed the envelopes back in the briefcase, then flipped it closed and placed it back on the passenger seat.

He pressed his hands to his forehead. What on earth was he doing meddling in such matters? He had killed two men and deserted his post. He was a dead man if he was apprehended. Surely he would do better to try and get to Berlin and hide until the war was over. He had heard rumors that there were thousands of soldiers holed up in the city already.

He had promised Anja that he would come home before the darkest hour descended.

But the Wenck farm on the Zossen Road near Müncheberg was just a few miles away now.

He had to know.

He owed it to Nicolas. He had done nothing that June night to protect his father. He would not walk away again; he had to go to the farm. Only there could he learn for sure what Dieter's terrible mission had been. Only there might he discover the danger to Berlin posed by Germany's doomed rulers.

He got back in the car and executed a three-point turn with much skidding of the *Kübelwagen*'s knobbly tires and drove back the other way toward Zossen. On his left, the west and sunshine, on the right, the darkness of the east.

He headed north for another half hour, following the road toward the farm. Without warning the car began to splutter. He examined the sole dial in the *Kübelwagen,* which was positioned on the dashboard midway between the driver and passenger. He was out of diesel. Damn. The meeting was supposed to be at six— he had two hours to get there, and he estimated that it was at least five miles away. He clambered out of the car into the misty air and set about unstrapping the jerrycan from over the front wheel arch. There would be twenty liters of diesel in there—enough to get him to Berlin.

The second he pulled it free Johann knew he was in trouble. The can was empty. Johann cursed and threw the metal container into a field. He looked up the road, which narrowed. There was nothing else for it now. He returned to the *Kübelwagen* and retrieved the briefcase.

He imagined that its contents were as incendiary as anything the Soviets could fire from their Katyushas. He would honor his father and expose the full awfulness of his brother. He would find his wife. As he trotted up the road he realized that he was now a lot closer to Berlin than he had been this morning.

He was halfway home.

Time was short. Johann consulted the map that he had sketched according to Lehman's description. There was no way he would make the rendezvous if he continued along the road, which offered a circuitous route. On foot it would be quicker to cut across fields and woodland. Johann found a gap in a hedgerow and squeezed through it, dragging the case after him. He was thirsty. He hoped there might be a stream in the woodland ahead. The field he walked across was wet and marshy. It appeared not to have been planted. He didn't like being out in the open like this, and hurried toward the tree line.

He reached the woods and looked back over the swampy land to see if he was being followed. He couldn't see anyone. He tried to get his bearings by checking on the position of the sun. He needed to continue northwest for about two miles, where he would encounter a road. From there he had to head north for another two miles through more woodland.

He waded through the decaying leaves and ferns as quietly as he could manage, stopping every so often to listen and watch for other people. As he marched, he shifted the briefcase between his arms, sometimes cradling it in both. He checked his watch. If he was right, he was making good time.

At last he saw water—a small brook, some of it obscured by dead foliage and branches. He let go of the briefcase for the first time and knelt down, scooping the cold water up and gulping it down. It tasted metallic, but it satisfied his thirst.

What was that?

Johann threw himself to the woodland floor. He was sure that he had heard a horse whinny.

There it was again. Johann flattened himself on the ground and pulled the briefcase toward him. Were those footsteps he heard? He reached down for his handgun.

He was sure there were people nearby.

He searched for the source of the noise. Through the trees he could see movement. He was close to the road. He inched forward on his knees, dragging the briefcase after him. He was perhaps twenty yards away now. Before him he saw a picture of pure human misery: thousands of bedraggled, haggard refugees streaming toward Berlin to escape the Russian advance. The convoy appeared to consist mostly of women and children, some of whom were being carried, while others stumbled after their mothers as if in a dream. Still others rode on carts or were pushed in carriages loaded with possessions. They were all silent, each absorbed in private wretchedness. There were elderly people too: some hobbling along as if each step might be their last. Many carried suitcases, and several had bedding draped over their shoulders.

He decided to go back deep into the woods and walk parallel with the road to ensure that no one observed him. Just as he was beginning to edge backward he heard a vehicle coming down the road. He watched as people scattered to the side of the highway. The vehicle pulled over urgently next to a cart driven by a woman.

Four children sat on top of a pile of household possessions. Johann peered through the trees at the *Kübelwagen*.

Feldgendarmerie.

The soldiers shouted instructions to the woman to halt the cart. Two of them climbed on the back, lifting the children to the ground. They then set about rifling through the furniture, bedding, and clothing. The woman gathered her children by the side of the road and began to shout at the soldiers.

"You won't find anything in there—let us be on our way. *Ivan kommt.*"

The soldiers ignored her and continued to search. One of them discovered a chest at the bottom of the pile of possessions.

The woman pulled her children closer to her.

The *Feldgendarmerie* officers flung open the lid of the chest and dragged a man, who looked to be in his early thirties, out onto the cart, shouting at him to raise his hands. The man wore a thick, bloodied bandage around his head and looked dazed. He gazed forlornly at his wife, who was hugging the children and screaming at the soldiers to let her husband go.

"He's honest and hardworking!" she shouted. "Let him alone. Let him live in peace."

The man was dragged from the cart. Johann could see that he was wearing a civilian coat, but on his lower body there were military-issue trousers and boots. A deserter.

The woman kept screaming. The soldiers ignored her pleas and the sobbing of the children. With weapons raised they pushed the man into the woods.

Johann was horrified to realize that they were heading directly for him. His instinct was to run, but he grasped that, if he moved, he would give himself away. He maneuvered his body deep into a cluster of ferns that were just behind him, sliding through the moist earth. The foliage was his only chance.

"Please," the deserter said. "What will become of my family? Let me live, please."

The *Feldgendarmerie* soldiers took no notice, pushing the man deeper into the woodland—closer to Johann. He was among the ferns now, but he doubted that they were dense enough to hide him properly.

Through the trees Johann heard the woman screaming. An officious male voice informed her that all deserters were to be executed by order of Army High Command.

The woman's wailing grew louder as the noise of the two *Feldgendarmerie* and their prisoner got closer to Johann. They were eighteen yards, then fifteen, twelve. . . . They stopped no more than ten yards from him. He was partly obscured by a tree that they were standing near. If they stepped beyond it they would almost certainly see him. Johann made himself as small as he could and leveled his pistol. If they saw him he would shoot.

The deserter was on his knees.

"Please," he said, reaching into his coat. "Look." He held up his *Ostmedaille*, the medal awarded to those who fought on the eastern front. "I have fought for the Führer for four years. I killed Soviets. I did my duty. All I wanted was to care for my family. To protect them."

Just then the deserter looked up, and—through the foliage—his eyes fell upon Johann. His face opened wide with surprise.

"Look!" he said to the soldiers. "Look, behind you! A deserter."

Terrified, Johann leveled his pistol. He would have to use the element of surprise to shoot the soldiers in the woods and hope that their comrades on the road didn't come after him. He rolled to the right, into the thickest part of the clump of ferns, and hoped the tree would continue to obscure him. He tried to flatten his body so that it would become part of the ground beneath him.

The *Feldgendarmerie* soldiers looked where the deserter had indicated. One of them kept his rifle on the prisoner, while the other turned to peer into the woods. Johann pressed his body as close to the ground as he could and watched in horror as the soldier began to walk toward him, his eyes scanning the woods. He kicked at a rotted tree stump before creeping farther into the forest.

"Can you see anything?" the other *Feldgendarmerie* soldier called.

Johann watched as a pair of boots passed five yards away. Surely the soldier couldn't miss him. . . .

He cocked the pistol. The boots stopped moving. Johann's finger tightened on the trigger. He aimed for the soldier's heart.

"No, nothing here," the soldier replied. Johann exhaled. The man moved back to join his comrade.

"No, no . . . ," the deserter pleaded. "I swear I saw a man, just over there. A deserter. Better to take him than a war hero."

The woods echoed with the loud bang of a single shot. Crows screamed and fluttered from the trees. The forest reverberated for several seconds. Johann looked up to see the two soldiers walking out of the woods. He could no longer see the deserter. Johann heard the engine of a *Kübelwagen* start and the vehicle pull away.

Finally he stood up. Johann could see the man slumped about twenty yards from him, his face on the ground. He started to run north, the briefcase banging against his legs.

He did not want to hear the screams of the deserter's wife when she found her husband.

10

Johann found the marker for the Wenck farm nailed to a tree by the side of the crossroads Lehman had talked about. The sign had been carefully hand painted onto a small oval of wood. Johann stood still and listened. There was no sign of life.

Then, out of the dark, came three quick barks, like rounds being fired from a gun. A dog. He looked down the lane toward the farm and saw something. What was that? Fireflies in March? He realized the orange lights in the distance weren't insects but the glow of a cigarette. Someone was standing at the end of the lane.

Johann began to walk down the track. Soon he heard the patter of paws and felt the nuzzle of a big dog in the palm of his hand. He petted the animal, enjoying the warmth on his hands. The dog fell in behind him, trotting along and panting contentedly. At the end of the lane he saw in the moonlight that he was standing in a courtyard. On one side was a house and on the other three farm buildings. He smelled animals and manure, the damp odor of hay that had gone bad. He looked around for whoever had been smoking.

"*Heil Hitler,*" a voice grunted. It was hoarse, full of cold. Johann heard the man come to attention.

"*Heil Hitler,*" Johann replied.

"They're waiting for you inside, sir," the soldier said.

Johann swallowed. He was terrified. Momentarily he thought about disappearing into the night. He regained his focus: Only by entering the building would he discover Dieter's secrets and the threat to Berlin. It was too late now; he must maintain his nerve.

"Which way?" Johann asked. He felt for the P38 on his hip absently.

"Where's your car?" asked the soldier. Johann could make out a large vehicle, perhaps a truck, behind the man. Was it a troop carrier? He feared this meant there would be large numbers of SS, and looked closer. It appeared to be a general-purpose vehicle—perhaps even civilian, although it had SS plates.

"It broke down," Johann said.

"*Kübelwagen?*" the soldier asked.

"Yes," Johann answered. The man wheezed.

"It's the transmission," the soldier eventually said. "Always is. Does your driver require assistance?"

"No," Johann cut in. "He has help on the way."

"Very good, sir," the man said. "Please, this way."

Johann followed the man through a stone doorway into a farmer's cottage. They passed through a kitchen area and into a dining room with stone walls and no windows. Two men were sitting at a table that was lit by a candle that had been stuffed into a wine bottle. Both of them stood up, and the three men exchanged the German greeting.

"Sturmbannführer Schnell?" one of them asked, extending his hand. Johann nodded. How strange to be addressed as Dieter.

"Sturmbannführer Schorner. And this is Obersturmführer Beckmann."

"Dieter Schnell," Johann said, shaking both of the men's hands. He looked around. There was a dresser with crockery piled on it randomly, some linen stuffed in a corner, a photo of a young man wearing a First World War uniform.

"Looks like they left in a hurry," Johann said.

"Most of the farms here are abandoned," Beckmann said. He was a large, lumbering man with dark hair and a ruddy complexion. Next to him was a half-eaten salami. The blade of a knife was stuck into the wooden dining table. Beckmann saw Johann gazing at it.

"Hungry?" Beckmann asked.

Despite his fear, Johann was starving. He had no idea when he might eat next. He nodded and Beckmann sliced the salami, cutting a deep mark into the varnished table. He handed a thick disk to Johann. The salty meat made his eyes water with pleasure.

"It's a lovely table, I know," Beckmann said, acknowledging the damaged veneer. "Oak, I think. But the heathen Soviets will only burn it anyway."

"Shall we get down to business?" asked Schorner impatiently, rubbing his hands together. He was smaller than his companion but looked muscular. His head was completely bald. A pair of wire-rimmed spectacles was perched on a minute nose. In the half-light, Johann wondered whether Schorner might have lost part of it in combat.

"Yes," Johann said. "I have the briefcase." He placed it on the table next to the knife. This was his ploy: offer them what he had in order to learn what it was that they had.

"Excellent," Schorner said. "We now have all the information in one place."

"All the information?" Johann asked. He looked inquisitively at Schorner, as if the man might not be revealing the entire truth.

"You know what I'm saying," he answered, waving his hand dismissively. "There are some files with Reinhard at the Ministry in Berlin, but I believe that if you have the microfilm and we have the paper versions then we have a record of every single prisoner who has passed through a KZ."

The two hard consonants hit Johann with a thud.

He felt like the air had been sucked from his lungs.

All Johann could hear was KZ. *Konzentrationslager.*

He was carrying the history of the camps.

All those names. All those people reduced to mere paperwork that had been copied dutifully onto microfilm. Of the seven departments in the Reich Main Security Office it would be the operatives in the seventh office, "Written Records," who would ensure protocol was followed to the letter. Lives extinguished, made real only by the functionaries who organized it with no more emotion than they would coordinate a train timetable. But why had they gathered the documentation into one place? What were they intending to do with it?

"So you are accompanying the documents to the Ministry?" Johann asked. He tried to make his words sound as if he was ensuring the safety of the data.

"Indeed," Schorner said, leaning against the fireplace. "What a shithole Poland is. Four weeks of driving from godforsaken place to godforsaken place collecting all these documents."

"Quite," Johann said, pretending to laugh.

"I don't know why they needed two units to do what one could have done," said Beckmann, cutting another slice of sausage.

"If one unit had done both, then if they were captured the entire archive would be lost," Schorner said dismissively, as if he had told Beckmann before.

The three men stood awkwardly. Johann still held on to the briefcase tightly.

"What are your orders after this?" Schorner asked Johann. Both SS officers looked at him curiously. Was this a test? Johann held their gazes, his mind searching desperately for a plausible answer.

"I'm afraid I can't tell you that," he said eventually.

Both men nodded. This was clearly not unusual. Johann felt some of the tension ease.

"And when you arrive at the Ministry with the documents and the microfilm?" Johann asked.

"I'm afraid I can't tell you that," Schorner replied. He kept a straight face before breaking into a smile.

Beckmann laughed and set fire to a piece of greasy paper that had been used to wrap the salami. It flared briefly before twisting and turning to carbon.

"Up in smoke," he said.

"Even now they are stoking the furnaces at the Ministry," Schorner said with a smirk.

They were going to burn the files and the microfilm. They wanted to erase history, to pretend that the deportations, the separation of families, the murder, had never happened. Johann had heard the stories, but many people were still oblivious, wouldn't believe the rumors, or just didn't want to know what had happened to their neighbors when they were marched off—what the authorities described as a "resettlement program in the east."

The Nazis hoped that they would never find out, that the rumors would remain just that.

Johann knew now what Dieter had been doing: cleansing history, removing the corroboration so that conjecture would take the place of truth. His half brother was a willing manipulator of fact, an adversary of light.

Johann tightened his grip on the handle of the briefcase. He held the truth in his hands.

And at that moment, it struck him: Hidden in the back of the truck was a file with the name "Meier" on it. If he could get inside the vehicle he could find out what had happened to his father.

"We have an early start," Schorner announced, stretching. "And tonight will be the first time that I have slept on a real bed for months. There are several rooms upstairs, Schnell. Feel free to help yourself, if you wish. They seem to have taken the bedding, but you might be lucky enough to find a blanket if you look around."

"The *Sturmbannführer* is very kind," Johann said, clapping Schorner on the back as the man moved past him to the staircase.

"Forgive us for not having some girls to keep you warm," Beckmann blurted, laughing at his own joke.

Johann followed Schorner up the narrow stairs. He noted that half of them creaked. He felt his way along the corridor and into a small room with a wire-framed bed. Johann approached the window and looked down into the courtyard. He watched as the driver stepped out of the cab of the truck into the moonlight and walked into the house for the night.

Johann heard a crunch beneath his feet. He looked down and moved whatever was on the floor with the toe of his boot. He saw that he was standing on a broken ceramic washbowl. As his eyes adjusted to the darkness, he could see that there were pictures of nursery rhymes on the wall. This had been a child's room once. Maybe only last week. His body ached. His eyelids hung heavily. He yearned for rest, but his mind was racing too fast for him to be able to sleep. He thought about how his half brother was complicit in this criminal act of denying the terrible fate of so many. It was almost inconceivable to Johann that someone could side with such cruelty with absolute passion and belief.

He leaned his head against the freezing wall and tried to displace the thought that Dieter was now only a few miles, if that, from Anja and Nadine.

Johann waited until he could hear Schorner snoring before negotiating the staircase. He had decided to tell anyone he might encounter downstairs that he was searching for some water. Beckmann was sprawled on the table, asleep.

Johann edged out of the kitchen door and into the still night. He moved slowly, feeling his way on the cobbled courtyard to ensure that a scrape of his boots didn't give him away. Any stray noise would be the end of him. He glanced back up at the house. None of the inhabitants appeared to be awake.

The body of the truck was coated with a thin sheen of frost. Johann worked his way to the rear of the vehicle and felt for the handle on the back door. He turned it upward and the doors were released.

He pulled the left door ajar slowly, lifting it slightly from its hinge to ease its passage, then climbed inside the vehicle, closed the doors carefully behind him, and fished in his tunic for his flashlight. He took what felt like his first breath since he had left the bedroom. He moved the beam of light around the interior. Cardboard boxes were stacked in rows two or three deep along the sides and backed up against the cab of the vehicle. Johann crouched and cast the light on a scuffed box at the bottom of the pile—it was bulging from the weight of others on top of it read "Belzec" in scrawled script. He had heard of the place: a town in the south of Poland. The one next to it said "Kulmhof." He moved the light beam to the next: "Dachau."

He stood up, reached toward the box on the top of the stack, and lifted the lid. He peered inside. He saw dozens—maybe hundreds—of manila folders. Each file had a tab on the top right-hand corner with a name typed onto it. The one at the front read "Aaronson." Johann pulled out the file and opened it. The light fanned out across the yellowing page that was embossed with the words "Konzentrationslager Sobibór." He followed a story that revealed itself in neat typewritten letters.

Name: Aaronson, Ruben
DOB: 19/10/22
Father's name: Eyou
Mother's name: Maia
Date of arrival: June 28, 1942

Notes: Jew
Date of death: February 12, 1943
Cause of death: Unknown

Johann stared at the word through the mist of his breath. *Unknown.* A deception perpetrated by liars. They could kill a human being, but not tell the truth about what they had done.

Unknown: a euphemism for what? Worked to death? Beaten by a guard for sport? Perished for want of medical care? There were so many ways to die in an unknown manner. So many opportunities to no longer exist, to slip from the memory of others without any reckoning.

Johann looked around the truck, overwhelmed. Here they were. Thousands of them. Every single file a life, every one a living, breathing person. Each box contained hundreds of them: notifications of unchallenged, unremarked deaths sandwiched between two pieces of manila paper.

Unknown. The word revolted him. A denial of action, of responsibility, of culpability. It needed human beings to obey orders, deliver beatings, and pour lime into pits. This tragedy didn't occur randomly—choices were made and paths were followed for horror to come to pass.

Johann looked around at the boxes and boxes of files, the thousands of souls.

"Someone did this," he whispered to himself. *"Someone did this."*

And someone—Dieter—was responsible for one of the files that might be here. He looked through the names on the boxes: Auschwitz-Birkenau, Belzec, Bergen-Belsen, Bogdanovka, Buchenwald, Dachau, Gross-Rosen, Jasenovac, Lublin, Poznan . . . His head spun at the scale of the monstrosity. He shut his eyes for a moment, like a climber with vertigo. He needed to take himself away from his current situation. He tried to loosen his limbs, to let the feelings of disgust and dismay drain away. He opened his eyes again. He didn't have time for this. He had to disengage his emotions and hurry. The house contained three members of the SS. Discovery would mean immediate execution.

His flashlight moved from box to box, but still he couldn't see what he was searching for. Then he moved one of the containers and realized that there was another layer behind them. He slid some of the boxes out of the way and scanned the beam deeper into the truck.

His eyes came to rest on one word: Sachsenhausen.

Johann slid the box out and paused. He was acting on a hunch. He had no idea if Nicolas had been sent there, but it was the most likely: Political opponents of the regime from Berlin had first been sent to Oranienburg, which had been set up in a former brickworks. In 1936 it was replaced by Sachsenhausen, a camp designed with a singular purpose in mind. He had sent repeated requests to the authorities for information about his father's welfare and whereabouts, but had never received a reply.

The air in the truck was thick with cold; he could virtually feel its weight as he moved about the vehicle. Johann lifted the lid and pointed the flashlight at the contents, which looked exactly the same as the other boxes he'd examined—hundreds of files organized alphabetically, with names typewritten in a cutout area in the top right of the file. Everything in perfect order: It could have been a filing system at a doctor's office. Johann leafed across the files, pulling the paperwork forward with his fingers to get a look at the names at the top. As he came to the letter *M* he wondered whether it might be better not to find any news than something conclusive. Or worse, something "unknown."

And then there it was: Meier, Nicolas. His father, documented by a bureaucrat. Johann opened the file quickly—he needed to know. He scanned down the document.

His blood ran cold.

He was sure he had heard movement in the courtyard.

Johann stopped breathing. There it was again: the *click-clack* of gravel moving. He stood up very slowly and took a step toward the door, his pistol raised. His legs were cramped from crouching, and his breath had clouded the small window at the back of the truck. The condensation had made the window opaque. He raised his arm and used the cuff of his jacket to wipe away a small area to see outside. There was enough moonlight to make out a large part of the courtyard. Johann craned his neck. A pair of eyes stared back at him. Johann steadied the pistol. His index finger tightened on the trigger before he lowered his weapon—he was about to shoot a dog. The mutt was standing in the courtyard looking up at the truck hopefully.

Johann crept back to the file he had been looking at. The paper inside was slightly yellowed. Nicolas's name, date of arrest, and supposed crime were written in elegant script. Johann ran his finger down the form, looking for more information.

There it was: date of death.

Johann experienced a moment of hopelessness: Nicolas had died in the winter of 1940 at the Heinkel factory. He had been a forced laborer. Although Johann had, in his heart, always expected his father to be dead, he had clung to the golden promise of hope: a pardon, a mistake with paperwork, an unlikely escape. His eyes filled with tears. He pulled out his handkerchief and wiped his face.

Damn this war. Damn Dieter.

He tilted his head upward and swallowed. He didn't have time for this now. He had to escape. To leave with the briefcase and to prevent its terrible secrets from being erased. More than that, he had a final task: to discover the true meaning of the directive that had so terrified Lehman, the executive order that menaced those he loved in Berlin. The SS man had suggested that the diktat was the final ignominy the Nazis would bestow upon the world.

Johann replaced the boxes where he found them. He needed to be quick. He must get back to the city before Dieter regained consciousness and Anja and Nadine were arrested. He took a final look at his father's file. The flashlight revealed one other detail. He had stumbled across it years before, when, as a newly qualified doctor, he had gone to the bank on Behrenstraße and opened the safety deposit box with the key that had not left his neck since the night his father had handed it to him.

Johann nodded to himself, satisfied by the confirmation.

He folded the document and tucked it inside his jacket. If nothing else, the last vestige of his father would remain next to his heart. Furnaces be damned.

Ten minutes later Schorner, Beckmann, and the driver, Glaezer, sat blinking at the table, their hands tucked behind their heads. Johann had used a technique that one of the doctors told him was employed by officers in the field: He had ordered the men to strip. Not only did it mean that Johann was sure none of them had weapons but also that each of them was vulnerable and—in March in Brandenburg—cold.

"Push your clothes toward me with your feet," Johann ordered.

Each of them did as they were told. Johann warily picked up a pair of trousers and threw it on the fire.

"What do you know about the Führer's directive?" Johann asked.

Beckmann looked at Schorner.

"You should know," Schorner said.

"Really," Johann said, and threw another item of clothing on the fire. It was March, but it was touching zero outside.

"Tell me anyway," Johann said.

"I take it that you are not Sturmbannführer Schnell?" Schorner said.

"Tell me now," Johann said, fixing his handgun on Schorner. Silence.

"You won't get away," Schorner said. "Not out here. There are *Feldgendarmerie* units everywhere."

Johann tossed a shirt and underwear into the flames, which were greedily consuming the woolen garments.

"Answer the question," Johann ordered them.

"I'm just a soldier," Glaezer said. Johann had found him asleep upstairs, snoring like a bear. "I do what I'm told. I don't know anything."

Johann desperately wanted to leave. It would be sunrise in around three hours and he needed to be far away from here by then.

"What is due to happen in Berlin?" he insisted.

Silence.

"None of us has any idea what you're talking about."

Johann picked up a broken chair leg, gripped it hard, and suddenly swung at Schorner, hitting the officer across the face.

"Don't tell me lies!" he shouted. "You sit here with a truck full of files that you intend to destroy. How dare you tell another lie!"

Schorner looked up from the flagstone floor at Johann.

"You're talking about the Demolitions on Reich Territory," he said, coughing. He spit blood onto the rust-colored tiles.

"The truth!" Johann ordered.

"I can hear a Berlin accent," Schorner said with a cackle. "Oh, dear . . ."

"What the hell are you talking about?" Johann demanded. There was a trace of desperation in his voice.

"Still got loved ones there, have you?" Schorner asked.

Johann didn't react. He would avoid revealing anything about himself.

"Well," said Schorner. "You won't have long if they're sheltering in the U-Bahn or going through a railway station, or anywhere near a fuel dump. Because if the British bombers don't get them, the Party will."

"What are you talking about?"

"They're destroying it all," Schorner said, suddenly serious. "The Führer issued the order on March 19."

"Anything of value within Reich territories," Beckmann said, acting as a chorus. "It's all going to hell."

Johann thought for a moment. Anything of value—that would be most of the city. "Railway stations, bridges, food supplies, factories, S-Bahn, U-Bahn, vehicles . . ." Johann recited the words as if in a dream.

"All gone," Beckmann said.

This was the final insult. After the misery and cruelty of the past twelve years, the Nazis had one last act of destruction that would make the lives of the ragged survivors of their folly even more wretched. Johann put his hand against a wall to steady himself. Not satisfied with erasing the records of millions of lives, Dieter was the enforcer of a decree that was pointless and cruel— the Nazis' final insult to a ravaged Europe. A ruling devoid of compassion or human decency.

Johann's head spun.

"But what about the people?" Johann asked. There was no artifice to the question; he simply couldn't believe what he was being told.

"The order makes no provision for the protection of civilians," Schorner said. "They will have to take their chances. Better that than the Bolsheviks get their dirty hands on it."

Johann's body shook as if he had been shoved.

He had to get back. He had to warn Anja and Nadine.

Johann picked up the briefcase while keeping the P38 trained on his captives.

"I'm leaving now," he said, backing away from them while holding the remaining clothing. He had confiscated the weapons he could find, but they might have others hidden. "And if any of you try and pursue me, I will kill you."

Glaezer remained passive. He was happy to see Johann leave. But Schorner and Beckmann stared back at Johann threateningly.

"You'll never make it past the *Feldgendarmerie*," Schorner said.

"I'm warning you," Johann said, pointing the pistol at both men, in turn. "Remember, it would be easier for me if I left you dead in this farmhouse."

The men suddenly straightened their arms anew, as if in recognition of the opportunity they were being handed.

"One other thing," said Schorner, clearly enjoying his role. "They have a name for it—the Nero Decree. You know, after the Roman emperor."

Johann thought back to one of Nicolas's talks—he would often regale him after dinner with tales of ancient Greece and Rome. Nero, the tyrant who burned Rome.

He backed out of the doorway and into the darkness. The soldiers, their teeth chattering, watched him until he was lost in the night.

At first light Schorner, Beckmann, and the driver clambered into the truck. Wrapped in makeshift clothing—burlap sacking, a thin rug, a pair of curtains—they were anxious to get to Berlin and report the incident. While it didn't reflect well on them, they were happy to be alive and thrilled to be avoiding the Soviets who would soon be passing through Brandenburg. As they advanced past the refugees and showed their documentation to bullyboy *Feldgendarmerie* units who were thrilled to see SS personnel humiliated in this way, they considered the afternoon of interrogation they would have to endure while the paperwork in the back of the truck was unloaded and taken to the furnace at the Ministry. They knew that the job was incomplete without the microfilm.

There would be consequences.

They drove through the suburb of Köpenick—where small farms and plots of land gave way to family houses—with some dread about the inevitable interrogation they would receive now that they were back in Berlin. They knew, of course, that the search for the film would become one of the top priorities of the Reich Main Security Office.

What they didn't know was that the briefcase containing the microfilm was in the back of the truck, concealed among the boxes, with its custodian, Johann Schultz. Still dressed as his *Sturmbannführer* half brother, Johann was contemplating what he had learned about the Nero Decree.

He now had his own task to complete at the Ministry.

11

Dieter woke up, his eyes flicking from side to side to try and determine his location. It was his habit: He had barely slept in the same bed on consecutive nights for months. His brain processed the information at hand. He was in the hospital still. He closed his eyes again and took a reading of his body. He didn't feel too bad. He had been wounded. There was pain. Extreme pain. But nothing he hadn't suffered before. Nothing he couldn't and wouldn't endure. His arm felt stiff from the bandages. There were dressings on his face, and his chest throbbed with pain. Every breath he took felt as though he were splitting skin. But he remembered what had happened and where he was.

Dieter had no idea where the farmer had gotten the phosphorous grenade from, but there was enough abandoned or forgotten ordnance lying between Berlin and Moscow to equip several armies. The device must have gone off in the old man's hands—if he'd thrown it at Dieter he would be dead now. He raised himself on his elbows. The pain was excruciating, but he had no time to convalesce.

He had to locate the briefcase.

He signaled to a nurse who was hurrying by. She did a double take before halting and moving to his side.

"Herr Schnell . . . ," she said.

"Sturmbannführer Schnell," he interrupted with a brisk tone of voice that belied his condition.

"Of course," the nurse said, her manner shifting from tender to businesslike.

"The men who visited me," Dieter said weakly, but with authority, "have them return here immediately."

The nurse paused for a moment as if she was going to ask Dieter if he felt well enough for whatever he was intending to do.

"Quickly," he said.

If he could have clapped his hands together he would have.

Pfeiffer and Vogt were back within the hour.

"This Schultz killed the *Obersturmführer?*" Pfeiffer asked Dieter. He looked over at his fellow officer, Vogt, who had removed his cap and was rubbing his thumb around the brim thoughtfully.

"In front of my eyes," Dieter confirmed. "And Ostermann only died because he disturbed Schultz when he was attempting to inject me with the sedative."

"Do you know anything of him?" Vogt asked, looking up. His eyes were narrowed as if he were questioning a suspect.

"No," Dieter said. The statement was partially true. Dieter's memories were from a decade before. He needed to keep Johann's real identity a secret. Should others discover that Schultz was his half brother, it would not bode well for Dieter.

Dieter sunk back in his pillow and shook his head. He had made a connection: The name Johann was not a casual choice. Johann Sebastian Bach had been Nicolas's favorite composer.

"Do you have something to tell us, Dieter?" Pfeiffer asked.

"No, no," Dieter said darkly. "It's just the medication."

"Well, you must rest, my friend," Vogt said.

"He's right," Pfeiffer added. "Those wounds will take time to heal."

Dieter was about to speak when a messenger walked quickly into the room with a cable for Vogt. The *Sturmbannführer* tore it open and scanned the paper.

"After we last saw you we asked our analysts to see if there was any mention of Johann Schultz in army dispatches recently," Pfeiffer explained.

"He's coming here," Vogt said, incredulously staring at the telegram.

Dieter sat up. "Why?" he asked. He felt a rush of excitement. It reminded him of how he sometimes felt in combat.

"One of Goebbels's awards ceremonies," Pfeiffer said. "Radio operators can't get through to the hospital, but according to Army High Command communications, Schultz is due to attend."

"Goebbels is still doing those?" Dieter asked.

Pfeiffer nodded grimly.

"Where is it?" Dieter asked.

"Doesn't say," Vogt said, smacking the back of his hand against the paper. "It will be easy to find out."

"Good," Dieter said. "Come back when you know."

"What are you talking about?" Pfeiffer smiled, thinking that his friend was joking.

"You can drive me," Dieter said.

Vogt and Pfeiffer looked at each other.

"You're not thinking of . . ." Vogt started gesturing at Dieter with upturned palms.

By now, though, Dieter was sitting on the side of the bed and getting his bearings. It was the first time he had been upright in nearly five days.

"No one gets to arrest Johann Schultz or Thomas Meier, or whoever he is today, but me," he said resolutely. "Do you understand?"

Neither of them said a word. They didn't need to. It was clear that they had little choice in the matter.

The ceremony was being conducted in a cavernous cellar in a semi-wrecked mansion near Pariser Platz. Vogt and Pfeiffer accompanied Dieter uneasily, aware of the sidelong glances that the disfigured, limping man attracted as they pushed through the crowd.

"I think that we've missed the actual ceremony," Vogt said to Dieter, who was casting his eyes around the wood-paneled room, searching for his half brother. Both Pfeiffer and Vogt nodded courteously to other officers they were acquainted with. While the SS men appeared sober, most of the others in attendance—all of them from parts of the military—were milling around, their faces flushed with drink. Some had formed groups and were singing raucously. Behind a long bar, staff in threadbare uniforms poured drinks and lit cigars. Dieter coughed. The room was clogged with smoke. He forced his way through clusters of oblivious men, wincing from every movement, every accidental elbow to his ribs.

"Careful, Dieter," Pfeiffer said at one point, steadying his friend. Dieter looked around. There was no sign of Johann. Vogt shoved his way through the crowd to join them.

The three of them worked their way around the room, with Dieter scrutinizing every face. After two circuits he shook his head irritably. The voices around him had stopped being just noise. He had started to hear individual conversations, and what he heard he didn't like. He had realized that this wasn't a ceremony at all. It might have started that way, but it had become something else: a wake.

"Best finish that brandy before Ivan gets his filthy hands on it. . . ."

"The British smashed Hamburg. . . ."

"They say they'll be here in a week. . . ."

"The Americans are allowing the Russians to get to the oil; then they take Berlin. . . ."

"No one has seen the Führer for weeks. . . ."

To Dieter's mind, none of these drunken men seemed to understand the ramifications of what they were saying. They saw what was coming and they would prefer not to think about it.

For Dieter, things were different; while some turned to frantic revelry, he had to fill his time judiciously and locate the microfilm. He rubbed his wrist—he could still feel the soreness from where the metal bracelet, attached to the briefcase, had been. While there was still life in him, he would fight, and he would ensure that the information he had worked so hard to procure would not end up in the hands of enemies of the Reich.

He would find Johann and the briefcase.

He started to push his way through the crowd again.

"He's not here," Pfeiffer said, gesturing to the exit. "Come, Dieter, you need to rest."

Dieter continued to cast his eyes around the room suspiciously as he limped among the guests.

"I don't believe it," he said, his eyes narrowing.

"It's no great surprise," Vogt said. "There's precious little air traffic and the road is almost impassable with refugees."

"Maybe so," Dieter said. "What I mean is that it's too convenient."

Vogt grabbed a glass of wine from a passing waiter holding a tray.

"It's plausible, though," he said, downing the glass with one action. "Oh, that's good. . . ."

"Plausible, yes," Dieter said, leaning on a wall. He felt like he was tiring. Leaving the hospital had been exhausting.

"Where would you rather be," Dieter asked, gesturing with his bandaged hand at the revelers, "Berlin or the front?"

Vogt and Pfeiffer nodded in agreement.

"He should want to be here, unless he's dead, which is possible. . . ." Dieter pushed back a strand of his hair that had fallen over his face. "But it's too damn convenient. Traitors like Thomas Meier—or Johann Schultz, as he has it—rely on opportunities like this for us to have our guard down."

Pfeiffer caught Vogt's eye while Dieter gazed off into the distance.

"Would you like a drink, Dieter?" Pfeiffer asked after a while. "It would be churlish to be here and not at least help them use up their reserves."

Dieter considered this for a moment.

"No," he said. "You have a drink. I have work to do."

He barged his way through the crowd again, locating the bureaucrat from the Ministry who was responsible for organizing this fiasco.

"What do you know of Johann Schultz?" he demanded.

The official regarded Dieter with distaste. Dieter noticed the man's assistant hovering nearby.

"His *Kommandant* claims that he was indisposed," the bureaucrat replied, examining some paperwork.

"You're sure?" It seemed unlikely that a commanding officer would not submit to Goebbels's whim, no matter how absurd.

"I'm sure," the official said, before acknowledging someone else over Dieter's shoulder and moving past him.

Dieter stood, frowning, in his wake. Then he noticed the assistant looking at him furtively.

"Well?" Dieter said, moving toward him. "Is there more?"

The man looked at the ground, as if he were breaking a confidence.

"Yes, *Sturmbannführer*," he replied. "I suspect my colleague didn't think that it was relevant. . . ."

"Spit it out, man."

"A communiqué was sent to Schultz's commanding officer to ask why he was unable to accept Reich Minister Goebbels's invitation."

Dieter stepped closer. "And?" he demanded.

"We received no reply for a few days. Eventually a cable came back telling us that Schultz was no longer at the field hospital."

Dieter tensed.

"Apparently the *Kommandant* has reported his absence to the *Feldgendarmerie,* which has issued a warrant for Schultz's immediate arrest."

The official had barely finished before Dieter was heading toward the exit.

His manhunt had begun in earnest.

Among the usual bustle of officialdom, long glances were cast at Dieter as he limped up the stairs to the third floor of a grand, neoclassical Wilhelmine building. He straightened himself as much as he could, determined that he should not look dispensable.

Standartenführer Keller, Dieter's commanding officer, was writing a letter to his wife—whom he had sent to stay with family near Minden—when his adjutant knocked on the door.

"Sturmbannführer Schnell here to see you, sir," he announced, a look of mild alarm in his eyes.

"Schnell?" the *Standartenführer* said, looking up from his letter. The pen was left poised over the paper, a drop of navy ink collecting at its tip. "Isn't he still at the Charité?"

"Not any longer, it seems," the adjutant said. He could feel Schnell behind him champing at the bit to get into the room.

"Well, send him in then," the *Standartenführer* said impatiently, slipping the letter into his top drawer.

Dieter walked into the room. It had high ceilings and large windows that opened onto a small balcony that looked out on some birch trees. The *Standartenführer* could see that Dieter's arms were stiff with bandaging. Livid red marks reached from beneath his tunic and curled up beneath his chin. The *Standartenführer* couldn't help thinking that the injuries suited Dieter. The wounded man raised his arm in salute, grimacing from the effort.

"Please, *Sturmbannführer*," said Keller. "Come and sit down."

He ushered Dieter to a pair of leather armchairs in front of a fireplace.

"I'm afraid that there is no wood or coal," the *Standartenführer* said. "It used to be my favorite thing about this office."

"It's certainly very pleasant," Dieter said. The *Standartenführer* couldn't tell whether he was being polite, or whether he was commenting on the circumstances that Keller had been living in while others froze at the front.

"We are in crisis," the *Standartenführer* said.

"The briefcase?" Dieter interjected.

"Yes," the *Standartenführer* said. "We know from our investigations that it was attached to you when you were brought to the field hospital, but no one seems to have seen it after that. Obersturmführer Ostermann was found dead. We're surmising that maybe he killed himself after discovering the theft of the information. Such sacrifice is not uncommon in matters of honor. The *Oberscharführer* . . . what was his name . . . ?"

"Lehman," Dieter said.

"Yes, Lehman—he hasn't been seen since the night after you arrived at the hospital. Maybe he might have something to do with the disappearance of the briefcase?"

Keller crossed his legs and placed his hands in his lap. This was Dieter's cue to talk, but he remained silent. He wanted to see if he was being tested. Were they aware of Johann? Did they know that Johann was, in fact, his half brother?

"Do you have any other information?" Keller prompted him. His gaze was intense now.

"Yes," said Dieter. "I do. I know who stole the briefcase. It was the same person who killed Ostermann."

The *Standartenführer*'s brow furrowed, but he nodded patiently.

"Was a postmortem conducted on Ostermann?" Dieter asked.

"There was no need," the *Standartenführer* said. "The man was found hanging. It was clear what the cause of death was."

"Really?"

"His neck either snapped or he was asphyxiated."

"I'm afraid that's not true, sir," Dieter said.

"How do you know this?" Keller was annoyed. He drummed manicured fingers on his thigh.

"I witnessed his death," Dieter said.

Keller gestured impatiently for Dieter to go on.

"There was a surgeon working at the hospital—Oberstabsarzt Johann Schultz. He attempted to kill me by injecting a lethal dose of painkiller. Ostermann disturbed him and he killed Ostermann instead of me. I have no idea how Ostermann ended up hanging from a rope. Maybe Schultz had an accomplice in order to get the body up there."

"Lehman?" the *Standartenführer* asked.

"Possibly," Dieter said, considering the question. "But I think that's unlikely. The man doesn't seem like the type."

"I know that I don't have to stress the importance of this theft to you, Schnell," the *Standartenführer* said. "The reason we sent two units—one for paper, one for microfilm, was insurance against such a mishap. But—"

Dieter met Keller's eyes.

"—there will be consequences."

He was being threatened.

"There is an intense rescue mission ongoing."

"Sir," Dieter said. "Respectfully, I'd like to request that I am put in charge of this investigation. The Gestapo is under the authority of the SS. I can lead the investigation. The documents were stolen while in my possession. I am fully responsible for their destiny, and I intend to ensure that I complete my mission and that the contents of the briefcase are brought here and managed in the way that was planned from the outset."

The *Standartenführer* considered Dieter for a moment. Surely this injured man wasn't intending to set off in pursuit of the Reich's most valued information?

"I assure you, sir," Dieter said, as if reading Keller's thoughts, "that I am fully capable of seeing this mission through. Duty and my honor respectfully demand it."

The *Standartenführer* stood up and strode over to the windows and stared onto the clear day. Workers had removed the blackout blinds. Keller was keen to enjoy the daylight while it lasted. He put his hands behind his back and clenched them tightly. Dieter saw one hand turn red as the *Standartenführer* squeezed blood into it.

"Why would this Schultz do something like this?" he asked wistfully. "Why might he want to kill you?"

Dieter remained still and silent, his eyes fixed on the back of Keller's head.

"It just seems so arbitrary," the *Standartenführer* said. "A doctor at a field hospital. The pressure affects people in different ways, I suppose. Maybe he lost his mind." Keller examined Dieter as if he didn't quite believe what he had said himself. There was something missing.

"It's hard to tell . . . ," Dieter said.

Keller turned, his boots squeaking on the wooden floor.

"Do you know anything else about this Schultz character?"

"I know nothing of Johann Schultz," Dieter replied truthfully.

What he did know was that he would find Johann Schultz—and he would kill both him and Thomas Meier.

The *Standartenführer* regarded Dieter. There was something badly askew beyond the theft of the briefcase, but he couldn't decipher what was making him uneasy.

"Let me find him," Dieter said.

Keller considered the request.

"Very well," he said. "You will lead the investigation with full authority over all military and *Staatspolizei* officers. I will issue a document insisting full cooperation with your every wish from all ranks of the army."

"Thank you, sir."

"I will have Gestapo resources secured for you as well as those of the *Feldgendarmerie*."

Dieter nodded. "One other thing, sir," he said. "Will you authorize a driver to take me to the field hospital?"

Keller picked up a pen. "When do you want to leave?"

"Now," Dieter replied, his eyes fixed on the *Standartenführer*.

Minutes later he was in a staff car heading east.

12

The all clear sounded. Inside the bunker the air was rank, laden as it was with the smell of unwashed bodies and stale clothes. Anja was thirsty. She reached down for the bag that she had brought to the shelter, but before she could get to it Nadine handed her the water bottle.

"Is this what you're looking for?" Nadine asked.

"Yes, thanks," Anja said, unscrewing the top. The water was lukewarm. The inside of her mouth tasted as if she was coming down with a fever. She looked at Nadine, who was standing and ready to go. The girl smiled at her aunt quickly, as if she was agitated, her mind elsewhere.

"How are you?" Anja asked, rising from the bench.

"I'm fine," Nadine said, hoisting the canvas bag over her shoulder.

Nadine nodded. She didn't believe her niece. It would be an unusual adolescent who would be unaffected by spending the night in a shelter while high explosives rained down in the streets outside.

"Did you sleep?" Anja asked.

"Not really." And then, as if she was concerned that she might be burdening her aunt, "I was worried about my math test."

"Do you think that you should go to school?" Anja asked. "You must be exhausted and it might be dangerous being out today—you know how unstable some buildings are after raids."

As they neared the exit their noses were filled with smoke. Anja quickly reached into her bag and produced two clean handkerchiefs. They held the cloths over their faces as they walked from the bunker. Flakes of ash lodged in their hair, carried from the fires started by the incendiaries. Sudden gusts of wind surged up the street, caused by the flames. Everywhere, it seemed, there were groups of firemen and members of the Todt—prisoners of war and so-called guest workers—pulling survivors from the cellars of collapsed buildings. In some parts of the road the smoke was so thick that they had to pause to wait for it to pass.

Underfoot they trod on glass and rubble. Anja worried about Nadine's feet—what leather was left on the soles of her shoes was thin and surely wouldn't offer much protection against anything sharp. Walking down one block, they saw an old woman sitting in the street on some salvaged bedding while an old man pulled at a heap of masonry and wood to try and salvage their belongings. A black cat picked its way across what had once been a roof that was now partially lying in the road. On Schumannstraße they struggled past a blazing building, which a fire crew was struggling to control. In the distance there was a loud explosion.

"That one must have had a timer on it," Nadine said. It was not unusual for them to hear explosions going off for several hours after an attack had finished. On one corner they passed an emergency field kitchen, which had been set up for those fighting the fires but had been overwhelmed with civilians. In some places housewives clutching ration cards waited patiently outside food shops in the hope that their owners would make it to work.

Anja and Nadine trudged drowsily through the streets. Much of the aftermath barely registered; they had seen it so many times. Anja looked up into what would once have been a bedroom—the room was completely intact but one side of the building had been sheared off. She saw a dusty limb protruding above some rubble. She hugged Nadine close to her. Some instances still had the power to shock. That was the end for school. She would get as much food as she could with her ration cards and then pack some essentials. She resolved that it was time to go.

She thought about Johann. Was it possible that he would make it back to this miserable place from whatever hell he was currently enduring? Casting her eyes along the bombed street, taking short breaths through the cloth, she allowed a feeling that she had suppressed for months to sweep over her: She would not see Johann again. Even if he was still alive there was little chance of him surviving this final reckoning. It had all gone to hell. These city streets, for so long hives of trade and business and social activity, were ruined.

She could barely remember what it was like not to be tired and scared and desperate. Her reserves of hope were exhausted. She had hung on to the possibility that Johann would come, but that now seemed absurd. Through her fear she felt annoyed with herself: Why hadn't she moved her and Nadine out months ago? Surely Johann could have found them if they had fled to the countryside. She glanced over at Nadine, who was shielding her face from the heat of a burning building.

Anja was suddenly distracted by something else: There was something in the air.

She gasped as she saw a piece of charred, burning masonry fall toward her niece—she shoved Nadine to the ground a second before a piece of wood landed on the street where the girl had been standing. Small fragments of burning charcoal sprayed outward, onto their clothes. Nadine coughed as she brushed the burning embers from her coat, before returning the cloth to her face. Anja pulled the girl forward, toward their apartment. She could no longer jeopardize their slim chance of survival by waiting for Johann.

They would leave Berlin tonight.

The airborne debris remained thick, but they were almost home. They passed people trying to decipher where a particular building had once stood, their faces ghostly with ash. They turned the corner into Oranienburger Straße, and Anja felt as if she had been struck hard in her chest. She reached out, her hand grabbing at thin air as she surveyed their building. One side of it remained partially intact—the Schneiders' apartment appeared undamaged—but the rest of the structure was a tangled mass of rubble and masonry. She felt her insides twist into an ugly, horrible lump.

"Flöhchen!"

Nadine's cry pierced the noise of the rescuers calling to each other and the wail of a trapped survivor. The guest workers sifting through the rubble paused and looked over. Nadine pushed her way through them and up onto the pile of bricks and wood. She moved back and forth across it. At first Anja thought that the girl was simply overwhelmed by the volume of rubble; then she realized that her niece was approximating where their apartment had been. Nadine pulled frantically at the rubble, tossing lumps downward, causing some rescue workers to move out of the way. She was fevered, distraught.

"Here, boy!" she shouted. "Don't worry, I'm coming."

Anja pulled herself up onto the ruins and began to move toward her niece. She had to be careful—sharp pieces of wood and jagged edges to the masonry made it treacherous. She had heard stories of people falling into hollows created when the building fell and impaling themselves.

Nadine was on her knees pulling at bits of debris and was covered in dust from the building. Blood ran through the layer of gray powder that had collected on her hands. She was talking to herself, to the dog in a low chatter, as if she were praying, or trying to hold on to something that, if she only kept talking to it, would remain with her. Water from a broken pipe cascaded nearby.

Anja reached down, her back aching, and put her hands on her niece's shoulders. She tried to lift Nadine.

"Come on, my dear," she said as soothingly as she could. "It will be all right."

The decision to leave the city was now less complicated. There were no longer any preparations to make. The procedure for those who had been bombed out was to register with the NSV, the Nazi Welfare Service. Anja had no intention of making the authorities aware of her location for the sake of housing vouchers and extra ration cards. She would find another way.

"Come on, Auntie, dig," Nadine said to her. "He was under the sofa. It might have protected him."

Anja stroked the girl's hair. It was full of soot from the embers.

"Please," Nadine said, returning to pulling at the bricks and collapsed plaster speckled with horsehair. "Flöhchen!" she called again, quite softly.

Anja stayed by the girl. She reached down and pulled at the heap of rubble. She had to give Nadine time. The two of them moved masonry from one small spot. For every piece they shifted there was another underneath. And another.

"Aaaaarrgghhh!"

Nadine's scream halted the rescue work that was going on around them for a second time. All activity ceased. The foreign workers and civilian teams straightened their backs and looked up at the teenage girl on top of the mound of debris. She was on her knees, sobbing and beating at the collapsed building. The sun had risen but there was precious little light. The air was dense, loaded with debris. It was as if they had been disconnected from the earth itself, like they were caught in an indefinite limbo. What was this place they found themselves? It was all so strange, so distant, but so familiar as well.

Anja pulled Nadine up gently. The girl allowed herself to be raised this time, falling onto her aunt's shoulder, crying and repeating the dog's name, over and again, as if this one word acted as a kind of mantra, an invocation of everything awful and hurtful and unjust that had befallen her and the city.

"Flöhchen," she repeated. Anja held the girl to her. There was nothing to say any longer.

Eventually Nadine stopped crying. Anja took her handkerchief and climbed over to the burst water pipe and wet it. She returned to the girl and wiped the dirt and tears from her face.

"That's better," Anja said, holding Nadine's face in her hands. "I can see you now."

"What are we to do, Aunt?" Nadine asked eventually. She stared at the devastation as if she were seeing it for the first time. "Our home, our things . . ."

"All gone," Anja said. "All gone. And we must go too. . . ."

"But what about Uncle Johann?" Nadine asked. "How will he find us?"

Anja found that it was she who might sob now. She swallowed her tears. Not here, not now. She couldn't afford this kind of indulgence.

"He will find us eventually," Anja said forcefully. "He will come for us. I have absolutely no doubt about that."

The prospect of certainty, no matter how hollow, seemed to buoy the two of them.

Anja led Nadine down from the debris. She felt like there was something almost biblical about coming down from the mountain of rubble. Everything had become different in a few moments— they now had, quite literally, nothing. They had no ties, no reason to be held back. They could just go.

They strayed back onto the road, which was littered with masonry and personal artifacts that been pulled from the wreckage. Anja could see that the guest workers had been detailed to pile bodies at the junction with Schlegelstraße. Anja steered Nadine away from the cart that had been sent to collect the cadavers. Women, children, and elderly people—the bombs didn't differentiate.

Anja knew that she had to say something that would distract the girl, would offer some kind of response to shift her mind. Anja could sense that she'd lost her, that the teenager now occupied another realm. She felt a small moment of panic—she had failed to protect the girl, to save her. She needed to redeem herself.

"We must leave now," Anja said, staring into Nadine's eyes, trying to make a connection.

The girl looked back up at the rubble where she imagined Flöhchen was lying. Anja reached out and held Nadine's hand, which was filthy from digging.

"Good," Nadine said eventually.

"I have ration cards in my pocket," Anja said. "We can stock up on supplies for the journey."

"Where shall we go?" Nadine asked.

Anja thought for a moment. She had no idea—they would go wherever a train might take them. But is seemed like it was important for the girl to have an objective in mind; a destination would give her something tangible to focus on.

"Somewhere in the country north of Nuremberg," Anja said confidently, as if she had been poring over maps late at night to mastermind their escape.

"Oh, Aunt," Nadine replied. "That sounds lovely."

The two stumbled across the rubble until they reached a passable thoroughfare. After a few minutes they came across a family who had managed to pull some furniture from their damaged home. They had arranged it in the street and were sitting in it as if they were drinking coffee in their parlor.

"Wait, Aunt," Nadine said urgently. "I thought that I saw the boy from the bakery, the one whose parents . . ."

Anja stepped forward and looked up the street to where her niece was pointing.

"You mean Lukas Balzer?" Anja said, looking around anxiously. "The delivery boy? Such a nice young man."

The two of them ran toward where Nadine thought she'd seen the boy.

"Lukas!" Anja called. "Lukas!"

Within moments the figure had disappeared and a cloud of thick smoke blew over them.

"He's gone . . . ," Nadine said. "I'm *sure* it was him."

"Maybe not," Anja said. "It's hard to tell."

They stood coughing for a moment before moving between the rubble and furniture again, heading west. In their haste, they didn't notice a large man, who had followed them from their apartment, emerge from the shadow of a derelict bus shelter and continue to trail them.

They picked their way along the street. Anja examined one of the messages chalked on bombed-out buildings by survivors to let their loved ones know that they were still alive. Anja heard a noise behind them—a can being kicked, perhaps—and looked around to see a well-built man picking his way along the cluttered street. He lurched as if he was stiff, negotiating one obstacle after another. Anja hurried after Nadine, who was slightly ahead of her, clambering over the hood of a burned-out car, its tires melted to the road. She glanced back again. The big man just kept coming. The edges of his large black trench coat were coated with gray dust. There was no doubt in Anja's mind now: They were being followed.

They came to a junction, and Anja pulled Nadine in one direction.

"Quick," she said. "This way."

Nadine immediately realized that something was wrong.

"What is it, Aunt?"

"Nothing," Anja said, walking briskly. She had chosen a street where there were comparatively few obstacles. The buildings here had been hit a long time ago and were either back in use or had been left as empty relics.

"Just follow me," Anja instructed Nadine. She put her arm beneath her niece's and darted up an alley. There she pushed the girl into a doorway and pressed both of them as close to the building as possible. She glanced down the passageway to see the man run past, continuing on his way. He was moving quickly now, as if in pursuit of someone.

"Is he following us?" Nadine asked.

"I think so," Anja whispered.

"Who is he?"

"I don't know. Gestapo maybe."

Anja and Nadine waited for a few moments before creeping back out onto the street. Anja peered around. People were hurrying about their business—women lined up for rations wearing helmets, bombed-out families hauled their belongings elsewhere, and there was even someone distributing *Der Angriff,* the Nazi free sheet that had become the only printed matter in the city.

After checking again, Anja and Nadine darted from the alleyway and moved quickly in the opposite direction—back toward a road that would take them to the station.

"I know that Andersen's is supposed to be open today," Anja told Nadine, trying to distract the girl, who was glancing anxiously behind them. "We can pick up some supplies there."

"Do you think the trains are still running?" Nadine asked.

"I don't know," Anja replied. "It will depend on whether there was any damage to the tracks or the station last night."

The pair of them hurried onward. There were virtually no businesses open any longer. The driving school, coal merchant, and tobacconist on the street they were passing along were all closed. All that was open was a pharmacy—which had been emptied of anything useful—and a hardware store. Berlin was only days away from shutting down completely.

Anja moved Nadine down the street as quickly as she could. She knew that if one Gestapo officer had come to their home, then the chances were that the search would continue throughout the neighborhood.

"I think that we should get our supplies elsewhere," she said to Nadine. "Let's get out of here."

They passed down the road, hurrying while trying to remain inconspicuous. There was a loud rumbling in the distance—another damaged building surrendering to the laws of gravity and collapsing. Anja moved them off the main street in order to take a shortcut. She calculated that they could be at the station in twenty minutes if they kept moving. They would see what the situation was. If it appeared hopeless they would head southwest on foot. They might be able to reach Potsdam by nightfall, if they were lucky.

Anja's thoughts were interrupted by a blast of fear: The man who had been following them appeared no more than ten yards before them from a side street.

Anja didn't hesitate; she grabbed her niece and ran.

"Wait," the man shouted, his voice thick and gravelly.

"Go," she said to Nadine, "just go." The two of them stumbled across a pile of fragmented bricks and through what had once been a small courtyard. They could hear the man grunting with exertion behind them. They ducked up the side of a building, attempting to confuse him, but the man was upon them, grabbing Anja. They tumbled to the ground, rolling inside an abandoned structure. Most of its entrances had been boarded up, but someone had pulled a piece of corrugated iron aside to create an opening.

Anja grabbed the man's face, attempting to gouge his eyes, but he was too strong—he held her wrists, his eyes purposeful.

"I need to talk to you," he said firmly.

"Stop!" came a shout. The man and Anja paused. They turned to see Nadine standing close behind. In her hand she held a knife that Anja recognized from their kitchen. "Let her go or I will kill you," Nadine said, moving the blade to within an inch of the man's spine.

"You don't understand," the man explained.

Anja pulled herself away from him. He was sweating from the exertion.

"You are Anja and Nadine, no?"

Neither of them answered.

"I am a friend of Johann's," he explained, wiping sweat from his forehead.

"I came from the hospital at the front where we were both working."

Anja felt something bloom inside her. Johann was alive still. Or he had been yesterday, at least.

"He asked me to give you this," the man said. He reached inside his coat. Nadine pressed the blade so hard against him that it was close to puncturing the cloth of his wool coat. One mistake and he was dead.

"It's okay," he said over his shoulder, trying to reassure the girl. "I'll remove it slowly. It's not dangerous."

He produced a crumpled envelope and handed it to Anja. She held it for a moment, examining the handwriting. She looked at the man and then at her niece.

"He's alive," she said to Nadine.

"Uncle?" the girl asked.

"Yes."

"Otto," the man said, extending his hand. "I was stationed with Johann."

"I've heard your name," Anja said. She had a dim memory of Johann taking a bottle of something to an Otto the previous Christmas. "When did he give you this?" Anja asked.

"Two days ago," Otto replied, examining the remnants of a fireplace.

"And how was he?" Anja said suspiciously.

Otto looked at her, not sure what to say. "He's as well as can be expected," he said diplomatically.

Anja nodded. There was no point in pursuing the line of questioning. It was implicit in what Otto had said that, if you were alive, you were as well as could be expected. There was no gray area of mood or physical well-being; you were either alive or you were dead.

"Is he coming to Berlin?" Nadine asked.

"I don't know," Otto said. "Perhaps there may be some news. . . ." He nodded at the envelope.

"What are you doing here?" Anja asked Otto, pulling the envelope apart.

"Johann asked me to deliver this and to see how you were."

"No, I don't mean that," Anja said, scanning the letter. "I mean Berlin—what are you doing back in the city?"

"There is a grave shortage of doctors at the hospital," Otto said.

"Well?" Nadine said to Anja, who was engrossed in the letter.

"He's coming," Anja said. Nadine clapped her hands. "But it might not be for a couple of days."

"But we have nowhere to stay."

"Of course you do," Otto said sternly. "You must stay with me."

"That's very kind," Anja said. "But we can't possibly . . ."

She wanted to keep moving, to head to the station, but she looked at Nadine—exhausted after a night in the bunker—and realized that the girl needed some respite. A day of rest would allow them to face what was to come. Besides, there was something in Johann's letter that compelled them to stay. . . .

"I absolutely insist," Otto continued. "I have no water or electricity, but there's a hand pump on the street and I have a bucket."

"That's very kind," Anja said after a beat.

"Good," Otto replied. "That's settled then."

"We'll make do, won't we, Nadine?" Anja said. She had folded the letter away and put it in her pocket.

"What does it say, Aunt?" Nadine asked.

Anja swallowed. "I'll fill you in on the details later," she said, raising a smile for Nadine.

"We should go back to our apartment and chalk a message for Uncle to let him know that we are with Otto."

"I'm afraid that we can't do that now—I will try tomorrow," Anja said. She was trying to sound businesslike and in control of the situation. "We should go. . . ."

"But, Auntie," Nadine interrupted, putting her hand on Anja's arm, "we need to let him know where we are. How else will he find us?"

"He'll find us," Anja said quietly, as if she didn't believe it herself. "We have a day to leave the message before he comes."

"I don't understand why we can't leave him a—"

"The Gestapo," said Anja briskly, waving the letter in her niece's direction. She turned to face Nadine. "They're looking for us. They're also looking for him. We can't ever go back to the apartment. They will surely be waiting for us. I'm surprised no one was there this morning."

"But why, Auntie?" said Nadine. She kicked an upturned pail gently.

"It's not important now," Anja said, taking her hand. "I will tell you later, once we are safe."

The girl nodded and lifted her shoulders up and down, as if shrugging off a disappointment. In the distance there was another explosion—a bomb with a timer going off.

"We should split up," Otto suggested. The Gestapo will be searching for a woman and a girl together, right? They're less likely to stop you and ask for your papers if you're apart."

"That makes sense," Anja said. "Nadine, you walk ahead with Herr . . ."

"Deitch," Otto said. "Otto Deitch."

"I will follow behind you," Anja continued.

The three of them moved toward the exit. Anja tugged at Nadine's sleeve and looked into her eyes.

"Promise me one thing," she said somberly. "If you see that they've stopped me just keep walking. Do not say anything. Do not stop. Just keep walking."

Nadine nodded. "I understand," she said, and moved toward the light and out onto the street with Otto.

"I'll be right behind you," Anja called after the girl, suddenly anxious about seeing her go. She waited a few moments before following them.

As she walked she kept her eyes locked on Nadine, never allowing the girl to leave her sight for a moment. She wondered if she could really trust Otto. He had the letter from Johann, but she knew little else of him. No one was to be trusted. She needed to keep focused, to place every footstep carefully to ensure that they weren't swallowed by the enormity of what they faced. She tried to console herself: At least Johann was alive and was attempting to find them in Berlin. Quite how he was proposing to reach the city, she had no idea, but Anja had always known her husband to have enormous reserves of determination. She had seen how the war had crushed so many people, had ground them, literally, into the earth. She knew that Johann was one of those who would never give up. Quietly and methodically, he would do what he needed to cling on to what—and those—he loved.

The letter delivered baffling and terrifying news.

Johann wrote of a half brother, Dieter, who would have Johann and his family killed at a moment's notice. Johann had always told her that he had no siblings; his mother had died while he was an infant, and his father had perished of an illness when Johann had been at medical college. Why had he told her this lie? Did he have a family whom she had never met? Surely that was an absurd notion.

She had to cling to a single thought—she trusted her husband; he was a good man and would never seek to harm her. On the contrary, he had done all he could to make her life fulfilled and happy.

Then a nasty, toxic feeling surfaced: What if the war had changed him? What if the Johann she knew and loved had suddenly become corrupted by the struggle to stay alive?

Walking warily along the streets, as the sun battled its way through the dusty miasma that surrounded her, Anja tried not to think too hard about it. She was scared and desperate enough without having to carry another heavy burden. The danger from the authorities scared her witless—she and Nadine had enough to contend with without glancing over their shoulders constantly, watching for the Gestapo. She could hardly believe what she was thinking—that losing their home in the air raid might have been a blessing. If the building was still standing the police would know where to find them both. Now they might even believe that she and Nadine had perished in the wreckage. She would do everything she could to keep hidden until they fled the city. It seemed they would be safe at Otto's—no one would think to look for them there.

She thought about the final part of Johann's letter. He had warned her that, should he not arrive within three days, then they must leave, no matter what. Anja passed a group of guest workers loading corpses onto a cart—an emaciated horse waited patiently, its head bowed almost to the ground, as if it were too weak to support its neck.

As much as she ached to see her husband, she would wait no longer than he had suggested. That is, she thought, if she was still alive to make the decision.

13

Dieter hobbled from the staff car that he had commandeered to bring him to the field hospital. He only had hazy memories of the place: sounds, colors, and voices more than the specifics of the geography. He limped through the mud, his walking stick useless as it sunk deep into the sticky mire.

"Where will I find Kommandant Henke?" he demanded of a passing worker.

"In the administration area," the man said, pointing to a series of green tents that were set up beneath camouflaged webbing. Dieter slithered off in search of his quarry before the man could say anything else. The *Sturmbannführer* didn't notice the bony orderlies avoiding his path as he picked his way across the ground, the collar of his greatcoat turned up against the driving rain. He was enjoying the downpour—the rainwater cooled the burned skin on his face.

Dieter pushed aside the flap of the tent to find Henke bent over a large white metal bowl containing some scummy water. There was a towel around his neck and his head was covered in white soapsuds.

"Kommandant Henke?" Dieter said, by way of announcement. "Dieter Schnell, Reich Main Security Office. I am here to conduct an investigation."

"I see," Henke said. He appeared unimpressed and bent down over the bowl again and continued to shave his head. "We have a terrible problem with lice here," he offered by way of explanation.

"Time is of the essence in my investigation," Dieter continued, listening to the noise of the razor scratching against the stubble on Henke's head. "I do hope that the *Kommandant* will be able to find the time to consider my questions with the necessary thoroughness."

"Of course," Henke continued. He gestured at a fold-up chair with his razor. "Please go ahead and sit down. Would you like someone to fetch you water or some terrible coffee?"

"Johann Schultz," Dieter said, ignoring Henke's offer. "When was the last time you saw him?"

Henke considered this while Dieter pulled out a small black notebook and flipped it open. "It's hard to remember exactly," he replied. "Time here has a tendency to blur. He was asked to go to some ceremony in Berlin. I couldn't spare him."

"Did he give you any indication that he might not be of sound mind?" Dieter asked.

"On the contrary," Henke said. "He continued to be a huge asset to this hospital because of his calmness and hard work." Henke cleaned his razor in the water and looked up from the washbowl. "I believe that it was he who treated you."

"There were two men with me," Dieter said. "One of them is missing and one is alleged to have committed suicide. . . ."

"I think that being found hanging from your own belt in the latrine is a little more than an allegation," Henke said.

Dieter wanted to smash the smug little man's face. He clearly had small regard for Dieter's rank or mission.

"Has there been no sign of Oberscharführer Lehman?"

"Why should there be?" Henke asked. "How do we know that he didn't go off somewhere else?"

"The intelligence I have was that he was last seen at your field hospital, *Kommandant*," Dieter said pointedly. "Where else would you suggest I conduct my investigation?"

"*Sturmbannführer*," Henke started, while pouring water from a jug onto his head. "While I would love the resources to send out search parties to see if the *Oberscharführer* is somewhere in western Prussia, I'm afraid that we are distracted by other matters."

Dieter cocked his head to the side.

"I should remind the *Kommandant* that I am conducting a criminal investigation," he said carefully. "Cooperation in this matter isn't at your discretion; it's required by law."

Henke appeared undaunted. He took the small towel that had been hanging around his neck and rubbed his head. When he was finished, he carefully laid the towel out to dry.

"One of the problems we have at the moment is getting clean laundry," he explained, never taking his eyes off Dieter. "It's a fairly basic requirement for a hospital."

"The autopsy of Obersturmführer Ostermann," Dieter persisted. "What were your findings?"

Henke picked up a shirt and began to dress.

"There was no autopsy," he said while securing the top button. His tone was offhand. He had had enough of Dieter.

"No autopsy?" Dieter said incredulously. He had witnessed how Ostermann had died, but he wanted to try and intimidate Henke in order to prize other information from him.

"Are you serious?" Henke said, his temper rising. "Sturmbannführer Schnell, I can only help you if you ensure that your questions remain within the bounds of reality. Last week I had close to one thousand men here. This field hospital has the beds for less than a quarter of that. I've managed to get most of them away to positions behind the front line, because the last thing we are going to need once the Soviet artillery opens up is to be caring for patients when there is work to be done in triage. This is my actuality, *Sturmbannführer*."

Henke picked up his jacket. "I am willing to do all I can to assist you in your inquiry," he said. "But I cannot conduct autopsies, nor can I speculate as to the whereabouts of an officer under your command. Is there anything else?"

Dieter looked intently at Henke. The *Kommandant* could see the anger flickering across his face.

"Doctor Schultz," he said menacingly. "He is no longer under your command?"

For the first time Henke showed vulnerability. "No," he said, looking around for his cap. "He hasn't been present for several days now."

"And is it unusual that officers under your command go missing?" Dieter continued.

"Surely you know this already?" Henke said. "Schultz took the vehicle that you and your officers arrived in. He hasn't been seen since."

Dieter felt a sudden pain running up the injuries on his left side. His half brother had taken the *Kübelwagen*. Could the documents have been inside, or was this just coincidence? And where had Johann gone with the vehicle? Surely he would be arrested by the *Feldgendarmerie* before he got too far. Dieter had asked that all field reports from *Feldgendarmerie* units in surrounding sectors be forwarded to his newly appointed assistant, a decrepit former Gestapo interrogator named Harald Kuefer, who had been sequestered for the investigation. Dieter had little faith in him. The man appeared to be suffering from chronic lung disease and was barely able to maintain a conversation due to a debilitating cough.

"And you informed the appropriate authorities as soon as Schultz went missing?"

"I did," Henke said, standing up. "*Sturmbannführer*, I really must go now; I have ward inspections."

"I understand," Dieter said. "Perhaps the *Kommandant* wouldn't mind if I accompanied him?"

Henke didn't comment. He held open the flap of his tent for Dieter to head back into the rain.

"Your injuries have healed remarkably quickly," Henke commented once they were outside. The rain had let up a little.

"I have nothing to compare my recovery to," Dieter said. "I continue in the only way I can—by serving my Führer to the best of my ability."

Henke looked over at the SS man, incredulous that he could make such a pronouncement without any hint of irony.

"It was Schultz who worked on you when you arrived in triage," Henke said. "Why would you imagine that someone who saved the life of one senior SS officer would want to end the lives of others? It doesn't make any sense."

"I would like to talk to other doctors who would have known Schultz," Dieter said, casting his eyes suspiciously around the complex.

"Be my guest," Henke said. "The officers' quarters are over there." He pointed to a tent about a hundred yards away on the edge of a tree line. "But be warned. Many of them are working more than twenty hours a day. You'll be lucky to catch many of them, and the ones you do will be keener on sleeping than answering your questions. I will have my adjutant deliver you Schultz's personal effects."

Henke pushed his hands into his coat and walked off toward the triage unit, his head unbowed even in the rain.

"Anyone would think that you didn't care whether we caught Oberstabsarzt Schultz or not," Dieter shouted after him.

The *Kommandant* halted and spun around on his heel. He held Dieter's gaze for a moment.

"You know . . . ," he said, his voice echoing across the field, before the words petered out and Henke continued onward. Dieter watched as the *Kommandant* walked quickly into the gloom.

The other doctors were useless—they were either too recently arrived to have met Schultz or they were full of praise for his professionalism. Most noted his private nature. None of them knew anything about his personal life.

An adjutant brought Dieter a small cardboard suitcase of Johann's belongings. Dieter picked through socks and shirts, casting items on the floor impatiently. There were toiletries and a fountain pen, but no letters. Dieter considered this for a moment. Almost certainly this could be explained by a pattern that he was beginning to determine in his half brother: caution. He appeared to offer little of himself to the world.

With good reason, Dieter thought.

Then, at the bottom of the case, his hand struck two hard objects. He pulled them from the case, energized with excitement: his first clues. He held one in each hand and considered them.

Two framed photos.

One he knew well. He had seen it every day of his early life: his stepfather, Nicolas Meier. The photo showed an austere, patrician figure. Dieter knew him differently—a weak man with a politically objectionable outlook. Dieter felt nothing; seeing an image of Nicolas for the first time in over a decade made no impression on him.

He put down the photo of Nicolas and focused all his energy on the other black-and-white image. It was a woman in her early twenties, her hair pinned back, looking into the distance. She looked calm, contented. And she was attractive.

Dieter smiled. His half brother had a wife.

There was now a new way to find Johann. Another means to take him down.

Dieter's driver met him outside the tent. Rain drummed on a large black umbrella he was holding. Dieter wasn't sure where he had gotten it from—incongruously the handle was made of bamboo. The driver pushed the umbrella over Dieter's head.

"That is not necessary," Dieter said, batting the man's hand away.

"Apologies, sir."

Dieter headed back toward the staff car.

"We must head back to Berlin immediately," Dieter instructed the driver.

"Absolutely, sir," came the reply. The man trotted to keep up with Dieter, who was making quick progress despite his limp. "Sir," the driver said. "The comms department just gave me this."

Dieter took the envelope that he was being offered. The field hospital had received a telegram from Kuefer back in Berlin. The old coot had come up with something: The *Kübelwagen* that Johann had stolen had turned up. It had been found by the *Feldgendarmerie* about thirty miles northwest of the hospital—about seven miles south of Müncheberg.

The name flashed across Dieter's mind—the rendezvous. Had Johann found out about the meeting and attempted to reach it? If so, what had happened there?

Such behavior seemed improbable, but then pretty much everything else about his actions had been out of character. The car was discovered to have run out of diesel, suggesting that Johann had had to abandon it. Where had he been heading? Maybe to the meeting, but far more likely he was traveling west—back to Berlin.

"We need to return to the Ministry as quickly as possible," he instructed the driver. "We have much to do."

Despite his persistent cough, Kuefer puffed on cigarettes constantly. Dieter waved his hand through the clouds of smoke as he entered the small, cheerless room at Gestapo headquarters that he had been detailed for the investigation.

"Are you still alive?" he said to Kuefer, who barely raised his head from the noisy typewriter that he was working on.

"Where do you even get those things from?" Dieter asked.

"One decade in the *Kriminalpolizei* and another in the Gestapo," Kuefer said, his eyes narrowing. "You think I don't know where to find a smoke when I want one?"

Dieter removed his coat and hung it on the rack. The smell of damp wool competed with the cigarette smoke.

"What did you find at the hospital?" Kuefer said, pushing himself back from the desk. His chair had small wheels on it.

"Schultz has a wife," Dieter replied. "And I think she's here."

"Do you have an address?"

"No," Dieter said. "Look for a Schultz in the records. Intelligence should at least be able to give you a first name."

"Once we know, I'll send someone to pick her up immediately," Kuefer said, reaching for a black Bakelite phone.

"No," Dieter said, easing himself into his chair gingerly. "Don't pick her up. Watch her. Wherever she is, Schultz will follow. Think of her as bait rather than quarry."

Kuefer made a call. Officers were instructed to locate the last known address of the wife of Johann Schultz.

"They are saying that they can locate a district soon, but an exact address will take longer as the records have been archived," Kuefer said after putting down the phone.

"Dammit!" Dieter thundered, thumping his desk. "I need an address!"

Kuefer put out a cigarette in the overflowing ashtray before him. "Once the district is known, we can at least alert all police and Gestapo units to be on the lookout," he said. "She might show up."

Dieter drummed his fingers on the table impatiently. He had never much liked the idea of police work and its interminable processes and waiting. Now that he knew how dull it was he longed to be back in a combat unit.

The phone burst to life. Kuefer snatched it up.

"Yes," he said, before pausing. "I see." Another pause. "Immediately. We will be there within the half hour."

"What?"

"That was the Oberst Reinhard's office," Kuefer said, suppressing a smile. "It seems that you are responsible for stripping three SS officers near naked and robbing them of official documents."

The three men were back in uniform and seated in a row behind an interview desk. They stood up when Dieter entered the room, and they exchanged the German greeting. Sturmbannführer Schorner, Obersturmführer Beckmann, and their driver, Glaezer, stared expectantly at Dieter, who remained standing when they sat down.

"I know that your superiors will have a great deal to say about this fiasco," Dieter said. "I am not interested in the consequences for any of you. I am here in my capacity as an investigator."

Schorner and Beckmann exchanged an irritated look.

"Forgive me," Dieter said. "I should have introduced myself more formally: Sturmbannführer Dieter Schnell."

The men looked at their boots.

"I believe that you have encountered someone else using that name," Dieter said, limping over to a corner of the room, where he stood in a shadow. "But I can assure you that he was an imposter."

Glaezer took a deep breath. He wanted nothing to do with this.

"Where shall we start?" Dieter said, clapping his hands together lightly. It would have been too painful to make anything other than the gentlest contact.

"I shall speak for all of us," Schorner said, folding his arms.

"I shall decide that," Dieter replied quickly.

"I think that the *Sturmbannführer* forgets himself . . . ," Schorner continued.

"On the contrary—I think you'll find that this investigation has the authority of SS-Obergruppenführer Doctor Ernst Kaltenbrunner," Dieter said. "Take it up with him if you'd like. He has expressed a personal interest."

Dieter was lying—the last thing anyone wanted was for Kaltenbrunner or Himmler himself to be aware of what had happened. The implicit deal he had made with Keller was that he would stamp this thing out before it made its way up the chain of command. It was also in the best interests of Schorner and Beckmann to make as little noise about the incident as had to be made.

"I insist on full cooperation," Dieter announced. Beckmann and Glaezer looked down at the floor, waiting for Schorner to speak.

"What would you like to know?" Schorner said.

"Obviously we were both aware of the other's missions," Dieter said. Schorner nodded.

"But the rendezvous was compromised. . . ."

"The information that led to the impersonator coming to the farmhouse did not come from my side," Schorner said coolly. "It might make sense for the *Sturmbannführer* to be asking questions of his own men rather than laying the blame elsewhere."

Dieter cocked his head. "This investigation is not about apportioning blame for how the incident came to pass," he said firmly. "This is the very least of our concern. Through your oversight we now have a Bolshevik on the run with state secrets. Orders from the Führer himself that, were they to fall into the wrong hands, would have enormous repercussions both for the people of Berlin and the defense of the Reich."

The men straightened their backs. The very mention of the Führer's name, even when the man hadn't been seen for weeks, was enough to make them sit up. If the documents were not recovered swiftly, Hitler would ultimately be told of the incident and would draw his own conclusions about who was responsible. There would be repercussions.

"This impersonator," Dieter said. "Was there anything else that he took other than the briefcase with the materials?"

"No," Schorner said. "When he left, we assumed that he would take the truck, but he just appeared to slip away into the night."

"He had a *Kübelwagen* and a driver," Glaezer added, keen to offer some insight. "He told me that they had broken down not far from the farmhouse."

Dieter noted the detail. It was consistent with the report from the *Feldgendarmerie*. It seemed likely that Johann was still somewhere in the country east of Berlin.

Schorner glared at the driver for speaking out of turn. Glaezer shrugged.

"Tell me about the conversation," Dieter asked.

"He arrived on time at eighteen hundred hours," Schorner said. "He was carrying the briefcase and introduced himself as you. There was nothing about him that appeared suspicious."

"Nothing?"

"He seemed a little odd at first—anxious," Schorner explained. "But I put this down to the fact that I thought he had been on the road for some time and was carrying highly sensitive information."

"Did he ask you any questions about your mission?"

"Yes, he wanted to know what we were doing next."

"You didn't think that odd?"

"Maybe in retrospect," Schorner says. "You'd imagine that an officer so intimately involved in the operation would have that knowledge, but who knows? He had fulfilled his part—he was bringing the information, and from that point onward his role was over." Schorner paused.

"At what point did it become clear to you that he had gone rogue?"

"When we were woken from our beds at gunpoint. . . ."

"You thought it wise to fall asleep?"

"He was an officer with whom we had a longstanding rendezvous," Schorner answered. "It seemed a perfectly natural thing to do."

"But why did he wake you?" Dieter asked. "Why didn't he slip off into the night? Surely it would have been much safer to do so."

Beckmann and Glaezer were now paying attention. They looked at Schorner.

"He wanted to know about the Nero Decree," Schorner said.

"What about it?"

Schorner shrugged and then sighed.

"What about it?"

"He seemed to be fixated on it—it was like he had just learned about it and was . . ."

"Was *what?*"

"He seemed to be particularly struck by it. Outraged, even."

"And he left with what, exactly?" Dieter asked. Schorner held his gaze and set up straight.

"Everything," he answered eventually.

The silence in the room was broken only by the sound of Kuefer's cough and then the sound of his boots on the floorboards.

"This is the suspect," Kuefer said, handing over a sheet of paper to Dieter. The three men had contributed to an artist's impression.

Dieter picked it up and examined it.

He concealed a shiver of recognition.

He knew this man.

Dieter strode across to the other side of the room. Schorner, Beckmann, and Glaezer watched him as he stood with his head bowed.

He knew now who had the briefcase - and there was no doubt in his mind that Johann was coming to Berlin.

14

Anja woke early and dressed quietly while Nadine slept. She needed to leave Johann a message in the ruins of their apartment—something discreet that would reveal where they were without revealing anything to the Gestapo. Then she would find some food and wake Nadine with breakfast. It would be like the old days. She padded through Otto's apartment. She had been surprised when they arrived yesterday by how grand it was—there were paintings on the walls and dark wooden furniture throughout. As she pulled her boots on, Anja realized she had only two more nights in Berlin. They would rest and try to find some food to give them strength; then they would leave, as Johann had written.

Outside the weather revealed an indifference to the mood of the capital—while the sky wasn't blue, it was at least bright. The acrid smell of smoke remained, but there was at least no rain to slog through. Anja imagined that this had once been a fashionable bourgeois neighborhood where families of the professional classes situated themselves to raise wholesome children. Now there were only blackened stumps remaining of the linden trees that had once provided shade for mothers pushing carriages in the heat of summer. Anja looked around. She couldn't see another human being. There were not even any birds.

She came to the end of the street and remembered that there had once been a famous pet shop here called Schnauzers, like the dog. On Sundays families would come to look at the puppies and kittens in the windows. There were also exotic birds, lolloping rabbits, and tropical fish. Anja had heard once that they even had a monkey for sale, although no one she knew had actually seen it.

Now there was nothing for sale. No mammals, no birds, no fish. Every building on the block had been flattened during a raid. Where once there had been a small department store, a café, and a haberdashery, there were just the husks of buildings. In front of each there were piles of rubble. Twisted metal appeared from piles of masonry, like plant tendrils reaching up from the earth. Anja noticed a streetlight that had begun to melt because of the heat it had been exposed to. Occasionally she would pass temporary structures that had been set up by the bombed-out: bits of tarpaulin engineered into tents with fires for warmth and cooking. Many of the parks in the city were now being used as campsites for the homeless. Thousands of them huddled together in a misery of mud and jerry-rigged shelters.

She felt the piece of chalk Otto had given her to leave Johann a message on the ruins of their former home. Anja knew that returning home was loaded with potential danger, but she reasoned that it was the only way Johann would be able to find them, should he make it to Berlin. She walked confidently through the streets, back to her old neighborhood, playing the part of a woman with an early-morning errand to run. She kept her head down, while maintaining an uneasy surveillance of everything around her—just one mistake or piece of bad fortune, and she would be found.

The street had been cleared of much of its debris. Anja marveled that even now, with the country's resources exhausted, there was still the wherewithal, manpower, and desire to sweep away the wreckage of attacks with such speed and thoroughness. It was one of the last vestiges of the city that she recognized—the determined, single-minded Berliner. She skirted carefully past their old building, checking to see if anyone was watching before crossing the road and retracing her steps on the other side to make sure that there wasn't something—or someone—that she had missed.

There appeared to be no one around this early in the morning. Writing the message on the front of the building was too risky—she might be seen, and it was more likely that, should Johann be pursued, this would be the first place the authorities would check. She moved around to the side of the building and, as close to the front as she could manage, added a brief, cryptic missive to the dozens already there. The second she had finished she threw the chalk down to the end of the passageway, thrust her hands deep into the pockets of her raincoat, and walked briskly away. Only when Anja was three streets away did she begin to feel like she wasn't being observed.

She came upon a road near Chausseestraße where she saw a queue of women. They seemed hopeful, although the shop had yet to open. Anja joined the back of the line, turning her collar up and pulling down a hat Otto had lent her in case anyone should recognize her.

"Morning, dear," an old lady in front of her said.

"Good morning," Anja said, smiling. Social interaction was the last thing that she desired, but she didn't have the nerve to let others know otherwise.

"No raids last night then," the lady said. She was dressed entirely in black with stout lace-up shoes, and her gray hair had been arranged neatly in a bun. She could have been on her way to church.

"Thankfully not," Anja replied. "It was nice to get a full night of sleep for once."

"I sleep through it, mostly," the old lady said. "I have a makeshift bed down in the cellar, and most of us have gotten so used to it that we don't even notice it unless it comes really close."

"There's a shelter in your building?" Anja asked.

"Yes," said the old lady. "And I'm on the ground floor, so I only have to walk down one flight of stairs. I suppose if we get a direct hit, they'll only have to bring my body up one flight, so it works both ways, I suppose."

She chuckled to herself and touched Anja on the forearm playfully.

"Do you know what time the shop opens?" Anja asked.

"Well, he didn't open until lunchtime yesterday—the queue was round the block by then, but I heard a couple of the girls say earlier that they'd heard he was in there already this morning and there was talk of fresh bread."

The lady squeezed Anja's arm in anticipation.

"That would be a treat indeed," Anja said. "If only there were butter."

"How wonderful that would be," the old lady said. "And maybe some rose-hip jam too, while we're at it."

"My husband always loved sour-cherry jam," Anja said.

"I'm sorry, dear," the old lady said, after a pause. "When did he leave you?"

"Oh, no," Anja said. "He's still alive." It was her turn to pause. "I think. He's in the east."

The old lady squeezed her arm again.

"Oh, well," she said. "At least he's not too far away, eh?"

Anja was surprised to see that the old lady had been right: The store contained basic provisions. She got some bread, potatoes, a jar of pickled carrots, powdered eggs, and a tin of herrings, and she had to suppress the smile playing on her lips as she walked past those still in the queue—some of them might not be as lucky. Anja could hardly wait to get home. She would make Nadine and Otto a fine breakfast, and then they would be able to look forward to a dinner of the fish with the potatoes and maybe some of the bread, if there was any left.

She hurried along the street, not entirely sure of the fastest way to get home—there were so many thoroughfares closed because of collapsed buildings that Berlin had become something of a maze. She passed through a series of streets that were almost entirely unoccupied. She noticed, though, that some of the bombed-out wrecks were occupied by pitiful families. Better misery in their own homes than misery in the unknown.

She came to a road that had been largely untouched—people busied themselves with their daily routines, many of them wearing scarves over their mouths for protection from the foul air. She had grown used to the noise of almost constant coughing. Anja wondered at an old man who was cleaning the windows of his tobacconist's shop—aside from the pointlessness of the task, she wondered where he had gotten the water. She assumed that there must be a standpipe somewhere nearby. She watched him as she started to cross the road.

"Watch out, madam!" The voice came past her quickly, out of nowhere.

Alarmed, she stepped back onto the pavement and watched as a series of bicycles streamed by her. Each was ridden by a member of the *Volkssturm,* the militia of young boys and old men that the Nazis had ordered into existence—a final roll of the dice once it became clear that German towns and cities were under imminent threat from the Red Army. None of them appeared to have a uniform—they wore mismatched items of Hitler Youth, Wehrmacht, and improvised clothing. Some of them had attempted to dye their garments a dark color, as advised by the authorities. The only thing each had in common was a *Panzerfaust*—a disposable bazooka that fired a single shot—strapped to the handlebars of their bicycles.

Anja watched them move past her, and the mood of excitement she had felt at foraging the food was erased by a terrible realization that the defense of Berlin was to be conducted in such a way. Some of these boys were no older than Nadine.

"Mrs. Schultz!" A voice came from one of the riders.

She looked up and realized that it was Lars Ziegler, the boy who had been taken from her class only two days before. He was the last rider, followed by what looked to be a police officer. The boy waved at her unsteadily, taking one hand off the handlebars.

"Mrs. Schultz!"

Anja waved at him enthusiastically as he passed, hoping that, in some way, her support might offer him a form of protection. Lars continued to ride with his hand raised once he had gone beyond her. The police officer, meanwhile, pulled his brake so hard that the back wheel of his bicycle lifted momentarily from the road. He had a thick gray scarf over his mouth to protect himself from breathing the debris that was thrown up from the road. He looked at Anja warily.

"Mrs. Schultz?"

Anja said nothing. She noted that Lars had stopped on the roadway ahead.

"Mrs. Johann Schultz?"

The man continued to stare at her.

"Are you Mrs. Johann Schultz?"

They know my name. They're looking for me.

It was too late for denial. Anja's hesitation had convicted her. She tugged at her coat as if she had felt a chill and headed off in the direction opposite from the one the cyclists had been riding in. She walked quickly, ignoring the stares of a few passersby who had witnessed the exchange. She glanced backward and noticed that the man was turning his bicycle around to come after her: He would be upon her in moments. She looked to her left and saw, no more than a hundred yards away, a collapsed building. Hoping that the officer would not follow her over the rubble, Anja crossed the road and broke into a run.

She glanced behind her. The man was standing while pedaling now to try and reach her. She had to be careful where she placed her feet—there were bricks and pieces of wood scattered nearby, and a misplaced foot while running could mean a sprained ankle and almost certainly capture.

She made it. She placed her boot on a section of wall that had ruptured outward and began to climb. How strange, she thought, that the buildings that had once dominated the city were now an obstruction. The going was slow; occasionally Anja would put her foot on what she thought was a solid outcropping, only to feel it slide away once she put more weight upon it. She trod carefully; she was terrified of falling into a hollow that had been concealed by part of the collapsed edifice. Parts of the building slid down behind her, as if she were clambering up a scree embankment.

Behind her the *Volkssturm* officer reached the bottom of the collapsed building and looked up at Anja.

"I order you to stop!" he shouted.

Anja ignored him. She had reached the highest point of the rubble and was able to see that, on the other side, there were several houses that were still standing. If she could get to the other side, she would be able to lose the policeman in the streets below. She looked back and saw that her pursuer had abandoned his bicycle and was laying his *Panzerfaust* on the ground gently. He began to clamber over the rubble after Anja—he was not giving up.

"Dammit," Anja said. She started down the other side, balancing her desire to get away as quickly as possible with a need for caution.

"There's no point running," the man called after her. "We will find you wherever you are."

His words echoed around the empty houses, repeating themselves in Anja's panicked mind. She stumbled. Dust flew around
her. Her relief at not damaging her ankle was offset by her dropping the shopping bag. She watched, horrified, as the contents
spilled among the bricks and dirt. She paused, unsure whether
she had the time to collect her belongings. The man was just over
the brow of the rubble now—heading down toward her. She felt a
rush of anger: She had gone out to get food for her niece and this
. . . this bastard was trying to capture her. He wanted to ruin the
one good thing that she was able to do in this terrible, terrible city.

She refused to leave the food where it lay. She would make
Nadine the breakfast that she had intended to make the girl. A
healthy meal should be the least that she could offer her. Keeping
an eye on the officer, Anja stooped to pick the items up quickly.
The officer saw his opportunity and started to clamber faster, taking greater risks than he had before as he descended through the
shattered masonry and splintered timber.

Anja found the bread and her onion quickly enough. She put
her hand into the hole where she thought the tin of eggs had
fallen and pulled it out. But where were the herrings? They were
to be the centerpiece of the meal—their oily smoothness offering
enough comfort and sustenance to keep them going for a few more
days. She had pictured it in her mind, but now she was standing in
a bomb site turning around in circles as a man pursued her.

There! She saw a silver glint—like a fish in a murky ocean—
and reached down to pick it up before putting it in her bag. The
man was much closer now; he was about halfway down the slope.
Anja started to run up the roadway, her legs feeling more vital as
she moved along a flat surface. She made a dramatic right turn
onto another street and looked for somewhere to hide. She ducked
into an abandoned building and realized that she was intruding—a
woman and her husband and children sat around a fire drinking

from tin cups, their possessions arranged neatly throughout the burned-out room. They turned to look at her, their faces wretched and smeared with soot.

"I'm sorry," Anja said, bolting back out the door.

She continued along the street. Some of the houses were intact, but many were damaged and blackened—it seemed that the RAF had used incendiary devices in this part of the city. She was breathing heavily now as she tired. The shopping bag felt heavy, its contents jumping around with every fearful step she took. Behind her she heard the crunch of footsteps. They sounded as if they were quickening. She was now too terrified to turn and see how close he was to her. She wasn't sure how much longer she could continue to run like this.

Anja realized with dismay that she wasn't going to be able to outrun the man. She made a quick right turn down a side street and almost immediately saw an alleyway. She thought that she had maybe thirty seconds before the man would be upon her. This was her opportunity to lose him; if he dithered over which way she had gone, she would be able to slip away.

She headed swiftly down the alley, which passed behind the backyards of a row of unblemished houses. Almost immediately she saw that it was a dead end. Panicked, she realized that she had no time to go back; by now the officer would be approaching the road she had first turned down. If she was to reappear from the entrance to the alleyway they would virtually bump into each other. The only way out was through one of the houses. She ran through the yard and tried a back door. It was locked. She knocked on the door—rapping quickly on it. An old lady appeared at a window and peered at her.

"Please, let me in," Anja implored as quietly as she could. The old lady considered her request for a moment before raising her hand and shooing Anja from her property. Anja had no time to explain. She ran to the next house and tried the door. It was also locked. She banged on it, fearful that the noise would alert her pursuer. There was no answer. She had no time to wait, quickly moving to the last house. She realized that by now, the man must be in the street at the end of the alley. If he was to investigate the passageway, the next time she appeared from a backyard he would spot her immediately.

She tried the third back door. It was locked, as the others had been.

She couldn't knock—her pursuer would surely hear her. She tapped with what was left of her nail on the pane of glass. She thought of Nadine. Asleep alone in Otto's apartment. The policeman's boots crunched ever closer. She tapped again—there was nothing left to do. It was a just gesture, a plea. It was hopeless. . . .

At the very moment Anja turned to face her pursuer, the door opened behind her. Anja tumbled into the scullery of the house, landing on a slate floor. She heard the door close and looked up to see an old woman, who was dressed head to toe in black. She had perfectly manicured gray hair, which Anja took to be a wig. The woman leaned over Anja and put her index finger to her lips. The two women remained motionless and listened to the crunch of boots in the backyard. An unseen hand rotated the handle a second after the old woman silently twisted the lock. The wooden object rattled in its frame. There was silence and then, after what seemed to Anja like an eternity, the noise of the boots receded into the distance.

The woman beckoned Anja to stand up, then led her into a dark, candlelit parlor with a threadbare sofa that had maybe once been covered in velvet. The woman floated through the room like a specter. Although the woman said nothing, Anja knew that she was supposed to follow her through the shadows. As she passed through the room, Anja made out a silver frame resting on a sideboard. She slowed slightly to look at the photo inside. The woman felt Anja pause to examine the picture. The two of them stood silently for a moment and took in the image before them: a couple on their wedding day.

The man was in his dress uniform, stiff on a gray background. Anja knew nothing about military insignia, but she thought she recognized a Luftwaffe uniform. He was clean-shaven, with a strong jaw and a playful look in his eye. She looked at the woman and half smiled, wanting to express her sympathy but also acknowledge the striking look of the man. They must have made quite a couple at one time in their Sunday best on the Kurfürstendamm. The woman nodded as if accepting Anja's respects and then continued through the house, eventually coming to a front door, just off the parlor. A plate containing a single slice of black bread with a layer of margarine smeared over it sat on a table nearby. The woman looked at it guiltily, as if she had been caught doing something improper, before leading Anja to the door.

She opened it carefully and peered outside. The gloom of the house made the day appear bright. There was the sound of a horse and cart coming by at quite a clip and even of a child laughing. The woman took a long look up and down the street. She seemed to have second thoughts, returning inside and reaching for a light-colored raincoat that was hanging on a rack by the front door. She lifted it down and beckoned Anja to turn before sliding it over Anja's wool coat. The woman turned Anja around so that the two women faced each other and examined her closely. The woman reached up and pulled out the pins that were holding Anja's hair up. It fell about her face. She handed the slides and pins back to Anja, who put them in her pocket. The woman nodded, pleased with the change in appearance. From a distance Anja didn't resemble the woman who had been chased through the rubble.

The woman opened the front door again before handing Anja another cheap bag to put her groceries in. A minor but maybe decisive change. The woman scanned up and down the street thoroughly, before ushering Anja outside.

"Thank you," Anja said.

The woman, still watching for danger, waved her away.

"Go," she said. "Quickly."

Anja scuttled along the street, back toward Otto's apartment. This morning she would make her niece breakfast.

15

Johann had slipped from the back of the truck as it passed through Kreuzberg and breathed the Berlin air for the first time in months. It was dense and left a residue of dust and smoke at the back of his throat. He coughed and cast his eyes around. It seemed that the majority of the city's muscular, elegant buildings were destroyed, the vibrant city a crooked shadow of its former self. As he walked down the street clutching the official briefcase, he noticed that civilians cast dark glances at him. Some even crossed the road, or went out of their way to avoid him.

Dieter's uniform marked Johann out as a *Sturmbannführer*. The SS had been feared but widely deferred to; now it seemed that they were feared and loathed. He strode as confidently as he could—only those hunting him would be aware of the panic in his heart. He needed to find Anja and Nadine to get them away from this hell. But first he must finish what he had started at the farmhouse. The violence perpetrated on the populace for years was terrible enough, without the terminal conclusion advocated by the Demolitions on Reich Territory. He stepped into a doorway, then pulled the top document—the army directive expediting the Nero Decree executive order—from the briefcase and scanned down the page.

The directive had been issued from the office of Oberst Erich Reinhard at the Reich Main Security Office. Overseen by the loathsome *Reichsführer* himself, Heinrich Himmler, the department was responsible for all matters of state security from the police to the most senior member of the SS. It was the same government department responsible for the KZ documentation.

Johann recalled while in the east having to listen to an interminable broadcast by its former head, Reinhard Heydrich, who raved about "enemies of the Reich both within and without our borders."

Johann knew its headquarters, the Ordenspalais on Wilhelmplatz, a grand neoclassical building by the famed nineteenth-century architect Karl Schinkel, like many in the government district. It sat opposite Speer's vast Reich Chancellery, which Hitler had funded—although the Führer was said to spend little time there, avoiding Berlin as much as he could. Johann calculated that he could reach it in twenty minutes if he hurried.

There were more buildings flattened than there were standing in Wilhelmstraße: Passersby wound their way around the neat V-shaped piles of masonry that were arranged on the pavements and street corners. Eerily, most of the street signs were intact or had been replaced by temporary wooden stands even when the buildings around them were gone, creating spectral versions of once-familiar streets. What had been the engine room of the Nazi state was little more than a skeleton—it may as well have been of an ancient civilization. As he approached Voßstraße, he could see that the Ordenspalais no longer existed.

For a moment, he forgot his mission and stood and looked at what had once been the home of Prince Charles of Prussia, who would have gazed from the building onto a large, neatly aligned grass square with a gravel path around it. There was nothing left except for a flag with a swastika planted in the rubble. Behind it two poles had been sunk into the ground. A banner fluttered between them proclaiming, "Führer, we march with you to final victory!"

A policeman stood on the corner of Wilhelmstraße. Johann approached him.

"Yes, sir," the policeman said, and came to attention.

"The Reich Main Security Office," he said. "What has happened to it?"

"Hit by the British on March 17," the man replied, staring over Johann's shoulder at the ruins. "A direct hit, I'm afraid. The bastards."

"I mean, where are they conducting their operations from now?" Johann continued.

"The annex," the policeman replied, gesturing along Wilhelmstraße. "It was built by Schinkel's student, Stüler. He built the Neues Museum, you know."

"Indeed," Johann said, walking toward the building. "He also built the Neue Synagogue."

"Yes, sir," the policeman said, not entirely sure how he was supposed to respond to such a comment, but clearly intent on not offending an SS officer.

Johann approached the building on Wilhelmstraße. The sandstone that had once been the color of wheat was stained gray and black by smoke and soot. Johann passed under a high arch, up a broad staircase, through a two-man security detail (the members of which simply nodded at him), and into a large lobby with vaulted ceilings. A young man sat behind an oval-shaped wooden desk. He stood up and saluted Johann, who assumed a casual air.

"On what floor will I find Oberst Reinhard?" he asked briskly, removing his gloves.

"The *Oberst*'s office is on the second floor at the back of the building," the corporal replied, pointing at one of the two staircases that led upstairs from the central atrium. Johann looked around. There was frantic activity throughout the building. Men and women in uniform carrying files and messages hurried about. Some gathered in small groups, in deep discussion. *Death throes*, Johann thought. Every lie told to the German people had been issued from this Ministry—or from Goebbels's Ministry of Public Enlightenment and Propaganda—and here, as time ran out, the obfuscators in chief went about their business as if they were running a department store, not a mass deception. Johann thought: Most of these people had never been in the field, but they were responsible for as much hate and falsehood as any group of human beings had ever produced.

He gripped the handle of the briefcase, his knuckles whitening. He would not allow any more falsehood.

"Let me call up . . . ," said the receptionist, lifting a telephone.

"That won't be necessary," said Johann, pushing his hand down on the cradle to cut the call off.

"But, sir, protocol insists that . . ." The receptionist appeared alarmed.

Johann spoke calmly and coolly, never taking his eyes from the functionary as he spoke.

"You would do well to remember that, after several years in the field, some of us don't need an appointment," he said. "You pen pushers need to relax a little."

With a couple of bounds Johann reached the staircase.

"I will find my own way," he said to the receptionist, who sat wondering what on earth he would tell the *Oberst* if there was a complaint.

Reinhard had chosen his secretary well. It had been hard to even obtain soap for several years, but the woman was immaculately groomed and appeared to have stepped straight from the reel of a Metro-Goldwyn-Mayer film. When Johann first saw her, as he opened the door to Reinhard's office, she reminded him of Snow White: pale skin, red lipstick, black hair. The woman looked entirely out of context.

He had forgotten that human beings could look like this.

The anteroom was tiny. Once Johann had opened the door he had to maneuver himself into the room and shut the door behind him before he had space to breathe.

"I'm sorry, sir," the woman said, acknowledging Johann's challenging entrance. "Space is at a premium since we lost the other building."

"I understand," Johann said, bowing to her over-courteously in the way that he had seen SS men do when they were trying to reenact an imagined and now long-lost Prussian courtly tradition.

The woman stood up. She was only just over five feet tall.

"There is nothing in the *Oberst*'s schedule," she said. She was clearly alarmed at having an *SS-Sturmbannführer* in her boss's office but didn't want to appear to be a pushover.

"I have come directly from the front, as the condition of my uniform indicates," Johann said. The woman looked him up and down. "I have come to the *Oberst*'s office because I have a matter of the utmost urgency to discuss with him."

The woman nodded in a way that suggested she was now slightly embarrassed and uneasy about the fact that she had questioned the *Sturmbannführer*.

"Of course," she said quietly. "Please, wait a minute."

She returned almost immediately and ushered Johann into Reinhard's office. The *Oberst* stood up behind his desk, and Johann saluted him.

"Please, take a seat," Reinhard said, indicating a simple wooden chair on the other side of his desk. He settled back into his own office chair that creaked under his not inconsiderable weight. The room was dark from the blackout over the windows—the only light was a desk lamp. He was young for an *Oberst*, probably midthirties, but he had taken to the trappings of middle age easily—his uniform was amply filled, and he had plastered his hair over his head to camouflage its thinning. He regarded Johann with heavyset eyes.

"Can I have Ursula fetch you anything?" he asked. Johann sensed that Reinhard was what was known by the people as a "golden pheasant": He had taken easily to the pomp and ornamentation of the military but knew his own limitations; he was fearful of the battlefield and in awe of those who embraced it.

"Yes," Johann said. He may have had just one purpose, but he was also aware that he must take nourishment where he could. "Some water and tea . . . or coffee, if you have it."

"Only tea, sadly," Reinhard said.

"That will do," Johann agreed. "Sugar, if you have it."

While Reinhard called in his secretary, Johann looked about the room. It was small and wood paneled. Once it would have had a bank of windows looking out onto what Johann imagined was a courtyard below. Now the glass was covered in black paper.

"So . . . ," Reinhard said. Johann was enjoying the *Oberst*'s discomfort. He was clearly finding it difficult having a field officer in his cozy room. "How are things at the front?"

"We are doing everything we can," Johann deadpanned. "I was there only yesterday, and all is ready for the Soviets. We wait; that is all."

"I hear that Busse's Ninth Army and Wenck's Twelfth Army are said to be coming from the south to defend the city," Reinhard said hopefully, crossing his hands on his belly. "Do you know anything of this?"

"No," Johann said. He had heard the rumor too, although he doubted its veracity. Frantic citizens were clinging on to false hope—as they had done throughout the war (Peace with Britain! Stalin is dead! Miracle weapons have been deployed!) in order to distract themselves from the horror of what was occurring.

"So you think that—what?—we might have a couple of weeks maybe?" Reinhard asked. The man was clearly apprehensive.

Ursula entered the room with a tray of tea, water, and biscuits.

"I found some *Lebkuchen*," she said brightly to Reinhard. She clearly knew what made her boss tick. Johann suspected there might have been more than a professional relationship between the pair, despite the gold wedding band on Reinhard's finger.

"It's hard to tell," Johann said as he sat back with his cup of weak tea. He wanted to convey to Reinhard that he felt comfortable. He moved the briefcase from his lap onto the floor between his feet. As his eyes adjusted to the dark of the room he saw several photos—Reinhard with his wife and children in formal poses. "What do you imagine that you will be doing in a week from now?"

Reinhard was momentarily thrown. Johann could tell that he was dismayed by the idea of having to fight. "Well, I . . . don't know. . . . I imagine—"

"How about a month from now?" Johann interrupted him. "Can you imagine that far into the future?"

Reinhard stayed silent.

"You have a family, I see," Johann said, acknowledging the photographs.

"Ah, yes," said Reinhard with an audible sigh. "Two daughters and a son."

He passed Johann a studio photo of three doughy children dressed in sailor suits. Johann was pleased—he had the man in the right frame of mind for his purposes.

"You must have high hopes for them," Johann said, passing back the picture in a businesslike fashion—he was keen not to drift too far from SS character.

"Oh, of course," Reinhard said wistfully. "They have all proved themselves to be good students. . . ."

A silence descended on the room. Johann let it settle. He wanted Reinhard to think about his children for as long as possible. Reinhard wasn't stupid. Even he and the other diligent servants of the regime who had never been near a firearm, let alone the front line, realized that the war was lost. Yet Reinhard waited, tight-lipped. It may have been the dog days of the Nazi regime but he still couldn't risk incriminating himself through loose talk. The punishment meted out to transgressors was as unforgiving as it had always been, and there was a chance that the *Sturmbannführer* sitting across the desk from him was a true believer. While it wasn't uncommon for civil servants or even members of the military to express dissidence, the SS remained the most loyal servants of the Führer. Created by the Party, they would go down with the Party.

Johann sensed Reinhard's unease. And with that unease came vulnerability. Johann knew that this was his opportunity. If he managed to mine along this seam there was a chance that he would find weakness that might be exploited.

"*Oberst.*" Johann crossed his legs and took a sip of his drink. He was trying to convey confidence, to exhibit control. "I hear from mutual friends that you are a man who can be trusted."

Johann looked hard across the desk. Reinhard looked down. A very slight smile played across his mouth: He was flattered by the comment, but he was fearful of it too.

"Oh, really, *Sturmbannführer?*" he said. "Is that right? What kind of friends are these that we have in common?"

Johann balanced the saucer on his knee and tipped his body toward the *Oberst.*

"I think that it's probably best," he said, "in these challenging times, if I remain discreet as to their identities."

"I understand, *Sturmbannführer,*" Reinhard said. "One can never be too careful. In the heightened atmosphere we find ourselves in we are well served to maintain decorum rather than offer our unexpurgated thoughts."

Johann began to feel confident about the role he was playing. Reinhard was listening to him as he would a senior SS field officer, with a degree of vigilance and watchfulness that befitted the potential threat posed by the *Totenkopf* insignia combined with the arrogance befitting a colonel of so tender an age. Johann pressed his advantage.

"I can assure you, Reinhard," he said, "that everything I have to say to you in this office is well considered. Nothing that comes out of my mouth will be unexpurgated. However, some of it may not be to your taste. I should warn you that should you decide to pass on what I tell you, then the consequences for you will be dire. Do you understand?"

Reinhard folded his arms in front of himself and looked Johann in the eye.

"These people are very serious," Johann said, and paused. "We have heard that you are someone who is to be trusted." He could see that Reinhard's body was tensing. Perhaps the *Oberst* was calculating whether being implicated in dissent was worse than the Soviet offensive to come. It was clear that his decision might influence the rest of his days: He would have precious few opportunities to see his chubby *Kinder* if he was starving in a gulag.

"I understand," Reinhard said. "All of us only have thoughts for the Reich." He had used the Nazi word *Reich*, the one beloved of the Party officials who dreamt of exercising power well beyond German borders. Was it just habit, or was he trying to tell Johann that he had no time for some unlikely putsch. Johann could tell that Reinhard had spent so long clambering up the greasy pole of the Nazi civil service that he was completely capable of masking his true sentiments. Notwithstanding that, Johann moved onward. He had no choice.

"Reinhard," he said, "you should understand that what is being discussed now isn't about a rearguard action or saving the country as it is. That war is over. The men I represent are senior figures within the Wehrmacht, intelligence, and civil society, and they are concerned about the future of Germany well beyond the spring of 1945."

"I have heard of such people," Reinhard said. Johann couldn't read his tone of voice. Was it dismissive? Malevolent? Or was it just the literal truth? German High Command was presently awash with rumors—they were the currency by which people communicated—so it was hardly surprising that Reinhard was aware of such things.

"I assume that you have read the intelligence briefings from the east, *Oberst?*" Johann asked. Reinhard nodded.

"Millions of Soviets are massed across the Oder. *Millions* of them," Johann said. "They have tanks and artillery lined up for miles the length of our border with barely enough space for a man to pass between them. When the offensive comes it will be devastating. They will crush our depleted defenses and arrive at our city within hours. Berlin and everything—and everyone in it—will be destroyed. There will be no quarter given. You know what went on in the east in forty-one and forty-two? It will be much, much worse than that. . . ."

Johann paused for a moment and let the thought settle. He leaned over and took a sip of his water, swallowing loudly for emphasis. "In the west, the Americans and the British have broken through our lines, but have stopped advancing at the Rhine. No one is clear as to why. The rumors you hear about the Americans arriving in Berlin first are untrue. The Soviets are knocking at the door already."

Reinhard took a deep breath as if imagining Red Army infantrymen storming into the Ministry, scattering paperwork and burning the desks, bringing chaos and disorder.

"For the future of our country, we must do everything that we can to prevent this from happening," Johann said urgently. "For the past few days, senior figures within Army High Command have been in contact with their counterparts in the American forces. We are trying to bring the best possible peace to Germany."

"How so?"

Johann thought that Reinhard's question suggested that the Oberst wasn't playing games. He had straightened in his seat a little as if genuinely intrigued. Johann wondered if it was possible to underestimate the degree to which people were desperate to leave the city.

"Our offer is that German forces will show no resistance if the Allies agree to advance quickly beyond the Rhine. The agreement is that they would secure Berlin before the Soviets can advance past what's left of Army Group Vistula, which is outnumbered by some estimates by ten to one."

Reinhard weighed this up. There were rumors circulating about secret deals of this nature. One version even had the Americans and the British joining with German forces to fight the Red Army.

"And who are these senior military figures, doing the negotiating?" Reinhard asked skeptically. Johann gave him the deadest eye he could muster.

"Do you think that I am at liberty to discuss such details?" he said irritably. "Those of us who are involved in this patriotic work are sworn to secrecy."

Reinhard pushed his chair back slightly and crossed his legs. "It's hard to know who you're talking to these days," he said.

"Indeed," Johann replied. "There is a great deal of talk in Berlin. As a military man you know that the only thing that matters are people's actions. When all is said and done, that is the only thing that shifts the universe—and it is what we will be judged by."

"And God?" Reinhard asked. Johann couldn't help a small, bemused smile. Were Nazi officials evoking long-repressed religious deities now?

"No," he replied. "Whoever comes after us once this mess is finished with will judge us alone."

Reinhard eyed him warily.

"Well, well, well . . . ," he said eventually. "Even the SS are thinking about the end of all this. . . ."

"I can assure you that the SS will do everything it can to serve the best interests of the German people," Johann said. He was amazed that he had spoken on behalf of the SS. It didn't seem possible. He tried to think clearly: Was this credible? Would a *Sturmbannführer* in the SS really talk in this manner to an *Oberst*, albeit even if he was simply a functionary? While Reinhard was testing him, it didn't seem that he considered the conversation unlikely. Johann waited, his right hand ready to reach for his pistol at the slightest hint that Reinhard would turn on him. He was confident that he could shoot the man, grab the briefcase, and escape from the building before he was caught—the Ministry was large and there was such distraction that the few security officers on duty would take time to get organized.

Suddenly he had his answer.

"You didn't come here just to tell me this," Reinhard said. "What do you want from me?"

Johann had his chance.

"The Allies have stipulated a number of conditions," he said. "Guarantees of one kind or another."

Reinhard appeared excited about being allowed into a secret brotherhood.

"The Nero Decree," Johann said flatly. "It must be revoked."

The two men sat across from each other in silence. Eventually Reinhard sat up and placed both his elbows on the desk in front of him. He formed a steeple with his hands.

"But you know that this is impossible," he said. "An executive order from the Führer is exactly that. No one has the authority to revoke such a diktat other than the Führer himself."

"Of course," Johann said. "The Allies know that as long as the Führer is in power he will never overturn the decision. However, if an order is issued from High Command to units in the field there is every chance that, by the time the Führer becomes aware of what has happened, events will have overtaken him."

"The Allies can move that quickly?"

"Without resistance, yes," Johann said emphatically. "They could have their forward units driving through Alexanderplatz within a day."

"The stab in the back," Reinhard said, almost to himself. Johann froze. He waited, but Reinhard remained quiet. "That is what they will say, eh?" he continued eventually.

"I have no interest in that," Johann said. "My interest is only in securing the best peace for Germany. We must protect Berlin and its people from further trauma." Johann worried that maybe he was letting his mask slip a little, that his passion had caused him to break from his cover as SS-Sturmbannführer Dieter Schnell.

"You . . . *Oberst,* you"—Johann paused—"are the only person who might plausibly be able to send such a message. The original order was transferred along the chain of command using your call sign. As long as an order revoking the Demolitions on Reich Territory has your call sign at the top, then telegraph operators and couriers will feel compelled to transmit the order."

Reinhard turned his head to look at some of the photos on his desk. Johann wondered what was going through his mind. He wasn't able to read Reinhard any longer. He wondered if there was a private signal between Reinhard and his secretary that would have security officers entering the office at any moment.

"You're the only one," Johann said. "This simple act could bring a bloodless peace."

"A simple act, eh?" Reinhard said, his mood souring. "You see this as a simple act?"

Johann put his teacup and saucer down on the wooden table next to him. He shuffled his feet so that they were touching the briefcase.

"Do you have any idea how much danger revoking the order will put me in?" Reinhard snapped. The *Oberst* stood up, moving his chair away from himself with his foot.

"As a colonel in the Reich Main Security Office, do you think that you will be any better off sitting at your desk and waiting for a Belarusian rifleman from the Second Shock Army to kick the door down?" Johann said in answer.

Reinhard stalked around his desk and sat on the edge of it, nearer Johann.

"I came past the Ordenspalais," Johann continued. "The building we're sitting in will be in exactly the same state as the palace once the Red Army moves its artillery closer. We cannot deny what is about to happen. We have but days before it begins."

"I've read the intelligence briefings," Reinhard said dismissively. "Our spotters say that they have more than two thousand tanks. . . ."

"Then we must stop them," Johann urged him, leaning forward. "It can be done by revoking the decree. The Allies will be true to their word."

"I wouldn't last the afternoon . . . ," Reinhard said. There was a wistfulness to his voice, as if he had thought about what might actually happen if he were to send the telex that would stop further destruction.

"You could go into hiding," Johann said. "You and your family would be protected. I can assure you of that. You think they will have time to start searching for a rogue colonel when there are Sherman and Comet tanks cruising into Spandau? The advance will begin as soon as the conditions of the agreement are completed."

Reinhard put his hand to his head, as if he were developing pain from even thinking about Johann's proposal.

"And think about after the war—if the Soviets get here first you'll be lucky to be shot dead quickly," Johann said. "With the Allies there will be a new order with a place for you. A chance for all of us to thrive rather than be enslaved."

Reinhard got up again and paced the small room, maneuvering around the furniture, his hands behind his back. His head was bowed in thought. Johann felt that he was close. He seemed to seemed to have won the Oberst to his side. He just needed one more push, one more way of making a human connection.

"Where are you from?" Johann asked. Reinhard stopped pacing and looked up at him as if shocked by the question. Then he smiled, as if the memory pleased him.

"Fünfseenland," he said, "it's just . . ."

"South of Munich . . . ," Johann said. He could see by Reinhard's face that he had completed his sentence.

"You know it?" Reinhard said, his eyes brightening.

Johann pretended to laugh, placing his clenched fist in front of his mouth.

"Fate has brought us together—my family is from Herrsching," Johann lied.

"I know the town well," Reinhard said, slapping the table. "We would go there in the summer!"

"To the lake?" Johann asked. This was something of a gamble. He was pretty sure that there was a lake in Herrsching, but he wasn't entirely sure.

"Of course!" the *Oberst* said. He gazed at Johann, as if they were somewhere far from a ruined city. "You know, I want nothing more than to be there this summer. When this mess is over, I will take my family and we'll swim in the lake. It's the loveliest place I know."

Johann shook his head, smiling. "I don't believe it," he said. He unbuttoned his shirt and pulled out the key that Nicolas had given him all those years ago. "You see this key? This is the key for our family lake house in Herrsching. I keep it with me always to remind me of happier times. *Oberst,* I insist that you come and visit in August."

"I would like that very much . . . ," Reinhard said. He had stopped his pacing and the two men were quiet. Reinhard stared flatly at Johann.

"I'd need a guarantee," Reinhard said.

"I understand. I can have that to you within hours."

"We all have skeletons in our closets," Reinhard said. "I need immunity from prosecution and a fresh start from the government in a comparable position."

Johann nodded. "That can be done. I can get a note of guarantee."

"How long?" Reinhard asked.

"Today," Johann replied confidently.

"When will you be back?"

"I need the telex to be sent first," Johann said.

Reinhard shook his head. "The letter first."

"There isn't time," Johann said. "The Allies need the guarantee by the end of the day or we're on our own. I beg of you. . . ."

Reinhard considered this. "I will write the order of revocation," he said. "You can watch me. But I will only have it sent across our communication channels once you have given me your letter."

Johann nodded. "Write the letter," he said. "Once I have seen it, I will return in an hour with your letter of guarantee. If you fail to fulfill our agreement, I promise you that I and my associates will take you down with us."

Reinhard moved behind his desk and pulled a small typewriter from inside a drawer.

"I keep it for the most sensitive material," he said, pulling off a gray cover. Johann stood up, placed the briefcase on his chair, and walked over to the desk. He wanted to see what Reinhard was about to do. As the colonel reached into his desk to pull out the official stationery, Johann noticed that the ends of Reinhard's fingers were chewed and raw as the colonel's hands tapped at the keys.

Wilhelmstraße 8–9, BERLIN, 6 April 1945

Executive Decree, dated 6 April 1945 on behalf of The Reich Minister for Armament and War Production ZA/Org. 372–381/45

For immediate attention:

Plenipotentiary General for Reich Administration with duplicates for the Reich Defense Commissioners.

Regierungspräsident, Landräte, and Chief Mayors

Chief of the Party Chancellery with duplicates for the Gauleiters

Armament Commissioners

Chairmen of the Armament Commissions with duplicates for the Armament Inspectorate Armament Detachments WKB, LWAE, Rue-Obm., Organization Todt Einsatzgruppenleiter

Chiefs of the Main Commissions, Main "Rings," and Production Main Commissions

Reich Minister of Communications with duplicates for the General Plant

Directorates and the Reich Railroads Directorates

Reich Food Minister with duplicates for the state farm leaders.

Inter Office Distribution A2

SECRET

Subject: Executive regulations for the Führer Decree, dated 19 March 1945, concerning measures for crippling and destroying the Reich territories.

I decree:

My present decrees and directives concerning the crippling of industrial installations of all kinds and public utilities (electric power, gas, water, food, economic enterprises of all kinds, transport) shall not continue to apply as before. All preparations for crippling that have been ordered are to be halted immediately.

[signed] SPEER
Official [signed] REINHARD Oberst [Seal]
Distribution:
Highest Reich authorities and Armed Forces Offices according to special distribution list.

Reinhard pulled the order from the typewriter and inspected it, before pulling an ink pad and a seal from his desk and stamping the document. He filled in both his own signature and Speer's.

"It's not hard," he said. "I've been copying it for years." Reinhard pulled out another sheet of paper. Johann could see that it was for the attention of the teletypist and contained the call signs that allowed the information to flow through the Nazi information system.

"You have done a great thing," Johann said as Reinhard sat back and examined his work.

Reinhard just nodded. "I have placed myself in your hands," he said. "Before we send this I need the letter."

Johann nodded. He couldn't leave the building without proof that the message had been sent. He needed to exert more pressure on Reinhard, or offer some proof that his bogus military leaders who were supposed to be negotiating with the Allies were in fact real. As Johann was weighing his next move, Reinhard stood up and marched toward the door. Johann could see that he had left the paperwork on his desk, meaning that the colonel wasn't taking it to the telex room.

"I think I need a brandy to steady my nerves," the *Oberst* said. "I have some in the officers' common room. Please will you join me?"

"Of course," Johann said, watching as Reinhard closed the door behind him. In the empty room Johann reached out and touched the papers that Reinhard had signed. He could hardly believe that he had managed to get this far.

Reinhard, on the other hand, couldn't believe that Johann had allowed him to leave the room after trying to inveigle him into a treacherous plot. He felt born anew as he hurried down the corridor. He would return with guards as soon as he managed to raise the alarm.

16

Anja was under no illusions about the situation she and Nadine were in. After her brush with the police, she determined that she could no longer take the risk of leaving the house. The authorities were hunting her, which she thought could mean only one thing—that Johann was on the run. The Gestapo routinely disappeared families as punishment for desertion or other such offenses. She prayed that he would make it to Berlin within the two days he had promised in the letter he had sent with Otto.

She had played out the scene of Johann's arrival dozens of times in her mind, had hoped that every small sound in the house was his footstep on the stairs. She didn't care how exhausted or broken he was; she would look after him. They would escape west beyond the ravaged city.

Nadine lay on a sofa reading. Anja was pleased to see her getting some rest. Anja turned on the radio, but there was no sound. She waited for a few moments, thinking that maybe the machine needed time to warm up—but it remained stubbornly silent.

"It's just us, then," Nadine said, noting what had happened. There was no electricity.

"I suppose so," Anja replied. "Do you want some tea?" Otto had a wood-burning stove in the kitchen and a small supply of wood left from months ago when he had last occupied the apartment. Anja supposed he wouldn't mind them heating a pot of water.

"Yes, please, Tante," Nadine said, stretching. "What time is Otto coming back?"

"I'm not sure," Anja replied. "I imagine that he'll be late again."

"I hope that there are no air raids tonight," Nadine said.

Anja made the tea using as little of the kindling as she could. The water was only lukewarm, but it was good enough. There was marmalade in one of the kitchen cupboards. She put a film on some hard black bread and brought it out to Nadine. As she passed her niece the plate, for a moment she felt like a human being again.

"I miss Flöhchen," Nadine said, breaking the spell. "I miss him so much."

Anja cupped the girl's cheek in her hand.

"And I miss our apartment," Nadine said, her eyes welling with tears.

It was too much for her, Anja thought. Way too much.

"I know it's hard," she said to the girl. "But we are still here, and we have to remain hopeful. We have to keep going."

"I know, Tante, I know," the girl said, wiping a tear with the back of a grubby hand. Anja watched the girl tamping down her emotion.

"I wish we could light the fire," Anja said. She curled up on the sofa next to Nadine and sipped her tea. Nadine polished off the bread.

"We need to rest tonight, if we can," Anja said. "Tomorrow we leave."

Nadine nodded. "I wish that Uncle Johann would come."

"We have done everything we can."

"I know that," Nadine said, "but I still don't like it. How will he find us in the west?"

It was something that Anja had thought about. Surviving the hell of Berlin and escaping to the country was one thing, but how would they live beyond that? And what of Johann? They would have no idea how to contact him. She supposed that they might try to do so through Otto, but what were the chances of him or his home surviving the next few weeks? She told herself that it was pointless to think like that. All they could do—all anyone could do, whether they were a gunner on the Oder or a grandmother Lübeck—was to hang on. To find the next meal and to survive whatever the night might bring. That was all any of them could hope for.

That afternoon Anja ignored an urge to go and try to find some groceries to make Otto dinner—a way of saying thank you for putting them up. She perused Otto's books and found some poems by Theocritus that she hadn't read since she was in college. Lying on the large bed, she fell asleep, hopelessly lost in the warmth and comfort of the eiderdown.

Nadine had become bored with her book and had gone to the back of the house, where she was able to pull at a piece of cardboard covering one of the windows and peek outside. There was birdsong and she could see that the sun was shining for what felt like the first time in months. There was an ancient key in the thick back door upon which generations of residents had layered paint. She turned it and felt the heavy lock shifting. The door creaked open, flooding the dark interior of the kitchen with light. Nadine squeezed through the crack.

She walked out into a courtyard, where there was a stone table. Six chairs that had once been arranged around it were scattered about the yard. On two sides there were stone walls about six feet high upon which ivy grew. Among the leaves there were strips of metal foil, dumped from the bombers to confuse the German civil defense radar. Nadine hadn't seen greenery for such a long time. She approached one of the walls and inspected the ivy. The leaves were covered in a layer of soot and gritty debris. She reached out and drew a line on the waxy surface of a leaf. She examined her fingertip, which was covered in grime. Beneath her feet she noticed chunks of razor-sharp shrapnel in the gravel.

"Hello," came a soft voice. Nadine whirled around, shocked at having been disturbed from her contemplation. She saw a young boy standing in the garden next door. He was thin and pale with floppy blond hair and a wide, toothy smile.

"I'm sorry, I didn't mean to scare you," he said. "It's just that I've been here all the time and I thought it best to let you know that I was here."

Nadine nodded.

"Do you live here now?" the boy asked. Nadine immediately panicked. She should not be telling anyone who she was or what she was doing here. This boy could be Hitler Youth, only too keen to claim another scalp for the Führer.

"I'd better be going," she said, hurrying toward the back door. The boy sensed her fear.

"We've only just arrived," he said. "We were bombed out a few months ago. We stayed with my aunt in Wedding until she lost her place too. Then the authorities sent us here to lodge with an old lady who lives in this apartment. She was killed one day; she just happened to be passing a damaged building when the chimney collapsed. Apparently they never found her head, but they knew it was her from the contents of her handbag. My mother had to go and confirm that it was her."

Nadine had halted. Hearing the boy tell the story had made her think that he couldn't be the kind of boy she feared he might be. He seemed too naïve, too unassuming.

"We lost our place too," she explained. "We lived in the north of Mitte, near the hospital."

"I didn't think anyone lived in Mitte any longer," the boy said. He picked up a piece of tinfoil from the ground and began to fold it. "I'm Hans," he said. Nadine decided it was best not to reveal her name just yet.

"There were some of us still there," Nadine said. "The authorities moved us here." Telling him that they had official sanction made her feel safe. As if she had right on her side.

"Do you have a father?" Hans asked. Nadine looked at him. He seemed so small and weak—what was he, maybe twelve?—but he asked lots of very direct questions.

"My parents were both killed," she replied.

"A raid?" the boy asked.

Nadine nodded. She wasn't about to tell a stranger they had died in a camp.

"I still have my mother," Hans said. "I'm lucky. My father died at Kursk. He was a tank commander. A hero."

Nadine remembered hearing the news about Kursk. She recalled Anja had talked with a friend long into the night about the mounting losses: North Africa, Kursk, Smolensk, Normandy . . . Nadine had lain in bed and listened as Anja and her friends drank homemade potato vodka into the night and ran through various scenarios that amounted to the same thing: The war needed to end to get rid of the Nazis. There was nothing else for it.

"What school do you go to?" Nadine asked.

"I don't go to school," the boy said. He put his elbow on the wall and pressed his hand to his chin and gazed into the distance. Nadine drew closer and could see that he was older than she'd thought he was. His extremities—his hands, ears, nose—were disproportionately large. She wondered if he might have an ailment—it wasn't unusual for Berliners to have dietary deficiencies now. Nadine looked at him shyly, not wanting Hans to think that he was being examined. There was something not quite right, as if he hadn't developed properly.

"My mother teaches me at home." He cast his eyes down as if not sure of himself. "We have an agreement with the authorities."

Nadine realized at that moment that both of them were telling lies.

"I see," she said. "That must be nice." She didn't really feel that way.

"It is," Hans said, but he didn't sound like he believed it.

"I don't go to school anymore anyway," Nadine said. "All my books were at home when we lost our apartment. And my aunt says that it's too dangerous—she doesn't want me out of her sight until . . . well, you know."

The boy nodded. "That's what my mom's like," he said. "Always worrying." He lapsed into an impression of his mother: *"Hans, be careful with your spoon when you eat your soup—you might slice your head off! Hans, don't swallow that soap when you wash your hands!"*

Nadine laughed at the boy's impression and he smiled broadly.

"I wonder if it will still be like that when you are grown up?" she asked. "Your mother will be coming over to your house to make sure that you don't cut your hand off when you're slicing bread."

"I wouldn't be surprised," Hans said. "I daresay she'll try and prevent me from even making a sandwich. *That cucumber could explode!*"

"Why didn't you leave Berlin?" Nadine asked.

"We did," the boy said. "After the first incendiaries were dropped in 1943, we went and lived out in the country for a few months. We moved around a little between guesthouses and lodging in people's houses, but we missed the city. This is where we're from. And people started saying that the bombing wasn't so bad any longer, so we thought that it was safe to return."

"A lot of people came back," Nadine said.

"A lot of dead people," Hans said, throwing a pebble toward a wall.

"I'm Nadine," the girl said, extending her hand. He took it. His grip was frail.

Just as their hands parted they heard a voice inside the boy's house.

"Hans!" There was a pause and it repeated itself. "Hans! Where are you?"

"Uh-oh," the boy said, looking at the house sheepishly.

"Hans!"

He returned his gaze to Nadine.

"I'm not supposed to be outside," he explained.

"The bombs?" Nadine asked.

"No," Hans said. "*Volkssturm*. All the boys my age are being forced into it. My mother swears that she would rather die than let me be rounded up."

The back door opened and a middle-aged woman in an apron stood with her hands on her hips in the entryway.

"What did I tell you about going outside?" she asked.

"I was just talking to—"

"Come on," she said.

"Mom . . . I'm tired of sitting in the basement," Hans said, trailing back toward the door.

Nadine looked at the woman, thinking that she should introduce herself, but Hans's mother didn't even glance at the girl. She wanted only to get her son inside. Nothing else mattered to her.

As he was led away Hans turned and waved meekly at Nadine.

She smiled at him and waved back before continuing to examine the plants in the garden to see what had survived the onslaught from above.

"Tante," Nadine said, standing over Anja. "Tante Anja . . ."

Anja began to surface from a vivid dream that she forgot the moment she regained consciousness.

"I made you a cup of tea," Nadine said, placing the cup and saucer on a nightstand next to the bed.

"What time is it?" Anja asked. The blackout made it impossible to tell.

"It's past five o'clock," Nadine said.

"Goodness," Anja said, sitting up with the mild dread of someone who fears that they might have slept through the day. "I wanted to have something ready for Otto when he came home. You know, to say thank you."

"It's good that you slept," Nadine said.

"Well, don't speak too soon," Anja said. "The RAF are likely to be overhead in the next couple of hours."

"I met one of the neighbors," Nadine said.

"Who? When?" Anja was immediately concerned. The idea of Nadine talking to strangers filled her with fear.

Nadine read her aunt's concern. "Don't worry," she explained. "It was just a boy who lives next door. I met him this afternoon."

Anja sat up. "This afternoon? Where were you?"

Nadine realized that she had crossed a line.

"Just outside," she said sheepishly. "In the backyard."

"Oh, *Nadine* . . . ," Anja said.

"But I saw the sun shining outside," Nadine protested, "and it just seemed so strange to be sitting inside in the darkness. I wanted to be outside in the world."

Anja reached out and stroked the girl's face. How odd that she should be thinking this way when all her niece had done was wander into a garden.

"Who is this boy then?" she asked.

"His name is Hans," Nadine said. "He's funny; he made me laugh."

"Well, that's a good thing," Anja replied.

"He looks awfully thin," Nadine said. "I worry that maybe he hasn't got enough food."

"Who's looking after him?"

"His mother," Nadine said. "She made him go back inside."

Anja felt an odd sense of relief. She wasn't the only one. She moved her legs over the side of the bed, then stood up and hugged her niece. Nadine held her tightly.

"Tante . . . ?"

"Yes, my dear, what do you want?" Nadine had used the tone of voice that she reserved almost exclusively for making requests.

"Well, I was thinking . . . ," she said. "Might we have just a little food for him?"

Anja rested her chin on the girl's shoulder. She and her niece had been the same height for two years now.

"You think that he doesn't have any?"

"I don't really know," Nadine said. "But he looked so very thin. He's pale too, but that's because they're living in the basement now."

"A city of basement dwellers, that's what we are now," sighed Anja. Many people had taken up permanent residence in whatever underground spaces they could find. It was easier to move beds down into the basement than traipse between living quarters and the only place it was safe to be when the Lancasters appeared overhead. Anja put her arms on Nadine's shoulders.

"Thank you for my tea," she said, and kissed the girl on her forehead.

"You should drink it while it's warm," Nadine said, laughing. She hadn't wanted to use much of the wood, so she had only had enough to bring the water up to a certain degree of heat. Anja picked up the cup and saucer and took a sip.

"Delicious," she said.

"Tante," Nadine continued. "Might we have just a little something?"

"My goodness." Anja smiled. "You really are persistent, aren't you?"

192

"It's just one of my qualities," Nadine said goofily. She was being silly in the way that teenagers sometimes did when confronted with the personal. Anja was proud that the girl felt so strongly about taking care of this stranger who she had only encountered that day.

"We will find something," Anja said, and began to stretch. She needed to see if she could produce something to eat. The air raids were likely to start around seven-thirty, and she didn't want to run the risk of being halfway through a meal and wasting food.

The two of them walked down to the kitchen, carrying Anja's candle with them. Anja pulled a piece of black cardboard carefully from a window so that she could replace it and blew the flame out.

"There," she said. "Some light for us to cook with."

"But is there any *food* for us to cook with?" Nadine asked. She was joking, but Anja was stung by the remark; the girl had known only shortages for years. Nadine's adolescence had been overshadowed by blight.

"How about this?" Anja asked Nadine, holding up a jar of marmalade. Otto seemed to have at least a dozen of them. A gift from a Spanish doctor friend, apparently.

"For what?" Nadine asked.

"Have you forgotten your friend next door already?"

"Oh, Hans," Nadine said, looking at the jar of marmalade. "Are you sure that's okay?"

"Otto told me to take one," Anja said. "He doesn't even like marmalade, apparently."

"He doesn't like marmalade?" Nadine said with a look of mock outrage. "He should be arrested for that."

"Here," Anja said, holding out the jar. "Take it to him."

"Me?"

"Yes, you."

"But I . . ."

Anja held it out insistently. Reluctantly Nadine took the dark orange object and moved toward the front door.

"Do I have to?" she asked, pausing.

"Why not?" Anja said, ushering her on her way. "It will be a nice gesture."

Anja walked to the door to encourage her niece and ushered her through the communal hallway and out the main door. She opened it and peered out to make sure that there wasn't any danger before steering Nadine into the daylight. The girl walked to the building next door and headed down the steps to the basement. Anja listened as Nadine knocked. After about thirty seconds she heard her rap on the door again, this time a little more loudly. There was silence for about another minute.

"Try one last time," Anja called out of the crack in the door.

Nadine rapped again. Almost immediately the door opened and Nadine was face-to-face with Hans's mother.

"Good day," Nadine said politely.

"Yes?" the woman replied. She looked quizzically at the girl as if she had never seen her before.

"I was just in the garden. . . ."

The woman stared at her impassively.

"With your son," Nadine continued, mildly flustered by the woman's frosty reception. "I thought that he might enjoy some—"

"I have no idea who you're talking about," the woman said, her eyebrows furrowing. "I lost my son in an air raid in forty-three."

Nadine held out the jar of marmalade. Surely this tangible object would make it clear that she meant no harm.

"But I brought something for him," Nadine persisted. "I brought something for Hans."

The woman looked beyond Nadine, casting her eyes around uneasily. She ignored Nadine's hand, which was held up toward her.

"I have no idea what you're talking about," she murmured. "There is no Hans here."

Nadine lowered her hand, but she kept staring at the woman, bewildered by what was happening.

"Don't you understand?" the woman continued, her eyes fevered. "There is no Hans here."

With that she closed the door. Nadine heard her shuffle away inside the basement. She looked down into the stairwell and then up at her mother, who was peeking from behind Otto's door. Nadine turned and looked up and down the street, taking in her surroundings. She was just about to step back into the house when she noticed movement: a piece of blackout being held wide enough for someone to look out of a bay window on the first floor. Nadine put her hand up to shield her eyes from the sun and saw a bald middle-aged man wearing a gray shirt staring back at her. She turned and went into the house, feeling his eyes on her back until she had closed the door behind her.

Anja knew that she and Nadine were unlikely to have a second untroubled evening in a row. The planes appeared, as they mostly did, around seven-thirty, by which time Anja had made a dish with potato and herring, which she and Nadine had wolfed down. There was enough for Otto to have when he returned from the hospital.

The raid was brief. It seemed like the bombings now were more about harassment than breaking the workings of the regime. Anja thought that a glance from an airplane would have revealed the truth of the matter, that Berlin was a broken city. What was the point of smashing it even further? There were three waves, lasting around twenty minutes. When the siren started Anja had thought it better to head to the nearest bunker than to hide in Otto's cellar, despite her wariness of being seen in public. She disguised them as best she could. She knew that she was taking a risk, but the shelters had served her and Nadine well enough, and they were far enough away from their apartment to feel that they were beyond the immediate reach of the authorities. To change things now seemed like an unnecessary complication. In the bunker was where they felt safest.

It was twilight when the two of them emerged from the shelter and were relieved to see that no bombs had fallen nearby. The planes appeared to have been heading to the east of the city. Anja wondered whether this was maybe a warning to the Soviets, a message that the Allies were able to strike wherever they wanted.

She and Anja arrived at Otto's street and were hurrying home when a middle-aged man started walking in step with them, his hands thrust into a raincoat.

"We got off easy tonight," he said breezily, weaving between a burned-out car and a pile of rubble.

Anja watched him carefully. He kept his eyes forward, not really looking at either her or Nadine.

"I suppose so," she replied. "Hopefully they won't be back."

"No, not tonight," he replied. "They won't be back tonight."

The three of them continued to walk along the road. The wind whipped up dust from a pile of masonry, causing them to put their hands over their mouths and turn their faces away.

"So I see that you've moved next door to my sister," the man said. Nadine suddenly recognized him as the man who had been watching from the house opposite. That explained why he had been watching, she thought.

"How is my nephew?" the man asked.

Alarm bells went off in Anja's mind, but before she could intervene Nadine had spoken.

"Oh, he's fine," she said. "I saw him today."

Anja stopped to do up her shoelace, hoping that the man would continue ahead. He stood and waited for them.

"I haven't seen him for quite some time," the man said. "I really must pay a visit, but you know how it is these days."

Just then there was the sound of footsteps.

"Erika, Joana . . ." It was Otto. He had chosen to address them with phony names. He didn't acknowledge the man. "We should be getting back home."

With that, Otto hurried Anja and Nadine along the street and into the apartment.

"What's wrong?" Anja asked him, her heart racing as they stood in the darkness still wearing their coats.

"Never speak to that man again," Otto said.

"Why not?"

"He's a *Blockwart*," Otto explained. "He's one of them."

17

Johann wasn't foolish enough to think that Reinhard had left the room to fetch a bottle of brandy. The second that he heard the *Oberst*'s footsteps receding outside the office he leapt up and rushed behind the colonel's desk. He grabbed a pen and added a note at the end of the executive order by hand. He rummaged through the top drawer of the desk, seeking that which would make the document legal—Reinhard's official seal. He rolled it in a pad of black ink and stamped it on the paperwork. Johann folded it crisply and put it inside his jacket pocket.

He picked up the briefcase, then went to the door and opened it slightly. The secretary, Ursula, was no longer there. Either she was doing something elsewhere in the building or Reinhard had warned her of the danger. He walked over and pulled down some blackout and threw a window open, causing a gust of air to blow in. Looking around he saw that there was a roof nearby that was reachable if he walked to the end of the ledge. His pursuers would hopefully believe that he had fled this way.

He left the office and hurried along the corridor. He tried to calm himself. He needed to hurry while remaining as inconspicuous as possible. He could see other functionaries through the frosted glass panels in office doors. Clearly Reinhard had not raised a general alarm; perhaps he thought that the resulting chaos would offer Johann the best chance of escape.

He needed to find the communications center quickly. He estimated that he had perhaps a minute to get off the second floor. A door next to him opened unexpectedly; he whirled around, reaching for the pistol on his hip.

"Forgive me, Fräulein," Johann said to a young woman wearing spectacles. She had appeared next to him almost without warning and, seeing his reaction, had dropped the files she was carrying. Johann bent down to help her.

"I'm awfully sorry," he said, handing the paperwork back to the woman. "I have only recently returned from the east. . . ."

"It's quite all right, *Sturmbannführer*," the secretary said, smoothing back her hair and swallowing. She was clearly scared. "I think everyone is currently on edge."

"Tell me," Johann said—it was as much as he could do not to glance along the corridor in search of pursuers. "I have an urgent cable I need to send. Could you direct me to the communications center, please?"

"It's been set up in the basement," the woman said.

"And is there a quicker way to get there other than the main staircase?" Johann asked with as charming a smile as he could muster.

"Us girls use the emergency staircase," the secretary said, pointing down the corridor.

Johann was already on his way by the time she had turned back to him.

"Thank you," he muttered over his shoulder.

He reached the door and pushed it open, finding himself in a dark stairwell lit only by lightbulbs that had been strung up haphazardly. He rushed down the steep stairs as quickly as he could, keeping hold of the handrail to prevent himself from slipping.

He passed down three flights of stairs and opened a door into a basement with a low ceiling. There was no lobby; rather, he found himself among rows of makeshift desks staffed by women who blinked at him in the low light. Smoke hung around him like cirrus clouds. The telex and telephone operators eyed him warily, unused to seeing a senior SS officer in the bowels of the building.

There was the chatter of machines and the voices of those passing messages on and connecting telephone lines.

"I need to send an urgent telegram," he said to the nearest girl. She was in her early twenties with brown hair tied back in a net. Johann could see that her clothes were threadbare—the elbows and cuffs had clearly been repaired time and again. She extended a bony hand toward him.

"Of course, *Sturmbannführer*," she said. She examined the document and did a double take before removing her glasses and looking up at Johann. One of the switchboard operators nearby realized something unusual was happening. She continued to connect calls through a large exchange in front of her, but was watching Johann. The telegram operator caught the eye of the girl on the switchboard. Johann needed to override their misgivings.

"*Well?*" he said impatiently. "Is there any reason for delay? This order comes from Oberst Reinhard himself and must be implemented with immediate effect."

The switchboard operator looked away.

"Yes, *Sturmbannführer*," the telex operator said. She put her glasses back on and began to tap a machine that looked like a typewriter that had been built into a rolltop desk. Johann watched the girl's fingers press down on the gray keys, each of which was stuck on the top of a lever. The message was recorded on a roll of paper that scrolled, with jittery movements, in a panel higher up the desk. Johann folded his arms, trying to appear in charge of the situation, a figure of authority having his will followed. In truth, his insides were tied in a thick knot. They would be looking for him now. He had to hope that they had been diverted by his having left the window open. The building was big enough for it to take more than thirty minutes to conduct a thorough search. If the girl sent the telegram quickly, there was a chance that he would be able to slip from the building, his mission complete.

He looked at the telex as it made its way through the machine.

"My present decrees and directives concerning the crippling of industrial installations of all kinds and public utilities (electric power, gas, water, food, economic enterprises of all kinds, transport) shall not continue to apply as before. All preparations for crippling which have been ordered are to be halted immediately."

And then there was his last, handwritten note that would make it harder for Reinhard to overturn what had been done.

"All subsequent orders on this matter are to be ignored. This decree must be prioritized over all others no matter the consequences. The penalty for enacting the Demolitions on Reich Territory will be severe."

At that moment the enormity of what he was witnessing hit Johann: He had undermined the Führer himself.

To undo this telegram, Reinhard would have to find his way up a chain of command that was increasingly fractured and agitated. Johann thought that, at the very least, it would delay the Nero Decree being restored by two or three days, perhaps more. He felt a momentary flush of satisfaction and relief—he had saved lives as he had set out to do.

The girl's hands came to rest on her lap momentarily before she handed the paperwork back to Johann. He knew now that the order was traveling throughout the Reich communications system. It was like a virus. Nothing could stop it. The order would be received and passed among senior officers and down through the ranks. He had revoked the Nero Decree. Even if it was only for a short time, he had done all he could.

Now he must think about himself and his family.

"Thank you," he said to the girl, who nodded in his direction without making eye contact. She just wanted the SS man to leave.

Johann walked across the communications center; the eyes of the women workers stalked him. He opened the door to the main staircase and found himself in the stairwell. He started up the two flights of stairs to the central lobby with the briefcase in his left hand in the event that he needed to reach for his weapon with his right. He had traveled a couple of steps when he heard the clatter of boots above. They might not have anything to do with him, but he couldn't afford to find out. He hurried back through the door and looked around for other means of escape. He cast his eyes around desperately; the emergency exit would have to do. He rushed back to where he had first entered the room and opened the door.

He ran up the stairs and opened a door at one end of the main lobby. There were two guards—old men drafted in for the final stand—waiting, peering up the staircase. He was out of sight, but they would notice him as soon as he headed for the door. He could try to make a run for it but they would almost certainly see him, and the chances were that he would be shot before he reached the street. He decided that he would fight fire with fire: He unsheathed his pistol and walked toward the men. One of them noticed the movement and looked around to see Johann. He turned and leveled his weapon. His fellow guard saw what was happening and turned and did the same thing. Johann was staring down the barrels of two rifles.

This is it, Johann thought.

"He's on the roof at the back, you idiots," he barked at the men. "Quick! Follow me!"

The men paused and glanced at each other. Johann didn't wait for a response—he ran from the building with the two soldiers in pursuit. Since they had yet to shoot him he assumed that his uniform had done its work. They may well have been told that they were looking for an *SS-Sturmbannführer,* but the power of the uniform was such that even those with suspicions came to be powerless when they encountered it.

Once on Wilhelmstraße he turned to face the guards.

"The fastest way to the back of the building?" he asked urgently.

"It's the same distance whichever way we go," one of them answered.

Johann momentarily pretended to consider the best way to proceed.

"Okay," he said, raising his pistol so it was pointing at the sky. "He has to come round one way. We'll need to cut him off. I'll head south and you head north. We'll meet at the back."

He started to move down the road. The two men headed in the other direction. Once the guards were out of sight, he wandered into the street and stepped onto the running board of the first vehicle that came down the street—a truck transporting sand. He crouched low with the vehicle shielding him, and watched as the two guards ran up the street in the direction they had last seen him walking, closely followed by three other soldiers and an apoplectic-looking Reinhard.

18

The records offices in the central government districts had been moved outside the city, mainly to small towns that were unlikely to face sustained aerial bombardment. As his driver ferried them across Berlin, making detours as the streets dictated—a stalled streetcar, a collapsed building, pipes and cables sprouting from the ground as if the very guts of the city had been ruptured—Dieter considered Johann's actions. There would be danger if it was discovered that it was his half brother who was responsible for stealing the microfilm. Dieter settled back in the car and moved his head slightly—the collar of his greatcoat was rubbing on the wounds on his neck. The bandages were making his body unbearably itchy.

Everything indicated that Johann was heading to Berlin with the microfilm. He could even be in the city. Dieter had to find out where. The bombings meant that hundreds of thousands of people were displaced. While the welfare organization attempted to keep track of where they ended up, it was an almost impossible task, especially in the past two years when the attacks had become more frequent and formidable.

Such was the chaos in the city that many fugitives were turning up at overworked offices of the NSV, claiming that their papers had been lost in a raid when their home was flattened. The offices generally issued new documents and ration cards without too many questions being asked and arranged temporary accommodation. Dieter passed a jerry-rigged soup kitchen that had been set up in the shell of an old cinema. Bizarrely, it was possible to see the rows of seats—many of them occupied by exhausted people—while the entire façade of the building had been demolished.

The car passed through the Tiergarten and the Zoo. The trees were gnarled lumps of charcoal. Those that hadn't been destroyed by the bombing had been cut down during the winter for fuel. Dieter ran through what they knew. Johann had last been seen leaving the farmhouse with the briefcase. The testimony from the SS soldiers Johann had duped at the farmhouse seemed to suggest that he was motivated by more than simply fleeing from the killings at the hospital. Dieter tried to coax some connections between what he knew and what he feared—Johann would hold on to the microfilm until he could hand the information over to the Allies or the Soviets. Dieter reasoned that, to hunt Johann down, he needed to know more about what had happened to him in the eleven years since they last had seen each other. The state, scrupulous in its gathering of information, would surely offer clues.

Many of the birth and marriage certificates for central Berlin were being stored in the basement of a bombed-out waterworks. His car pulled up at a ruined hulk of a building. It reminded him of a wooden ship that had been washed up on the shore and had slowly deteriorated so that only the timber frames remained.

There was a small white sign next to a metal staircase that ran down to a basement. Someone had carefully painted the words "Records Office" and an arrow pointing down the stairs.

"Wait here," Dieter said to his driver, who had come around to open the door. The man had offered his hand to help Dieter from the car, but he had refused it. His boots crunched over glass and debris before ringing on the metal stairs as he walked to the basement. The smell of a cigarette wafted up from below. He entered through a red brick archway and entered a vast open space that contained dozens of rows of metal shelves. On each shelf were large boxes.

Dieter heard the shuffling of footsteps, and an old man with spectacles perched on top of a balding head approached him. He wore a battered black suit, his tie was askew, and the collar of his shirt was filthy. He licked the palm of his hand and flattened the wisps of hair that remained on his head when he saw Dieter.

"Good day . . . ," he said. He peered at Dieter's uniform, attempting to decipher the wearer's rank. "*Sturmbannführer,*" he said.

The man straightened his tie a little and leaned forward as if he was hard of hearing.

"We have no SS records here," he said. "I'm not sure where the Ministry has secured those. . . ."

"I want civilian records," Dieter said. "Specifically births in Charlottenburg in the first two decades of the century."

Dieter would start at the beginning—his own and his half brother's.

"Ah, well," the man said. He seemed pleased to be able to deliver good news. "You're in the right place." He shuffled over to a large box that was resting on a table near where Dieter had entered.

"Normally," he said, "I would ask you to fill in a form and then I would ensure that your documents are ready for examination within forty-eight hours of the request. However, as you can see, things are fairly quiet today, so I'll be happy to facilitate any request you might have."

Dieter was momentarily stunned by the notion that the clerk wouldn't do what he asked immediately.

"And I need to see the wedding registry for the past decade," he said, removing his leather gloves and putting them in his pocket.

"There will be several volumes," the man told him.

"Don't you have them cross-referenced?" Dieter asked irritably.

"In some instances, yes," the man replied, scratching the side of his face anxiously. "It depends on the church and the district."

"Bring me everything," Dieter said.

"Of course," the man said. He pulled a flint from his waistcoat pocket, lit a lantern, and scurried off. Elsewhere in the archive, skylights above the shelves had somehow, miraculously, remained intact. Large swathes of light broke through occasionally when the clouds moved away from the sun.

The man returned within minutes with three large volumes. Each was two feet wide and a foot long.

Dieter snatched at the register of weddings. Before his own and his half brother's birthdays, he would discover more about his marriage.

"It will be in here somewhere," the man said, as if reading his mind. Dieter opened the book and examined it. The weddings were in chronological order starting in 1919. As he turned the pages looking for 1934, the year he had last seen Johann, it crossed Dieter's mind that many of the people in these pages were dead. There were comparatively few weddings immediately after the Great War, but they picked up toward the end of the 1920s. These husbands and fathers were now lying in the frozen wastes of Silesia, the deserts of Libya, the mountains of Italy.

"You're lucky you came when you did," the librarian said. "We received word that everything is being transported to Bavaria for safekeeping. The trucks were supposed to come two days ago, but there has been a delay."

Dieter didn't even hear him. As drained as he was, he remained focused on the task at hand: discovering what had happened to his half brother. How had Johann reinvented himself? What kind of man had he become? How had he managed to evade Dieter for so long? And he tried to calm his fantasies about the great trophy he knew now Johann had stolen from him: the security box. The thought of the key around his half brother's neck—he had seen it at the hospital—was never far from his mind, but a further concern preyed upon him: Who knew if whatever it was that Nicolas had secured was still even there?

As he thumbed rapidly through the pages of the records, probing the black ink for any familiar name, Dieter couldn't help fantasizing about the box's contents. Surely it would offer him a shield from the inevitable grinding Soviet retribution to come. His belief in the Party and the Führer was absolute, but he knew that he must start to plan for his own survival. He understood that the war was over. He must prepare for what was to come afterward. There were plenty of fanatics, the true believers who would rather die under the wheels of a T-34 or in a bunker that would double as a mass grave. Dieter would fight, but he planned on living a long and prosperous life. Dieter had always been a survivor.

What kind of a life could a disfigured former *SS-Sturmbann-führer* look forward to? His record would mean that he ended up in a gulag, or a POW camp at best. Whatever was in the box was his opportunity to escape an unknown but unquestionably grim future. Finding Johann would give him a life beyond the horror of imprisonment.

The librarian stood awkwardly waiting on Dieter to give him direction.

"Is there anything else I can get you?" he asked.

"No," Dieter replied, thumbing through the books, his eyes scanning the pages.

"Perhaps I could help with your search?" the librarian offered.

Dieter looked up from the ledger.

"Perhaps you can," he said eventually. "I am looking for a man called Schultz. Doctor Johann Schultz. I believe that he was married after 1934."

"Ah, well, there is only one book then," the man said. "And you have it. Plenty of weddings back then. I suppose people were feeling, you know, optimistic."

Dieter knew that it was his duty, as an SS officer, to question why the man wasn't feeling optimistic now. Defeatism was, after all, a crime. But, looking around the ruined, gloomy basement, he realized the question was not a plausible one. Even this place was soon to be evacuated. He continued to run his index finger down the page, looking for the telltale curve of an *S*, the letter itself shaped like a snake, the creature that best described his half brother.

And then there it was. "Schultz, Johann. Married to Welge, Anja, on June 20, 1938." They were married in Mannheim, but registered the union in Berlin. His half brother doing what all liars do—compounding the lies. Did his bride—as she stood there at the altar wearing a dress she had dreamed of stepping into her entire life—did she know that the man standing next to her was not who he said he was? Dieter was suddenly thrilled at the prospect of interrogating her. These kinds of devastating revelations didn't come along too often. Pull someone from a cell and shock them with news like that and chances were you wouldn't be able to shut them up.

Dieter pulled out a notebook and recorded the details. With this he would be able to discover where she lived.

"Found what you're looking for?" the man asked.

Dieter closed the ledger with a thump.

"I need the register of births from 1915 onward," he said to the librarian, straightening his back. The librarian nodded, then picked up the large volume and shuffled back toward the shelves. Dieter was left in semidarkness. If he moved quickly, he thought, he would be able to compare the housing records with those of the state at the *Standesamt*. He would have Johann's wife in custody within twenty-four hours.

The old man shuffled back with a box. He held the lantern before him. It cast the shadow of a giant across the basement.

"Here," he said, placing the book on the table. "Births from 1915 onward. Anything else?"

Dieter turned and looked at the man. He could tell that the archivist wanted to help: The war had taken his role from him, and any opportunity he had to demonstrate his knowledge and to rummage around the records was something that he was eager to grasp.

"No," Dieter said. "I would like to examine these documents in private."

"Of course," the man said. "If you need anything else I will be outside." He made to walk off before turning. "I need some air every now and again."

Dieter didn't acknowledge the man. He had already opened the box. Inside there were several hundred four-by-six-inch cards. On each was a name of a child, the date and place of his or her birth, and the names of the parents. Each was typed. The way the letters fell on the cards—the placing, spacing, and organization—was slightly different on each card, as if typewriters had the same idiosyncrasies as handwriting. The box he had was organized alphabetically, and Dieter quickly flipped through. . . .

There was no card for Johann Schultz. Satisfied that he was right that his half brother Thomas's name was indeed a fiction, he pulled a box containing the letter *M* toward him. He flipped through the cards.

Found it.

There he was: Thomas Meier, born July 21, 1918. Charlottenburg, Berlin. But wait . . .

He read it again and it still didn't make sense.

There, on the card, the word "Orphan."

Dieter put the card down and massaged his temples. He was exhausted. He was injured. There was too much going on to make sense of. Clearly he was losing his mind. After a few moments, he pulled the card up to his eyes and took another look at it. There it was again, the word "Orphan."

He rifled through the box; surely there must be another Thomas Meier. The name was not that uncommon. It was not impossible that there was someone with the same name as his half brother who had been born on the same day. His fingers prized at the cards to make sure that two of them had not somehow become joined together. He rummaged through to the end of the box and then went through it again. So many names beginning with *M*, surely he might have overlooked one. Or maybe a distracted archivist had placed one back in the wrong order. . . .

But no.

There was a single card with his half brother's name written on it.

What did this mean? He immediately went to the box where he would find his own card. He leafed through, spurred on by the discovery. There it was: Dieter Schnell. Name, birth date, birthplace, and . . .

Dieter flinched. The same word: "Orphan." He put the card down and paced along the rows of files, his head spinning.

This was not possible. Had he lost his mind since he was injured? Were the memories he had of his childhood and that of his half brother fictions created by the trauma of battle? This made no sense.

He returned to the table, his boots crunching on the crumbling concrete floor. He looked at both cards. There was no question. The word "Orphan" appeared on both in the place allotted for the names of their parents, their mother and their different fathers obliterated from history. It made absolutely no sense to him. It was feasible that yes, a mistake could be made on one card, but for both of them to have been the subject of a clerical error was surely not possible.

He felt a twinge of excitement; this had been done on purpose. There was a secret to discover.

He examined them again and noticed something he hadn't seen before. Placing the cards next to each other, he could see that they were of exactly the same stock. He fanned some of the others out and examined them. Each had slight differences in color, texture, size, the way the rulings lay upon them, but his and his half brother's cards were exactly the same. And there was another similarity: Whereas the makeup of each of the other cards was slightly different—the keys of the typewriter falling in slightly different ways, the point at which the names or the other particulars were typed varied slightly—these two cards were identical. He laid one on top of the other and compared them—the words fell in exactly the same places in exactly the same way. The cards were the exactly the same size, texture, and color.

They seemed to have been written at the same time by the same typewriter.

His head spun.

Was it really the case that two people born a few years apart would find themselves having their details typed by the same bureaucrat in the same way using the same types of cards? In addition, he had been born in a different district from Johann, so how likely was it that two administrators in different offices at different times would type official documents in exactly the same way? Not impossible, but very, very unlikely.

Dieter took a deep breath. His chest and neck ached. Clearly, he thought, these two documents had been produced by the same person and, it seemed highly probable, were produced at the same time.

Who?

He walked toward the exit, passing by the archivist. The man was standing at the door as if he were about to go out to promenade through Potsdamer Platz on a Saturday afternoon. He nodded at Dieter, but the SS man was lost in thought and hurried up the stairs to his waiting car without even the briefest acknowledgment.

The two cards were in his pocket—both he and his half brother were now excised from the public record. Neither of them officially existed.

The NSV office where the housing records were kept was chaos. The place was besieged by bombed-out people clamoring for somewhere to stay and food tokens. Dieter commandeered the attention of a large woman in a tweed jacket who appeared to be in charge and insisted that she prioritize his request. She gave him a look of disdain. Dieter could tell that she was one of those rare creatures who was completely unintimidated by his uniform.

"What is it?" she asked eventually in a way that suggested she would take care of it just to see the back of him.

"I need an address for Frau Anja Welge," he said. "Urgently."

"It's all urgent," the woman said to him before disappearing to the back of the premises. Dieter watched crowds of desperate people being helped by a group of seemingly unflappable, prudent women. A young boy sitting on a bench pointed at him and asked a question. Perhaps he was fascinated by Dieter's injuries. His mother shifted him around so that he was no longer facing Dieter. The woman in tweed reappeared five minutes later with a scrap of paper.

"There is no record of her being bombed out," she told him. "The most up-to-date address we have is this . . . ," she said, handing it to Dieter. "It's the official address of her niece too." Dieter took the paper and examined it. "There's no guarantee that the place is still standing, though," said the woman, before engaging with an old couple who had been patiently standing at the counter with two cardboard suitcases. The old man had fragments of masonry in his thin, brittle-looking hair.

"How far along Invalidenstraße is this?" Dieter asked, but the woman either couldn't hear his words or chose to ignore them.

As he picked his way toward the apartment block where his half brother's wife had once lived, Dieter could tell that there was little point in searching. There were families camped out in the rubble, people salvaging belongings, and workmen trying to repair broken mains. All was chaos and destruction.

"This was number 52?" he asked an old man with a cart who appeared to be salvaging scrap metal.

"The next building," he said. "They're all gone, though."

Dieter stumbled forward, sending pieces of glass from a picture frame flying as his boot caught it accidentally.

"Be careful," the old man said. "These places are a devil for tetanus."

Dieter persevered. He could make out the shape of the next building. Some of it remained, but it was uninhabitable. Floors sloped to the ground at precipitous angles, the remains of ordinary lives visible within—crushed furniture, pictures on walls, curtains flapping in the wind. Part of one floor remained stubbornly horizontal despite its supporting wall having been destroyed. It appeared to have been cantilevered. A sole armchair remained in place. Was this where Johann sat? Which apartment was it that his half brother and his family had called home? The address on the card suggested that it was the second floor. Dieter wished he could sift through the wreckage to look for clues.

Around him, pieces of paper fluttered in the wind. Each contained a message to loved ones. "Helena and Gretl are living with Cousin Helmut." "Petr, we are safe. We have gone to Brieselang and are with Maria." "For the attention of the Hauser family: Lottie and Inge are looking for you. Are you with Harold?" Fragments of information about splintered lives. Dieter scrutinized every message before moving on to the versions that had been chalked up on the remaining masonry.

He walked across the building, sometimes having to stand on piles of rubble in order to read the messages. There was nothing that he could decipher. He moved back to survey the entire building, standing on a shattered wooden beam. There was a clue here that would lead him to them—he just needed to open his eyes and recognize it. He tried to look afresh, to consider whether there was anything he'd missed. He realized that there was one wall that was running perpendicular to the front of the house. It must have been an alleyway at some point. It was now mostly full of rubble, but there were a few feet into which people could walk. He stepped from the beam and slid himself into the former alleyway. There were half a dozen messages left in different hands. His eyes scanned for familiar names. . . .

He found one: Johann. Not the entire word, but enough.

He read the script hungrily. "J. We are all right. We are with your friend." The message was cryptic. Why hadn't she revealed which friend they were with? Surely it would have made sense for her to reveal more information. Dieter's mind raced. He told himself to calm down: this "J" might not even be Johann. The letter *J* wasn't, after all, an uncommon first letter of a name. But the enigmatic nature of the message made him think that he was onto something. Whoever had written it was holding something back.

All the other notes had been clear about whom the message was for, whom it had been left by, and where they had gone. Whoever had left the communiqué for "J" hadn't left his or her name, had been purposefully obscure about where they had gone, and hadn't left any form of signature.

Dieter pulled a pencil from within his jacket and copied the message into his notebook, then folded it away and began to walk back through the rubble to his staff car. If the message was for Johann, then the author assumed—or knew—that Johann would inevitably come to this place. He was expected in Berlin.

For the first time he felt like he was getting closer—as if finding his half brother wasn't just a possibility but an inevitability. He now had to fathom who this friend of Johann's might be who was harboring his wife. His driver held open the door for him and he got into the car. As they headed back to Prinz-Albrecht-Straße he watched the streets pass by and remembered how many of them contained memories for both him and Johann. Their identities were woven into the fabric of Berlin.

Dieter was sure that Johann would return—he couldn't not. And when he did, Dieter would be waiting for him.

"Anything?" Kuefer asked as Dieter took off his overcoat and placed it on the ancient wooden coatrack behind the door of the office.

"He's coming back," Dieter announced. "I want a twenty-four-hour watch from Gestapo officers on his apartment block. I located the address, here."

Kuefer took the piece of notepaper he was offered and picked up the phone and checked to see if he could get a line. He watched as Dieter sat down at his desk and settled into his chair.

"He's coming," Dieter said impassively. "I know he is."

"Let me call operations," Kuefer said.

Kuefer's finger became hot from turning the dial—he must have tried at least two dozen times—before he managed to get a line through to the Gestapo duty officer for the appropriate section. Kuefer suspected that he'd been asleep from the hazy way he answered the phone. His voice came into sharp focus once he realized he was speaking to the office of Sturmbannführer Schnell. The Gestapo feared little, but since its secret police had come under the control of Himmler, the SS had treated it as a subsidiary.

"Don't be fooled," Kuefer stressed to the person on the other end of the line. "Schultz is likely to be wearing the uniform of an SS officer. He is impersonating Sturmbannführer Schnell."

Kuefer replaced the handset in the cradle.

"There will be someone watching the apartment within the hour," he said. Dieter said nothing. The right side of his face glowed from his desk lamp. In the dark room—the shadows were forgiving—it didn't look like he had been disfigured.

"Looks like an hour," Kuefer repeated.

"I heard you the first time," Dieter said.

"Do you want anything?" Kuefer asked, before descending into a coughing fit that lasted a minute. "There is some water left in the pot," he added after catching his breath.

Dieter shook his head. He continued to sit at the desk silently. Kuefer pulled some paperwork—another roundup of criminals—from his tray and signed an order for them to be shipped to Oranienburg. He checked through the names, the tip of his pencil tracing down the paper as he verified them against reports from the arresting officers. The process took about ten minutes. He looked up once he had finished. Dieter remained at his desk, motionless. It was eerie. There was the sound of footsteps and voices outside. Kuefer started racking his brain to think of an excuse to get out of the office. There must be some errand that he could run.

The phone rang, interrupting his strategizing.

"Yes," Kuefer said.

It was a female voice.

"I have Oberst Reinhard for Sturmbannführer Schnell," the operator said.

"Put him through," Kuefer answered, waving to Dieter. He put his hand over the mouthpiece. "I have an Oberst Reinhard for you?" he said.

Dieter snatched the receiver.

"Sturmbannführer Schnell," he announced.

"Good afternoon," the *Oberst* replied. "I understand that you are heading up an investigation into a Doctor Johann Schultz."

"Indeed," Dieter replied. "We have reason to believe that he is responsible for the theft of important documents and is headed back to Berlin."

"Your information is incorrect," the *Oberst* replied. Dieter felt his hand tighten on the telephone. The man's tone was arrogant.

"And why is that?"

"Because Schultz is already in Berlin," Reinhard answered.

"Oh, really?" Dieter replied skeptically. "And what's the source of your information?"

"There is no source," the *Oberst* continued.

"With due respect, sir, I can hardly be expected to run an investigation on rumor—"

"You're misunderstanding me," Reinhard said, cutting him off. "He was in my office in Mitte only yesterday morning."

"Yesterday morning?" Dieter asked. "You're sure?"

"He was wearing your uniform," Reinhard said dismissively.

Dieter clenched his teeth. He remembered trying to comfort an injured comrade while they were sheltering in a ditch. As he had arrived to help the man, he had slipped on something. He looked down to see it was the man's entrails. Being spoken to in this way by a bureaucrat who had never left his office made his blood boil.

"There is more," Reinhard said self-importantly. "It seems that not only has Schultz committed capital crimes, but he has also committed treason."

The colonel paused for effect, enjoying the moment—he could tell that Dieter ached to know more.

"He attempted to send out a message through the Army High Command communications channel that sought to overturn the Demolitions on Reich Territory decree."

Dieter closed his eyes. The theft of the briefcase already meant that his time in Poland was a disaster; it was hard to believe it could get worse.

"The express wishes of the Führer," Dieter said, incredulous. He could barely force himself to ask his next question: "Was he successful?"

"Thankfully not," Reinhard said, the relief palpable in his voice. "A quick-witted operative in the communications center sensed that there was something amiss and inserted the incorrect call sign. Without that the system protocols don't come into effect."

Dieter felt a wave of contentment wash over him. Johann had failed. His attempt to derail the Nero Decree had been in vain.

"I will need to interview you in person," he told Reinhard.

"I understand," Reinhard replied dryly.

Dieter made an appointment for that afternoon and put the phone down.

He took a deep breath, reached into his pocket, and rubbed his thumb across the edge of the cards he had taken from the *Standesamt*.

He had been right: He knew his half brother would come. Ten years on from Nicolas's arrest, they would face each other in the city of their birth as it collapsed around them. Johann would try to prevent the implementation of the Nero Decree, but he was destined to fail. They would leave nothing for the Soviets.

One day soon it wouldn't be the cards that he was touching in his pocket—it would be the key.

"Kuefer," Dieter said. "Call operations again. Tell them that the fugitive Schultz is in possession of a briefcase and a key. They are of the utmost importance and must be recovered."

"Right, sir," Kuefer said, snatching up the handset.

"And one other thing," Dieter continued.

Kuefer looked up at his superior.

Dieter could not risk Johann revealing the identity of his half brother, if he was captured.

"The rules of engagement have changed," he said. "Tell them to shoot to kill."

19

Johann moved quickly through the shadows. After what had happened at the Ministry, they would be coming for him. He passed north through Mitte and over the river. The carcass of the Reichstag loomed to his left like an ancient monument. The Allies had no need to bomb it—the Nazis had burnt it down long before. Few buildings on the south side of the Spree were undamaged; many were still occupied. Those who survived the coming Soviet revenge would inherit a city so ruined that there was little hope of returning to the life they had before the madness had begun.

A couple of old men stood on the bridge in ragtag uniforms. Johann suspected that they were supposed to be checking identity cards—he had heard that one of the many anxieties suffered by Berliners was that guest workers and slave laborers from the east would act as fifth columnists. Many had already been confined to their quarters for fear that they would rise up and do the Soviets' work for them. But the old men ignored Johann, who nodded severely in their direction to maintain the deception of his uniform.

The area directly north of the Spree didn't appear to be as badly damaged. He had seen the ruin along Unter den Linden: the university, the museums, the cafés. He headed toward Charité Hospital; there were rows of apartment buildings where there appeared to be some normality—washing hung from balconies, a tailor's shop remained open, and people hurried along the street, going about their business.

He was not far from the home that he had briefly shared with Anja and Nadine. They had moved there a year before he had received his call-up papers in 1941. Back then, before the opening of the front in the east, it was hard to believe that they had been at war.

Before him, a damaged water main pumped water into the air like a fountain. An old man stood by the side of it and collected the falling liquid in a tin pail. Johann turned onto a street that was almost entirely rubble. Nevertheless, there were some families who were trying to make the best of things, living in jerry-rigged constructions made from tarpaulin—damaged doors propped at the side acted as walls. Someone had constructed a makeshift oven from bricks. A woman was cooking something on a skillet with a group of hungry-looking children gathered around. Johann was surprised by the number of children still living in the city. Parents had been told to send them away, but most were unwilling to be separated.

He turned onto what had once been his street. It was unrecognizable as the vigorous thoroughfare he remembered. The neighborhood had been largely lower middle class—low-ranking civil servants, teachers, and shopkeepers had formed its backbone. Now the men were either dead or at the front, and the women had joined them in the graveyards in Lichtenberg, Schöneberg, and Weißensee, or had fled, or were living the lives of scavengers enduring the daily toil of survival in the capital.

He almost didn't dare approach the building. Clouds of dust were being whipped up by the wind; a stray, emaciated dog clambered over wreckage; and a telephone cable hung loose, wildly slapping against the façade of a building that had somehow managed to stay upright.

"Herr Schultz!" came a voice. "Herr Schultz!"

Johann turned to see an old lady who used to work in the nearby laundry. He couldn't remember her name. She hobbled toward him. Johann cast a wary glance up and down the street. He didn't want anyone using his real name.

"Since when did you join the SS?" she said, her face a combination of confusion and concern.

"Oh, recently," Johann said. "I was briefly transferred to work at an SS hospital attached to the Third SS Panzer Corps. A braver group of men I have never known."

He looked up the street warily.

"And Anja?"

"You don't know?"

Johann felt his whole body go numb. He shook his head.

"The apartment . . . Only a few days ago . . . ," the old woman said.

Johann nodded, trying to hold his emotions in check. His mind immediately tumbled to dark conclusions. He pulled air inside him as his head spun. The woman from the laundry continued to talk, but he didn't hear a word. He just kept repeating to himself.

They weren't here.

They weren't here.

They weren't here.

He assured himself that Anja would have taken them both to the bunker or the U-Bahn station.

He momentarily felt more composed, but dread quickly rose again unless he maintained a firm grip upon his mind. What if they hadn't made it to the shelter? What if this had been one of the American daytime raids that offered little warning? What if the SS had already implemented the Nero Decree somewhere Anja and Nadine happened to be?

"You haven't heard anything?" the woman asked.

"The Feldpost isn't entirely reliable at the moment," Johann explained. "We get our letters in fits and bursts. And my unit has been moving a lot. . . ."

The old woman nodded.

"And you?" Johann asked.

"I came back to see if I could find some things," she said. "My Heinz's medals from the first war."

Johann nodded. "I hope that you find them," he said.

"I'll keep looking," the old woman said, casting her eyes to the ground. "They're all I had left of him."

Johann moved along the street, trying to breathe. Had he gotten here too late? He cursed himself. If he hadn't gone to the farmhouse he would have arrived in Berlin sooner. Maybe he would have been with Anja and Nadine and they would have been on their way west. At the very least—and he could hardly believe that he was thinking this—then he would have been able to die with them. He kicked tamely at what was left of a truck tire. It was partially melted to the ground, the rubber spilling sideways from the vehicle.

He told himself to get a grip. There were plenty of people who survived the raids. As long as the bunker or U-Bahn station was sound, then they were alive. He needed to calm himself; his emotions were running high because he was exhausted. He had to find them—but where to start? First he needed to visit the building itself. Anja knew that he was coming, so it was likely that she would have left some sign or a message for him. He peered around the front corner of a blackened bus. He gambled that Reinhard would not know his real identity, but the soldiers from the farmhouse were back in Berlin now and might have been questioned. Even if neither of these things had happened he must still avoid encounters with any form of authority—if Dieter had regained consciousness, the Gestapo would be after him. He thought about

the Walther P38 on his hip. He hadn't fired a round since officer training, but the idea of doing so no longer troubled him. He
would kill whomever he needed to should they try to prevent him
from reaching his family—if they had survived the bomb.

All appeared quiet near the apartment. He edged forward up
the street. A couple of women carrying pails of water passed by
him, their bodies lopsided from the weight of the water. There
was a small fire burning in the remnants of the building opposite.
Johann could see faces inside lit by the flames.

He got to the building and took a deep breath—his attempt
to conceal a sob.

Even knowing what had happened to his family home couldn't
prepare him for what he saw. He and Anja had come here for the
first time when friends had told them that it was available to rent.
It was bright and airy with a modern kitchen and an indoor bath-
room in a good location and was well within their budget. They
had shaken hands with Herr Kessler the landlord that afternoon
and had moved the few things they had before their marriage into
the apartment one cheerful autumn day. Johann could remembered the sting of the cold October wind—the first real chill of
the winter—as he and a friend had carried a dining table Anja
had bought at a flea market into the apartment. What seemed
strange was that—after all that had happened in the intervening
years—it seemed so recent. If he had returned to find the street
still tidy and the apartment well cared for he could almost have
imagined that what had happened in the east had been something
he could discount as fantasy. Rediscovering his Berlin life would
have compensated for the horror of war. He could have walked
in the park, eaten at restaurants in Charlottenburg, bought vegetables at Hackescher Markt, visited the theater. Life would have
been as it once was. Now it was something totally different.

He approached the building with the swagger of an SS officer with nothing to fear. He surveyed the property. Old Mrs. Matthaus's apartment had been entirely crushed. The Petersons once had a third-floor apartment—now they had easy access to the street. He could see belongings strewn about inside. Water cascaded from shattered plumbing in one part of the building. He glanced around. There didn't appear to be anyone watching him, so he began to examine the messages that had been left by survivors. As he moved between them he began to feel a degree of optimism: It appeared that many of the residents had left messages. It seemed that most of them had survived.

But, even as hope flowered within him, he still couldn't find a message from Anja. He checked through the rubble systematically for a second time, clearing away dust and sand where he thought it might have covered a message. Was it possible that they had left a note and that it had been blown away in the wind? Or maybe it had been removed, either by a mischief maker or by the authorities. . . .

He examined the building thoroughly for a third time, alarm spreading through him—if so many of the residents had survived, surely this meant that, statistically, it was less likely that Anja and Nadine had escaped. . . .

Think *clearly*, he told himself.

How else might they have thought to communicate with him? He checked the messages chalked on the front of the structure again.

Still nothing.

He prayed he was missing something. Then he saw the narrow passageway that had once run between his apartment block and the adjacent building, along which the caretaker had moved the rubbish bins from the rear of the building and the coal merchant had made his deliveries. He hurried toward it. There were several messages chalked on the wall. He scanned them quickly and didn't recognize any handwriting. He tried to compose himself. He needed to take his time and make sure that he didn't miss anything. He told himself to work from top to bottom, ensuring that each message was examined carefully.

He forced himself to take in each and every letter.

No. No. No.

There it is.

"J. We are all right. We are with your friend."

It was Anja. He was sure of it. It was like her to remain cautious, not to take unnecessary chances if she could avoid them. He stood there and ran his hands over the letters, knowing that if the old lady was right and the bombing had occurred only two days before, then Anja had been here, maybe only hours ago. She was still alive and she was still here, in Berlin. He would find her. He puzzled for a moment about who the "friend" she mentioned might be before realizing that it was likely to be just one person: Otto, who had brought the letter to Anja. He knew that Otto lived in Moabit. He even recalled him living on Wiclefstraße, but he wasn't entirely sure of the number. He would remember the building when he saw it.

His family was alive; he still had the briefcase. It was enough.

He heard a pile of rubble sliding near the road—the clinking sound of bricks knocking together mixed with the rush of aggregates. He looked up to see two men picking their way over a pile of twisted metal and masonry.

Johann immediately knew their identity from their fedoras and long coats: Gestapo.

He was so close to reuniting with his family. He would not let them take that from him. Johann looked around for a quick means of escape. But every path was either filled with rubble or had obstacles in front of it. He reached down to his leather holster, pulled the flap open, and pulled his pistol out, holding it level. He pointed the weapon at one of the men and then the other, not knowing which to fire at first.

A shot rang out, surprising him with the volume of its noise. He had been too slow, but he had been lucky—the Gestapo man had missed. He squeezed off a round before throwing himself behind a cast-iron bathtub that was lying nearby. He could hear the Gestapo men shifting toward him, searching for cover. Johann risked peeking out from behind the tub. They had taken shelter, but he wasn't sure quite where. Another shot rang out, and he ducked back behind the bath. He needed to move; no doubt one of them was trying to pin him down while the other outflanked him.

He leapt up, lugging the briefcase, and fired off another round at the officer who had shot at him. The man ducked back behind the shattered wall he was sheltering behind. As he did so, Johann scrambled out from behind his shield before throwing himself inside the shell of the building next to his own. He found himself in the hallway of a residential block he had once visited to drop off mail that had been wrongly directed.

He lay behind the wall, desperately running through his options. There were footsteps outside, two sets—both men were on the move. He looked around. As far as he could tell the back of the building was still intact; there was no easy escape. He peered from behind the bricks and saw one of the men edging toward him. He fired another round. It missed, but the bullet kicked up a cloud of dust near the officer's feet, causing him to dive behind a pile of rubble. Johann reached into the leather pouch on his belt and picked out some replacement ammunition. He had per-haps another dozen rounds. He needed to think fast. The two men were closing, and he was trapped. His fingers shook as he loaded the ammunition, dropping a bullet. He reached down to the floor—stone flagging that now had an inch or so of dust settled on it—and fumbled for the brass casing.

Johann told himself that he needed to stop thinking and act: If he stayed where he was, he would either be killed or captured.

He began to crawl toward the stairs before standing and rushing up the steps. Shots rang out, peppering the steps with traces of gunfire. They knew that he was headed upstairs. He needed to use the building as a maze in which to lose or kill them. He got to the first-floor landing. He was out of his pursuers' line of fire now and peered down. There was no way the Gestapo officers could get up the stairs without him being able to shoot them. But he knew that time wasn't on his side; they would muster men to overwhelm him in a short time, and his ammunition was limited. He ran to the back of the building to see if there was a fire escape. He crept as close to the edge as he could risk—maybe he could jump?—but at the back of the building was a tangled mass of ironwork. Johann liked his chances of surviving the drop but knew he would almost certainly injure himself on a sharp piece of metal.

There was no other means of escape that he could see other than the roof. He knew that, on the left, his own building was semi-derelict and there were no other ways of getting out of the front or the rear of the structure. This left only the building on the right as a possible escape route—if he could reach it. Johann racked his memory to try and remember whether it was still standing. Even if it was partly destroyed, he might be able to get over to it and climb down to the floor and get away.

Johann returned to the landing and peered down cautiously, aware that his pursuers would be looking for an opportunity to take a shot. He crept along the hallway, trying to make as little noise as possible. He stopped moving and listened—he could hear whispering. They were in the building. He craned his neck over the staircase and saw, in the lobby area, a pair of large, dusty shoes poking out from behind a doorframe. They were just a floor down from him.

Johann experienced a moment of dread. How many steps were there? Maybe twenty? They could be up here in a moment. He needed to get away, to put some distance between them in order to reach the roof and see what his options were for escape. And what if he was unable to get away? He would need to find a place to hide and wait for his adversaries. With the element of surprise he might be able to shoot both of them, as long as his aim was true.

Johann ran up to the next floor and waited. He heard boots cautiously following him up the stairs. He waited for a moment before rushing up to the third floor. Again, they came after him. He repeated himself, getting to the landing on the next floor. The second he imagined the two men were edging along the third-floor landing, he appeared at the top of the stairs and took a shot. He saw the first of them—a big man with a walrus mustache and a face pink from exertion—drop his weapon and fall to the floor, cursing. Johann flung himself back to the top of the staircase. A piece of plasterwork puffed into the air as a bullet lodged in the wall a foot away from where he was lying.

The incident bought him a few moments, and he rushed along the walkway on the top floor, passing through a door that was hanging from a single hinge and out onto the roof. Outside, the sun was beginning to set. The lack of light didn't make a huge difference. The gloom just appeared to be getting heavier. Johann looked around. The remaining Gestapo officer had yet to start up the final staircase. He scanned the roof. One edge was completely shattered, but the other three appeared safe to walk on.

Johann oriented himself. He knew that three sides were useless. He needed the fourth to offer him an escape route. The officer would be up the stairs soon. He needed to hurry. He ran to one edge and peered outward—it was the side adjacent to his old building. This meant that the opposite side was his potential escape route. He rushed over, barely able to contain his dread. As he crossed to the other side he realized the roof offered no cover. He held his weapon up as he approached the edge in case the Gestapo officer came through the door.

He looked over and distinguished a solid roof, about ten feet below. But the gap between the buildings—perhaps eight feet—was such that he would need to leap. From where he was standing, Johann thought the roof appeared to be solid. He had no choice anyway; he had to get away, even if there was a chance it wouldn't support his weight.

Johann backed up so that he could gather pace for the jump—the weight of his briefcase would slow him, so he needed to gain as much momentum as he could.

"Wait right there!"

The voice was as loud as thunder. The order came from the Gestapo officer who had appeared on the roof. Johann had his back to the man. Should he dare turn and try to shoot him?

"Drop the gun!" the man instructed him.

Johann hesitated. Once he was unarmed there was no hope.

"Drop the gun or I will shoot!"

Johann held out his arms horizontally, but held on to the pistol.

"I will count to three," came the voice. "One . . ." There was a pause. Johann listened to a loud diesel engine starting somewhere in the distance. "Two . . ."

He made a decision: Being alive and in the hands of the Gestapo was marginally better than being dead. He dropped the pistol and the briefcase.

"Now turn around slowly," the officer instructed him.

Johann rotated and stared at the man. The officer was tall, with dark hair that had a severe center part. The skin on his face was florid. A drinker, perhaps.

"I think he's dead," the man said, nodding back toward the exit to the roof. "Aren't you in enough trouble already? Killing a member of the *Staatspolizei* is just going to get you deeper in the shit. Mind you, you were so deep in the shit already that there was nothing you could do to keep yourself alive beyond nightfall. I suppose it's all relative."

Johann's arms were aching from holding them in a position of surrender. He let them sag a little.

"Up!" instructed the officer. "What's a little discomfort when you're on the scaffold?"

Johann forced his hands high into the air.

The Gestapo officer edged toward him.

"I need the briefcase," the officer said.

Johann looked down at the leather bag.

"And the key," the Gestapo officer added.

Johann froze—the officer was acting under orders from his half brother.

"Quick!" the man ordered.

Johann looked up at him and then back at the bag. He could feel the key against his chest now, warm from his body heat. Would he really just hand them over?

The Gestapo officer gestured with his gun impatiently. Johann was out of time. He thought of Anja and Nadine. If only he could get off this rooftop he could be with them within an hour. The thought was almost too painful.

"If I give you them, will you let me go?" Johann replied.

The man considered this for a moment.

"All right," he said.

Johann paused before reaching down and pulling the chain from his neck. The key twisted as it hung in midair in front of him.

The Gestapo officer reached forward and snatched it and kicked the briefcase away from Johann.

"Our friends in the SS will be extremely appreciative of this," he said, stepping backward.

"Now turn around very slowly," the man added. Johann complied. "Walk to the edge of the roof." Johann took six steps forward until he was a few inches shy of the four-story drop. He looked out across what was left of the Berlin rooftops.

"Now get on your knees," the officer ordered.

"But I gave you—" Johann started.

"Be quiet, fool," the man snapped.

Johann took his time. He had expected arrest and torture, not execution. He cast his eyes around, desperately looking to see if there was a means of escape. There was nothing to jump onto if he threw himself over the edge. There was no object nearby to grab hold of and throw at his captor.

Johann heard a fresh magazine being slid into a P38. He probably only had a few seconds left. He felt an overwhelming sadness that he had gotten so close to seeing Anja and Nadine again. He had failed them: His heroics had cost him his chance of being reunited and—who knows?—maybe even escape. There was a part of him that wished he had never heard of the Nero Decree. He wondered whether he should say a prayer like some of his patients would do when they were dumped before him in the operating theater, but nothing came to his lips. All he could think was that he had failed those he loved.

"Let him go!"

The voice came from nowhere, piercing the hushed anticipation. The noise was so out of place that Johann wondered if he had even heard it at all, or whether it was a figment of his fevered, preexecution imaginings.

"Let him go!"

The voice was high-pitched: a boy. The words this time were spaced out. Grittier. More determined than the first order, which had been full of trepidation.

Johann shifted his body slightly so that he could see what was happening behind him. The Gestapo officer still had his handgun trained on him. The man's body was angled toward Johann but his head was shifted to his right, where a boy of around twelve stood with a pistol pointed at the policeman. The officer regarded the boy coolly, seemingly untroubled by his intervention. Johann could barely believe what he was seeing. Then a smile spread over the face of the Gestapo man, his eyebrows rising up an inch in amusement.

"Really?" the man said. "You're really going to shoot?"

Johann could see that the boy was continuing to hold the weapon, but that the end of the barrel was quivering slightly. Johann could tell that the words of the Gestapo officer had affected him. He was losing his nerve.

"You've never fired a gun in your life, have you?" the officer said.

Johann wondered whether he could get up and rush the Gestapo man before he could fire his weapon, but it wasn't feasible—the man would have plenty of time to fire at him before he could cross the roof. If he could maybe create some kind of a distraction, it might help to break the sway that the Gestapo officer had over the boy. Johann saw the boy beginning to cry. His face was dirty, his hair unkempt. His lower lip trembled with emotion.

Johann needed to help. He shifted his position, causing the officer to shout.

"Don't you move!"

He gestured toward Johann with his weapon, instructing him to turn around. Johann remained still. He stared at the boy, trying to give him courage.

"Turn around now!" the Gestapo man commanded. There was a little more urgency in his voice than just moments ago. "You think that some kid who hasn't even started shaving is going to save you?"

Johann looked at the boy. The young man's clothes were ripped and grimy, his face appeared to be covered in dirt, his hair was disheveled, but he had piercing blue eyes that suggested the unfulfilled promise of youth. He didn't want to be on a roof pointing a gun at a Nazi, but he was doing exactly that. Like everyone else in this chaotic city he found himself doing something he could never imagine he would ever do. The boy was trembling. Johann saw a tear well up in his eye. It dripped onto his cheek. The boy dared not wipe it for fear of removing his hands from the weapon.

"You've never fired a gun in your life," the Gestapo officer repeated. His body was still twisted—the weapon was leveled at Johann, but his eyes remained on the boy. Johann could see the young man beginning to melt. He needed help. . . .

Johann moved again, and this time the Gestapo officer edged closer to him. Then the boy began to edge forward as well.

"Get away from him!" The boy ordered the Gestapo officer. The man kept his head turned toward the boy and shuffled sideways. He was the same distance from Johann as before, but he was now perhaps four feet from the edge of the roof.

"I said get away from him!" the boy insisted.

"I did as you asked," the officer replied. "Now how about you and I come to an agreement. You walk away from this and I'll pretend that I've never seen you."

The boy blinked several times, trying to clear the tears from his eyes. The pistol was waving wildly now. Johann watched as the boy began—ever so slowly—to lower the gun.

He could wait no longer.

Johann leaped at the Gestapo officer. The policeman must have noticed the movement out of the corner of his eye—he began to turn his head to look at Johann, who was now crouched and perhaps two feet from him. The man's eyes narrowed as he realized what was happening and determined that he must pull the trigger. Their eyes locked at the very moment Johann heard the explosion of gunfire and tumbled to the ground.

There were a few seconds of silence. Stunned, Johann ran a mental inventory of his physical state: Despite the explosion he felt no pain. Had he gone numb? Was he in shock? He reached up to his shoulder and felt grit from the roof embedded in the cloth of his jacket. Johann sat up and felt himself all over. The boy stared at him, incredulous, before walking to the edge of the roof and peering down. Johann stood up, staggering ever so slightly, and moved to where the boy was standing. The two of them looked downward at the Gestapo officer, whose body lay splayed in awkward angles—like the victim of a car crash. There was blood on the remains of a wall nearby. His head must have collided with it.

Johann felt nothing. No relief. No guilt. He was alive, that was all.

"Thank you, Lukas," he said to the boy.

"You're welcome, Herr Schultz," the boy replied weakly. "We all thought you were dead."

20

"**F**uck the *Sanitätsstaffel!*" Dieter said, throwing the telephone handset into the cradle.

"The SS Medical Corps won't help?" Kuefer asked. His chair creaked as he turned to talk to Dieter.

"They say they're too busy to help," Dieter replied, tossing a file across his desk in disgust. "I ask them to offer assistance with a simple matter and . . ."

Dieter had returned to the cramped office in a foul temper. He had slept badly the night before—despite medication, his injuries were acutely painful—and he was frustrated by his inability to find Johann's family. The chaos among the official bodies that might be able to facilitate crucial information had left him fuming.

"Is it too much to ask, Kuefer?" he snapped. "This is an investigation of the utmost significance, and the *Sanitätsstaffel* can't even make the most basic inquiry for me. I need to know who this friend might be who is harboring Schultz's wife. I need records of other doctors who Schultz might have come into contact with."

Kuefer wanted to help. The relationship between the two of them had been awkward—although he was the more experienced investigator, protocol dictated that he take a back seat to the SS man.

A match flared in the stuffy office and a plume of smoke coiled around Kuefer's face.

"We are no longer able to communicate with the field hospital," Dieter continued. "So I can't even talk to that asshole commanding officer Henke and question more of those who saw this Schultz before he left the facility."

Kuefer stood up and placed a file carefully on Dieter's desk before retreating back to his chair.

"What's this?" Dieter asked suspiciously. He was in no mood for understatement.

"If you can't get to the field hospital, then maybe elements of it can come to you," Kuefer said. He felt foolish now. He had attempted to garner the *Sturmbannführer*'s respect, but had overplayed his hand.

"Enlighten me," said Dieter sarcastically, without touching the file.

Kuefer cleared his throat. "I sequestered all the dispatches from the field hospital," he explained. "Take a look. Since Schultz disappeared, two of the doctors he worked with have been sent back to Berlin to work at hospitals."

Dieter flipped open the file and examined two documents that Kuefer had placed at the top. He had circled two names: Andreas Karl and Otto Deitch.

"Karl is at the Rudolf Virchow in Wedding, and Deitch is at Charité."

Dieter stood up.

"I'll visit Karl; you find Deitch," he growled. "Meet me here at thirteen hundred hours for a debrief. We will find Thomas Meier. And we'll find him soon."

Dieter walked from the room without a further word, leaving the door open behind him. He had offered no thanks for the breakthrough.

Kuefer took a deep drag on his cigarette and pondered what Dieter had just said: He had called the suspect Thomas Meier, not Johann Schultz.

He leaned over his desk, opened his notebook, and wrote the name down. He could tell that Dieter was holding back sensitive material on the case; his manner and investigative trips had been furtive and abnormal. Although this wasn't an unusual practice for the SS, the slip of the tongue suggested something conspiratorial. He didn't know what, but he imagined that there was more to the *Sturmbannführer*'s interest in resolving this crime than he had thought.

He threw his cigarette butt on the filthy floor, stamped it out, and pulled on his leather coat.

Dieter had visited the Rudolf Virchow Hospital years before when a friend had his gallbladder removed. He recalled admiring the elegance of its pavilion-style architecture—the stucco-fronted main building and the elegant approach along an avenue lined with chestnut trees.

Any semblance of grace had been diminished by years of bombing. The building's classical façade was damaged and the trees were mostly gone. Dieter bullied his way through four different bureaucrats before he found one who could tell him where Andreas Karl might be found. Although Karl wasn't a surgeon by training, he had been posted to general surgery because of his experience in the field.

Dieter peered through a round window into an operating theater and saw Karl at work—he looked small, apprehensive, and he wore thick glasses. As soon as the operation was finished Dieter burst into the room. The nurses and doctors stared at him in alarm.

"Andreas Karl?" Dieter asked self-assuredly.

Karl blinked up at him.

"Are you Andreas Karl?" Dieter repeated. He heard the others in the room scurry off.

"I am," the man said.

Dieter led him to a nearby office, which he commandeered. He positioned Karl in an armchair and stood over him.

"I recognize you from somewhere . . . ," Karl said tentatively.

Dieter's face remained impassive. "I'm sure you do," he replied.

"Yes, yes, of course—in the east," Karl said. "I, um, apologize. You understand that we see so many people that it's hard to—"

"How well did you know Johann Schultz?" Dieter demanded. He felt that this one was scared, easily manipulated.

"Schultz?" Karl repeated. He straightened. "I heard . . ."

"You heard what?"

"That he had disappeared," Karl said. "That he couldn't face the Soviets, so he fled."

"Did you hear anything else?"

"No," Karl said. "I left the field two days after he left. I've been here since. When I'm not working I'm sleeping."

Karl moved to stand up, but Dieter pushed him back down. He didn't want them at the same level.

"What was your opinion of Schultz?"

"He was a good doctor," Karl said guiltily, as if he knew that he was giving the wrong answer. "I didn't really know him well beyond that. He was quiet. Got on with his work."

"What else?"

"I really wasn't there for long," Karl explained.

"What else?" Dieter persisted, his voice harder this time.

"I don't know . . . ," Karl pondered miserably.

"There must be something."

"He had a wife and niece," Karl said, his face somehow brightening. Surely this would be enough for the SS man? Dieter knew he was getting closer now: Karl was telling the truth—and there was more. "He mentioned them a couple times. I remember before the last time he went back to Berlin that—"

"Where in Berlin?" Dieter asked.

"Somewhere in Mitte, I believe," Karl said. "I'm pretty sure that he grew up in the city."

Karl put his hands under his armpits, as if hugging himself. Dieter noticed the man's thinning hair—from the top it was possible to see how little was left on the crown—his thin, trembling hands . . . He would not make it.

"When was the last time you saw him?" he asked.

"The day before he, you know, disappeared, I think," Karl answered.

"How did he seem?"

Karl considered this for a moment. "Not himself," he explained. "He seemed preoccupied. Agitated, even. I remember he came into the doctors' quarters in a hurry. Usually he slipped in and went straight to his cot. He wrote a lot of . . ." He paused. "I remember now: He borrowed some writing paper from me."

"Did you see him write the letter?" Dieter asked.

"No," Karl answered. "He left immediately."

"And that is definitely the last time you saw him."

"I think so. . . ."

"I don't want to hear 'I think so,'" Dieter said impatiently. "Was this the last time you saw him? Think about it."

"I'm thinking, I'm thinking," Karl replied, his head bowed. Dieter sensed that Karl had more to say, that he had suddenly realized there was something pertinent he had not thought of before.

"I saw him talking to another doctor, Otto Deitch, very briefly," he said. "In triage. They had a short conversation, but it seemed like there was something serious going on. Usually Deitch is, you know, voluble and fun-loving, but he talked quietly with Schultz, as if they didn't want to be overheard. I can't be sure, but it looked like Schultz gave Deitch something."

"What?"

"I wouldn't like to speculate. . . ."

"*What?*" Dieter said irritably. He shoved Karl's head.

"A document maybe," Karl replied. "A letter. I don't know. It was dark, but he seemed to be holding something and then he wasn't."

"Do you know where Deitch is?" Dieter asked to confirm that Karl was telling the truth.

"They transferred him back to Berlin, to the Charité," Karl said. "I was jealous of him, and then they sent me back too."

Dieter looked at Karl. "A shameful sentiment," he said after a while. "You do a discredit to yourself, your comrades, and your country."

Karl looked up at him, anger in his eyes. "What honor is there in *this?*" he demanded. He virtually spat the words.

"Make no mistake, Karl," Dieter replied. "When you lose your honor, you lose everything."

Karl said nothing. He pressed himself back in the chair.

The connection had been made. Dieter thought of the chalked message: "We are with your friend." The friend had to be Deitch. He needed to call the records department and the NSV to see if they could identify where he lived. Dieter was convinced that, if he found Deitch's house, he would capture his half brother's family—and eventually Johann himself.

For a moment he considered teaching Karl a lesson. A beating he would remember. He clenched his left fist and felt the pain in the side of his body. He needed to save his energy. He wasn't even sure that he had the strength to deliver blows of the kind that Karl deserved. He walked from the office quickly, throwing the door wide. There was no need for him to concern himself with Karl— the Soviets would take care of that.

21

Anja was ready. She had bathed as well she could, knowing that this was the last opportunity she might have for some weeks. She had washed her and Nadine's clothes and packed them in a rectangular leather case that Otto had given her before he said farewell and headed to work at the hospital. He had also offered her any of his mother's clothes that were in the house. The woman was long gone, and Anja found the idea slightly repellent, but the idea of new undergarments and hosiery was too tempting to turn down. Such things had been rationed for years.

She had gone through the woman's clothes and found items that might fit Nadine as well. She was thankful that it would soon be spring and after that summer. There was less need to pack bulky winter clothes. Otto had also donated a water canteen that she had filled to the brim from a standpipe at the end of the street. They would drink from the same faucet on their way west to make sure the supply lasted as long as possible. They had spent the night in comparative ease—there had been an early raid, which had finished by 8 p.m., so both of them had managed to get a solid night's rest. It seemed like a luxury—even sleep felt like it had been rationed over the past few years.

Anja placed the bag near the front door and ran through her mental plan. They would try the train stations. Perhaps there were trains still running west. If not, they could flee to the south, down to Bavaria. Failing that they would start to walk west. She had heard that the authorities were preventing people leaving the city for fear of causing mass panic, but she believed that she would somehow be able to smuggle herself and her niece out. There had to be a way.

"Nadine!" she called up the stairs. "Are you ready to leave?"

"Yes, Tante," Nadine called down. "I'm just tidying the room."

"Good," Anja said. "Let's be gone in five minutes, shall we?"

"I'll be down in a minute," Nadine promised.

Anja was anxious and at a loose end. She had already checked the contents of the bags and ensured that the paperwork was in her pocket several times, but she did it again before surveying the apartment for anything that was out of place.

"Nadine," she called. "Let's go."

She was ready now. It was time to leave.

The girl appeared at the top of the stairs, and Anja was suddenly and unexpectedly almost overwhelmed with love for her, this girl who had had her world turned upside down, had had so much taken from her. As Nadine walked down the stairs there was a straightness to her back and a firmness to her jaw that Anja prayed she could emulate. The girl refused to be beaten. Anja would hold a mirror to her and live the same way. It made Anja stronger knowing that she had a companion like this. Together they would face as one whatever it was that they had to confront.

Nadine arrived at the bottom of the stairs and they stood opposite each other across the hallway.

"Are you ready?" Anja said, brushing some lint from the collar of the girl's coat.

"Yes," Nadine replied firmly. "Are you ready, Tante Anja?"

"I am," Anja said, busying herself with smoothing the girl's hair back as if they were on their way to church. She didn't want Nadine to see the doubts crowding her mind.

"Let's be on our way then," Nadine said. "Oh, wait . . ." She ran to the rear of the house and started to open the back door.

"What are you doing?" Anja asked the girl.

"I saw a cornflower growing yesterday," Nadine said. "I found a vase and wanted to leave it for Otto."

The girl opened the door and left the back of the house. Anja stood at the door uneasily, switching her weight from foot to foot. This delay was playing on her nerves. She wanted to go now, and hanging around was causing her to consider what was ahead. She felt relief when Nadine reappeared.

"Got it," she said, locking the back door. She walked over to a vase on the kitchen table and carefully placed the stem of the flower in the water.

"There," she said, considering her work.

At that moment a roar of engines and screech of brakes broke the quiet of the house. It was a noise that seemed alien to Berlin streets now, such was the shortage of fuel.

"What's that?" Nadine asked. Her face had clouded.

Anja raised her hand, as if asking for silence. Had they come for them?

"Quick," Anja said. The two of them ran to the kitchen, abandoning their suitcases. They could hear the shouts of men outside in the street.

There was a loud banging and cries of "Open up! Open up!" Anja froze before realizing that it wasn't coming from Otto's front door. The noise was so loud that it must have been close. The pair of them edged out of the kitchen and up the corridor to the front of the apartment. The shouting continued. The blows to the door became more staccato—the door was being broken down. With a crunching noise the door gave way. Nadine and Anja could hear the sound of boots clattering on a wooden floor. The shouting continued and was broken only by the shrieks of a woman.

Anja felt a sickness in her heart as she recognized the voice of the woman next door.

"Let him go!" she screamed. "Let him go!"

The footsteps and screaming continued through the house. There was the occasional thud. One of Otto's family photographs jumped. Nadine looked at Anja, who put her finger to her lips. Anja wondered whether they should flee through the back door as a precaution. Then she heard the voice of the woman next door.

"Let him go, you bastards! Let him go! He's just a boy."

Anja and Nadine stood frozen behind the door, just feet from the drama.

"Help me!" It was the woman's voice.

"Mother!" came the voice of a boy.

Anja's hand hovered over the door handle before she pulled it back.

"Let him go!" came the woman's voice again.

Anja opened the door, and from the hallway she saw the woman from next door, who was mostly hidden behind a large man in a uniform. A truck idled at the curb outside the building. The flap at the back of the vehicle was down. There were four soldiers: Two of them were wrestling with the young boy Nadine had met, one was searching in the cab of the truck for something, and the other, an officer, was holding the woman from next door by her shoulders.

"There are no exceptions," he said to her calmly as she wriggled to escape his grasp. "The order from Gauleiter Goebbels was clear on this—all males aged fourteen and above are to defend the Reich."

"He's not fourteen!" the mother said, her eyes darting about frantically, searching for her son, who had been brought beside the truck. Anja could see faces peering out from behind blackout, and there were others in the street who had heard the commotion, but no one wanted to be a witness. Anja walked down the steps of the building.

"What are you doing?" she asked one of the soldiers, who was holding the boy's arm firmly. The boy's face was puffy and red, his cheeks streaked with tears; he looked hopelessly feeble next to the soldiers. The private ignored her, choosing instead to look up at the officer who continued to talk to the boy's mother.

"You should have thought about your mother's duty . . . ," he was saying. "While our patriotic sons are fighting the Soviets, your offspring cowers in a basement afraid to shed his blood for the Führer and the country."

"He's just a boy," the mother said. "Please, please, let him go. He's all I have left. My husband and brother both died in the east. Just leave my son. Is that too much to ask?"

The officer raised his hand dismissively.

"What possible relevance has any of this to your crimes and the crimes of this malingering boy?" he asked, his voice incredulous.

Just then Anja saw what the man in the cab of the truck had been looking for. He jumped down onto the street holding a thick piece of rope with a noose tied in it. The woman flew at the officer, scratching and biting, her face a blur of anger. The soldier with the rope ran to help the officer restrain her.

"No!" the woman screamed, over and over. *"No!"*

That was when Anja felt herself moving toward the soldiers. She pushed at one of the men holding the boy. His shoulder was firm beneath her shove. He looked at her with astonishment, his cloudy eyes framed within a dark circle of ragged tiredness. The boy saw it as his cue to thrash against the men holding him captive. He wrestled one of his arms free and kicked the soldier who held him. The soldier reached and grabbed the boy by the neck before delivering a powerful punch to his solar plexus. The boy immediately dropped to the ground, doubled up and groaning. One of the soldiers made to kick him. Anja stepped forward and grasped at the private. She wasn't really sure whether she was pushing him or hitting him. What she knew was that she had to intervene before he could hurt the boy again.

The soldier lost his balance and stumbled to his right before regaining his poise. That was when she felt the force of a shove so powerful that her neck snapped back and her legs went weak. She hit the pavement next to the boy and lay there trying to gain her bearings.

"Stupid bitch," she heard one of them say. "That will teach her."

As the world gradually came back into focus she saw Nadine's face appear before her.

"Aunt! Aunt! Are you okay?" she said urgently. "Can you hear me, Aunt?"

Anja could just about hear her niece's voice above a ringing in her ears. She needed to get up, to look after Nadine. They had to get away from here. They had to escape. The bags were in the hallway. They were leaving Berlin.

"You bastards . . ." It was Nadine's voice. A fourteen-year-old girl talking to soldiers like that! Part of Anja was terrified; part of her was thrilled. The girl had spirit. She was proud. Anja tried to move, but her body wasn't doing what her mind was asking it to. She could hear scuffling and shouting around her. Loud voices and boots crunching on the pavement. There was movement all around her. She felt someone stumble over one of her legs.

Then she was up, her body now able to function again as she required it. There was still the piercing ringing in her ears, but she was able to see what was going on. One of the soldiers was holding Nadine, another the woman next door. A few feet away a third soldier had put a ladder against a lamppost and was securing the rope to it with practiced knots. The boy was now held by the fourth soldier.

It took a moment for Anja to realize what they were doing. She put one foot in front of the other and stumbled toward the soldier, who eyed her coolly, aware of what she hoped to do. He thrust the boy at her, shouting something about loyalty and using the teenager as a human battering ram, shoving him at Anja as if the lad were nothing. Anja could see that his body had gone limp, his head jerking around like a marionette. She wondered what had happened to his arms; he no longer appeared to have any. Anja focused and realized that the soldier had tied the boy's hands behind his back—he was now powerless to claw, rip, or punch.

And it wasn't just his head that was moving; there was something else, something oblong, moving around in front of him. Anja realized that it was a sign. It was attached to a piece of cord that had been placed over the boy's neck. The thing was swinging so fast that she couldn't read the black letters that had been painted by hand about half an inch thick.

She glanced over and saw Nadine shouting at the soldier gripping her arm, her face undaunted. The man looked away from her, his jaw set awkwardly as if he were tasting something he didn't like. There was a deep razor cut in the middle of his cheek, the result of pressing too hard with an ancient blade.

The mother of the child was now on her knees in the street, pleading with the officer. He appeared unconcerned by whatever it was that the boy's mother was telling him. His coat flapped violently about him as he moved between the soldiers, giving orders.

Suddenly the boy appeared to take flight. His mother uttered as loud and desperate a scream as Anja had ever heard. Nothing had ever sounded so desolate. The boy was traveling vertically, hoisted up onto the lamppost by a rope around his neck. He swung from side to side, his legs kicking wildly, trying to gain purchase to take the pressure from his throat. He made a low gurgling sound as he moved back and forth. Flecks of spittle sprayed from his mouth. Anja ran toward him, trying to support his feet. She felt a tug on her shoulder and turned to see the officer, who was shouting at her.

"Leave him alone! Leave him alone!"

Then, as suddenly as they had arrived, they were gone. The truck roared away.

Anja went over to the woman, who was on her knees beneath the swinging feet of her son. He had stopped his deathly shuddering. She embraced the woman, who was emitting low, primal groans. Nadine joined them, wrapping her arms around Anja. The three of them remained like that for some minutes, until they heard the sound of another vehicle pulling up.

Anja looked up to see a Mercedes at the curb. An SS officer, his scarred face a livid red, heaved himself from the rear seat followed by another man, who coughed raggedly.

The two men looked at the boy hanging from the lamppost with little interest, and headed toward the women.

Anja regarded the officer—his eyes burned intensely as their gaze met. She knew that he had come for her.

"Anja Schultz?" he asked.

She nodded slowly.

"I am arresting you for crimes against the state," the officer said.

He kept talking, but Anja was no longer listening. She had long dreaded this moment. Now that it was happening she wondered why it had taken them so long to find her.

22

Lukas led Johann through the unlit streets. Johann struggled to keep up with the boy, who moved nimbly through the debris. Eventually Lukas clambered through a small gap in what was once an entrance to a courtyard. He picked his way over a ten-foot-high mound of rubble, with Johann following behind. The two of them stood momentarily in the darkness at the top of the heap. Johann realized that the courtyard on the other side remained relatively intact.

"People don't come in here," Lukas said, standing in the small cobbled courtyard. "They think that the entire place is a ruin."

The boy pulled open a wooden door twice the size of him, which made a piercing creaking noise.

"If anyone tried to get in here at night I'd know about it," he said. Large panels of moonlight came through rectangular windows that ran the length of the room. Strangely, many of them were still glazed. Johann smelled sawdust.

"It used to be a carpentry workshop," the boy explained proprietarily. "It was closed down a couple years ago. The men went to fight or to the munitions factory. I suppose nobody wanted doors and cornicing any longer either."

"You live here?" Johann asked. He had known the boy from the neighborhood. His parents had had a successful bakery, and Lukas had delivered its products around the locality on a black bicycle that was too big for him. The bread was always piled high on a basket on the front, but it never seemed to topple out.

"Yes," the boy replied. He walked up a metal staircase onto a gallery. "Up here," he said, encouraging Johann to follow him.

Johann walked up the stairs. His legs felt heavy. The briefcase, key, and gun, which he had retrieved from the roof, was feeling heavier. The boy lit a candle. Johann could see that he had arranged salvaged household items—some blankets, plates, a chair, a desk. There were even some books.

"How long?" Johann asked.

"About six months," the boy said. He pointed to a chair. "Sit down, please."

Johann accepted the offer unwillingly; he knew that he should be trying to get across the city to Anja and Nadine, but he didn't have the strength.

"There's a toilet in the back that still works," the boy said proudly. "And a water pump too."

"Aren't you afraid?" Johann asked.

The boy considered this for a moment. "Yes," he said cautiously. "Sometimes at night. But it's no worse than the air raids. What is someone going to do to me that the British aren't trying to do already?"

Johann closed his eyes. Now that he had stopped, the full extent of his tiredness had crashed upon him like a wave. He felt physically crushed.

"Why are you back in Berlin dressed like this?" Lukas asked the question slowly, unfolding it like it might be explosive. Johann didn't say anything.

"I didn't recognize you at first," Lukas said. "But then I saw the Gestapo trailing you, so I figured that maybe you had done something wrong and maybe that might have to do with the uniform. You never seemed like the type."

Johann smiled at the small affirmation and opened his eyes to see that the boy was offering him a hunk of black bread. Johann didn't feel hungry, but he knew that he had to eat.

"Thanks," he said, taking the bread. He bit down on a small part of it. It was tough, but not stale. A treat. "Ignore the uniform," Johann said. "Just enjoy the food."

"I got it this morning," the boy said triumphantly. "The women at the NSV, I tell them that I'm getting it for my grandmother. There are so many bodies after the raids that it's easy enough to pick up ration cards."

The two of them chewed on their bread.

"I need to move on," Johann said quietly after swallowing. It felt as if his body was now one with the armchair. Would he ever be able to rise again?

The flame from the candle crackled.

"Where?" the boy asked. Johann noted a tone of disappointment.

"You remember my wife, Anja?" Johann asked.

"Of course," Lukas said. "She liked our doughnuts."

Johann smiled, his memory stirred. He remembered Anja going into the bakery and getting one after they had been to watch a movie on Kurfürstendamm at the beginning of the war. It felt like so long ago. Another lifetime.

"And you had a daughter too . . . ," Lukas said, settling on the rugs and blankets that formed his bed.

"A niece," Johann corrected him.

"Ah, yes," the boy said. "I remember now."

Both of them remained silent for a while. They had conjured other lives and neither of them wanted to return to the present. Being able to live in a delightful past was a skill that passed as entertainment.

"What happened to your parents?" Johann asked, breaking his reverie.

"Oh, dead," the boy said matter-of-factly. "In a raid. I was out on a delivery and went to the bunker on Reinhardstraße—you know the one the railway company built?"

Johann nodded. He had sheltered there and in the bunker at Gesundbrunnen when he was in the city. Anja and Nadine used the same place.

"They were in the bakery cellar," the boy continued. "But the building caved in on top of them. They tried to dig them out but—well, you know."

"But why are you here, like this?"

"I was sent to a home for orphans," Lukas said. "I'm not even sure where it was, somewhere in the west, way past Spandau. It was horrible: bread with worms, thin cabbage soup. . . . We weren't cared for. It was like they were keeping us alive because they had to, not because they wanted to. There were some lessons, but the teachers were brutal. So I decided to leave. We were locked up at night, but it wasn't too hard. I opened a window and climbed down a set of pipes outside my room. I asked others to come with me, but they were too scared."

"Don't you have any relatives outside Berlin you could stay with?"

"Yes, there are some," Lukas said, "but I don't have their addresses. Those went with my parents. And it's not like the phone lines are up so we can call them."

Johann thought about Anja for a moment. How he wished that he could pick up a telephone and call her.

"When were your parents killed?" Johann asked.

"November last year," Lukas replied. "I suppose I should think myself lucky that I was in the institution for the first winter. But this year wasn't so bad, I suppose. It's dry in here and there's an old stove over there. And I manage to find quite a bit of wood on the bomb sites if I get there before the other scavengers."

"You can't stay here; you know that, don't you?"

The boy cast him a dark look. "Why not?"

Johann closed his eyes again and leaned back in the chair. As much as he wanted to get across Berlin, he wasn't sure if he was going to be able to stay awake. He was overcome by the quiet, warmth, and apparent safety of the workshop. He could still taste the bread in his mouth. The situation felt as good as he might hope for.

"How old are you now?" Johann asked the boy, who had gotten up and was now fiddling with a clock that appeared to have been salvaged from a bomb site.

"Fifteen," the boy said.

"*How* old?" Johann repeated.

"Thirteen," the boy replied, quietly this time.

Johann sighed. The expelling of air relaxed him. He felt guilty; how could he feel relaxed, knowing that he was so close to Anja and Nadine? The chalked message was obscure to others, but he was sure now what it meant: They were at Otto's apartment in Moabit. If he started out soon, he could be there in—what?— maybe two hours. He stood up, trying to energize himself. He couldn't afford to sit around. For all he knew his wife and niece were leaving tomorrow morning and he would miss them. Then another, terrifying thought occurred to him: They could already be gone.

He tried to gather his thoughts: It was around twenty-one hundred hours. He desperately needed rest. He hadn't slept for two days. If he just allowed himself a few hours' sleep he would be rested and in a better position for them all to escape. But he felt that if he allowed himself to fall asleep then he might not wake for days. No, he had to leave this place. Had to trek to the northwest and then lead them south to Lehrter Bahnhof and away from the city.

He paced around a little, trying to boost his body for the walk to Moabit.

"A thirteen-year-old boy shouldn't be living alone in an abandoned building," he said. "Nor should he have a weapon."

The boy looked at him as if he was absolutely insane.

"I'm sorry," Johann said. "That was a very stupid thing to say."

"Herr Schultz," the boy said. "I'd like my pistol back, please."

Johann realized that he had pocketed the weapon after the incident on the roof.

"How did you come to have this?" he asked Lukas.

"It was when I first came back to the city," he said. "I tried to find some friends and people that my parents knew, but I couldn't find anyone, so I decided that I needed to take care of myself. I wasn't looking for a gun. I'd found this place. But one day I had gone out to get some food and there was a raid. I was used to helping myself to ration cards afterward, but then it suddenly occurred to me, I should take a gun. The Red Army. Criminals. Who knows? So I saw a dead soldier, and the pistol was sitting there in his holster. He had no further use for it, so I took it."

Johann pulled the gun from his pocket. Every bone in his body told him that giving a child a weapon was wrong, that this was a lunatic path. Battle-hardened, front-line troops would not hesitate to kill anyone they encountered with a weapon—even if it was a child. But he thought about the opportunists and predators who were now prowling the city. The boy needed protection.

Then something else occurred to him.

"Here," he said, and put the weapon on a small bookcase. "I pray to God you never need to use it."

"I already have," the boy answered, perking up a little. "I shot a rat last winter. It was eating my rations. Killed it with one shot."

"Just try and remember who you were before all this," Johann said. He had resolved to remain on his feet to stop himself from falling asleep.

The boy considered the question. "You know what happened to my parents?" he said. "I blame the National Socialists for it. I blame them for everything. My parents hated them, but they weren't able to say anything. They just wanted to be left alone to get on with the bakery. And I know that there's no way things are going to go back to the way they were, you know, before, but I often used to think about what it would be like if I could just get a gun and kill all of them. And I suppose, since I've had the gun, I've wondered what it would be like to get rid of one of them. And I saw you running from them and remembered that my parents liked you, and I thought to myself, well, here's my chance. I wasn't going to let them kill you."

"Thank you, Lukas," Johann said.

"It's nothing." The boy shrugged. "I'm sorry that . . ."

"Don't be silly," Johann said, thinking back to the boy crying on the rooftop. "Killing is something a child should never have to think about."

The boy stood up and went over to the piece of bread and pulled off another hunk. He handed the piece to Johann.

"So what did the Gestapo want with you?" Lukas asked, his mouth full of the food. Johann noticed that his hands were filthy.

"I left the front," Johann said.

"So you're a deserter?"

Johann looked at the boy. Was he really a deserter?

"They're saying that all deserters found in the city will be executed," Lukas said. "I heard it from some Party member on a megaphone. They were going about the streets in a car. And it was in the newspaper. Orders from the Führer himself."

Johann reached into his pocket and pulled out his worn and flattened wallet. He opened it up and pulled out a photograph.

"Here," he said, handing it to the boy, who took it with his grubby fingers and examined it using the candle.

"Your wife and daughter," he said, running his fingers over their faces as if touching their cheeks.

"Niece," Johann corrected him with a smile.

The boy continued to examine the photo, apparently lost in the image.

"That's why I'm back," Johann said.

The boy nodded and returned the photo to him.

"I saw them," Lukas said. "Two days ago, I think."

Johann felt a kick of excitement. The thought of such proximity was almost more than he could bear.

"Go on," he said to the boy urgently.

"They were like all the others who had been bombed out," the boy said. "I had come to see what had happened during the bombing and they were there. They were covered in dust and ashes, but I knew it was them."

"They looked healthy, though?" Johann asked, desperate to know more but aware of the foolishness of his question.

"Well, you know . . . ," the boy said.

"Do you know where they were going?"

"I tried to say hello to the girl, but they were both distracted," Lukas said. "I don't think that they saw me. Did you check the messages at your old building?"

Johann nodded. "I think that they're with a friend in Moabit."

"I see," the boy replied. He set about tidying some blankets that were resting on a chair before walking over to the bookcase and reaching for the weapon.

Johann stepped in front of Lukas before the boy could grasp the gun.

The boy looked at him, an expression of confusion and alarm soon adjusting into determination: If Johann wouldn't let him have the pistol, then he would take it.

"It's okay," Johann said.

"Give me my gun," the boy demanded.

"I have to find my family," Johann said resolutely. "But I'm not going to leave you here."

"I'm fine . . . ," the boy said, his eyes blazing.

"No, you're not," Johann told him. He used his greater size to emphasize his point, moving closer to Lukas. "I won't have it; do you understand me?"

The boy's mouth softened.

"I want you to come with me," Johann said. "I want you to have a chance even if your parents are dead."

"What if your wife and niece aren't in Moabit?" Lukas asked.

"Then we go to Lehrter Bahnhof," Johann said, trying to distract him from the gun. "It's our fallback plan. We'll escape west."

The boy stared past him.

"I want the gun," Lukas said.

Johann sighed and turned so that the boy could reach past him. The boy tucked the metal object inside his coat and walked to the other side of his makeshift bed. Johann watched as Lukas reached down and pulled a backpack from behind an oil-stained workbench.

"I have this packed so I can leave at a moment's notice," he explained.

Johann nodded, a small smile playing at the side of his mouth.

"What are we waiting for?" Lukas asked.

23

Anja could hear something that sounded like wailing, but she couldn't detect the source. Perhaps her hearing had been damaged. Nadine sat beside her, leaning against a wall, her legs drawn up tightly to her chest. The girl had her arms wrapped around her shins and her chin on her knees. The girl noticed that her aunt had opened her eyes.

"Auntie," Nadine said, moving toward Anja. "How do you feel?"

"I'm okay," Anja said. "Just a little groggy."

She looked around the room. The walls were covered from top to bottom in cream-colored tiles. The floor was concrete and there was a small barred window high up behind them. Anja knew exactly where they were. She had heard about this place, dreamed about it, dreaded it. She heard the noise of vehicles on the street outside and assumed that the automobiles were passing along Prinz-Albrecht-Straße between the Air Ministry and Gestapo headquarters.

"How long have we been here?"

"Only a few hours," Nadine replied.

"I can't really remember what happened . . . ," Anja started.

Nadine scooped some water from a pail and gave it to her aunt.

"They came for the boy," Nadine said flatly. "Then they came for us. We were ready to go as well. I wonder if our things are still at his house."

Anja looked around the room in alarm.

"Have you seen my coat?" she asked Nadine.

"They took them," the girl said. "All our other things are at Otto's apartment."

Anja nodded but didn't reply. They had no identity cards.

There was another jolt of dread: The letter from Johann had been in her pocket as well.

"They pushed you over," Nadine said. "One of the guards shoved you so hard that you lost your footing and banged your head."

The two of them sat listening for a while. The trucks passed outside. Anhalter train station was nearby, but there was no noise from trains—the place had been flattened. Occasionally they heard a pair of boots in the corridor behind the metal door that confined them.

"I'm sorry, Nadine," Anja said.

"What for, Auntie?" Nadine asked.

"I shouldn't have opened the door to the apartment," Anja explained. "If we hadn't gotten involved trying to help the boy and his mother we wouldn't be sitting here. We would have been gone by the time they came for us."

Nadine shrugged.

"We have all been involved for years," she said eventually. "It's really only a question of time before something dreadful happens."

Anja didn't reply. Did the girl really believe what she had just said? Is that what growing up in Germany over the past fifteen years had taught her? A grim certainty that, sooner or later, the water would rise above her head?

Anja searched for some words of comfort but couldn't find any.

"Perhaps the Soviets will come before too long," Nadine said. "Or perhaps we will be put in a camp."

"Time is on our side," Anja said, laying her hand on the girl's arm. "If we can just survive in here until then, we will be freed. These people don't have long. You can tell."

"Poor Hans," Nadine said.

Anja recalled her last, blurred memory of the boy strung up from the lamppost. She realized that the noise in her head wasn't the result of an injury—it was something she had preserved—the boy's mother's wailing. It had pierced even the rumble of the truck that had spirited her and Nadine to this place.

"We'll be okay—you know that, don't you?" Anja said, reaching out to Nadine. The girl rested her head on her aunt's shoulder. It seemed to Anja that the teenager was too exhausted even to embrace her.

Without warning there was a rattling of keys outside their cell. Anja pushed Nadine toward the corner of the room and stepped toward the entrance. The heavy metal door swung swiftly inward toward her. There was an older man on the other side, his face dented with scars. He looked at Anja and Nadine as if he was surprised to see them.

"Anja Schultz?" he asked testily.

"Yes."

The man stepped into the room and nodded to the corridor before coughing violently. Anja made to step forward, but before she could move she felt a hand on her shoulder. She was being pulled backward and turned around at the same time. It was Nadine. The girl hugged her. Anja let herself be held for a moment before pulling away. She turned to look at the girl as she reached the doorway and captured a mental image of her niece to cling to in the coming hours. Moments later she heard the door shut and the jailer's key refasten the lock.

Anja was led to an ancient freight elevator. The jailer—whom Anja recognized as one of the two men who had stepped from the staff car—closed two sets of sliding metal doors and threw a lever to one side. The contraption shunted shakily upward, the floors passing in front of them slowly. Anja wondered if she might find a way to overpower the man. He looked weak and disinterested—he was hardly the Gestapo man of the popular imagination—but she wondered what the real chances of escape were.

She felt fearful knowing that they would confront her with the letter Johann had sent her, but Anja had little time to consider a possible strategy before the elevator came to a halt with a shudder as the man threw the lever the opposite way. The contraption smelled of oil, the kind that Anja had once used on her sewing machine. She was led along a corridor and into a dark office. The room was small; there were two desks. The door closed behind her, and the man who had brought her upstairs disappeared into a corner.

As her eyes adjusted, Anja realized that the red-faced man she had seen with the soldiers who hanged Hans was seated behind one of the desks. He still had his coat on and was waiting with his elbows resting on his desk, his hands clasped together. Anja noticed that the man who had brought her here was now leaning back on a chair—which was up on two legs—regarding her curiously, as if he had never seen her before.

"We appear to have forgotten ourselves, Kuefer," Dieter said. "There is a lady present, and both of us are lounging around without offering her a seat."

Neither of the men moved.

"I will stand," Anja said.

Dieter got up.

"How very modern of you," he said, taking his chair and carrying it around his desk toward Anja. "But Kuefer here and myself are very old-fashioned, and we absolutely insist that a lady should be comfortable when she visits us."

She heard Dieter place a chair behind her.

"Sit," Dieter instructed her. Anja hesitated, wondering if there was even a chair behind her. Moments later she felt him press down on her shoulder, and she was forced into the wooden seat, which was still warm. There was a smell of damp wool from his coat and maybe boiled food. She had noticed that he had walked carefully toward her, as if exertion might cause him pain.

"So," Dieter said, "you are facing some serious charges."

An image of Hans flashed into her mind, and she could not control herself.

"Why did they hang that boy? How can a fourteen-year-old be the enemy?" Anja blurted out.

She cursed herself. She had vowed to remain quiet and compliant, yet within moments of entering the room she was admonishing the Gestapo officer.

Anja heard Dieter move across the floor. He appeared in front of her.

"Do you hear that, Kuefer?" he asked. "She wonders how a young man, who is perfectly physically capable, choosing not to defend the Reich, is not a traitor? Frau Schultz, apart from the boy's cowardice, Gauleiter Goebbels has decreed that every able-bodied man should be willing to defend the capital of the Reich from the Soviet assault. What kind of weakling or coward chooses not to do his utmost in this struggle? Do we really want people like this in our society, or are we best rid of their weakness and defeatism?"

Dieter left Anja an opportunity to say something, but she chose to remain silent. She had learned her lesson. The officer's mood had shifted from calm to agitated. He looked around at his companion, who remained seated and regarded her with curiosity.

It was as if he were studying the scene rather than participating. Anja noticed beads of sweat forming on her interrogator's brow. As if acknowledging this, he began to take his coat off. His movements were slow and tentative. The man in the corner's chair scraped as he stood up, intending to help.

"It's not necessary," the officer said abruptly. It took him perhaps two minutes to remove his coat, the garment peeling from him like a second skin that he was hoping to take off in one long movement. Once it was done he tucked in his shirt carefully and wiped the back of his hand on his brow.

"Your husband is Johann Schultz, is he not?" the man asked. He virtually spat the words. This was an accusation, not a question.

Anja nodded, resolved to try and maintain a level of control. She would not succumb quickly to this bullying. Dieter hurried to the desk where the other man was sitting and flipped open a manila file.

"And you were married on June 20, 1938?"

A flush of warmth flowed through Anja. What a wonderful day it had been: the friends, the food, the dancing beneath the stars. . . . All this just seven years ago. Her mind alighted on the day briefly. It seemed both distant and immediate.

"Answer the question," Dieter demanded, still standing on the other side of the room. His voice was flat, impatient, as if he was hurrying through preliminary material in order to get to something more meaningful.

Anja nodded again.

Dieter paused.

"So, Mrs. Schultz"—he stressed her surname heavily—"your husband is something of a hero, isn't he? A field surgeon for almost four years in the east, he has received numerous commendations. You must be very proud."

There was a sneering tone to the interrogator's voice that pained her even more than the threat of violence. It was the disdain for her husband that she could not bear. She could remain silent no longer.

"I am immensely proud of my husband," she said, her voice rising a little more than she would like. "And I know that he feels the same way about me."

She raised her chin unconsciously as she talked and realized that her aspect was one of defiance. She thought of Nadine back in the cell and tempered her movement. She sensed Dieter smiling slightly, as if amused by her passion.

"I'm glad to hear it," he said eventually. "That's as it should be, of course, but your position is, perhaps, slightly different."

Anja could sense him building toward something.

"Would you feel so proud of your husband if you discovered that he wasn't who he said he was?"

"I don't even know what you mean," Anja said. "How can I possibly answer a question like that? It's absurd."

"Absurd!" Dieter said, clapping his hands, a noise that shot through the fug of the room. "Absurd, she says." He limped toward her slowly. As he got close he raised an eyebrow.

"Would you also consider it absurd that your husband's name isn't Johann Schultz, but Thomas Meier?"

Anja narrowed her eyes. What kind of foolishness was this? How did he expect her to respond to such a ludicrous premise? Had she missed something? Was this some type of SS interrogation technique that attempted to throw its subject into a state of confusion? She had heard that interrogators often deprived their subjects of sleep, or that they exposed them to light or noise in order to throw them off.

"No, it's not," she replied simply. "My husband's name is Johann Schultz. You clearly have our wedding certificate. You can see for yourself. You can speak to him yourself at the front, if you wish."

Dieter peered at Anja.

"Why are you lying to me?" he asked, his voice flat now and quieter.

"I'm not lying to you," Anja told him.

"But you know you are."

Dieter walked over to the desk and opened the file again. He produced the letter from Johann that Otto had given her, the one that revealed that he was coming to Berlin. He held it by a corner and waved it in her direction. Anja didn't react.

"I believe that you are supposed to meet him at Lehrter station," Dieter said. "Better hurry . . ."

"That isn't my husband's handwriting," Anja said. "I don't know its source. It arrived a few days ago and I was surprised to receive it. All other correspondence from my husband states that he is still in good health and doing his duty at the front."

"So you deny that your husband is the author of this letter?"

Anja nodded.

Dieter examined the piece of paper as if seeking to determine its provenance through close inspection.

"In which case, would you deny the following: a thin scar on his right arm, a dislike of oysters, a passion for Bach?"

Anja listened. All three of these things registered with her. How did this terrible man know these things about her Johann? Had they captured him too? Was he also languishing in one of the cells after being captured while on his way to the station?

"The first was done while trying to climb over a barbwire fence into a farmer's field during the summer of 1927. The second was discovered the following spring during a trip to Langer See.

The last is a legacy of his father, Nicolas Meier, for whom young Thomas would play the piano."

Anja stared at Dieter. She was confused, but was determined not to show it. She knew that Johann loved Bach, but she had never heard him play the piano. There was a gleam to her interrogator's eyes now. He thought that he had trapped her. And maybe he had. Anja knew that she had run her fingers along the scar many times. She had swallowed oysters as Johann had pulled contorted, comic faces. And Johann had taken her to any and every performance of Bach that he could. He had even admitted to her that he had been named after the composer.

There was too much about what Dieter had said for it to be conjecture.

Either her interrogator really did know Johann, or he had her husband locked in one of the infernal cells in this hellish prison.

The sound of Kuefer striking a match broke the silence.

"Such a revelation must be a shock to you," Dieter continued. "I understand your silence. What wife wouldn't be surprised to discover that her husband has spent their marriage pretending to be someone else?"

Anja steeled herself. She would not let his words pierce her skin. He could throw barbs, accusations, and innuendos, and she would ignore every one. She knew that her Johann was loving and kind; even if the SS bully's words were true, it mattered not to her. She would be the judge of her husband. After years of war, she had little left, and she would not allow her faith in Johann to be shaken. To survive the conflict she had clung to her belief in her husband, and she refused to allow it to be contested by someone who had no capacity to love.

"I know my husband," Anja said more hotly than she would have liked. "You can tell me what you wish. It will change nothing."

"Ah, the devoted wife!" Dieter said. "Just as it should be. Dinner on the table at six. The children to bed and then a night of pleasantries, maybe something later on . . ."

Anja's mind was abuzz. It made no sense that an SS man had such a deep fascination with her husband and her life. What on earth did he want with her?

"Now," he said, leaning down to face Anja eye to eye. "You and I have something in common."

Anja tilted her head to one side.

"Really," she said, feeling a chill pass through her. She wondered what he could possibly have in mind.

"I am SS-Sturmbannführer Schnell, assigned to the Gestapo," Dieter said. "I doubt my name means very much to you, but it should."

His voice now was low and hard. Like he was sharing something elemental. Something that Anja absolutely had to know.

"Tell me," he said. "Does the name Schnell mean nothing to you?"

Anja shook her head. She was wondering if maybe she had encountered someone of that name before. Had she maybe taught a Schnell at school?

"I'm sorry," she said. "I can't think of anything."

Dieter chuckled and stood up, placing the palms of his hands on his lower back. He stretched backward before crouching so that his face was on the same level as Anja's. She crossed her legs just to break the tension.

Dieter said something so quietly that she couldn't quite hear him.

She thought that he had said, "We're related," which of course was absurd. She sat impassively, waiting for Dieter to say something else. He looked at her warily, suddenly less sure of himself.

"Did you hear what I said?" he asked.

Anja, fearing a trick, was wary of telling him that she hadn't.

"I asked you if you heard what I said," Dieter said. This time his voice was loud, filling the small, stuffy room.

"I'm sorry," Anja said, suddenly frightened. "I . . . I . . ."

Dieter took a breath.

"I'll tell you again then, if I have to," he said. He paused and then spoke again, this time enunciating his words and using his mouth to make out the shapes of the syllables. "We. Are. Related."

Anja tensed. She felt like she had been dealt a blow to the abdomen. She had a flashback to the letter that Otto had brought her: Of course, this was the half brother whom Johann had warned her about. The knowledge flickered across her face.

"Yes," Dieter said. "That's right."

He waved Johann's letter before straightening his back and looking at her in a way that no one had before. "I know all your secrets," he said.

Sitting at the back of the room, Kuefer made a connection—the slip of the *Sturmbannführer*'s tongue the previous day, when he'd said "Meier" instead of "Schultz," had been because the man they were hunting was his half brother.

Anja folded her hands in her lap and looked at Dieter as coolly as she could manage. Her instinct was that this damaged and dangerous man was completely deranged. But there was something about the way that he was looking at her that made her doubt her instinct. She had a clear-cut feeling that he was looking through her.

"You see, Anja," Dieter said, drawing out her name as he pronounced it, "I am in a strange situation. I need to find your husband, my half brother, as part of an ongoing investigation, and I had hoped that you might be able to tell me where he was. Only I don't need you or that niece of yours any longer. . . ."

Anja sat straighter. Dieter was beginning to get down to business.

"I already know that he has been in Berlin."

Anja's eyes widened—Johann was here? Why hadn't he come to find them? Had he been captured or injured? Surely the very first thing that he would have done would have been to find her?

"He paid a visit to the *Reichssicherheitshauptamt* here, just along Wilhelmstraße. . . . There was some lunatic, treacherous scheme."

Dieter let the thought float around the room.

"He was here, Anja, fewer than five minutes from this room only yesterday. He tried to undermine the war effort but failed in his attempt. He managed to escape, but it will not be long before he is captured."

Anja's spirits lifted a little—Johann was still free. He had come back for her and Nadine, just as he said he would. What she had been told about his past was irrelevant. He was the man that she had always believed he was. She wondered where he was at that exact moment and about the message that she had left him outside their former apartment. Had he located it? Did he know that they had gone to Otto's apartment?

"So you see, Anja, you have little value to me and Kuefer here since we have the letter that reveals your husband's plans," Dieter said. He was leaning against a desk now. He seemed tired, but was trying to hide it. "We can do what we want with you."

Dieter poured some water from a flask into a coffee cup. The cup was much too fine to belong in this office. He must have taken it from somewhere else. Kuefer shifted in his chair, leaning forward on his desk now, opening a file and examining its contents. The inactivity preyed on Anja's mind: She wanted only to get back to Nadine. Locked in a jail cell they could at least wait for rescue from the Soviets or Allies. She thought of Nadine curled up and alone. She needed to return to the girl. She could not allow her niece to be alone in this terrible place.

"What do you want?" Anja said. Her voice was bold. Dieter took a sip of his water before resting his palms on his legs. "Are you keeping me here solely to torment me, or is there a purpose to this?"

"I think you'll find that it is standard practice for the family of traitors to be detained," Dieter snapped. "And your conduct in this interview makes it very clear to us where your sympathies lie."

"But he has served his country!" Anja shouted.

"He is a traitor!" Dieter shouted back, standing up. He lowered his voice. "And so are you."

Anja swallowed. She wanted nothing more than to stand up and walk away. Every part of her body itched to rise from the seat. To flee from this terrible place. But she was trapped, no more able to escape Dieter than she was able to protect Nadine. Dieter finished the water in the cup and then slowly poured some more from the flask.

"There is something that might help," Dieter said eventually.

Something inside Anja flickered. She knew that Dieter's methodology was crude, but she couldn't help but want to move toward the shaft of light that he was offering.

"There is an object that I am searching for that is of great national importance," Dieter said, his eyes narrowing as if he were imagining the item. Anja said nothing, allowing him to savor his vision.

"A key," Dieter said emphatically, immediately staring hard at Anja to gauge her reaction.

Kuefer's ears pricked up. Here was something else for his notebook. Schnell seemed preoccupied with this key.

"A key to what?" Anja asked.

"That was not my question," Dieter said.

Anja thought for a moment. "I don't follow you," she said.

"Your husband has a key."

Anja thought of the key that Johann wore around his neck. She knew what it opened: the security box where he stored the family valuables. She had accompanied him to the bank on several occasions. She looked upward, as if trying to jog her memory.

"Well, he used to have a house key, and there were some others for his work . . . ," she said thoughtfully. She saw Dieter take a deep breath. "Is that what you mean? The key to the house, or to his office?"

Dieter stood silently before approaching her and placing his hands on the arms of her chair. He leaned in close. Anja could see every blemish on his cheek, every red vein in his eye.

"You *know* that's not what I mean," he said to her.

Anja stared back at Dieter as calmly as she could muster. His breath was foul, his teeth khaki.

"But those are all the keys that I can think of," she said.

"Fine," Dieter said, and stood up. He turned and communicated something to Kuefer, who walked out of the room.

"You should think carefully," Dieter said. "Some reflection on how you approach the next few minutes will serve you well. Who knows? You might even make it out of here alive."

Anja heard the door close. After a few moments she realized that she was alone. She wondered if she was being watched. If she stood up, would she find herself in deeper trouble? She shouldn't worry about that: *Is there deeper trouble?* she asked herself. She gently tried the handle of the door. It was locked. Pulling the blackout to one side, she tugged at a window, but they were all impossible to open. She looked around feverishly—there must be something in the room that would help her.

Anja rushed to Dieter's desk and began opening the drawers. They were full of office supplies—forms, pencils, tape, paper clips.

There was nothing for her. She pushed them closed and sized up the windows. She scanned the room for other options while trying to listen to what was happening in the corridor. Surely she didn't have long.

Then, out of the corner of her eye, she noticed a metallic flash from beside the other man's desk. She fell on her hands and knees and reached into the space between the edge of the desk and a radiator. She stretched desperately, her hand inching forward for the object. Her fingers were just inches away when she heard footsteps in the hallway. With one almighty effort she snatched it up: There—in her hands was a metal letter opener. She felt the sharp edges as soon as she grasped it, before quickly throwing herself back into the chair. As soon as she was seated she tucked the thing inside her skirt where it met the base of her spine.

Seconds later the door opened, and Dieter walked back into the room. He stood in front of Anja.

"I have someone to see you," he said, and gestured someone forward.

Kuefer led Nadine into the room. The girl walked past Anja, her arms crossed defensively. Anja gasped and stood up.

She turned to face Dieter.

"So this is what we have come to—terrorizing children?"

Dieter considered this for a moment.

"There has been no terrorizing," he said coolly. "Believe me, if there had been, the girl would be in a very different frame of mind."

"Take her back to the cell," Anja said. "There's no need for her to be here. I will tell you everything I can."

Dieter considered the offer before nodding to Kuefer, who led Nadine from the room. As the girl walked past she reached out quickly and squeezed her aunt's shoulder as the woman sat down.

Anja looked up at the girl and smiled. She wanted to show Nadine that she wasn't broken.

The door closed again.

"I warn you," Anja said. "If anything happens to her I swear that I will kill you."

"Really?" Dieter said disinterestedly. "I'm fascinated to know how you think you might accomplish that."

"What do you want to know?" Anja said contemptuously.

"The key," Dieter said. "And the bank where the security box is stored. I need to know."

Anja nodded.

"All right," she said, swallowing hard. She knew that Johann would forgive her.

There was no electricity in the corridors on the way back to the cell. Dieter had detailed Kuefer to escort her. The man kept a loose grip on her bicep, as if she might bolt at any moment. Anja noticed that he kept clearing his throat. She had heard the symptoms before. Breathing the smoke and debris caused by the raids had left many Berliners with chronic coughs and wheezes. The lights flickered on as they stepped around a pool of water that had collected on the concrete floor.

Anja recognized that they were nearing the cell that she and Nadine had been slung into earlier in the day. A set of keys jangled in her captor's hand.

"Inspektor Kuefer," she said, slowing down. "I understand that you are a man of integrity who is doing his duty for his country, but I wonder if there is any influence you could bear in the case of my niece and me?"

The man stopped. He was still holding her shoulder, but he was not looking at her unkindly. Anja decided to push harder.

"We are simple people," she said. "We have never done anything unpatriotic in our lives. All of us are just individuals living in a time of crisis."

"I understand," Kuefer said. He raised his chin a little and looked her in the eye. "Do you feel remorseful?"

Anja tensed. The question appeared genuine, but it filled her with fear.

"Of course," she said. "We understand that officers of the Reich are required to do their duty, no matter how harsh their behavior might seem to civilian eyes."

Kuefer grunted and nodded as if satisfied. "I have influence over the *Sturmbannführer*," he said. "If you are to escape this place you will need help. He is not a man known for his willingness to compromise."

"I can see that," Anja said.

"But first," he said, "there needs to be some compromise on your part."

He looked at her slyly, and she knew exactly what he meant. Hadn't it always been so with men and power? She noticed that there was a cell door open next to them.

"Here," Anja said, and led him into the room. It was exactly the same as the one in which she and Nadine were incarcerated, except that there was a single bunk lying against one wall.

"Sit down," she said to Kuefer, pushing him gently to the bunk. She put her hands on his shoulders and began to rub the muscles at the base of his neck.

"This understanding . . . ," she said to him, tracing her index finger along his jawline. "I want you to release my niece and me. Say what you want to Schnell; it won't matter. He's got what he wants."

"You know that I can't release you," Kuefer said. "That would be the end of me."

"Hush," Anja said to Kuefer, and moved her finger to his lips. "Be quiet for a moment and think about what you can do for us. Relax. You must be tired. Close your eyes just for a moment."

Kuefer's lids fell heavily, his eyes creased and dark with lack of sleep.

Anja continued massaging him with her left hand. With his eyes closed, the man looked old and dejected. Anja felt deep trepidation but, staring at the door behind which her niece was imprisoned, she felt a sense of righteousness as well: She would free them both. She reached around with her right hand to the back of her waistband and felt for the letter opener. The metal felt true in her hand, as if it were welcoming her grip.

The blade hit resistance for a brief second before slipping through into something soft that she assumed was brain tissue. She had committed the act as quickly and violently as she could. She supposed that this was the most humane—and effective—way to commit murder.

Kuefer slumped on the bunk, his body making a much louder noise than she had expected. The thump had a percussive effect around the cell. Anja didn't want to look at him, but she had to get the keys that he had been brandishing. She cast a sideways look at the man. There was a pool of blood—so much more blood than she ever would have expected—gathering around his head. She had seen many dead bodies after the raids. She tried to imagine that this was just another of those. Another casualty of war.

She felt along Kuefer's arm and down to his hand and felt the keys that were still hooked around his fingers. As she tugged at them there was a resistance—it felt almost as if the dead man were trying to hold on to them. Anja momentarily panicked that he was still alive and stepped back. She stared at his chest to check his breathing. She couldn't bring herself to look at his face. She would wait for his hand to wrap itself around her throat before she would look at his eyes.

The keys slipped free of Kuefer's fingers. Anja exited the cell with a prayer of thanks and made her way along the corridor. She tried to dampen the keys' metallic rattling as she went. While it seemed that she and Nadine were the only captives, she had heard footsteps along the corridor at regular intervals while she had been locked up. She imagined that they had perhaps five minutes to effect their escape before Kuefer was missed.

There were a dozen keys on the chain. She fumbled through them, desperately trying each to see if it would release the door. She reached the last key—nothing. She started again, working her way through them systematically. She thought of poor Nadine on the other side of the door, oblivious and undoubtedly terrified by what was going on. Anja wished she could risk calling to her. She tried key number five for the second time. It rattled uselessly in the lock. Six . . . Seven . . . Eight . . .

Come on, come on, she said to herself, becoming convinced that Kuefer had picked up the wrong set of keys and that she would be reduced to kicking and shrieking at the door to try and free her niece.

Nine . . . Ten . . .

The key turned sweetly in the lock and spun around twice. It was the most wonderful noise Anja had ever heard. She shoved the door open, and Nadine stared at her from a corner of the room where she was pressed against the wall.

"Aunt?" she said, a relieved smile breaking across her face. The two of them embraced. "But . . . ?" Nadine gestured, expecting an explanation.

"I'll tell you later," Anja told her, taking the girl by the hand. "We need to hurry." They stood at the exit to the cell.

"Hold yourself as if you work here," Anja instructed Nadine. "Things are falling apart, so the building is half empty. No one will question us if we look as if we belong here."

The two of them tidied their hair and arranged their dirtied clothing as best they could.

"There," Anja said with a rueful smile, pulling Nadine's soot-stained collar straight. "Typical Berliners. Now remember to walk confidently. We will be fine once we are out of this basement."

The two women walked silently along the corridor. Anja thought that it would be more plausible if they chatted, but she couldn't bring herself to speak. The corridor echoed with their footsteps. She was barely breathing because of the sour smell of the cells.

They came to the main door that secured the corridor. Anja found the larger key that she had seen Kuefer use and opened the exit swiftly. Passing into a hallway, they found another door opposite, which clearly led to another corridor with cells. They worked their way into another corridor, which had rooms that seemed to have been abandoned. Anja suspected that maybe these had been the guards' rooms. She checked on Nadine, her face fragile and tense. If they could only get up a level then they would find an exit from the building.

She needed to be calm, to remain in control. There must be a way out somewhere. . . .

There.

Anja saw a staircase at the end of the corridor. The pair of them hurried toward it and began to move up the steps carefully. Just then she heard the thump of boots—someone was coming down. Anja and Nadine looked at each other. Anja glanced behind them to see if there was somewhere they might hide, but there was no time to escape. Anja nodded to her niece and the two of them moved upward as the noise headed toward them. Anja's head was spinning with anxiety. She feared that she might vomit.

"It was such a relief to hear from him. . . ."

The voice was Nadine's.

"Absolutely," Anja replied as they climbed the stairs. "My last two letters went unanswered, so to hear that he received the care package I sent him was wonderful. . . ."

Above her, at the top of her sight line, she saw a pair of men's boots. They faltered in their downward progress for a moment. The man hovered on a step.

"Although I suspect that maybe he won't be needing the gloves you knitted him any longer," Nadine said, smiling.

"Oh, I imagine that he will find a use for them," Anja replied.

As they rose up the stairs a man's body came into view. He was wearing a uniform that she didn't recognize. He was some functionary, a janitor perhaps. She looked him square in the eye and nodded.

"Good morning, sir," she said.

He eyeballed her for a moment before continuing on his way. At the bottom of the staircase he looked back up at Anja and Nadine. By then they were gone.

Anja squeezed Nadine's elbow as they reached the ground floor. They were almost free. The two of them maintained the pretense of their conversation as they walked down a corridor with a parquet floor. The concrete of the basement had given way to wood. They were headed in the right direction, Anja was sure of it. They passed along a wide corridor with high ceilings. There were dark lines on the wall where artwork had been removed. On the opposite side of the walkway large oval windows had been covered in tape and blackout. Workers hurried past; Anja and Nadine mimicked the movements and bearings of those around them.

But where was the exit?

They were close, but they were still trapped in the building and time was short. The chances of their being recaptured grew by the second. Anja opened a formidable door at random and peered inside a large room containing a long table—a dining room. She pulled Nadine behind her and led the girl to the other side of the room and opened another door, which led to a passageway. She assumed that this would lead to a kitchen. They pushed their way through swinging doors into a room where a few old women sat glumly knitting and reading among steaming pots. Each of them looked up.

"Oh, I apologize," Anja explained pleasantly. "We've just been transferred here and seem to have lost our bearings. Could you let us know the way out, please?"

One of the old women raised a withered arm drowsily.

"That way," she instructed them. None of the others said a word, but they continued to stare at Anja and Nadine as if they hadn't seen anything so intriguing for years. "Go through those doors—one way will lead you to the front lobby, the other to the service entrance."

Anja started moving toward the door.

"If you're trying to get out of here discreetly, I recommend the right turn," the woman added.

Anja halted in her tracks. Had the woman actually said that? The kitchen staff returned to their knitting and reading. Anja and Nadine bolted for the door and moved to their right. Her heart leapt: She could make out daylight at the end of the passageway. They reached a metal gate that afforded access to the exterior of the building. The two of them peered out. There were three officers smoking next to a vehicle and a guard who controlled access to the courtyard.

"This doesn't feel right," Anja said to Nadine.

"Let's go the other way," her niece agreed. "We'll look believable if we chat."

"I'm afraid that's not going to work," came a voice.

Anja turned to see Dieter standing behind her.

"I was just on my way to fetch your husband," he said, "when one of the attendants let me know that he'd made a rather nasty discovery. Poor old Kuefer. I know how much he was looking forward to his retirement."

Anja felt a wave of exhaustion wash over her. Had they worked so hard just to be thrown back in the cell? With a murder on her hands she was sure to be executed. Her mind spun in a whirl of calculation: She would throw herself at Dieter and instruct Nadine to run. The guards outside would be distracted by the gunfire from Dieter's weapon. Maybe her niece might escape.

Suddenly a siren began to blare. Then another. The Americans would come in the daytime, flying so low it was as if they might brush the chimney pots. These raids offered very little time to prepare—the attacks were quick and unexpected.

"This way," Dieter said over the noise of the sirens, gesturing back up the corridor with his gun. "Quickly."

There was an explosion a few streets away, and then another, closer. The bombing pattern was moving toward them.

"Move!" Dieter said urgently. Farther up the corridor people were running to the shelters.

Another explosion—this time enough for them to feel the tremors. The three of them stopped moving. Each was now experienced enough with the bombardments to know what was coming next. Anja counted in her head: There would be a six-second gap until the next explosion. Her eyes met with those of Dieter. She sensed that he too was counting down the seconds to impact.

There was a percussive *whump* that sucked the air from them, and the building shook—the walls seemed to bend, and each of them was thrown to the floor by the displaced air. Plaster and timber crashed around them. There were screams from within the grayness that enveloped them. After a moment, Anja realized that she was unharmed. Her first thought was of Nadine. She lifted her hand to discover that her arm was wrapped around her niece's body. She must have acted to protect her instinctively.

"Quick," she said to Nadine, pulling her to her feet. The two of them stood up. They could see flames through the dust and smoke. Anja took Nadine's hand and they picked their way through the debris. The part of the building they were in appeared to be structurally sound, but there was significant damage to the interior shell. They worked their way along the corridor to the exit. Anja checked to see if Dieter was behind them before looking outside. The three officers she had seen earlier were gone—perhaps they had fled to the shelter. Their vehicle was partially covered in debris. The guard at the gate lay dead.

"Come!" she said to Nadine. The stairs down from a loading dock into the courtyard were impassible, so they worked their way downward by sitting and inching slowly across the rubble on their backsides. Once at the bottom, they picked their way across the courtyard, avoiding flames pouring from a ruptured gas pipe. They arrived at an archway, and Anja could see the street at the end of a passageway that was perhaps seventy-five meters long.

"Stop right there!"

Anja turned to see Dieter at the entrance to the building, his pistol leveled at them. She didn't think twice. She ran toward the exit, pulling Nadine with her along the long tunnel that led to the street. Shots rang out over their heads. Dieter slithered down the mound of rubble and hobbled across the courtyard toward them. He had no line of fire, as Anja and Nadine had disappeared through the archway. He arrived at the arch and saw the two of them running for their lives toward Prinz-Albrecht-Straße, their silhouettes framed by the tunnel. He thought about the key, and the riches of the security box. He would have his prize—and he would take Johann's family.

His right arm ached as he raised his pistol. Already damaged, his arm had been hit by something heavy during the raid and had gone numb. Looking down the barrel, he aimed at Nadine—the woman would stop when the girl went down. Then he would take them both. His index finger tightened on the trigger. He couldn't miss.

He pulled the trigger, and felt the satisfying thud of minor recoil. But Nadine was still moving. She didn't even appear to be injured.

Damn his blasted arm.

He fired two more shots. Still Nadine didn't hit the ground.

He tried again, but just as he had the girl in his sights there was a flash and a deafening detonation from an incendiary close by. Dieter got his shot away, but he knew in his heart that he had missed—the barrel of this weapon had jerked upward at the crucial moment.

Dieter cursed and leveled the weapon again; maybe there was still time. . . .

He fired again and missed.

He realized it made no difference: They had not eluded death.

In the distance, where the tunnel exited onto Prinz-Albrecht-Straße, he could see Anja and Nadine entering an inferno of fire and smoke created by the incendiaries.

Berlin was ablaze, and the two women were running into the fire.

24

The morning was so hazy that it was hard to tell whether the sun had risen or not. A few people scurried along the pavement in a hurry. Johann was of the same mind. Lukas moved nimbly through the streets beside him, his eyes scanning the road ahead for danger. Every hundred meters or so, the boy checked furtively behind them. When the pair crossed major junctions he scrutinized every direction before rushing across the road as if exposing himself to peril.

"It's okay," Johann assured him occasionally. He wanted to convince the boy that it was no longer necessary to conduct himself as if he were being pursued, to persuade Lukas that now he had an adult with him who would protect him. The boy remained unconvinced, his eyes shifting constantly, his body tense and prepared to confront a threat.

As they made their way west along the north side of the Spree, Johann felt utter dismay at what he saw. In the distance, it appeared that most of the university and Neue Wache—the tomb of the war dead—appeared intact, the buildings' neoclassical façades remaining like healthy teeth in a mouth full of smashed dentistry. Elsewhere, the city resembled photos he had seen of classical antiquity: a ravaged environment that had been abandoned to the elements centuries ago. He remembered being taken to see the Pergamon Altar on Museumsinsel as a teenager. He recalled how the ruins told the story of a distant culture that seemed almost mythical. Now the idea of Berlin as a center of commerce and culture seemed as hard to imagine as the court of King Eumenes—whose altar he had stared at one Sunday afternoon, brought to life in Europe almost two millennia after it had been abandoned to the elements.

Lukas pulled him sharply into a ruined shop. Overwhelmed by the stench of the charred building, Johann watched as a pair of SS men hastened past, their faces dour and strained. Both gripped MP 40 submachine guns tightly and had folded the stocks for use at close range. Johann knew that standard practice in civilian areas was to carry them so that the barrel was facing into the air. Neither of them was following procedure any longer. Rule book be damned.

"Well spotted," Johann said to the boy, who nodded in response. Johann ruffled Lukas's hair before checking that the street was safe and stepping back onto the remains of a stretch of pavement. Even though the city was close to being cut off, there were people—groomed and presentable, some of them clutching newspapers—heading to work. Most appeared to be ready for labor at the munitions factories, but there were also office workers maneuvering through the debris. Johann found it hard to believe that one man in navy overalls appeared to be wearing recently polished boots.

"How far?" the boy asked.

"Probably a mile and a half," Johann said. "As long as we can pass through all the streets we need to."

They continued beneath the gray, unforgiving sky, Johann barely registering the desolation around him for fear it would diminish his resolve.

At first Johann wasn't sure what the object in the distance was. Although the sun was now midway through its ascent, the day remained hazy, with occasional clouds of black smoke drifting across the blighted cityscape, shrouding the wreckage momentarily. Sometimes, when the stain lifted, it was as if it were revealing the carnage for the first time.

As Johann and the boy moved cautiously down the street, which appeared to have recently been cleared of debris, it became obvious that whatever they could see was hanging from a wrought-iron lamppost. Johann's eyes began to make out the object more clearly, and the horrible truth of what he was looking at became apparent. His first impulse was to stop; he wanted to avoid putting the boy through the dreadfulness of seeing a human being strung up in a suburban street. But the sight was now, it seemed, as customary in a residential area as postboxes and children's bicycles.

"A deserter," Lukas said, his voice hushed. He halted. "There must be an SS unit close," he added, pulling his body nearer to a wall.

"Come on," Johann said gently. There was a sickness in his stomach. A cloud of thick, acrid smoke had blown over them moments before, but he knew that it was his mind, not his body, that was the cause of his nausea. What if this was Otto? Had his friend been betrayed in some way? And if so, what might have happened to Anja and Nadine? The Führer's orders were straightforward: The family of a so-called traitor was to suffer the same fate as the transgressor himself. There was no mercy shown to civilians, no matter how distant they were from events.

Johann and Lukas crept down the street, moving from the road to a position where they could duck into shelter should they need to. There appeared to be no one around. Johann noticed a baby carriage, twisted and abandoned, in a front yard, its frame a ghostly white from dust. He felt a lump appear in his throat and swallowed it hard.

The two of them approached the body. It gradually dawned on each of them, silently and terribly, that they were looking at the corpse of a boy. The cadaver twisted slowly in the wind; Johann had to wait for it to revolve 360 degrees until he was able to read the crude sign that was hung from the victim's neck. He wore no shoes, his face was twisted grotesquely, his tongue hanging out. His trousers were soiled.

A pair of crows pierced the silence.

"This is what they are doing," the boy said eventually. "If they think you are a traitor or a deserter the end is quick. They say the SS executed a soldier on Mohrenstraße only two days ago. No questions asked." He formed the shape of a pistol with his thumb, index, and middle finger. "Boom. Just left his body there."

Johann recognized Otto's apartment building from a brief visit the previous Christmas when on leave. The construction was unfussy on the exterior, but inside most of the apartments were spacious, some extending to two levels. There was wood paneling on the walls in the lobby, tin ceilings with patterns stamped into them, and a large, ornate wooden staircase that creaked terribly.

If he had read Anja's chalked message correctly, this is where he would find them. He walked up the steps and reached for the buzzer.

"Come on," he said to Lukas. "We can rest a little before we leave. They might even have some food."

Lukas looked up at Johann from the pavement and shook his head. The feet of the corpse dangled above his head.

"I don't like it," the boy said. His eyes were dark and untrusting. Johann nodded his head, gesturing that the boy should join him on the stairs. He watched as Lukas did the opposite, positioning himself on the other side of the street near a ruined building that offered a quick and uncomplicated escape.

As desperate as he was to see Anja and Nadine, Johann was willing to wait another minute if it meant that Lukas didn't disappear. He walked across the road toward the boy.

"Come on," Johann said. "I'm sure that they'd love to see you again."

"Are you sure that they're in there?"

Johann wasn't sure—who knew anything in Berlin these days?—but he didn't want to offer Lukas an opening for doubt.

"They left a message," he said. "My friend Otto returned to the city days ago with a letter."

"Your friend Otto . . . ," Lukas started. The boy was perspiring a little. He had walked a long way with his backpack. Johann couldn't help but worry that maybe he had a fever. "Are you sure he . . . ?"

"I have known him for years," Johann replied. "We worked together. He's a good man, even if he is a little fond of his pipe."

The boy shook his head. "People change," he said.

Johann suddenly felt impatient—he wanted to see his wife and niece.

"Okay," he said. "How about this: I'll go into the apartment and get Anja, and she will come out and let you know that everything is okay?"

The boy said nothing. Had he been so damaged by the previous months that he had no belief in those he had once known and trusted?

"Anja will be pleased to see you," Johann said. He could see the outline of the pistol in the boy's coat. Lukas nodded.

"I'll ask her to come out and fetch you, all right?" Johann said, flicking the boy's chin playfully. He was still unable to get a smile from Lukas. "Just promise me that you'll stay right there."

The boy nodded, his face inert.

Johann couldn't wait any longer; he was bursting to be reunited with Anja and Nadine. He trotted across the street, his boots causing dust to rise up around him, his pulse quickening. Part of him regretted the quest that he had undertaken the past few days. Life would have been so much simpler if he had returned to the city immediately. He told himself to stop feeling self-pity—he was still alive, and so was his family. At that moment, nothing more could be hoped for.

Johann rang the bell and waited.

He imagined the pair of them wondering who it might be at the door. They would, of course, fear the authorities—everyone had learned to fear the unexpected stranger at his door—but he ached with the thought that they still had enough optimism to believe that it might be him, returned from the front, standing on the steps.

There was still no answer. He tried the bell again, this time pressing the buzzer longer and harder.

He felt a mixture of apprehension and fear. What if they were in there but decided not to answer the door for fear of the authorities? Worse: What if he had missed them?

Then he heard an internal door open and footsteps shuffle through the hallway. Someone was coming. He glanced back at Lukas, who was now waiting in the shadow of a building, and he stood tall, bursting with anticipation.

The door creaked open, and Johann's excitement quickly dissipated, his eagerness turning to edginess.

"Hello?" a middle-aged man said, squinting in the light that flooded through the door.

"I'm looking for Otto Deitch," Johann said. He tried to sound official. He was, after all, still wearing the uniform of a *Sturmbannführer.*

The man opened the door wide.

"Come in, come in," he said.

Johann waited on the stoop, his body aching to enter the lobby.

"And you are . . . ?" Johann asked.

"I live here now," the man said, scratching his bald head. He smiled, his mouth a mess of rotten teeth and gums. "Our basement shelter is flooded. I think that it must be coming from a broken main somewhere. Otto and I are trying to make it usable again."

"I see," Johann said. He crossed the threshold of the house. "I am looking for a pair of women, or I should say a woman and a girl, who are staying with Otto. They've been bombed out, you see."

"I know, I know . . . ," the man replied, wiping his nose with a filthy handkerchief. "You're the surgeon come from the front, aren't you?"

Johann paused. It wasn't like Anja to share sensitive information. He stared at the stranger and wondered if maybe Anja and Nadine had perhaps befriended him. Maybe, in extreme circumstances, he had become a confidante. War and desperation caused all kinds of strange alliances to be formed.

"Come in, come in," the man said, waving him forward. "What's wrong with you?"

Johann saw that one of his hands was so twisted with arthritis that he could barely open it. "They are excited to see you, but they don't want to show themselves on the street. They believe that they are in danger."

Johann walked into the lobby.

"We're all in danger," he said flatly.

"I know, I know," the man said, ushering him forward. "If it's not the British, it's the Americans, and they say the Soviet offensive will start within the week. Apparently there have been Bolshevik planes seen over the city."

Johann heard the sound of his boots on the wooden floor. It felt good to be inside a home again. He looked at the cheap art on the lobby walls. It felt like greeting old friends. He was glad that

Anja and Nadine had come here—this place was safe. While there was no protection from aerial attack, he was glad that his wife and niece had not been reduced to the wretched fate of the millions who were living lives of daily desperation.

"Go through," said the man, gesturing in the gloom. Johann walked into the darkness of Otto's apartment. He was immediately struck by a bad smell, something that reminded him of the terrible nights and days he had spent at the field hospital forlornly trying to save the lives of men who were unlikely to see the following day. Dying on Johann's table rather than in a ditch was the extent of their good fortune.

"Where are they?" he asked, turning to the man.

Total darkness descended: From nowhere a bag was placed over Johann's head. His wrists were grabbed and roughly tied behind his back.

It was over.

They had found him and—if they were at Otto's apartment—they must have Anja and Nadine too. He hoped only that the end would be swift for all of them.

The briefcase was stripped from his grasp, and he was bundled outside in a flurry of shoving and growled orders and lifted abruptly onto the back of a truck, which raced off toward Mitte in a cloud of diesel fumes.

The bald man closed the door of the apartment building and glanced about him. It had been a busy day. After informing the SS about the traitorous boy, he had been asked to help with the capture of a deserter. He had been a *Blockwart* for eight years and never before had he felt quite such a sense of accomplishment.

The wind kicked up a sheet of dust as he crossed the road. He sensed someone was watching him, and cast his eyes around.

Lukas shrank behind a mass of bricks that had been piled in an abandoned lot where a house once stood. His distrust was absolute. He had watched Johann being led from the house by the guards, one of whom had stopped momentarily to examine the boy hanging from the lamppost.

Then the bald man who had opened the door to Johann shuffled across the street carrying some bread.

Lukas knew that he must reach Lehrter Banhof.

If he was to be the last Berliner standing, then he would be the one to escape.

25

Anja and Nadine stood in the relic of a building on Zimmer-straße, their lungs aching from coughing. The older woman put her hands on the girl's shoulders and examined her niece. There were black smudges under the girl's nose from inhaling smoke. The girl gasped for air.

"Take your time," Anja said, "take your time."

She looked out into the street. Buildings were ablaze on almost every side of them; structures that had been burned out months ago were on fire again. Molten phosphorous dripped through the structures, causing the buildings to burn for a second time. There was the ringing of bells in the distance. The fire crews—composed of fatigued middle-aged men—would be there soon.

"You should rest for a minute," Anja said, leading Nadine to a pile of disused sandbags that had been placed in the burnt-out shell of what had been a grand building. Anja wanted to keep moving. She was aware that Dieter and other soldiers might come after them, but she couldn't risk going out into the open unless her niece was strong.

The fire trucks arrived, and the men jumped from their battered, filthy vehicles and began running out lengths of hose and locating a water supply. Some wore the dark green uniform of the professional firefighter, while others wore the blue of volunteers. All of them wore the signature fire service helmet, with its brass piece running from front to back.

Anja wondered if she and Nadine could go much farther. They were physically and emotionally shattered. There was now surely no chance of finding Johann. Nadine was spitting onto the ground—olive-colored chunks mottled her phlegm. God only knew what she had breathed in.

"We should go," Nadine said, wiping her mouth on her sleeve. Anja had to stop herself from scolding the girl. That kind of maternal reaction was for another world.

"You need to rest," Anja replied.

"I'm all right," the girl said. "I just breathed in something horrible after the blast. My hearing isn't right either."

Anja realized that her ears were still ringing too. It had become such a common part of living in Berlin under siege that she barely even noticed it any longer.

"We need to get to the train station," Nadine said.

Anja nodded. That was the plan. But she knew that it might now be too late to get out of the city. There had been talk even a few days ago that officials were preventing people—or "defeatists," in Party terms—from going west. To get on a train, in the unlikely event that they were still running, would involve procuring a so-called red card, the travel passes that allowed freedom of movement from Berlin.

Nadine stood up. Anja knew then that she had to steel herself. She had to keep going; she had to keep believing that they could escape from the city. And she had to have faith that she would see Johann again.

"We'll get into the U-Bahn at Friedrichstraße," Anja said, taking control. "It will be safer there. Once the raid is over we'll head to Lehrter."

She grasped Nadine's hands, and the two of them climbed over chunks of masonry and timber and stepped back onto the street. Hoses snaked in every direction over the road; the firemen worked in pairs to control the force of the water that was being directed upon the buildings. It seemed like a futile pursuit; the water, a tiny stream of liquid, was entering a voracious mass of flame. Both women put handkerchiefs over their mouths and ran east.

Anja had her head bent so low to avoid the floating embers and chunks of soot that she could barely see where she was going. She knew that they both needed to get belowground as soon as possible. She could hear the antiaircraft fire from the Zoo flak tower, which meant that another wave of aircraft would soon pass over them. The bombers could be on a mission to hit the nearby Reich Chancellery from which, Goebbels had announced, the Führer was directing operations for a famous victory over the Bolsheviks. Dodging through the ruins of the government district, Anja considered the absurdity of the notion.

Without warning, she felt herself crash into something. She wasn't hurt—the impact had been relatively gentle. She looked up to find herself staring into the weary face of a fireman, his eyes a seemingly impossible olive color. He grasped her arms and fixed his gaze upon her.

"Are you all right?" he asked. "You shouldn't be here. This building might collapse."

"Yes, yes, I'm fine . . . ," Anja said.

"Get to the end of the street and get underground," the fireman said. "Go now. Quickly."

"We're trying to get to Friedrichstraße U-Bahn station," Anja said. "Is it still open?"

"I believe so," the fireman answered. "But go quickly."

It had been the first time in years that she had spoken to a man in uniform other than the postman and not felt a level of anxiety. She returned the handkerchief to her mouth and continued along the street, more quickly this time, until she caught up with Nadine. The two of them continued until they were forced to move into the middle of the street by the heat and flames emanating from the Air Ministry, its façade turned a hellish black by soot. They passed onto Leipziger Straße and headed east, looking for a hole in the ground into which they might plunge to escape the fire above.

Dieter pulled the collar of his coat across his mouth and walked onto Prinz-Albrecht-Straße and into what resembled an inferno more than a city. Still angry at missing his shot, he was determined to make sure that Johann's family was dead. He wanted bodies.

His eyes cast both ways along the street. Heading west, the road appeared to be blocked by a collapsed building, which was still ablaze, a sheet of flame reaching into the sky. He doubted they would have attempted escape in that direction. As he walked the other way, he checked in possible hiding places to make sure he wasn't passing his quarry. He would not be returning them to Prinz-Albrecht-Straße; elimination was the only possible course of action following Anja's murder of Kuefer. He knew, of course, that was what he had wanted to do all along.

There appeared to be no sign of the women, but he remained convinced that they would have come this way. A fireman ran past. Dieter grabbed his arm.

"Have you seen two women come this way?" he asked. The man pulled his arm free abruptly.

"I'm busy," he said, and ran toward a colleague who was uncoiling a hose.

Dieter approached another who was spraying water into a building through a window and asked the same question.

"No," the fireman said. "I wish that I had time to keep an eye open for women."

Dieter continued along the road until he saw another fireman, this one turning large metal wheels on a fire engine.

"Two women passed this way," he said to the man, not bothering with formalities. "Did you see them?"

The fireman said nothing. Dieter sensed that he was being stonewalled.

"Tell me," he ordered the man, who held his gaze with intense olive-colored eyes.

"Why should I help you?" the fireman replied to Dieter, turning squarely toward him now. "Look at this. *Look at this.*" He raised his arms to gesture at the destruction around them. Dieter held the man's audacious glare. The noise from the fire, the explosions, and the flak was thunderous.

"You will tell me," he yelled, "because I am an *SS-Sturmbannführer.* If you don't do as I say, I have the authority to execute you on this very spot."

The man didn't lower his gaze. He stared at Dieter with contempt.

"And I believe you would," he said. "I've come all the way through this hell, out every night for three years with the RAF dropping death from the skies, pulling bodies from the wreckage, getting into homes to save the living, and you'd end it all here. I know you would. That's how we ended up in this madness."

Dieter pulled his weapon from its holster flawlessly. Still, the man didn't seem to lose his resolve. A senior firefighter came over to the pair of them.

"What's happening here?" he shouted. "This is no way for us to conduct ourselves when under attack."

"He has information vital to state security," Dieter said, not altering his gaze from the man in front of him. "I expect him to give it to me."

"What kind of information?" the officer asked.

"The whereabouts of two women who are responsible for killing a Gestapo officer."

This appeared to make no impression on either of the fire-fighters. Indeed, it seemed to Dieter that perhaps his words had had the opposite effect from what he had imagined.

"I have the authority to execute this man if he doesn't help me," Dieter continued. "I will ask for a final time."

"Come on," the officer said to his fellow firefighter. "Whatever it is you're doing, it's not worth it."

"Last chance," Dieter said to the man. There was steel in his voice.

The firefighter turned his gaze as if examining one of the burning buildings.

"You're headed in the right direction," he said nodding toward the east.

Dieter sensed that there was more.

"The rest of it!" he roared at the man. "Now! I do not have time for your foolish prevarication."

"They're going to Friedrichstraße U-Bahn station," the fire-fighter said. "And I pray that you never find them, the poor wretches."

Dieter began to laugh. It rolled up in huge waves through his body, the noise rising above the rowdy cacophony that surrounded them on all sides.

The two firemen looked at each other.

"They're going to Friedrichstraße station?" Dieter asked, holding his hand to his chest as he struggled for breath.

"Yes," the fireman replied. "That's what they told me."

Dieter's laughter rose up again in a second wave, his face twisted and glowing as if the man had told him the funniest joke he had ever heard.

"That really is . . . quite extraordinary . . . ," he said, as much to himself as to the men around him.

He lowered his weapon. The firemen hurried away, the junior glancing back at the *Sturmbannführer* with a hateful look. Dieter stood in the middle of Prinz-Albrecht-Straße, buildings ablaze around him and the deafening blasts of ordnance close by. His eyes welled with tears of laughter, the flames reflecting in the moisture.

There was no need for him to pursue them. The gates of Friedrichstraße station were to be locked within the hour—the station was to be flooded to prevent the Soviets from using the U-Bahn to move around the city.

He had seen the order: It was part of the Nero Decree.

Johann would be in Gestapo custody soon. Then they would all be dealt with.

The bombing continued as Anja and Nadine made their way from Leipziger Straße to Friedrichstraße. Anja had hoped that they would be able to get underground at Mohrenstraße, but the entrance had been blocked off by a collapsed building. The noise from the Zoo flak tower was constant, although the attack appeared to be focused elsewhere in the city for the time being. Anja clasped Nadine's hand and pulled her north up Friedrichstraße toward the ruined steel-and-glass structure that had once covered the S-Bahn station. The pair of them trod on glass and rubble from theaters and cinemas that had once lined the street. Anja recalled coming here to see American films in the early thirties. She had watched Garbo here for the first time, transfixed in wonder. Had been to plays at the Friedrichstadt-Palast. Now, she and her niece were almost the only people visible. A few others fled, seeking shelter. Everyone else was either in hiding or dead.

They arrived at the entrance on the east side of the street and hurried down the steps. The noise from the skies warned of a new wave of bombers over Mitte soon. Two policemen stood at the entrance to the subway.

"Come on, come on," one of them said. "They'll be here soon."

Anja pushed Nadine forward, and the two of them squeezed through the gate and into the gloom. Groups of people huddled in the lobby area, while others sat on the steps leading down to the trains. There were elderly people, some soldiers, women with children, foreign workers . . . all that was left of Berlin. Doctor Goebbels's plan for the defense of the city had proved utterly irrelevant to these people; they just wanted the end to come as soon as possible.

The water from the fire crews had made the floor wet and slippery; the soot and cinders from the fires had mixed with it, streaking the mustard-colored tiles black with filth. The deeper that Anja and Nadine pushed their way into the station, the more tightly it seemed that bodies were packed. Lighting had been jerry-rigged from a generator that had been placed next to a former ticket booth. After searching through the crowd, Anja found the staircase down to the platform. She reasoned that she and Nadine would be safer the deeper underground they were. If there was a direct hit on the station they would be able to escape along the tunnel.

As they walked down the stairs to the platform, she and Nadine were faced with a heaving mass of humanity. As the noise of the generator abated they could hear murmured conversations that were punctuated by the sound of explosions from above. People sat silently, looking upward as if watching to see if the paneled ceiling might collapse.

In the middle of the platform the booths that had once sold snacks and periodicals had long since been emptied. Families squatted inside, filthy and exhausted. A woman cut chunks of cheese for her children, who resembled urchins. Anja noticed that the woman also had a bag of rice. Her mouth watered.

"Where do you want to go?" she said to Nadine, looking around for a place for them to sit.

"Look," Nadine said, indicating a train that was parked at the station, its doors open. Anja peered inside to see dozens of injured soldiers lying on stretchers. Most of them were wearing uniforms and lay motionless beneath gray blankets. A few had wounds that had been patched with bandages and medical compresses. Anja wondered whether Johann had treated any of them.

"It's too dangerous in Berlin even for the soldiers," Nadine said. "Are we all to become subterranean? People will eventually go blind, like moles, foraging under the ground for grubs and worms."

"We will rest here," Anja said, leading the girl to a tiled pillar that had space for both of them to sit at its base. "And once the attack finishes we will get to the surface. We can make it to Lehrter in fifteen minutes. We will board a train there."

"Auntie, we don't have the papers," Nadine said.

Anja didn't reply. The girl was right, of course, but Anja was damned if she was going to admit it. She would find a way. She had to.

"As long as the station and tracks don't get hit today, there are still trains running," a man sitting near them said. He wore the uniform of a postal worker but was wearing an armband that showed that he had been drafted into the *Volkssturm*.

"South and west, so they say," he continued.

Anja felt a stab of anticipation. "Good luck getting on a train, though," he told them with a chuckle. "They're full of the families of Party officials. The golden pheasants are escaping the nest of their own making, while those of us who loathed them are left to take the punishment. It's all wrong."

Anja, still mindful of informers, said nothing. She turned to Nadine to see how her niece was. She looked frail now, her body that of an adolescent rather than of a woman. As much as they needed to get to the station, the pair of them needed rest.

"Is there water here?" Anja asked the old man.

He waved his hand down the platform. "There's a tap down there," he said. "It's still working."

"Thank you," Anja said. She picked her way through the wretched people huddled on the platform, all of them waiting for the end. As she walked she wondered what she should do about papers: The SS had taken her and Nadine's identification and ration cards. If they were stopped they would be arrested immediately. She consoled herself with the thought that the Gestapo and SS units on the streets hunting for deserters were not looking for a woman and a teenage girl. Most of them were fanatics focused on vengeance against those they considered responsible for the demise of the Thousand Year Reich.

Nevertheless she had much to fear: Dieter. He was dogmatic and remorseless enough to come after them. And he knew their plan to meet at Lehrter Bahnhof. Despite the risk, Anja determined that she had to go to the station. It was her only chance of encountering Johann, no matter how slim the odds of their meeting.

She had to keep moving, keep ahead of Dieter, even if it meant leaving Berlin without Johann. She could survive, she knew that: There were soup kitchens, and she would get ration cards from the NSV by telling them that she had been bombed out and had lost everything. A false name and address would not be checked; the places were full of women clamoring for help for their families. She would keep them alive by her wits. She would use the chaos as cover until the pair of them was safe.

She took a deep breath. The station was putrid; how she longed for some clean air. A battered pail had been left by the tap. She filled it with rust-colored water and made her way back to Nadine, trying not to spill any on people. The two of them scooped water out of it, drinking silently. Then both of them used it to rub the soot and dirt from their faces.

As Nadine leaned over the pail, it suddenly struck Anja that the girl needed a haircut. She wondered at the triviality of the thought.

Anja returned the pail and sat on the platform next to her niece. The girl leaned her head on her aunt's shoulder. Anja saw that, despite the water, the girl's hands were filthy.

"We will rest here," Anja said. "But not for too long. We must get to the station before they stop running the trains. Even if that SS man is looking for us"—she couldn't bear to think of him as Johann's half brother—"we must stick to the plan we made with your uncle. We must be very careful but leave as soon as the bombing halts."

Anja realized that Nadine wasn't listening. Her niece was fast asleep.

"This will be our last Berlin air raid," she said to the dozing girl, closing her own eyes. "Tomorrow we will be gone. I promise you that."

With that, Anja's head nodded forward and, as thousands of pounds of explosives were detonated only a few meters above, the pair of them was lost in a deep slumber.

26

Johann blinked as the bag was removed from his head. Two desk lamps, which had been set up only three feet away, were producing a blinding light. He wanted to raise his hands to shield his eyes, but they were secured to the wooden chair onto which he had been forced. It was impossible to see anything and the heat was stifling. The rest of the room existed only in shadow, although Johann suspected that two darker spots might be guards, silently watching.

Somehow they had found him.

He had feared this day for almost half his lifetime. Memories of that awful night his father was taken away were not buried that deep. Dieter's presence had revived the part of him that he had been happy to let lie dormant for so long. Then a powerful thought rose above all other considerations: Where were Anja and Nadine? Were they here in the same loathsome building?

He heard a dull thud. Something had been dropped on the floor.

"You have been busy."

Johann felt sickened. It was Dieter, somewhere out beyond the lights. He had hoped never to hear his half brother's voice again. He knew, surely, that this was the end for him. After what had happened at the hospital, Dieter would exact the ultimate revenge. He wondered at his half brother's resilience in the face of terrible injury.

Johann looked around, but he still wasn't able to see his half brother's face. He longed to stare into his eyes, to communicate how much he despised him, but Dieter remained disembodied—a ghostly presence disconnected from the earth, as much in Johann's dreams as in the real world.

"Medical school, married, on the eastern front . . . ," he said. "I'm surprised that I didn't bump into you. I imagine that you were one of those snobbish army types who wanted little to do with the SS."

"I believe that the SS were busy rounding up civilians and executing them," Johann said.

"Tut, tut . . . ," Dieter said. "I believe that you should presently be at the front tending to our brave soldiers, not hiding in Berlin with the other cowards and deserters."

There were brown shapes floating in front of Johann's eyes now. He looked down—his shoulders ached as he was unable to alter the position of his body.

"Not only do you kill at least one SS man, you attempt to kill me as well," Dieter said slowly. "By the way, whatever happened to Lehman? The fat driver? We know that you were seen with him the night before he disappeared."

Johann didn't wish to see anyone dead, but he recalled Lehman being a particularly nasty piece of work. The amount of death he had witnessed over the past three years made it hard for Johann to grieve for the driver.

"He fell," Johann told Dieter. "He was pursuing me through the woods in the dark and he ran after me and tumbled into a ravine. I don't think he survived."

"Sounds to me like it was as much his fault as your doing," Dieter said. "We are probably best off without oafs like that."

Johann was beginning to sweat now. A bead rolled down his nose and clung to its tip. He shook it off and it flopped on the floor. His half brother was standing perhaps only two meters away to his right, but still out of sight.

"How strange to see you dressed in this way," Dieter said to Johann. "In every army officer there is a secret aspiration to join the SS. You wear it as a costume, though, in your vain attempts to change the course of history."

Johann raised his head. It was only the day before, but his attempt to end the Nero Decree seemed an age away.

"Ah, I see," Dieter said. "Now I have your attention. I have to say that I was impressed by the daring of your escapade in the farmhouse, but your visit to Reinhard at the Ministry was even more reckless. Not like you at all. At first I found it hard to believe, but the officers at the farm identified you when they were shown a set of photographs. Reinhard did the same. 'We have an impressive fifth columnist here,' I thought to myself. ' Would that he had shown the same commitment to the Reich. '"

"I was doing my duty as a citizen," Johann said. "I will not stand by and allow Berlin to be destroyed and its people terrorized and killed. And I tell you this, for every fanatic—every self-described *Werewolf*—who is going to lurk in the ruins and continue the fight even when Stalin himself is sitting in the Reichstag, there are dozens more who will welcome the advancing armies with open arms, because nothing—and I mean nothing—could be worse than what you have done."

There were stars floating in Johann's vision, following a beating in the back of the truck that had brought him here. They seemed to cross from his eyes to his mind, floating like bubbles that he could catch if only he could reach out. There was a sudden slapping noise as Dieter began to clap slowly.

"Bravo," he said, moving his hands close to Johann's right ear. "I bet you've been thinking of that speech for quite some time. Rehearsing it in your head at the operating theater perhaps, or on your lonely bed somewhere between Smolensk and Minsk."

Johann tried to recollect his thoughts. Suddenly Dieter, his face scarred and discolored, appeared in front of him.

"If only your wife and—what is she, niece?—had been around to hear it."

Johann's heart ached with an overwhelming intensity.

He wondered: Had Dieter captured them at the house too? How he wanted to know if Dieter had them, but to raise their names would only demonstrate vulnerability.

"Yes, yes," Dieter said, "they have spent some time with us here at Prinz-Albrecht-Straße."

Johann sagged. He imagined them in the infamous basement. They were just a few flights of stairs away. He ached to see them one last time. He doubted, once Dieter got what he wanted, that he would last long. This was likely to be the last hour of his life. As the realization pulsed through his being, he was mindful that the threat of death had hung over him almost for as long as he could remember. Every minute was simply an extension; all you had to do was keep surviving for another hour, and another hour after that. If you added them all up then the total grew to be a lifetime.

"Your wife really is quite attractive," Dieter announced.

Rage captured Johann's entire being. He stood up and tried to swing his body and the chair in Dieter's direction before feeling a violent blow to the side of his head. Unprepared for the impact, and unable to use his hands to break his fall, he crumpled to the linoleum floor. He lay for a moment, drool sliding from his mouth.

"They are not dead yet," Dieter announced. His words were enough to make Johann sit up.

"It turns out that you and I have some unfinished business," Dieter said. "I am not a vindictive man, so I will give you a choice. If you tell me where the key to Nicolas's safe deposit box is and identify the bank, then I will let your wife and the girl go free."

Johann's head began to clear. He knew that he was being manipulated, but he no longer cared. Part of him was amazed that Dieter was still obsessed with discovering what was in the box.

"I want to see them given passage to the west," he said. "Then I will cooperate."

"Ha!" Dieter snapped. "You should be aware that there is no room for negotiation." Johann heard him move a chair. There was a grunt. It sounded like he had sat down.

"I want to see them board a train to—" Johann said deliberately.

"Shut up!" Dieter responded quickly. "Take it or leave it. Either way, you're not going to make it."

Johann kept his head bowed to protect his eyes from the light. He heard footsteps and then hands lifted him upward until he was vertical again.

"What will you do?" Johann asked.

"You're going to make a leap of faith," Dieter replied. "We will simply turn them out on the street and let them fend for themselves."

Johann was taken aback by Dieter's candid answer. Did this mean that he was telling the truth?

"You know full well that it's a killing field out there," Johann answered. "They won't last long. . . ."

"Yes, yes," Dieter interrupted, "and then the Soviets will be here—we all know what happened in the east.' I'm afraid that none of this is my concern. I want what I want; that's all there is to it. I have made you an offer—a generous one at that, given the crimes that your wife has committed—and you are in no position to decline it."

"All right," Johann replied, wondering what Dieter meant—Anja had never conducted a criminal act in her life. He heard Dieter stand up. There was suddenly silence in the room. "The bank is the Danat-Bank on Behrenstraße on the corner of Glinkastraße—if it's still there."

"It still exists," Dieter blurted. There was excitement in his voice.

"The box number is 1518," Johann continued.

"That's . . . ," Dieter started.

"Yes," Johann said. "The years of our births: 1915 and 1918."

There was a longer silence. Johann's skin was burning from the light now. He heard something being picked up and the sound of swallowing. A cup or glass was then set down.

"And . . . ," Dieter said. "The key . . ."

"Let me loose with Anja and Nadine and I'll take you to the key," Johann said. "I'll take you to the apartment—I give you the key and you turn your back."

"I won't do that," Dieter said. "Impossible."

"Then I'm afraid that you'll never know what is in the box," Johann said. He felt as if, just maybe, Dieter was ready to give some ground.

He was wrong.

He felt another blow to the head, this time a slap to his face. A big, jagged canary flash joined the stars in his line of sight. The perspiring face of his half brother, a man almost trembling with rage, joined them in his vision.

"Your choice," Dieter said.

Johann was hauled to his feet. He was led to another room where there was rubble on the floor from plaster and brick that had been shattered during a raid. As he regained his sight he could see deep cracks in the walls of what appeared to be a storage or utility room with low ceilings. There was some daylight coming through one of them; he knew he was aboveground. His handcuffs were unlocked, and Johann was silently and forcefully maneuvered beneath a piece of pipework that had been painted over many times with black paint. His hands were then raised and handcuffed over the pipe. He could just stand on tiptoe.

Johann heard the same thudding noise that he had identified in the other room. He turned his bleary eyes to decipher its provenance: Dieter dropping the briefcase on the floor. He was carrying it from room to room, unwilling to let it out of his sight.

"I will pay a visit to your wife and niece and tell them what you decided," Dieter said, closing the door behind him. A key turned in the lock. Johann pulled on his handcuffs. Surely his half brother wouldn't harm Anja and Nadine until he had what he wanted? Johann tried to think the situation through. He knew that he couldn't trust a single word Dieter said. The pretense of releasing Anja and Nadine onto the street was simply a ploy. There would be no release. Johann tried to steady his mind, which had become a storm of dread and alternatives, all of which seemed dismal.

There was only one thing he could do: hang on for as long as he could without revealing anything. If, as everyone said, the Soviet assault would be over within a few days, then he had to find a way of delaying Dieter from killing them. Anyone held by the Nazis would surely be freed. Johann tried to convince himself that the approach was plausible, but he found it hard to have a great deal of faith: Dieter had no time for prevarication.

He would die in this room; that much was clear. He must accept his fate.

Now all that mattered was planning a way to save Anja and Nadine. If he could convince Dieter that he would accompany him to the bank it would use up some time. Moreover, moving around the city was so fraught with danger they might be killed. With Dieter dead, Anja and Nadine might last until the Soviets arrived.

Johann pulled against the cuffs. His hands were numb and he couldn't feel his shoulders any longer. He stared at the crack in the wall. A sliver of light shone through, illuminating part of the room—a few inches that proved that there was a world beyond the terrible place he was trapped within. He might not be able to wedge his body through the masonry, but his mind exited the room.

He would find a way out.

The door opened and Dieter entered, this time alone. He was clutching what looked like a wooden staff.

"Your wife and niece are too keen to leave the building," he said. "I informed them that their fate is in your hands, and they found it hard to believe that you wouldn't help them."

"What's the point?" Johann said. "You won't free them."

At first the thud on the right-hand side of his ribcage stunned Johann. Then he realized that he was unable to breathe. His body began to shake before he was able to take several low, hard breaths.

"Enough of this," Dieter said. "The location of the key. Quickly."

Johann was still trying to regain his breath when his half brother approached and grabbed the front of his shirt with his fist.

Johann closed his eyes.

He no longer had anything to bargain with.

Dieter looked down at his fist and then up at Johann, his face cracking into a broad smile. He loosened his hand and examined the front of Johann's SS shirt before ripping it open. Johann felt the chain with his army dog tags snap. He had protected the key his father had given him for eleven years in an attempt to prevent this moment.

Dieter grasped the object triumphantly.

"Hoping to keep it all for yourself, were you?" he said.

"Yes," Johann said. "It was for after the war. To help us start again."

"Surely you know by now that there will be no 'after the war' for you?" Dieter said, his face disbelieving. "Did you really think that you would be able to do what you have done and get away with it?"

Johann looked at Dieter incredulously. "And you think you'll just walk away? After all you've done?"

"I am not planning on eating cabbage for the next few years," Dieter said. "There will be places for us in Bavaria where we will be able to live well—"

"You have nothing to say to me other than this bragging?" Johann said, interrupting Dieter. "You kill my father, then—"

"I didn't kill your father," Dieter cut in. "Your father was the master of his own demise. His ideas were dangerous."

"Dangerous!" Johann scoffed. "He was no more dangerous than the Christmas tree you helped him decorate."

"He had no place in the Reich," Dieter answered. "If your father had his way, this country would be burdened by the weak and outsiders."

"You threw my father in the back of a truck and had him transported to Oranienburg!" Johann shouted. Flecks of spit shot from his mouth. "What on earth would make you think that he might survive such treatment?"

"Do not raise your voice to me," Dieter ordered, coming closer to his half brother. "You *still* think that you're superior. There you are, strung up, wearing a uniform that's not yours, desperate to save yourself and your family, and you have the audacity to lecture me? You and your father sat on your high horses, masters of condescension both. You thought that you were above the real world, above those of us who didn't possess minds equal to yours. Look where it got you both."

Johann shifted his weight. His entire body was throbbing. He was desperate for water.

So, this is how it would end: in a damaged room in a government building, a victim of fratricide. Johann had spent years burying his true identity, yet it eventually pulled alongside him and pushed him over a cliff.

"Dieter," he said. "I know nothing I say will affect what is going to happen in this room. But I'd like one final request: Anja and Nadine have nothing to do with this—they have no knowledge of you or my past. I ask you—in our mother's name—to let them go free."

Dieter smoothed down his uniform. His hands were as ruddy as a farmer's. He was still wearing a coat despite being inside.

"You mention our mother," Dieter said flatly. "Do you think that such sentimentality will affect my judgment, or prevent me from doing my duty as an officer of the SS who has captured an enemy of the state?" He paced across the floor, kicking at pieces of masonry as he went. "There you go again—you see, thinking that your weasel words will persuade me to divert from honor and duty."

Johann pulled against the handcuffs, which bit into his wrists. If he could get to Dieter he would gladly kill him. There was nothing, not even the most remote seed of a human bond between them any longer.

"I mention our mother because I am hoping that you might remember something other than your ideology," Johann persisted. He had nothing left to fight Dieter with other than words. "I want to see if I can stir any remnants of compassion and decency that might remain. My wife and niece do not deserve your brutal street justice; they are innocent of any crime."

Dieter stepped closer to Johann, who steeled his midsection for another blow from the staff.

"Not true . . . ," he said calmly. "On either count."

"Don't lie to me!" Johann shouted at him.

"Your wife killed an SS officer only a few hours ago," Dieter said matter-of-factly. She stabbed him in one of the cells in the basement as she was being returned to her cell. She used his own paper knife. Funny . . . ," he continued, "he could never find that knife."

Johann didn't believe what he was hearing—Anja a killer? It wasn't credible. Yet, he had done things in the past few days that he would never have imagined himself capable of. Desperation and fear had made slaves of them all.

"But this is before she escaped," Dieter said.

For a second time in a few moments Dieter's words made Johann flinch. The negotiation they had just undergone had been a charade? Dieter had pretended to have his family while it had been he alone who was captured? It took him a moment to process the new information.

"And the girl?" he asked. "What of her?"

"Oh, she went too . . . ," Dieter said. "During the middle of a raid."

Johann no longer felt the pain in his arms. He was content: Dieter could do his worst. Anja and Nadine had a chance of surviving. That was all that mattered. There was silence for a moment; the two men stared at each other. Johann noticed a smile creep into the corner of Dieter's mouth.

"You think that this is over, don't you?" he said. "I kill you and your wife and niece escape."

Dieter held up the key.

"I have what I want, you have what you want, the end. Correct?"

He reached into his coat pocket. Johann heard the key drop onto something else metallic.

"But you see, your wife and niece have stumbled inadvertently into another unfortunate and difficult situation."

Johann tugged on the handcuffs again. He looked up and realized that the pipe was narrow enough for him to grasp—if he got his hands around it he might be able to swing his body and kick Dieter off balance. The gesture was futile, he decided. He would still be chained to the thing.

"You see, they were seen heading down into Friedrichstraße station."

A color flashed into Johann's head: the yellow tiles that extended from the platform up to the lobby. He thought for a moment: The U-Bahn was one of the last safe places in the city.

"They couldn't know, of course, but they have made a considerable error," Dieter continued.

Johann watched him intently. *Here it comes*, he thought, *another lie*.

"You may know something of this, as you are, of course, well versed in the executive order Demolitions on Reich Territory."

Dieter lingered for a moment. He appeared to be enjoying himself. "The Nero Decree, remember, Johann?" he said.

Johann's heart began to race again. He took a deep breath and tried to control the panic that threatened to conquer him.

"You see, there is no need for me to kill Anja and Nadine," Dieter continued. "They have done it perfectly well themselves."

Johann was trying to fathom exactly what it was that he was being told. He shook his head. He understood Dieter's words but needed to process them.

"Am I not making sense to you?" Dieter said eventually. "You know the compass of the order. The Führer will not allow the enemy use of the tunnels to move around the city freely."

Dieter reached up and patted Johann on the cheek.

"Your wife and niece have just climbed into a mass grave," he said calmly.

Johann felt his stomach clench tight. The words were crushing. He felt as if his mind was shutting down. His thoughts coalesced around a single fact: His wife and niece were doomed. The Nero Decree was in effect. Everything he had attempted to do on his return to Berlin had come to nothing: He had failed to save his family; he had failed to stop the destruction.

Madness had prevailed. The strain on his shackled body was exhausting. Sweat poured from his face. He could take this no longer.

"It seems that time is up for our reunion," Dieter said. "This one has taken far too long to come about, and I'm afraid that there won't be another."

Johann watched as Dieter's right hand began to slide toward the pistol in his holster.

"Thank you for your gift," Dieter said, patting the pocket of this coat where the key rested as he continued to reach for his weapon. "I will use it well."

This was it, the denouement, Johann thought.

He thought of Anja and Nadine in the darkness and the cold of the station, the crash of ordnance around them. He saw Dieter unfasten his holster and begin to pull the pistol free.

This was his last chance.

As Dieter leveled the gun at him, Johann reached up and gripped the pipe, lifting his feet from the floor and using every ounce of his energy to pull downward. Dieter looked startled for a moment, as if astonished by the resistance. The brackets holding the pipe to the damaged ceiling gave way, and Johann was suddenly falling. As he had intended, the pipe smashed Dieter flush on the top of his head. Johann's half brother fell to the floor, groaning and holding his head. Plaster dust hung in the air around them. Johann was still chained to the pipe. He knew he had to act quickly while Dieter was stunned. He moved along the pipe, sliding the handcuffs along the metal until they ran clear. His arms ached, but he was able to move freely at last.

Dieter lay on the floor. Johann fell upon him and pulled the keys to the cuffs from his half brother's belt and quickly undid them. He rubbed his wrists and shoulders; the pain was severe, despite the adrenaline coursing through him.

The briefcase was sitting against the wall where his half brother had dropped it.

Just then he noticed Dieter moving. His half brother was reaching for his weapon, which lay nearby. Johann dived for the gun, grabbing it from his half brother's grasp. He felt the weight of it in his hand. At last, he was the one with the power. He pointed the pistol at his half brother's head. Dieter didn't flinch.

"Go ahead and do it," he said to Johann. "You can kill me, but you won't survive this. It's over, Johann. We're finished. All of us."

"Speak for yourself," Johann answered. His finger tightened around the trigger. He prayed to his mother for forgiveness.

There was a click.

The weapon had jammed. Dieter, realizing what had happened, was suddenly roused from passivity; he rolled to one side and began to push his body from the ground. Johann turned the gun in his hand and began to hit Dieter. His half brother roared and flailed with his arms, pushing himself around the floor to try to avoid Johann's blows, but his bandages and wounds slowed him.

Johann was exhausted. He gave up using his arms, both of which were numb, and proceeded to kick Dieter, showing no mercy. Eventually Dieter stopped defending himself. Johann could tell that his half brother was still alive, but he was surely unable to pursue him.

He reached for a brick to dash Dieter's brains out, then stilled himself: He knew what, to Dieter, would be worse than death itself. And Johann and his family would be gone before Dieter discovered it.

He reached down into his half brother's pocket. The key was still nestled there. He left it.

The security box would be his half brother's first port of call.

Johann straightened his uniform, picked up the briefcase, and walked into the corridor. As he fled from the building, a lone security guard saluted him.

SS units were gathered around Stadtmitte station—where an SS panzer division was said to have set up its headquarters—and along Friedrichstraße. Johann thought that they must have received the orders to erect a second ring of defenses beyond the one on the outskirts of Berlin. Clearly they were preparing to defend the citadel—the government buildings in the middle of the city—on the assumption that the outer defenses would be breached. Johann could hear the flak towers firing at enemy aircraft above. There were distant explosions of ordnance.

He was almost too excited to imagine that—finally—he would encounter Anja and Nadine. Had Dieter been lying when he revealed that this was where they had gone? He cast a glance back at the edgy SS soldiers farther down the street and gripped the briefcase tightly. He had to get them out of the U-Bahn quickly before the Nero Decree was enacted. He might only have minutes.

Johann reached the U-Bahn and pushed his way down into a scene of human misery that, even after years on the eastern front, he found hard to imagine—filthy women, children, and elderly people cowered in the darkness, exhausted and haunted. They no longer looked like living human beings but like the damned. They were waiting for the end to come. Johann felt a sense of dread: If this was his family's best option, the others must be unimaginable.

He searched the desolate faces, some impassive, some staring at him in terror. Others saw the SS uniform and glared at him with unconcealed disdain; the pretense was over, and those who had once feared to confront the agents of dread now felt that they had—literally—nothing left to lose. The sick and injured lay alongside families sharing their meager rations. The blue light flickered on and off. There must have been a generator somewhere, as the electricity had failed elsewhere in Mitte. He thrust his way through the crowds, examining faces, each time telling himself that his loved ones would be among the next group.

One of the wounded soldiers on a train parked in the station gave out a curdled groan. Johann glanced aboard and witnessed a scene familiar to him: a filthy space full of wounded men with little chance of recovery. A few fatigued nurses bustled about, but there was no sign of a doctor. With some guilt, Johann continued along the platform, stopping to adjust his eyes wherever the gloom deepened.

And there they were.

At first he hadn't recognized them; their hair was unkempt, their faces smeared with soot. Their worn clothes looked like they were the property of some other, larger person. But he had no doubt about their identity. It was his Anja, his Nadine.

"Anja," he said, keeping his voice quiet. He couldn't be sure he could trust those nearby. His wife had her eyes closed. There were still explosions going on overhead, but she appeared to be deep in sleep. Johann crouched down next to her.

"Anja," he said, more intensely this time. He took her hand and squeezed it. His wife awoke, tumbling into consciousness, falling forward as if in a hurry.

"Wha . . . ?" she said, momentarily alarmed. Then, more slowly than Johann could imagine possible, a smile of recognition spread across her face.

"Anja," Johann repeated, leaning into her and holding her close. "Anja."

"We knew you would come," she whispered into his ear. How light she was. Her shoulders felt scrawny, her body almost weightless.

"I'm here now, I'm here now," he said, examining her from behind his tears.

"Come on now," she laughed, "no time for crying."

She held his face and kissed him, her lips encountering stubble and chapped lips. He stroked her hair. It was full of cinders and grime.

"Onkel Johann!"

Nadine was hugging him now. He took the girl in his arms. She was so much bigger than he remembered her only a few months before, but she too was perilously slight.

"I knew you'd come," she said, holding him to her. "I *knew* you'd come."

She pushed him back to get a better look at him.

"I can hardly believe my eyes," Nadine said. "Are you sure that you're not an illusion?"

"No, no . . ." Johann smiled. "I'm here. We're together now."

He noticed them examining his uniform. "Ignore this," he said. "I'll explain another time."

He reached his left arm around Anja and brought Nadine closer with his right. He held them both to him, feeling the warmth of their bodies, their redeeming presence. They were together again, and he would not allow them to be separated. They would break out of Berlin together. They would survive.

"They say that there are trains still leaving from Lehrter station," Anja said to him. "There are still people trying to get west. Maybe we—"

"We need to get out of here now," Johann said urgently, interrupting her.

"Of course," Anja replied, although she didn't move.

"No," said Johann. "*Right* now. We are in terrible danger."

Anja looked at him as if he were insane. Did he think she wasn't aware of their predicament?

Johann bent down and lowered his voice. "They are going to destroy the U-Bahn."

Anja's expression shifted from confusion to pure terror.

"Let's go," Johann said. They began moving through the crowd quickly. He put his arm around Nadine, ushering her through the mass of people, most of whom were sitting miserably on the platform. Suddenly Johann heard shouting ahead of him—many of the voices were women, and some of the male voices were old. These were not military voices, but civilian ones. There was a scrum of people on the stairs up to the exit.

"They locked the gates," said one woman.

"Who has?" another asked.

"The SS," the first woman said.

"*Why?*" the woman asked, panic in her voice.

The other woman ignored her. Instead she joined the chorus of voices screaming up at the entrance. No one was able to see what was happening; alarm was rising.

There was no way out of the station.

"Coming through," Johann said, raising his hand to guide his way through the crowd.

As people saw his uniform the mob parted. Angry, emaciated faces watched him, incensed.

"They left you behind, did they?" said one sneering face.

"Get them to open the gate, you bastard," said another.

Johann was shoved; he felt blows on his back and head. The infuriated crowd wanted a scapegoat. He managed to make his way to the top, where he checked that Anja and Nadine had followed him.

"Keep close by," he insisted.

There were people pressed up against the sliding metal gates calling up to the soldiers above, begging to be freed. Johann came close to the gate. Maybe he could use his uniform to order them to reverse their actions.

But then he realized that he was too late; the Demolitions on Reich Territories was more powerful than one officer. Johann looked for a soldier nearby with whom he might negotiate to at least allow the people trapped inside to leave. The soldiers had retreated to street level at the top of the stairs, perhaps to avoid the screams of those trapped below. He looked at the people around him: None of them knew what was to come. The rank air that each and every one of them was breathing would be the last they would inhale. Johann pushed his way back through the crowd, dragging Nadine, Anja, and the briefcase with him.

"What's going on?" he was asked.

"Why don't they open the gates?" demanded another petrified person.

"Let us out!" commanded someone else angrily, shoving Johann.

Johann kept moving, steering Anja and Nadine through the scrum. They arrived back where they had first met, toward the rear of the platform.

Johann whispered to Anja, "We can't have long now."

"The tunnel," she replied. "We can escape along the tunnel."

There was more agitated shouting and screaming from above. Johann nodded.

"There are no trains and no electricity," Nadine added.

"Let's go," Anja said, heading toward the end of the platform. The three of them passed the end of the hospital train and clambered down onto the tracks.

"This direction will take us to Lehrter, right?" Nadine asked.

"Yes," Johann said. "It shouldn't be more than a twenty-minute walk, and we'll be safe from the bombing."

After about fifty meters the blue glow of the light in Friedrichstraße began to ebb. The three of them were in total darkness. Johann turned and looked back at the station. It existed now only as a receding and distant indigo blur. As remote as a star. There was nothing to guide the three of them forward. The next station would be Lehrter. It was either too far in the distance for them to see, or its generator had failed.

"What if there are no trains running?" Nadine asked, her feet clattering on the stones beneath their feet. Every so often one of them would trip over a railroad tie or an electrical installation.

"Unless it was hit today, the trains are still running," Anja said. "That's what people are saying."

"But we don't have travel documents," Nadine said.

Johann heard Anja groan—but it wasn't because of the question. She had tripped. He groped his way through the darkness and helped her to her feet. Nadine sensed what was going on.

"Are you all right, Tante?" she called. She was slightly ahead of Anja and her uncle now. Johann's eyes were adjusting to the darkness a little, but it was still hard to see much other than the outline of objects.

"Yes, yes, I'm fine," Anja replied through the gloom. "Keep going, Nadine, keep going. . . ."

Her mind cast back to what Dieter had said about Johann. Now wasn't the time to question her heart. Her husband's return for them told her all she needed to know about who he was.

Johann helped his wife forward. He was expecting a blast at any moment, if Dieter was to be believed. They continued to trudge along the tunnel. Johann's shoulders ached. For a moment the noise of their shoes on the gravel beneath the tracks made him think of a beach he had once visited on the Black Sea. For years afterward he'd imagined that all beaches had stones. It came as a great surprise to him to discover, while a student, that some were sandy.

His thoughts were interrupted by a noise. It wasn't the usual flash of ordnance from above, the crack of a bomb exploding; this was something else: a rolling, deeper detonation, as if coming from the center of the earth itself.

"That was it," he said to Nadine and Anja. "They blew it up."

Numb with shock, the three of them tried to block thoughts of the poor wretches who had perished—they stumbled forward in the darkness, their eyes searching for a light that would mean deliverance.

They knew that very soon Berlin would become a battleground that would make the Allied bombing seem like a mere thunderstorm. Life meant continuing west along a subterranean tunnel.

Dieter had been right: The regime might be dying, but it would take everything else with it as it perished.

27

ohann had never seen rats like them. Not that they were clearly visible: The creatures were scurrying presences, specter-like and swift around their feet. As the city had fallen apart, the creatures had thrived, the ruined buildings providing a rodents' paradise of niches and recesses for them to shelter and breed. The creatures were no longer frightened of human beings, and they moved around the city as if it were they, not the humans, who were in control.

Johann glanced behind him: Friedrichstraße was receding, its blue light glowing in the distance. There was a powerful smell of sewage now. Johann cupped his hand over his nose to try and reduce it, but the odor became stronger the deeper they went into the tunnel. There must be a damaged pipe somewhere, he thought.

"Hurry now," Anja reminded them. Johann heard her stumble as she said it. "The trains will not continue for long."

Johann stopped himself from declaring what he was thinking: That was assuming Lehrter Bahnhof still existed after the day's air raids. He tried not to think too hard about what they would do when they reached the station. He didn't doubt that the place would be in a state of chaos.

"We can do it," Nadine said. "This time tomorrow we'll be in the country. We can find a farm or a guesthouse somewhere safe."

"We have no money for a guesthouse," Anja said, not unkindly. To Johann it sounded like they were discussing plans for the weekend, not survival.

"I have a plan," Nadine said. "We shall offer to work for them—I can sew and you can cook, and Uncle, well, I'm not sure what he's good for, but maybe they can have him work in the fields or something. . . ."

"He can pull a plow," added Anja, clearly trying to keep up the girl's spirits.

Johann was thinking about the people back at the station. Was the explosion they'd heard what he thought it was? The implementation of the Nero Decree gnawed at him like a growing sickness. He wondered what other targets they were intending to destroy. Lehrter station could be next.

In the darkness he felt his wife's hand—cold and frail—reach for his. There was a weightlessness to it that was unfamiliar. He had always thought of her hand as solid, tenable. What she offered now felt feeble. Her fingers tightened into a squeeze.

"I'm sure that we will see the light of Lehrter Bahnhof soon," he said a little too loudly. His voice echoed off the slippery walls. He knew that he was using volume to block his thoughts. He didn't want to think about the past any longer. He didn't want to think what had happened to the people on the platform at Friedrichstraße. He wanted only to know how he would get Nadine and Anja out of this tunnel and onto a train.

"Is that it?" Anja asked. In the distance there was a blue light, similar to the one they had left behind at Friedrichstraße. Johann peered into the distance.

"I think that I see it too," Nadine said.

Johann could perceive no light. He was exhausted, virtually seeing double with fatigue, so he closed his eyes to rest them for a moment. He opened them again and—what relief!—he saw what Nadine and Anja described. It was difficult to judge in the darkness, but he imagined that it was at least a half mile away. They had had a glimpse of what might be their salvation.

"Come on then," Nadine said, stumbling ahead with renewed vigor.

Johann stepped forward, but as he placed his foot down he heard a splash of liquid. The thought of treading in sewage turned his stomach. He placed his other boot on the ground and the same thing happened. He told himself to put it out of his mind—the bombing had meant that there were pools of water and effluence all over the city.

But within a few steps, the three of them were wading—water was running past them further into the tunnel.

"It's getting deeper," Anja said.

Johann realized that it had risen above his boots. Every step he took meant getting soaked.

In the dark of the tunnel a moment of horror gripped him: He had been right—the noise farther back in the tunnel had been an explosion. The water was from the river that flowed on the other side of the tunnel wall.

Not satisfied with destroying Friedrichstraße station, the SS were attempting something even more terrible.

They were flooding the U-Bahn.

He tried to shut down his imagination. Conjuring the panic and desperation of the poor souls they had seen only minutes ago would not help him get Anja and Nadine to safety.

"It's getting harder to walk," Nadine said. "The water level is rising." Johann said nothing. He couldn't tell them what he thought was happening.

Within twenty feet the three of them were wading through water that was up to their knees. Johann felt the water rushing against his calves and realized that this wasn't a puddle that they were fighting through—the water was moving, as if a river had started to flow through the tunnel. And the water wasn't just cold, it was freezing. Already his feet felt numb. Johann cast a look at the tunnel ahead. The blue light seemed impossibly distant now.

Johann moved so that he was closer to both Nadine and Anja. He could hear both of them thrashing through the deluge.

"Are you all right?" he called to them.

"Johann!" Anja shouted. The noise of the water was so loud now that they had to yell to be heard. "We should hold hands."

Johann panicked—what to do with the briefcase? For a brief second he considered abandoning it; he must think of survival first. But no, leaving it was impossible—he had risked too much salvaging it. He undid his belt and stuffed the briefcase into the back of his trouser waistband, so that it was strapped to him once the belt was tightened again. Their fate would be one and the same.

Johann then moved so that Nadine was between him and Anja, and each grabbed the hand of the person next to them. The water was rising quickly; it was past Johann's thighs and climbing. His legs began to tire. He thought about cramp. The power of the water was such that it was becoming hard to keep a footing. The three of them stumbled along the tracks, their legs—already fatigued—becoming heavier at every moment.

"Keep going," Nadine called to her aunt and uncle, her hands clenching theirs tightly. It felt to Johann as though the girl was strong enough to drag both him and Anja to the next station. "Keep moving."

The water level continued to rise. Within a few minutes it was at Johann's waist. He realized that this meant it was more than halfway up both Anja's and Nadine's bodies. The going was tough now; each of them was using deep reserves of energy to remain upright. And the torrent rose higher and became more powerful. Despite the noise, the three of them could hear one another making involuntary sounds as they thrashed about.

"We can't keep walking much longer," Anja said. "The water is too powerful. We should just let go and allow ourselves to be carried. We will use less energy. We won't be fighting it. We can just drift."

"Tante is right," Nadine said.

Johann felt something brush against his leg. There was now a cascade of solid objects in the water buffeting them.

"That makes sense," Johann said reluctantly. "Let yourself drift with the flow of the river, but don't let go—or we will lose each other in the darkness."

Each of them dropped down into the water, their heads submerged in the frigid liquid momentarily before rising to the surface. Despite the cold, Johann found his brief moment beneath the surface a relief from the din of the tunnel. They gasped from the chill as they resurfaced, the water dragging them forward. They clung to each other tightly; if they lost touch, they would never find each other again in the murky pandemonium. Johann was concerned that the briefcase might slip from his belt, but it appeared to be stable, for the time being.

He reasoned that they had no choice but to sink into the water; it was becoming impossible to walk, and the flood would carry them down the tunnel toward Lehrter Bahnhof. He tried to put his foot down and realized that he could no longer touch the ground. They were at the mercy of a surging torrent of water that continued to increase in ferocity by the moment. Johann could only wonder at the volume of water flooding into the tunnel. The three of them were now being carried along like the pieces of flotsam that they could feel alongside them in the stream.

Johann shivered uncontrollably. The water was so cold that the only part of his body that didn't feel frigid was his left hand, which was wrapped tightly around Nadine's. He focused on that task alone. He would never let the girl go. He would hold on to her until the end of the earth if he had to.

The water rose ever higher, the pace of its flow increasing with every additional gallon flowing from the river.

"Where is the station?" Anja shouted. "We should be there now."

She was right: They had been traveling long enough to have reached the light they had seen before. Johann craned his neck above the waves, but all he could see in the distance was blackness.

Then, suddenly, there in the water beneath them, they saw something—a light of some kind.

There!

Johann twisted and tried to look down.

His heart sank: What he saw was a lone flashlight. Somehow it had remained active, its light still on. Perhaps its batteries were somehow protected within a watertight container? Johann had no idea, but what the beam illuminated filled him with horror—a sign for Lehrter Bahnhof U-Bahn station.

The station they had hoped to escape from wasn't ahead of them; it was now below them, submerged in twelve feet of water.

Anja must have seen the same thing.

"Oh, my God!" she cried, her voice echoing in the diminishing space above them. It was the first time Johann had heard her express dismay.

Johann cast his eyes around the space they found themselves in. He saw the outline of Anja's and Nadine's soaking heads and the vaulted ceiling of the station above as the three of them hurtled forward. He looked for anything that might offer them an opportunity to escape. There were no exits to be seen—all were several feet below the surface of the water. Johann grew even more fraught. There must be something, he thought.

There must be something. . . .

And then he saw an opportunity careering toward him. A steel support for the tunnel about a foot in width that jutted out from the wall. Johann was almost upon the object when he reached for it. His hand was so cold that, at first, he could barely tell if he had made contact. Then he felt his hand slipping a little and knew that he had purchase. He found a lip on the edge of the beam and felt himself stop moving. As the water gushed against him he summoned his strength and pulled Nadine and Anja toward him.

Nadine came close first.

"Grab it! Grab it!" Johann shouted to the girl, who snatched at the beam, clasping it. Once she had hold of the pillar, Johann moved around to help haul Anja toward them. When she had a grip Johann carefully moved her and Nadine around so that they were upstream of the object—that way they were being pushed into it rather than dragged away from it.

Each of them gasped for breath, the water bubbling wildly around them.

"What's happening?" Anja asked. Her teeth were chattering.

"It's fresh water," Johann replied, trying to get a better grip on the metal frame.

"It must be from the river," Anja said. "Or the canal."

"We must find a way up," Johann said, looking around. He knew that there were ladders built into the U-Bahn that allowed workers to access parts of the track directly from street level. "There must be something nearby."

"What happens if we just keep drifting?" Nadine asked. "The water must end at some point, mustn't it?"

Neither of the adults said anything. They had no idea. It was unlikely that they would find themselves washed gently onto their feet; more likely they would be trapped—against a grate, forced into a chamber filled with water—and would drown. The temperature of the water was also a problem. None of them could feel their extremities any longer. Before long their bodies would begin to shut down in order to protect their vital organs.

But there was a more pressing problem. The small amount of light allowed them to get a sense of their surroundings. Johann had realized that they were perhaps twenty feet above the tracks. This did not leave much room for the water to rise. He reached up and his fingertips ran along the damp indentations of tile. They were probably no more than four feet beneath the highest point of the arched tunnel roof now. Before too long their heads would be pressed against the ceiling, sucking the last vestiges of oxygen. After that . . . Johann figured there was probably a foot or two more breathing room in the center of the tunnel, but the rapid movement of the water would make it impossible for them to hold their position: They would be carried where the torrent took them. They would effectively be stuck in a pipe full of water.

"It's still rising," Nadine cried, as if having had the same realization as Johann. Anja looked upward, her chin dripping with water. Her face was resolute, but Johann could see mild panic in her movements, which were twitchy and uncontrolled.

Suddenly the tunnel was filled with a different noise: A scream echoed above the gushing of the water.

It was Nadine.

Johann spun around. Her face: distorted, animated, horrified.

She pushed at the water frantically, summoning a level of intensity that was matched by Johann as he too thrust his hand into the water, pushing whatever it was away from himself and the others. He found his palm pressed against cloth with something firm beneath it. Something hard. Johann shoved harder—the force of the flood was driving the object against them. It pulled away momentarily, before revolving toward them again as it became caught up in the torrent.

It was then that Johann saw what Nadine had seen: the bloated, injured face of a dead man floating above the waterline. The skin on his face was so pale that he looked like an apparition, moving toward the three of them like a ghoul gliding through the dark water.

Nadine screamed again as the corpse nudged her. She went to push the body away farther.

And then, in an instant, she was gone.

It had happened so quickly, and the light was so dim, that Johann couldn't tell how she had lost her grip on the pillar. All he and Anja knew was that she had been there only a moment before. Now she was tumbling, alone, through the tunnel. Johann and Anja exchanged a look of horror.

"Quick!" Anja said. She reached out to Johann, who took her hand. The two of them plunged back into the surging water in pursuit of their niece. Unidentifiable objects—rubbish, vermin, rocks—struck them as they were driven downstream.

It was as if there was no cohesion to the world any longer; everything had fallen to pieces. They were tumbling toward an end that, despite all they had seen over the previous years, they could never have imagined. They were thrown forward into frothing, violent darkness, their fingers gripped tightly to each other, their hearts heavy with hopelessness: How would they ever locate Nadine in this subterranean tempest? Johann held out the hand that wasn't grasping his wife's, casting around helplessly with the prospect that he might find Nadine.

Johann looked for her frantically. He could make out the arch of the top of the tunnel and could tell the difference between the curve of the masonry and the water. Suddenly he made out a shape that interrupted the uniformity. After a moment he could tell by the object's shape that it was human.

"Here!" Nadine shouted. "I'm here." He couldn't tell whether she had seen them, or was shouting blindly in the hope that they would hear her.

They came rushing toward her. Johann realized that she could see them, as she was reaching her hand in their direction. He would only have one chance to grab her hand. If he misjudged, then he and Anja would be past in an instant.

He attempted to swim toward Nadine, but there wasn't time to move as much as he would like. He realized that he needed to stabilize himself and offer Nadine as big a target as possible to grab on to. He tried to keep afloat while reaching over to her. . . . He had maybe three seconds until he and Anja reached Nadine. . . .

He felt her wrist. He closed his fingers around it before feeling her do the same to him.

He had her.

He gripped Anja's hand fiercely and attempted to haul them both toward Nadine. The girl was clinging to a metal pipe that ran up the wall and through the top of the tunnel. Nadine cried out as she struggled to haul them toward her, every sinew of her body straining as if her very being depended on it.

And then, Johann felt a shudder pass through her body.

Something had given way. . . .

She was on top of him now, flailing in the water to find some balance, thrashing to try and get her breath.

The water swept them away again.

Johann clung to Anja and Nadine as the three of them tumbled, helpless and freezing, deeper into the darkness.

ieter rolled over. The floor beneath his back was sticky; he was lying in a pool of his own blood. He remembered now. Johann had done this to him. He pressed his palm to his scalp and felt a gluey residue. It had clotted. He could have it dressed later.

The key.

His hand reached down to his pocket in a flash. It was there.

He pulled out the trophy and examined it. There was nothing distinctive about it: a simple metal object with a number of prongs at one end and a loop at the other. But to Dieter, its value was immeasurable; it signified the end of an eleven-year quest. The riches that Nicolas has squirreled away would be his. From the day Johann had disappeared, Dieter knew that his half brother had walked away with the key. He remembered where Nicolas had kept it in his desk. As an adolescent he had often opened the drawer to examine the object and contemplate its secrets.

Now he held it again.

The briefcase.

His eyes searched frantically around the room. He winced with pain—Johann had taken it. *Damn him.* Dieter was furious with himself—how had he been so foolish as to let it slip from his grasp again?

He scrambled to his feet and made his way outside to discover that his staff car was buried under a pile of bricks that had fallen from a damaged part of the *Führungshauptamt* security headquarters. He limped over to a corporal who ran the garage and demanded a vehicle.

"Of course, *Sturmbannführer*," came the reply as the man fretfully tried to secure Dieter a car. Eventually a *Kübelwagen* whose occupants had recently been killed was secured. Dieter sped off, ignoring the slashes in the vehicle made by shrapnel and the blood that appeared to have been sprayed on the seats. There was a thick yellow blanket of smoke throughout most of the government district and little wind, meaning that Dieter had to drive slowly, the wheels of the jeep bouncing off bricks and other obstacles littering the road. Dieter found a rag in the car and cleaned the windshield, which was smeared with something ochre. There appeared to be more troops in the city than there had been only that morning. The last remaining units were being pulled back for the final stand.

There had been little direct talk among the SS officers about the coming days, but it was clear from the manner and individual traits of some that there were those contemplating escape to the south—he had heard many of the Party officials had already fled to Bavaria. Others, of course, would fight fanatically to the end. Those in the latter group had no intention of surviving; they would die defending the city or take their own lives—the prospect of a Soviet gulag was not worth contemplating. Most of the soldiers he saw in the streets were SS units, the most uncompromising of the formerly formidable Nazi war machine. The old men of the *Volkssturm* and units of the Hitler Youth with their *Panzerfäust* would make up the numbers.

Dieter would fight. He would kill Bolsheviks with pleasure. There would be no stepping backward until the last minute when he would find whoever was left and join the much-talked-about breakout of Berlin. The Fourth Panzer Army was said to be coming from the south and would enable remaining forces to escape the city. Some would regroup to face the Soviets elsewhere.

Others, Dieter included, would head south and lie low until the call came again, as it was sure to.

He needed to focus on more pressing matters and retrieve the briefcase. He knew Johann would eventually head to the station—it was the only exit point from the city. He would capture him there. No, not capture—kill. Even so, he was being pulled elsewhere by an irresistible force.

He pulled up at the bank on Behrenstraße. The façade was pockmarked with holes from flying debris, but the building's structure appeared sound. He banged on a thick wooden door. There was no answer. It was 3 p.m.; they were supposed to be open. He would need to judge it right. And he would need to have the means to start again. Dieter still marveled at how many of the city's institutions—the post office, the factories, the civil service—continued to function, despite the collapse of the state. The chaos occurring in government and military buildings was unmatched in parts of the civilian world. Even most banks were still open, although staff was largely going through the motions.

Dieter continued knocking and eventually a middle-aged man with slicked-back hair and a black suit opened the door.

"Come in, sir," he said graciously.

Dieter walked in and saw a number of women sweeping the floor where some windows had shattered. There was paperwork strewn throughout the lobby.

"I apologize for the mess," the man said. "We only just came up from the cellar. The last raid was rather a long one and I'm afraid that we suffered some damage. It appears to be largely inconsequential and we are, of course, open for business."

The bank manager did not seem intimidated by Dieter's uniform, or the fact that the SS man was smothered with both his own blood and blood from inside the *Kübelwagen*. The banks had remained largely untouched by the Party, which had been careful not to alarm the population with changes that would cause the public to doubt their financial institutions. A phone rang in the background. One of the women put her broom down and hurried over to pick it up. She answered it as if it were a bright summer day and all was right with the world.

"I have a personal matter to attend to," Dieter said, producing the key and holding it in front of the manager.

"Very good, sir," the man said. "Please follow me." As Dieter proceeded after him toward a metal gate, he noticed pieces of plaster nestling in the manager's hair. He unlocked the gate and allowed Dieter to pass through. Locking it behind them, the man led Dieter down a marble staircase. The brass on the handrail looked as if it might have been polished that morning. The grandeur impressed Dieter: It was the kind of place where the rich discreetly went about their business, where conversations were held in whispers. It felt entirely cut off from the collapse that was occurring beyond its doors.

"If I may be so bold, sir," the manager said, lowering his voice, "you should be aware that, despite the circumstances, we are confident that there has been no decline in the high standards we hold ourselves to. As you can see, we are several meters belowground now. The basement is entirely safe. Should the main entrance become impassable, we have other methods of allowing our clients access."

"I'm heartened to hear that," Dieter said.

They arrived in an anteroom, which was lit by several candles.

"I'm afraid that we no longer have electricity down here," the manager explained.

"It must be a local problem," Dieter said.

The manager looked at him with disbelief, before correcting himself. "Quite so," he replied, approaching a desk. "Now, I need the name and number of the account."

"Meier," Dieter said. It felt odd speaking his stepfather's surname as if it were his own.

"And the security identification number?" the manager asked, sliding a piece of paper and a pen toward Dieter, who wrote the four digits. The man compared them to a column of numbers in the back of a ledger and nodded.

Dieter wanted the process to progress more quickly. As sweet as it was to finally have the key, Dieter's victory was hollow without the briefcase. He knew that Standartenführer Keller would sacrifice him without hesitation if the microfilm was not retrieved.

The manager produced another leather-bound ledger. This one was thicker than the first. He ran his finger along several columns before it hovered over some numbers.

"Right," he said, then produced a fountain pen and wrote the date in a neatly ruled column. "Very good. Sign here, please."

Dieter scrawled his name. The man blotted the ink dry.

He left the ledger on the desk and walked toward a thick metal door that had been decorated with fleurs-de-lis. He turned a key twice, and two levered bolts, top and bottom, slid open. The manager pushed the door and the two men walked in.

Dieter felt a sudden rush of exhilaration.

Here, in this room, his search would end. Whatever it was that Nicolas had decided to hide all those years ago, the gift that he had seen fit to hand to Johann but not his stepson, would now be his.

It had taken eleven years, but Dieter had finally won.

Inside the room there were two rows of thick iron cabinets, each with a number of drawers, which contained the security boxes. There were probably twenty stacks, with five boxes in each stack. Dieter felt a thrill: all these secrets. He imagined people furtively coming down into this basement to hide precious items, to preserve confidences from their loved ones and from government. He had always thought that all human beings harbored undisclosed thoughts and intentions, had always felt compelled to root out these mysteries and enigmas with vigor and inquiry. He didn't just ache to see what was in Nicolas's box; he longed to open each and every one of the containers to determine their contents. The manager passed between the rows of cabinets, moving decisively down one aisle until he reached the middle of the row.

The manager produced a key from the pocket of his waistcoat, slipped it into the slot in the front of the box, and turned it.

"Your key, please, Herr Meier," he requested.

Dieter felt the object, dull and hard in his hand. Here it was, this small piece of shaped metal that he had searched for for so long, returned from whence it had come. It had been created for just one purpose: to open the box before which he was now standing. He passed it to the manager, who repeated his action and then reached forward and slid the box from the casing that held it.

"Please, sir, follow me," the manager said. He led Dieter back along the aisle to an alcove that contained a wooden desk, a chair, and three candles that burned bright enough to give the impression of electric light. Dieter noticed that there was a thick purple, velvet curtain that was drawn back. The manager placed the box on the desk before stepping backward.

"I will be waiting for you in the anteroom," he said. "Please call me when you are ready."

He nodded deferentially before closing the curtain. Dieter heard his footsteps echoing down the hallway. He thought: In the end it has come down to being alone with a metal box in a basement. He hadn't imagined that the conclusion would have happened in this way. Nonetheless, he had believed irrevocably that he would fulfill his intentions. He would prevail—of that he had no doubt.

Dieter lifted the box and moved it slightly. He remembered doing a similar thing when he was a child opening Christmas presents. Other children would tear into the wrapping, but he would wait, contemplating the object, feeling and weighing it in order to distinguish its contents. He considered the box. One of the candles crackled momentarily, but other than that the silence was profound. He lifted the lid carefully; it creaked a little before coming to rest once it had passed a vertical position.

He took a deep breath and looked inside. There was a manila folder, which was immediately familiar: It was the same as the type used internally within the SS. He reached down and felt to see what was beneath the file.

A hard shot of alarm tore through him: The box appeared to contain only a large ream of paperwork. For so many years he had imagined that opening it would reveal tangible assets—gold, currency, jewels—so to be faced with something that resembled the in-tray of a Party functionary was startling.

Dieter's fingers felt along the edges of the paper to see if there were any gaps where objects might have been concealed, but all he sensed were the borders of the paper. It was strange, unexpected. He steadied himself and recalled Nicolas, who he remembered as a methodical man—an academic who believed in thoroughness and systematic approaches. Maybe there was something within the papers that would take him in an unforeseen direction but which might, nevertheless, prove to be advantageous. Bonds, deeds, or promissory notes, perhaps.

Dieter pulled the documents out of the box and placed them on the desk. The pile was perhaps two inches high. He opened the top file, which was smeared with dirty fingerprints. He had never seen a document from the Reich Main Security Office that was in such a condition.

The information had been collected on white paper on which typewritten boxes had been created for the purpose of collecting standard information.

At the top of the document, he could see that it was created on June 29, 1934.

Next to the date, the name: Nicolas Meier.

He had been transferred to Oranienburg a week after Dieter and his comrades had delivered him into the hands of state security officials. Dieter thought back: He remembered the journey to the police station, how Nicolas had begged him to help, to turn from the path he had chosen. His pleas had made no impression upon Dieter. He would not be swayed by the pathetic ramblings of a man whose loyalty lay somewhere other than National Socialism.

As Nicolas was unloaded from the truck and bundled into the police station, the final words that Dieter could remember him shouting were, "You'll find out one day, you'll find out. Maybe then you will understand."

The words had stayed with Dieter as he rushed home to find Johann and discover the whereabouts of the key for the security box. A candle crackled again—their quality was so poor now that they tended to burn unevenly. He continued to scan the page.

His stepfather's birthplace and the date. His address, his marital status . . .

All was in order.

He read down the form. Halfway down the page there was a box containing information about prisoners' children. Here, he paused with wonder. It read "None."

Surely the officials and bureaucrats would have simply cross-checked in the archives to see if this was true? The search for enemies of the state had been nothing if not thorough and unremitting. All means at the Party's disposal were used to investigate and root out those who had no place within the Reich. A multitude of bureaucrats were employed to comb through records to ensure that evading one's heritage was not possible. The Party would not be fooled by fabrication. How was it possible that they had failed to detect this?

He cast his mind back to what he had discovered at the state archives—the birth records for both him and his half brother had been doctored—before moving the file to the side and picking up the documents beneath. This was confirmed by the next item on the pile—his birth certificate. He scanned down it and saw that all the details were as he thought: the names of his father, Wilhelm, and mother, Hannah. The place and date of birth were all correct. How was it, then, that when he had looked in the archive he and Johann had been listed as orphans? The next document was Johann's birth certificate, and Dieter understood the details on the certificate to be correct. His father was Nicolas and his mother Hannah.

His mind reeled with possibilities. Then it struck him: This is what Nicolas had meant by "Maybe then you will understand." As an academic he would have had easy access to all state archives. With a little careful manipulation of the staff and prudent adaptation of the official record, he would have been able to change his son's and stepson's legacies, thereby protecting them from pursuit should he be arrested because of his political beliefs. Nicolas knew that he would be targeted by the Nazis. If it had been him who changed the certificates in the state archive, it had been done to protect Dieter and his half brother.

Bewildered, he put the document to one side and looked at the next item in the file. He started. At the top of the pile was a plain envelope with his name written on it. He ripped it open. Inside he found a letter, which was clearly old. He unfolded it and realized that it had been sent to his mother.

January 14, 1915

Dear Mrs. Schnell,

With great regret I write to inform you that your husband, Wilhelm Schnell, was found dead in his quarters this morning. It is my sad duty to inform you that he died at his own hand.

My condolences to you and your family. It may come as some comfort to you to know that, as a result of some of the clinical techniques and modern medicines we have been administering since his arrival in September last year following his injuries in Mons, his condition had greatly improved and, as of late, he had been in good humor.

Please contact me by return so that we may make arrangements for his body to be sent to his family for burial.

I remain at your service.

Yours sincerely,

Joerg Hartmann

Dieter looked at the address at the top of the letter. Psychiatric hospital, Rheinau. He found himself hardly able to breathe.

This could not be right. His father had died as part of the Sixth Army at Neuve-Chapelle in March 1915. He was sure of it. It was what he had been told since he was a child.

He read the letter for a second time and then a third. . . . He put the piece of paper down, looked away, and then tried again, hoping that its words might have altered.

But they were still there.

Dieter threw his arm out and knocked over one of the candleholders. He clawed at the curtain, tearing it from its fastenings. He brought his hands up and held his head as if to try to contain the tumultuous thoughts inside, before smashing a clenched fist onto the wooden desk in frustration, smearing wax with the back of his hand. He grabbed another candleholder and brought it closer to the letter.

Had he been told a lie? Was it the case that his father had not died gloriously in battle, but had taken his own life in an insane asylum?

He reexamined the piece of paper. The words made no sense to him. His mind was able to discern their shape and their literal meaning, but the significance was so shocking, so intolerable, that his mind could barely process them.

This simply couldn't be true.

He paced around and tried to think matters through clearly.

While it was clear that it was Nicolas who had placed the birth certificates and the letter in the security box, it was impossible for him to have included the document from Oranienburg-Sachsenhausen or addressed the envelope—and the document had been arranged carefully at the top of the pile so that it could not be ignored.

Of course.

Johann.

He had meant Dieter to find the key and come here all along.

The revelation of how Nicolas had protected them was his revenge.

Dieter stood up, his heart racing. The disclosure affected every aspect of who he was—and what he believed. Dieter's father—the hero of the Great War—had been but a figment of his imagination. The shockwave was compounded by his belief that Nicolas, whose demise he had engineered, had altered the records solely to protect him and Johann.

He couldn't bear it—he began to burn each of the documents. The dry paper flared and began to burn vigorously, warming him in the frigid vault. He felt as if the foundations of his being had been torn from him. He was rootless now, lost and without significance.

There was only one other person who knew: Johann. That is, if we wasn't dead already in Friedrichstraße station.

In the corridor the manager smelled burning paper.

"Is everything all right, Herr Meier?" he called. The smoke became stronger, and he stepped toward the curtained-off section. It was strictly forbidden for him to disturb clients when they were in the middle of inspecting the contents of a security box, but the odor of burning was highly irregular.

"Herr Meier?" he called out again. "Do you require assistance of any kind? Herr Meier?"

The manager pulled opened the curtain, and Dieter—thunder-faced and apoplectic with rage—pushed past him and into the corridor.

"Herr Meier, would you like me to replace the box?" the manager blurted out as Dieter bolted.

"Do with it what you will!" Dieter shouted, his voice echoing on the staircase.

The manager stared at the table. It was covered in wax from one of the candles that had been knocked over. The security box remained open and the key had been left inside. Beside the box was a set of charred documents, a tiny pile of ash and smoldering paper.

The bank manager hurriedly began sweeping away the mess, unaware that he was clearing away a vast catastrophe that could not be set right through practical-minded assistance.

Dieter got into his car and sat for a moment. There was a light drizzle falling. Perhaps it would clear the foul air that hung over the city like a shroud. A few yards from his car a wooden carousel horse lay on top of the mangled remains of a vehicle that had part of a building collapse on it. The horse's eye was trained on him, sightless and sinister.

He tried to calm his breathing. The discovery had thrown his entire world out of kilter. He had perhaps not expected riches, but he had hoped for enough to see him through the peril of the coming years. Despite the imminent downfall of the city he had dared to imagine a life beyond the grim privation of his current situation. Should he have found something of worth he could perhaps have built a life in the south without attracting any attention. He could have slipped from the city at the last possible moment before the noose tightened.

Now, he had nothing.

Worse than nothing: He would have to live with the horrifying truth about his father that had been revealed to him by that traitorous snake Johann who had gotten to the vault before him.

Then it occurred to him: When Johann planted the file in the security box he could quite easily have removed items of value. They would now be in his possession, along with the briefcase containing the microfilm. Maybe Dieter still had a chance. He would take back what Johann had stolen and he would kill his half brother this time.

He felt the rage coursing through him now. He would have his revenge.

He roared recklessly through the chaotic streets toward Lehrter Bahnhof in the *Kübelwagen*. What he had to do was clear to him now. He needed to finish the job; he needed to ensure that his half brother would end his days in Berlin.

29

They were swept down the tunnel, hurtling toward an unknown end. Johann, wild-eyed, watched for opportunities to halt their progress. He held Nadine's hand on one side and Anja's on the other, knowing that if he saw a fixed point to claw at, he would be forced to drop one of their hands in order to grasp it.

The tunnel walls rushed past, and any glimpse of salvation passed in an instant. Johann glanced upward—the water continued to rise. There were perhaps only three more feet of air. Pretty soon the water would carry them so high that their heads would scrape the roof. Beyond that there was only so much time before the water level would rise above their mouths. He could feel only a fuzzy, indistinct movement below his knees when he moved his legs; there was no longer any sensation in his feet. Each of them would soon go into shock. The cold was shutting down their systems. If they remained in the water much longer they would develop hypothermia. The symptoms—shivering and muscle miscoordination, turning to amnesia and major organ failure—were wretchedly familiar to Johann after years at the front.

"Look!"

It was Nadine. She was gesturing above the water, but Johann was unable to distinguish what she was pointing at. Then it came into focus; there was a split in the tunnel ahead where the tracks divided in two directions. The parting meant that there was a large tiled column in the middle.

"There's a ladder!" Anja shouted above the noise of the water. The metal structure was about two feet across. Johann looked up to see where it might take them but realized it was pointless unless they managed to grasp it. He felt Anja trying to move her body farther into the middle of the channel. Nadine was doing the same on the other side of him. Johann would have to trust them; there was nothing he could do but continue to clutch their frozen hands.

As the tunnel widened for the two separate tunnels, the water began to speed up and its level began to diminish. The three of them could see the walls rising next to them, and the tunnel opening began to appear larger. Nadine and Anja were both poised, ready to grab the ladder, although it wasn't clear which tunnel the water would drag them down. After a few seconds they felt themselves being carried inexorably to the left. Each paddled wildly to the right, trying to compensate for the pull of the current. The water was too powerful, and Johann realized that only Nadine had a chance of seizing the ladder.

As Johann and Anja kicked with every ounce of their reserves of strength, Nadine reached toward one of the struts, urging her slender fingers forward, stretching them with her entire being. Johann looked down the tunnel before them; to be dragged into that opening would surely be the end. He kept the arm attached to Nadine flexible, while stiffening his body and yanking Anja as close as he was able toward him.

Suddenly they stopped moving.

He could barely believe it. Nadine had hold of a ladder rung. She shrieked with effort as she held tight. Johann and Anja were still at the mercy of the water while the girl hung on.

"Climb across me!" Johann instructed Anja. He was unable to grip the ladder as he was holding both Nadine and Anja, but perhaps his wife could get over to Nadine. Anja frantically kicked and struggled her way past him. He expected that, at any moment, Nadine would lose her grip. Her body was surely at its limit; the force of the water and the weight of his and Anja's bodies must inevitably push it beyond its capacity.

But Nadine held firm.

"Yes!" the girl shouted, and he knew that somehow Anja had made it to the ladder. Then, a moment later, he was astonished to feel his body being dragged against the current until he too was within reach of the ladder, to which Nadine and Anja were both clinging. He grabbed a slimy rung and hauled himself up so that his shoulders were above the water. Once his head was clear of the freezing froth he looked to see Nadine and Anja, both of them shaking with cold, but both smiling through chattering teeth.

Johann looked up to see, through a hole about three feet in diameter, a manhole about fifteen feet above them. He began to climb. The ladder was slippery and his body was shaking, but he progressed steadily, checking for both Nadine, who was directly below him, and Anja, who was at the rear. Every so often he paused for breath, clinging to the structure without looking downward; heights had never been a strong point of his. He closed his eyes momentarily as if to convince himself that he was resting.

"Johann?" Anja called above the noise. They were all well above the water now, although it remained a menacing presence below. "Johann, are you all right?"

"Yes, yes, I'm fine," Johann said, forcing himself back into the world. He was certain that he could have fallen asleep clinging to the ladder given the opportunity.

"The trains, Johann, the trains," Anja shouted after him. Johann's sodden clothes pulled upon him like lead weights. His fatigue had such depth that he felt it to be interminable. No matter how long he lived, there would never be sleep enough to satisfy his exhaustion.

"Come on, Uncle," Nadine said. Her tone wasn't chiding— she could see that he was having a moment of repose.

With gargantuan effort, Johann began to climb again. He worked carefully, ensuring that he had a firm handhold and that his feet were properly positioned before stepping upward. Each of them was doing the same thing. To fall now wouldn't just be disastrous; it would be foolish—they were so close to being back on solid ground.

Johann reached the top of the ladder and examined the manhole above him. He had never lifted one of them in his life. Was there a technique, or special tools, that were needed? Fearful of letting go of the ladder, he positioned himself directly beneath the object, lowering his head and raising himself so that the top part of his back and his shoulders were pressed against it. He tried a gentle push and felt resistance. He wondered what was above. Perhaps they had happened upon a place where a building had collapsed or a vehicle was parked. Any kind of obstruction on the roadway would make the metal cover impossible to move. They would be stuck.

He heaved his body against the manhole cover, thrusting upward. His legs shook and his knees ached, but the object wouldn't budge. He relaxed for a moment and tried again. He could feel the anxious eyes of Nadine and Anja upon him. They all knew that if Johann wasn't able to move the manhole cover then this was the end: There would surely be no more chances for them to escape their subterranean prison. Johann glanced down at his wife and niece and pressed again, forcing the object with all his might.

What was that? Johann felt a shower of dirt or sand fall upon him from above. He must have moved the cover enough to release some of the debris that had collected in the gap between the road and the cover—proof that the metal disk could be shifted.

"Can you open it, Uncle?" Nadine called from below. Her voice was still patient and controlled. He heard her take a sharp intake of breath as a shiver passed through her.

Johann didn't reply. He paused again and summoned his energy. For a third time he pushed his body against the manhole cover. On this occasion he tried a different approach: explosive power. He would knock the object free with abrupt and concentrated exertion.

"Uncle?" Nadine asked again.

Johann counted down: three . . . two . . . one. . . .

His drove his body upward as hard as he could, his legs powering him and his back slamming against the iron of the manhole cover.

And there it was: movement. He felt the object shift. Swiftly Johann leaned forward to lift the plate onto the ground above. His back burned, but he felt the edge of the metal lid scrape against the street. His body was spent, so he set it down, praying that he had done enough for it to rest on the ground. He looked up, fearful of what he might see.

There was a slice of light. The gap wasn't more than two inches, but a part of the manhole cover was resting on the surface above. Johann gasped, sucking air into his lungs. There was a lick of breeze from above. He looked down at Nadine and Anja and experienced a moment of release. Their faces—filthy and soaking wet, but relieved—were illuminated by daylight for the first time since they'd entered the U-Bahn at Friedrichstraße.

"Give me a second," Johann said, clinging to the ladder. Dust blew down from above, collecting on his damp face. He pushed upward again, thrusting his body to the side. This time the cover shifted more easily, and he heard it scrape against the grit on the roadway. He looked up and saw clear daylight above him. There was enough of a gap to squeeze through. Johann clambered up the ladder. He reached up and placed his hands on asphalt before hauling himself from the hole. He cast a glance around, trying to work out where they were, before reaching down and helping

Nadine then Anja—blinking and drenched—up into the daylight. All three of them sat, shattered, in the roadway. Water dripped from their clothing onto the road, forming dark puddles.

"You did it," Nadine said to him. "You pushed it open."

Johann hugged her before reaching over to Anja.

"We're still here," Anja said flatly. She looked at Johann. "I didn't think you would be able to do that."

There was no relief in her voice. It was simply a statement of fact.

Johann wanted to tell her that neither did he.

He loosened his belt, pulled up his tunic, and released the briefcase.

"What's that?" Nadine asked.

Johann's eyes met Anja's. From his gaze she knew immediately that its contents were important.

"Just my stuff," he said to Nadine breezily. He could tell that the girl didn't believe him. He extended his hands to the women. If he sat any longer he would never be able to get up.

"We need to warm up," he said, hauling them to their feet. "We need to move around."

"We need to get to the train station," Anja added, taking off her coat. "Grab one end of this," she said to Johann. The two of them twisted the coat, squeezing the excess water from it. They did the same for Nadine.

"We're not far from the station," Nadine said.

Johann looked around. Almost every building around them had been damaged irreparably. It appeared that they had arrived in an unknown city, not somewhere he had spent most of his life. Johann spun around, searching for a familiar landmark. There was nothing; the city was a homogenous ruin. The remaining buildings had become merely the residue of what had once existed. Johann didn't recognize any of it. The city was alien.

How odd, he thought, to find a place so integral to the notion of oneself to be utterly foreign.

"We're on Lüneburger Straße," Nadine said eventually. She pointed to a row of buildings. "That's where the post office used to be, and that's where we went to get a birthday present for Tante Anja once, remember?"

Johann squinted. He remembered the day. He had picked Nadine up from school to enlist her help in buying a pair of gold earrings. The exterior of the shop had been vandalized by the SA; large Stars of David had been painted on the window and posters were pasted to the glass. A member of the Hitler Youth had been stationed outside to intimidate potential customers into going elsewhere. Johann remembered fixing the boy with such an intense glare that he shuffled away meekly, not daring to say a word. Johann and Nadine found a pair that Anja loved, but Johann had never enjoyed seeing her wear them. The street as it had once been reformed in his mind's eye. He could see what Nadine was showing him now.

"Come on," Anja said, stumbling over a pile of brickwork. "If we hurry we'll be there in a few minutes."

"Hey!"

The voice appeared to come from nowhere. Johann whirled around and saw a man sitting inside a ruined shop. He must have been watching them all along. Instinctively Johann moved so that he was shielding Anja and Nadine from potential danger. He realized there was little cause for concern when the man moved toward them—he limped over with a crutch under one arm to compensate for a lost leg and then looked down into the subway.

"That's a first," he said.

They didn't reply. Each of them was too tired to expend the energy necessary to manage this encounter.

"You're all wet," the man said. He was unshaven and dressed in—Johann estimated—at least three coats. He swayed slightly on his crutches as if he had been drinking. "Do you need clothes?"

"You have women's clothes?" Anja said skeptically.

"Of course," the man laughed. With a crooked arm, he gestured to the building he had appeared from. "This place I'm living, it was once a women's clothes shop. There are boxes in the back. Come . . ."

The man hobbled back toward the store. Anja, Nadine, and Johann exchanged glances. Who knew if he was telling the truth?

"What do you think?" Johann said quietly.

"I want dry clothes," Nadine said. Anja nodded.

The man stopped outside the former shop and waved his hand again. "Come," he said. "I won't eat you, I promise." He chuckled to himself.

"Let me go first," Johann said to Anja and Nadine, and followed the man inside the building. At the back of the ruined shop was an open door. The man hopped inside and pointed to a stack of cardboard boxes, which were piled next to a makeshift bed and kitchen.

"Help yourself," the man said. "I have no use for them. I have no idea where the owners of this place are, but I doubt they'll be back soon."

Johann exited the shop and waved to Nadine and Anja that it was safe.

"We'll be quick," Anja said on her way inside. The man followed Johann back into the street while the women went to work, searching through the boxes.

"You were at Friedrichstraße, *Sturmbannführer?*" the old man said to Johann. The inflection in his voice made Johann think that the man doubted he was an officer in the SS.

"We were," he said.

"My friend just came past," the man said. "He told me that they killed hundreds in there. Filled it with water. Apparently they're destroying anything that is useful to the Soviets. Will they leave us with nothing?"

"We were lucky," Johann said.

"It's true then?" the old man said. "We're not waiting for the Soviets; we're finishing the old girl off ourselves?"

"The old girl?"

"You know, Berlin."

Johann nodded. "There's no 'we' about it," he said.

"How bad will it be?" the old man asked.

"Who knows?" Johann replied. "You'll be okay. They'll leave someone like you alone as long as you're unarmed."

"I'm ahead of you there," the old man said, chuckling. "I had a Luger. I buried it in the garden only this morning."

Johann started. He needed a weapon—his had been taken from him when he'd been captured.

"Sir, you'd be doing me a great service if you'd let me have the Luger," he said.

The old man considered the request for a moment before gesturing with his thumb. "It's out back," he said. "You'll see a couple of large pots—it's in the dirt behind them. You'll find a box of ammunition too, if you look hard enough."

Johann retrieved the weapon, checked that it was still functioning, and fully loaded the magazine.

"It's well cared for," he told the old man, who nodded. The two of them sat in silence waiting for Anja and Nadine to appear. Moments later they were leaving the shop wearing completely new outfits. To Johann, it was like seeing different people.

"Thank you," they both said to the old man, who acknowledged them with a half smile.

"Good luck," Johann said to him as they departed.

The man just grunted.

Johann wasn't sure what was worse, the stench of human effluvia beneath the ground or the choking smoke above it. The three of them trekked toward the station, coughing as they went. They came upon Washingtonplatz, and the air cleared to reveal that the station was still standing. Dozens of wounded people were lying outside, ignored by the hundreds of others hurrying past into the station, their numbers swollen by the lull in the bombing. Johann felt guilt, remorse, and a degree of shame. He should be tending to these people, not leaving them to die. He watched as soldiers distrustfully prowled the crowd looking for deserters and malingerers.

They were here at last. Surely he should be joyful that there was a possibility of escape. But the sight of hundreds of others crowding the station filled him with dismay. The very idea that they had held so dear—that had sustained them through great darkness—now seemed utterly implausible. He felt Nadine waver on seeing the mass of humanity and took her by the arm. He would smother his own doubts to protect those he loved. He stepped forward, leading his loved ones.

"Coming through, mind your backs . . . ," he declared as he maneuvered them through the bewildered hordes and into the station itself. The three of them paused at the entrance, taking in the scene. There were hundreds of people, all of them in varying states of desperation. Almost everyone carried several bags or suitcases. Some simply had bundles of belongings tied up in blankets. Frightened elderly people sat on abandoned armchairs. Order was being kept by policemen and harried railway officials in navy uniforms.

Above the chaos huge metal girders arced over the station with a latticework of smaller metal supports woven across them.

Each square had once been filled with a pane of glass; Johann remembered the station was once encased in a semitransparent shell—smoke on the interior and the effects of the wind and rain had caused the glass to become milky and translucent. Now barely a pane of glass remained. Lehrter was now almost entirely open to the elements. The steam of a train drifted upward, crossing the threshold of the roof before blending with the smoke and clouds outside.

They walked on, passing a woman pleading with two soldiers to be let through to the ticketing area, which had been sealed off by security personnel.

"All the trains are full," one of them said. "If you don't have a pass then you should go home."

"But I don't have a home!" the woman cried, gesturing to a young girl standing, dazed, next to her. The child was wearing a canvas backpack stuffed with her belongings and was hugging a large toy bear.

"There's nothing we can do, madam," one of the soldiers said. "You'll have to look for other arrangements. There is an NSV tent outside. They will find accommodation for you and make sure your daughter eats."

"Please, sir," the woman continued.

The soldier turned his back, muttering, "There's nothing I can do."

Johann nodded at the soldiers, his uniform—sodden as it was—guaranteeing him and the others safe passage to an area reserved for those who had the right documents to be able to travel. They struggled through the throng to reach an information board. Each of them stared upward.

"There are no trains," Nadine said. "Look, no destinations, no times, no nothing . . ."

"But there are trains on the platforms," Anja said, turning and looking behind them. "This makes no sense."

A man carrying a large suitcase barged past Johann, knocking him back a step. At first the man appeared blasé about the mishap. His demeanor changed when he realized who he had bumped into.

"Apologies, *Sturmbannführer*," he said, tipping his hat obsequiously. "My mistake."

Johann nodded. From the corner of his eye he noted Nadine and Anja watching the exchange. He had grown used to the power of the uniform over the past days. To his wife and niece, the garb was still that of the enemy, someone to be feared. There had been such terror over the previous twelve years that it had become the default setting for existence. It was what people had come to know, because if they weren't fearful, they would end up dead.

Johann looked around the station. The place was full of people frantic to escape. Each was likely to be willing to offer his or her worldly goods to board one of the two trains that idled beyond the barriers, engines belching out sudden bursts of steam as if agitated.

He would have to make the fear work for them.

"Come," he said to Anja and Nadine. "Let's find out what's happening here."

They battled their way through the swarming, restless crowd until they chanced upon a besieged clerk, his back to an information kiosk. The three of them approached, jostling with others to overhear what was being said.

"I keep telling people," the clerk said, his uniform somehow immaculate, a silver watch chain dangling from his waistcoat pocket, "there are two trains going west as far as we know. This is not guaranteed. There could be an air raid at any moment."

"Where are they going?" Johann asked over the head of a man in front of him.

"Who cares!" someone else shouted. The clerk persevered, his face demonstrating that he very much cared where the train was going, as the railway company was not in the businesses of simply sending trains into the beyond without a clear destination.

"That's what is being decided by management," he said. "We are trying to ascertain the extent of track damage in various areas."

"But you think that there will be more trains leaving at some point later today?" Johann pressed him.

"We have every intention of running a service today," the clerk said.

"What about tomorrow?" asked a woman wearing a maroon hat, her face drained. The clerk gave her a weary look and shrugged his shoulders.

"Who knows?" he said. "We hope so, but matters are not in our hands I'm afraid, madam." Then he added, as if he was explaining that a tree had fallen on the line and there would be a minor delay to a journey, "I do apologize for any inconvenience caused."

Others began to bark out questions while Anja, Nadine, and Johann slipped away.

"So the trains *are* running?" Nadine asked eagerly.

"Yes, there are two," Anja said.

The three of them had to keep twisting their bodies to allow people to pass by.

"But what about the paperwork?" Anja asked.

"We'll find a way on board," Johann said.

"Let's try one of the platforms," Anja said.

They forced their way through, stepping over people who had taken to sitting on the station concourse. A large scrum of people was huddled against the entrance to one of the platforms, their bodies tightly pressed together.

"We'll never get through," Anja said to Johann.

Johann thought of the uniform, the fear it could generate.

"Step aside," he ordered the people at the back of the huddle. Their attention was entirely consumed by what was happening in front of them.

"Step aside!" Johann snapped at them. There was a part of him that loathed what he was doing, but his determination was such that he was focused on getting to the officials holding up the queue. People moved aside, their voices quieting as an SS officer came between them. Beyond the guards at the platform edge he saw a train that already looked to be fully loaded. Officials hurried about the platform shouting orders into carriages; steam billowed from the chimney of the engine.

Johann saw the faces of the guards—unyielding and skeptical—before him. He decided to go on the offensive.

"We have places on the train," he said to the guards. "Who is in charge here?"

An army captain stepped forward.

"That would be me," he said.

"I have authority from the Reich Main Security Office to board this train with these two women," Johann said.

"With the greatest of respect, *Sturmbannführer*, the SS has no authority here," the captain said. "The army is in charge."

"I was told by Oberst Reinhard himself that I would be allowed to board a train," Johann continued.

"Where are your documents?" the captain asked, extending his hand.

"This is my point," continued Johann self-assuredly. "Such is the urgency of our journey that there has not been time to issue emergency documents."

"Then I can't let you on the train," the captain replied. Johann could tell that he was playing to the crowd of people, none of whom wanted to see others allowed on the train.

"What do you expect me to do?" Johann asked. "Do you want me to return to the Ministry and ask Obergruppenführer Kaltenbrunner himself?"

"No one is able to travel without the correct paperwork, sir," the soldier said. He cast a glance at the crowd behind Johann. "I'm sure that you understand that."

Johann fixed the soldier with a menacing glare. "You should think carefully before making this decision," he said. "There will be no second chances for you if you get this wrong."

Johann could feel those in the crowd pressing around him, Anja, and Nadine; it was as if they wanted to force the three of them away from the barrier. With them gone it would mean three fewer people trying to get on the train, which appeared to be primed to go—officials were closing doors and squeezing the last few people on board.

The soldier looked unyieldingly at Johann.

"I don't think there are going to be second chances for most of us," he said grimly.

Johann glanced at Anja and Nadine. They were stranded in Berlin.

30

He had sensed that there was something wrong all along.

When Lukas saw the body of the boy hanging from the lamp-post, he knew that nothing good could come from Johann bringing him to that place. He had spent months holed up in his hideout for this very reason. The streets were unforgiving. Whether you were a soldier, an old lady, or a young boy, something terrible could happen to you in an instant. A piece of shrapnel could pierce your skull, a building might collapse on you, or someone could slip a noose around your neck. There were countless ways to die in Berlin. Avoiding each of these endings was something Lukas prided himself on.

The face of the boy twisting in the wind haunted him. Lukas had no idea how the lad had ended up like this. All he knew was that it could be him. They had killed most of the men, so now they were starting on the boys. He had seen others with signs around their necks, their heads lolling sideways and their hands tied behind their backs.

There would be others—he was sure of that. He would make sure that he was not one of them.

So when he saw Johann, a canvas sack over his head, being led down the steps from the building, he was not surprised; this was the type of thing that happened every day. He had felt another emotion in addition to fear—anger.

He liked the way Johann had treated him. He had felt connected to another human being again after months of stealthily moving about the city shunning interaction. He knew that a visit to the NSV would provide him with care, but it also meant being sent to a home for orphans. He was better off on his own; he didn't want to have to rely on a soul. Soon the war would come to an end. Beyond that, who knew? What he was sure of was that he wouldn't be put in an institution and left to rot. They would have to leave him swinging on a lamppost before that happened.

He had waited until the truck containing Johann had pulled away before crossing the street. Diesel fumes hung in the air. He stood on the sidewalk and watched a woman—he assumed it was the hanging boy's mother—come out of her house carrying a chair and a knife. She placed the chair next to the lamppost and climbed on it, but even with the added height, her head only reached his knees. She encircled the part of the body she could reach with her arms and clung onto it.

Lukas suddenly felt embarrassed: He was intruding. He needed to leave this woman to her private heartbreak. He had begun to move away, his boots abruptly disturbing a brick from a pile of rubble. The woman looked up, her grief interrupted. She continued to sob, but the noises were muted now, low and involuntary.

"Hello," Lukas said somberly.

The woman nodded at him, unable to find any words. The two of them looked at each other for a few moments, the breeze blowing dust over both of them.

"You should be gone," the woman said. "It's too dangerous in the city. Where are your parents?"

"I'm sorry about what happened," Lukas said, swallowing hard.

The woman closed her eyes as if trying to expel the thought from her mind. Lukas walked back across the street and toward the building—he would move through the city, avoiding the streets where he could.

"Come back!" the woman shouted. He couldn't tell whether it was aimed at him or the boy in the noose, as he didn't turn around.

It took Lukas less than an hour to reach Lehrter Bahnhof. He had grown skilled at moving along the quickest and least populated routes.

The station appeared to still be functioning. Like dozens of other places in the city, there were people camped outside; whole families sleeping, cooking, and washing among injured and dying soldiers. The smell of decay and sickness hung in the air as powerfully as the sulfur, smoke, and brick dust from the bombings. Several bodies had been left wrapped in gray blankets to be collected by the civil authorities. He felt safe in such numbers. Soldiers and policemen would assume that he was part of one of the families. He could move swiftly through the crowds without being noticed, and if he was challenged, he would be able to disappear into the throng. This was as safe as it got in Berlin, he reasoned.

Lukas moved into the station. He would recognize Johann's family when he saw them. He remembered Mrs. Schultz from the bakery—she would come in during the afternoon after she had finished teaching to buy bread for dinner and sometimes pastries or a cake at the weekend. Lukas had always thought that the girl—Nadine was it?—was their daughter, not their niece. He had seen her in the street, on her way to school with friends, but had always been too scared to talk to her; older girls had little time for younger boys.

He wanted to tell them what had happened to Johann. He wanted to warn them so that they could choose to leave. He imagined the SS were taking Johann to Prinz-Albrecht-Straße. He would be killed or sent to a camp, if they were still able to transport people with the Soviets closing in. Lukas had remembered Johann telling him before they set out for Moabit that he had a fallback arrangement with Anja and Nadine: They would meet at Lehrter Bahnhof and escape west. Lukas wanted Anja and Nadine to be able to do that, even if Johann couldn't. There was no point in waiting for Johann now.

He passed through the doors and into bedlam. There were people everywhere, many of them shouting, running, or pushing. Fear, exhaustion, and uncertainty were etched on every face, as if imprinted by the unforgiving Berlin rain. A few sat—powerless and feeble—on suitcases and bundles of belongings, apparently reconciled to their fate. Most of them wore extra clothing as a way of carrying possessions; some women were wrapped in two coats, and there were men with jackets and coats over knitwear and multiple shirts. Lukas could almost smell the torment and anxiety— the train represented a final, desperate roll of the dice. Failing to get on a locomotive would mean, within days, facing Soviet artillery falling from the sky and infantry kicking down doors.

Lukas looked around. How would he ever pick out Anja and Nadine from the crowd? Finding two individuals among the teeming masses was nigh on impossible—there were too many people swirling about him, a multitude of faces glimpsed only for a brief moment. There was a chance, of course, that Anja and Nadine weren't even able to come to the station, that they had been killed, injured, delayed, or arrested. But in a city where everything had been transformed, where there were few fixed points any longer and where a simple human exchange was a marvel, Lukas wanted to make a connection.

Finding Anja and Nadine could make Berlin seem like a decent place once again, a city where he could go to school, play with his friends, and help his parents in the bakery.

Lukas wriggled his way to one end of the concourse, maintaining a wary eye on any soldiers or policemen he encountered. Such was the scale of the unfolding drama that the security forces were oblivious to him. He searched the faces of those overwhelmed or worn-out souls slumped at the edges of the frenetic activity and tried to process snatched glimpses of waves of refugees, their faces etched with defeat and—uncommonly—with the faintest glimmer of expectation.

He was tired by the time he reached the far end of the station. The effort of pushing his way through the swarm caused him to pause and lean against a wall. He had no idea how he would find them, even if they were in here. He looked over to where most of the people in the concourse were heading and realized that there were great clusters of humanity gathered near the entrances to the platforms.

He resolved that, if Anja and Nadine were among the thousands of restless, fretful people clamoring to board the train, he would find them. The crowds grew tighter and harder to move among when he got closer to the platforms. He could feel the level of anxiety became feverish.

There were voices all around him.

"Excuse me!"

"Do you mind!"

"I have to get through!"

"My family is waiting for me in Münster!"

Lukas whirled around. In every direction, he saw people who had once been dignified, productive members of society reduced to wrestling with each other to get on trains that were already full, might not run, and could suffer aerial attack the moment they left the city.

Bewildered and confused, Lukas searched the crowd. Johann was a prisoner of the SS, and Anja and Nadine were nowhere to be found. He was bumped and shoved. His feet were trodden on. As the crowd buffeted him he felt himself losing his bearings, lost and alone in a city in disarray.

Holding the briefcase under his arm, Johann turned to Anja.

"We need to try the second train," he said, nodding along the platform where the other locomotive was preparing to leave.

"Do you think there's any point?" Anja asked. "We don't have documents. They won't let us through."

Such was the pandemonium around them that, although they were crushed next to each other, they were forced to shout. Johann put a protective arm over Nadine's shoulder as she was jostled by two large women barreling through the crowd.

"You want to stay here?"

"Of course not," Anja said, thinking that Johann meant they should remain in the middle of the mob.

"Let's try the other platform," Nadine said to Anja. "Look at this place. We have nothing to lose."

"Come on then," Anja said, leading the way. She thrust herself between two men, presumably Party officials, who were waving red cards over their heads in order to get the attention of the soldiers at the gate, who beckoned them forward. A hand rose out of the air and attempted to snatch one of the passes, but its owner pulled it away in time and quickly buried it inside his coat.

The crowd thinned a little once the three of them escaped from the immediate vicinity of the platform. Each of them adjusted their clothes slightly, which had been pulled out of place by the crush of bodies. Johann piloted Anja and Nadine through the swarm toward the other platform. As he walked through the frantic multitudes, he realized that, quite literally, every person in the station was trying to do the same thing.

You can no more escape death than you can prevent those you love from passing, he thought to himself. He had seen it on the battlefield and on the surgeon's table. There is an end for all of us.

"It's the same situation," Nadine said as they approached the platform. She was right: an unruly crowd was gathered around the entrance.

"Coming through!" Johann shouted. He plunged forward into the crowd, dragging Anja and Nadine behind him. He had decided he would get them onto the train by sheer force of will.

The crowd parted unwillingly for the SS officer, and there were even a few muttered comments about "golden pheasants," but Johann's field-gray uniform was still enough to move them in front of the three bedraggled soldiers who controlled access to the train. Behind them, through clouds of steam, Johann saw groups of people loading bags and loved ones onto carriages. The sight made him focus all his energy and desire—they were agonizingly close to escaping Berlin.

"I have orders from the Reich Main Security Office," Johann began as severely as possible. He would not let them question his authority. "We have been authorized by emergency edict to obtain passage on this train."

"Where are your papers?" the soldier said.

"Do you question the authority of the SS?" Johann said sternly.

"Sir, we have simple orders that expressly forbid anyone getting on the train other than those with the correct documents."

"My commanding officer, Oberst Reinhard, has spoken with your commander," Johann continued, "and authorized an exception."

The soldiers looked at each other. Johann sensed that they doubted themselves in the face of his authority. The uniform was doing its work again.

"Well, how many of you are there?" one of them asked.

Johann hadn't had a chance to answer before another of them, who had frowned at his companion's question, spoke up. Like the soldier on the other platform, he spoke loudly, for the benefit of the crowd, which had settled for a moment to hear the exchange at the gate.

"We are unable to authorize passage onto the train for anyone other than those with the correct authorization."

"But we have authorization," Johann said. "From the Reich Main Security Office."

"*Sturmbannführer,* unless you have the correct paperwork we are unable to let you through," the soldier insisted.

Johann stood tall, his eyes boring hard into the men.

"Do you understand what you are doing here?" Johann said. He wanted to unsettle them. To make them doubt their actions.

The men looked unmoved. The crowd behind Johann was almost silent.

"Yes, we understand our orders," the soldier said eventually. "I suggest that you address any further comments to the ranking officer at the command post."

As if to underline their comrade's comments, the other two soldiers took their weapons from their shoulders to show that they were ready to use them, if necessary. Johann couldn't help wondering if they actually had any ammunition. He stood and stared at the enlisted men for a moment before turning and looking at Anja and Nadine, their faces ashen and dejected.

"Let's go," Anja said, aware that the crowd was becoming restless. Johann stood still and returned his gaze to the guards. Beyond them the train emitted a high-pitched whistle.

"Come on, Uncle," Nadine said, her voice raised for those watching them. "We can get the paperwork."

He looked over the guards to the train beyond. He saw the driver talking to one of the conductors, who looked at his watch. They were preparing for it to leave. And while he knew that his mind should be ruthlessly focused on the present, he was distracted by thoughts from the past. His recollections were colored by the previous days; the extremity of the experience had caused a dense layer to calcify over the rest of his recollections. He pulled away as if viewing his life from a great height. He remembered his father and his university years. And he remembered first meeting Anja, how she had touched something elemental in him. He recalled her kindness and her toughness during the years before the war, her stern refusal to entertain the slightest compromise to the way she conducted her life, despite the risks of not being seen to publicly embrace Nazi ideology. And he thought of Nadine, the scared, traumatized child who lit up their lives despite the collapse of all else about them.

The driver climbed up the steps of the locomotive as the final few carriage doors thudded closed.

He was back in the moment.

He would not let it end like this. He would get them on the train whether the guards would allow him to or not.

"Don't worry," Johann said. "You will leave Berlin—I promise."

An army sergeant cursed Dieter as the *Sturmbannführer* pulled up outside the station and splashed him with rainwater from a puddle. Dieter, usually fastidious about respect for rank, ignored the man and ran from his vehicle into the station, shoving people as he went. Time was short; he must stop Johann and his family from escaping and retrieve whatever it was that his half brother had taken from the security box.

Pushing his way through a stream of people, Dieter was oblivious to the confusion around him. He had seen shivering survivors of the flooding of the U-Bahn during his journey from the bank to the station. The civil authorities had persuaded the SS to open the gates to release those who had managed to squeeze onto the steps or otherwise avoid the deluge. He would not be surprised if Johann and his family were among them; his half brother's determination and appetite for survival was admirable—equal, perhaps, to his own. Even so, Dieter would ensure that the station was where they suffered their final reckoning.

He prowled the length of the concourse examining faces agitatedly.

He strode through a security detail to the area where great crowds had gathered to attempt to get onto the two remaining trains. If Johann and his family came to the station they would have to pass through this point to escape. He would wait for them. He limped through the crowd, his physical appearance attracting furtive glances. Dieter knew that he was being stared out, but he quite enjoyed the sensation: A limping, disfigured SS officer struck even more terror into the multitude than a physically competent version.

The volume of the crowd around one of the platform entrances rose the closer he got to it. People standing shoulder to shoulder barged into each other to get farther to the front. He imagined that they were all trying to get the attention of whoever was making the decisions—eyes bulging with desperation, the smell of fear in the air, each of them willing to kill the others for a chance to avoid being present at the city's dreadful demise. He was excited. He hadn't felt this way since he had been in the east. This was just another aspect of the struggle—the fight for those on the home front was as intense and demanding as for the combatants facing the Soviets only a few miles to the east.

He was conscious that he was dragging his foot behind him slightly as he moved toward the crowd. He saw an old man hold back his wife, who had been oblivious to Dieter, so that she wouldn't cut in front of him. As she raised her eyes, she flinched. Dieter moved on, amazed that in a city where there was so much that was awful, he could cause someone to recoil.

When he reached the crowd in their multiple layers of clothes he didn't even have to say anything in order to be given passage;

his very presence was enough to make the multitude step aside, as if they were able to sense the menace behind them. He worked his way through the bodies, toward the front and . . .

Was that them?

He thought at first that perhaps his mind was playing tricks on him. There was a tall *SS-Sturmbannführer* at the gate. This was hardly surprising. But there was something about the way that the guards were looking at him that made it seem as if there was an ongoing exchange that was not collaborative—the SS officer was arguing with the guards, who looked as if they were becoming agitated. Dieter continued to move forward and kept his eyes on the scene, while casting around for other clues.

He noticed two women, incongruous in brand-new clothes, waiting by the officer; their bodies were tensed as if scrutinizing every word of what was being said. He moved closer, the anticipation speeding his pace. He felt exhilarated, alive to possibility again.

He got closer, and there was something else. . . .

The SS officer's uniform looked . . . wet. Dieter could see only the upper part of the man's body, but it seemed that his tunic was plastered to his torso and his hair was slick with damp.

Dieter inched forward, the density of the crowd slowing his progress as he approached the entrance to the platform. With every step the pace of his heart increased with expectation.

Was it?

The SS officer turned to the right to look at the woman next to him.

Johann.

In his eagerness, Dieter began to wade through the crowd now, shoving people as he went. He lost sight of his quarry as people moved before him. He anxiously pushed forward, knowing that his time had come. The women were there still. He was only yards from them now. As the crowd scattered before him he saw Anja and Nadine watching, horrified, as he approached. It was all he could do to restrain himself from smiling.

Nadine slipped her arm through Anja's and faced Dieter wordlessly. There was defiance in her eyes but, for the first time, Dieter could see defeat as well. He had them. He had won.

Just as he was savoring his triumph, Dieter felt something sticking in his ribs: the cold metal of the barrel of a pistol.

"You were always late, Dieter," Johann said.

Dieter turned his head slightly to look at his half brother, who was standing to his side and slightly behind him.

"What is it you are intending to do, Johann?" he asked. "This place is full of troops and police officers. I am an SS officer with the Reich Main Security Office working for the Gestapo. You will not leave this building alive."

"You are someone with a gun barrel pressed against your vital organs," Johann said. "You will do as I tell you." His voice was low and quiet, as if the conversation were nothing out of the ordinary.

"And for how long do you expect this to continue?" Dieter asked calmly.

"Until my wife and niece are on that train," said Johann, his eyes flicking toward Anja.

"Johann . . . ," Anja said, her face heavy with worry.

Johann smiled at her briefly, but Anja felt bereft, like she had swallowed a bag of stones. This was Johann's plan? To put her and Nadine on the train while he remained here in Berlin? Surely this ran counter to everything they had been striving for. It couldn't be that Johann was thinking of upending their agreement—meet here at Lehrter Bahnhof and leave the city.

"But, Johann . . . ," she started again.

"The women get on the train, no strings attached, or I blow your liver all over those soldiers," Johann said, jerking the gun forcefully into Dieter's ribs. "That's the deal if you want the brief-case and what was in the security box."

Dieter looked at Anja, perhaps hoping for dissent, but she remained silent.

"What makes you think that I can get them on the train?" he said.

"You're assigned to the Gestapo, aren't you?" Johann said. "The army might have military authority here, but the Gestapo is a civil institution. You have the power to overrule them. Do it."

"That explains why you're still standing here . . . ," Dieter said. "It's a shame that my old field uniform doesn't carry the same weight. An SS uniform is a powerful thing, but at the very moment you need it to carry you to freedom it proves useless."

"It's not my freedom I'm thinking about," Johann answered, pushing the barrel into his half brother. "Get the women on the train."

Dieter remained silent. The intimacy of the moment, consider-ing the pandemonium that surrounded them, was oddly thrilling.

"Very well," Dieter said. "Surrender and the women shall go."

Johann felt Anja grasp his arm tightly. He wanted nothing more than to cling to her.

But he had to tell her to leave.

He glanced over at Nadine. The girl's eyes filled with tears. He shook his head ever so slightly; he wanted to tell her that he loved her, that he would see her again before too long, that he wanted only one thing more than to be with her and Anja, and that was for the pair of them to be far, far away. His future was inextrica-bly linked to theirs, but it was Dieter who had a hold over their destinies in Lehrter Bahnhof. Johann would take his chances with Dieter if the trade-off would ensure their survival.

"Then do it," Johann hissed at him, pushing Dieter forward toward the guards.

The voice was so familiar to Johann, but for those who hadn't grown up with Dieter's growl, it could cause alarm.

"Which one of you decided to disregard the request of the Sturmbannführer?" he snarled, shoving a piece of paperwork under the noses of the soldiers. "This document, signed by Standartenführer Keller of the Reich Main Security Office, gives me full authority over all ranks of the army in my capacity as an investigator of a matter of national security. Disregard it at your peril."

The three guards looked at each other before the one who had confronted Johann spoke up.

"We are following orders," he explained.

"This is why you are still a sergeant," Dieter replied dismissively.

"Sir," the guard started. He addressed Dieter fearfully. "We are doing all we can to follow our orders to maintain control within the station."

"That's not my concern," Dieter said sneeringly.

Johann felt his arm being squeezed. It was Anja. He turned and their eyes met.

"What are you doing?"

"You have to go," Johann said.

"You do too," Anja said firmly, her eyes wild.

Johann looked at her as kindly as he could. He met his wife's eyes with his hand still on the trigger of his pistol in case Dieter decided to renege on their agreement.

"You have to go, Anja," Johann said. Dieter was shouting at the guards now, gesticulating wildly. "Take Nadine as far as you can. Be safe."

He wondered if it might be the last time he would see her.

"I won't go without you," Anja said. Her knuckles were white from squeezing his forearm.

He paused before he spoke.

"But you have to," he said gently. "You have to do it for me."

He thought about the ruined city outside. He was the opposite of some of those buildings: On the surface he appeared undamaged, impervious to whatever had been thrown at him. Inside, the entire structure had broken down. He felt near to collapse.

"You *have* to come," Anja implored him, her eyes wide and passionate. The two of them were brusquely interrupted by Dieter. Johann couldn't hear what he was saying, but the guards—who had raised their weapons to prevent a mass rush for the train—were waving Anja and Nadine through the temporary barrier with their rifles.

Anja and Nadine looked at Johann imploringly. Both of them were frozen, paralyzed by the decision they had to make. The eyes of the crowd and the guards were on them. Dieter remained still, a gun in his back.

"I don't want to . . . ," Nadine started, her eyes filling with tears.

"Johann, this doesn't make—" Anja started to say.

Johann felt everything within him fall apart. There was nothing inside but dust. He looked at his wife and niece and knew he had to save them from themselves. If they delayed much longer the opportunity would pass—the guards would become suspicious, Dieter could have a change of heart, there could be an aerial attack. . . .

"Don't you hear the soldiers!" he snapped. He summoned every bit of military authority he could find. "Go!"

Anja and Nadine appeared momentarily stunned by his outburst.

"Move! Now! Before we decide to change our minds!" he shouted at them, his throat closing with emotion. Anja released his arm, realizing she had to maintain the fiction. She led Nadine hurriedly toward the front of the queue, glancing back just once, her face set hard with determination.

By the time she and Nadine were near the barrier Johann was no longer able to speak, the sensation of loss was so strong within him. He watched as they hurried toward the platform. He held his nerve, refusing to wave or show emotion for fear of undermining their escape. He watched them squeeze onto a train—the loves of his life, anxious and desperate, leaving the city they had lived in all their lives, to be borne on a dangerous journey to an indefinite destination. He had no idea how he would ever find them.

He held the pistol in his half brother's back until the train—thundering and filthy—had pulled from the station. Many of the people in the group around him had become hysterical at not having been allowed to board the train, screaming and shouting angrily at the guards and at the indifferent gods above.

Johann tapped Dieter on the shoulder. His half brother turned slowly.

"It's over," Johann said, and handed him the pistol and briefcase.

31

Dieter took the weapon from Johann and checked that it was loaded before turning it back on its owner.

"Why didn't you just kill me?" he asked, his eyes narrowing distrustfully.

"A shoot-out would not have helped my family," Johann replied with loathing. "I would have done it joyfully otherwise."

The crowd had cleared a space around the two men—the largest area not occupied by a human being in the station.

"So what now?" Johann asked.

"You know the answer to that," Dieter said flatly. He wiped his nose with the back of his hand. Johann examined his half brother's face. The wounds appeared to have become infected. He could see clear fluid on the surface of his burned skin in several places. The man was a walking miracle—when Johann had first seen him, he hadn't expected him to survive. Now, several days later, surviving a phosphorous grenade had served only to increase his spite.

"Out," Dieter said, gesturing toward the station exit with the handgun. People stood and stared at the scene: an SS officer apparently marching another out of the building with a pistol at his back.

A soldier approached Dieter and asked him if he required help. "Another traitor?" he asked casually.

Dieter didn't respond.

"We have rope," the soldier offered.

Johann continued walking. He didn't regret giving Dieter his gun; it was the bargain he had struck in order to secure Anja and

Nadine's passage on the train. He thought of them on their way west, and prayed that the train would be given safe passage. Surely the Allies must know the carriages were full of civilians? Eradicating the few Nazis on board could not be worth slaughtering hundreds of innocents.

He knew Dieter would not keep him alive for long; if he was locked up in Prinz-Albrecht-Straße the cell door would be opened next by an infantryman speaking Russian or Ukrainian.

No, it was just the two of them now: half brother versus half brother, neither owing the other anything, both of them with nothing but loathing for the other. Johann knew that this encounter was intractable. He determined to go along with whatever Dieter was planning; there would be a moment when he was distracted or not paying attention. Johann would come at him then.

Dieter marched Johann out of the building and into daylight. Feeling the cold breeze against his face, Johann told himself to focus. He had to forget Anja and Nadine. He had to remember that they had escaped the city. He had done what he had promised to do. Now he must survive himself. A group of teenagers holding shovels walked past, on the way to dig fortifications, a tank trap maybe. He wondered what had happened to the boy Lukas. He hoped that he would return to his hideout, that someone else would find him and care for him.

"Over there," Dieter snapped at Johann, directing him to a clearing on one side of Washingtonplatz where a building had once stood. It had been hit early in the war, and the rubble had been removed. Now it was a dusty plot of ground specked with patches of weeds. The only object nearby was a *Kübelwagen*, which had been left carelessly on the edge of a large puddle. Johann couldn't help wonder if all Berlin would resemble this dismal spot once the Soviets had finished with it. The few survivors would be the only ones able to interpret the bleak landscape littered with occasional traces of what had once been there.

Was this desolate place where Dieter planned to finish matters? Johann didn't doubt it. Eleven years after killing Nicolas, his half brother would leave him dead among the wreckage.

Johann walked slowly. He had never been so acutely aware of his back: At any second he expected a bullet and then blackness.

He needed to find a route of escape, a way of keeping Dieter from pulling the trigger. . . .

Johann heard Dieter's footsteps come to a halt. Now came the reckoning. He closed his eyes tight and thought of Anja and Nadine.

"Turn around," Dieter ordered. Johann breathed again. He pivoted heavily and looked at his half brother. The sight sent a shudder through him. As menacing as he was, Dieter looked physically ruined. There was a bloody cut on his forehead, the part of his face that wasn't burned was sagging, his body was slumped sideways, and his eyes were swollen with exhaustion. Yet within them, Johann detected a believer's zeal. His conviction in what he was doing was pure, his willingness to do the unspeakable undiminished.

Johann had absolutely no doubt that Dieter would kill him. His sole focus was to prolong the encounter; every minute, every second he lived longer would give him more opportunity to turn the tables.

"What are you to do, Dieter?" Johann asked.

"With you?" Dieter scoffed. "What do you think?"

"I mean when the Soviets come," Johann continued. There was a rumble of artillery in the distance, sending an eerie growl over the city.

"What does it matter to you?" Dieter asked. Johann noticed a small, wry smile creep into the corner of his half brother's mouth.

"How ironic that the great objector, the champion of freethinking, Doctor Johann Schultz, should be found dead wearing the uniform of a *Sturmbannführer*," he said. "It seems that your sensibilities were not entirely offended when it suited you."

"I wear it through necessity, not choice," Johann countered. He glanced around, searching for the nearest piece of cover, should he find a way of distracting Dieter.

"You and your moral high ground," Dieter said. "It always held you back." He lowered the gun. Johann knew that this was no sign of reconciliation; it was because he was exhausted. Dieter was too far away to rush him—his half brother would have plenty of time to raise his pistol and shoot if he made a move.

"As interesting as this discussion is . . . ," Dieter said, seemingly drained. He waved the pistol around as if dismissing what had been said, then added, "We are here for another reason."

"Tell me," Johann said.

"Where are the contents of the box?"

"Oh, yes, the box," Johann said, furrowing his brow.

"You stole whatever was in it," Dieter said. "It is my birthright too."

For a moment Johann forgot the twisted disquiet inside him. He was able, momentarily, to think of a matter beyond Anja and Nadine's departure and his own survival. Dieter wanted to know what was inside the box. . . .

Johann smirked, shaking his head.

"You laugh . . . ?" Dieter said quietly. Then, in a blinding rage, he hobbled over toward Johann, the pistol raised. He pressed the barrel of the gun hard enough against Johann's head that it left a deep mark. "You would leave me that letter about my father's death, as if it were nothing?"

Johann was concentrating so hard on the weapon that he failed to see Dieter raise his hand and deliver a punch to the side of his head. Caught unaware on the soft side of his skull, Johann collapsed to the ground.

"Get up," Dieter said, kicking him. "Get up now."

Johann looked in the dirt for a brick or a stone that he might use as a weapon—Dieter was planning on ending it at any moment—but there was nothing large or weighty enough.

"Get the fuck up," Dieter said. "You and your pathetic bourgeois superiority."

Johann clambered to his feet, heaving. The fall had knocked the wind from him and he was having trouble breathing. Yet the violence had given rise to a feeling of liberation: If Dieter was so intent on killing him, he would have his say. He was dead either way.

"With all this"—he gasped, gesturing around them—"you can't think further than what was in the security box? What do you think was in there? And where do you think it will get you?"

"None of that is your concern," Dieter snapped.

Johann sucked oxygen into his lungs before standing upright. He noticed that Dieter had left the briefcase on its side in the dust. The tip of the Luger was trembling; Dieter was shaking, either through anger, or exhaustion, or both.

"The box was emptied long ago," Johann said. "You remember the day after you had Nicolas taken away, when you were searching for the key? I took it from under your nose. I went to the bank as soon as I was eighteen. I showed them my papers. As long as I signed my name and possessed the key and the code, there were no questions."

Dieter was suddenly still, listening hard.

"And, Dieter, you will never guess what was in the box. . . ." Johann let his words hang in the air. "You see, for all your criticism of him, Nicolas was a prudent and thrifty man. He had planned for hard times. He had seen what happened to the economy after the Great War and wanted to make sure his family would always have something to fall back on."

Johann paused again.

"Nicolas knew that the *Reichsmark* was vulnerable, could be rendered valueless, so he made sure that his wealth was in something more tangible. He left hard assets: gold and jewelry."

Johann looked at Dieter, whose face was framed by a smoky, thunderous sky.

"And there was one thing, Dieter, that was quite incredible, a necklace made of sapphires." Johann paused for effect. "It was the most wonderful thing that I've ever seen. Down there in the basement of the bank, that piece of jewelry illuminated the room. It was as if it was midday in midsummer, it was so bright in there. . . ."

The end of the pistol had stopped trembling. Johann could tell that he had Dieter's total concentration.

"You have never seen anything quite like it in your life. The object, it was . . . mesmerizing," Johann continued. "And there was a note from Nicolas. It said that it was our mother's, and that it was only to be sold in times of crisis."

Johann paused.

"I didn't want to sell it, Dieter, I really didn't, but you know how things have been, and I needed money to bribe officials when Nadine's parents were taken away. . . ."

Before Johann could step back to avoid the blow, Dieter had charged forward and smashed the pistol across his half brother's face. Johann felt the crunch of cartilage in his nose, and his mouth filled with blood. He spat strings of it onto the ground, along with fragments of a shattered tooth as he fell to his knees.

"You bastard!" Dieter screamed. "That was mine!"

He pressed the pistol against the crown of Johann's head and cocked the trigger. Beneath him he saw Johann shaking. Dieter paused. At first he had imagined that it was fear, but after a moment he realized that the rocking of Johann's shoulders wasn't dread. It was laughter.

"What are you doing?" Dieter seethed. This isn't how he had envisaged the execution. He had wanted Johann cowering, begging for his life, pleading, admitting his mistakes.

Johann spat blood and mucus and wiped his mouth. The liquid pooled beneath him.

"Your mind has done powerful things to you, Dieter," Johann said, once he had finished laughing. "Just as you believed in a mythical Germany, you could almost touch that necklace, couldn't you? You felt like it was within your grasp. . . . Well, here's the news, Dieter: There was no necklace. Nicolas had no wealth. He didn't aspire to money or to power. He believed in justice and decency and social responsibility. He left us fodder for bureaucrats: insurance contracts, deeds to the house, legal documents, valueless keepsakes."

Dieter looked down at Johann and stepped back slightly, as if trying to process the information. He had imagined that the box contained his fortune, that he could wrestle the riches from his weakling half brother. . . .

The reality of his situation became apparent: He had nothing left. There was only the here and now. It dawned on him that he had failed. He may have recaptured the briefcase, but he had no future in the Party. The fracture was irreparable.

"You have always thought yourself superior," Dieter spewed angrily. "You think that you're clever with the files, certificates, and the letter that you left for me. To what end? What do you prove? You think that it is news to me that your father ended up in Sachsenhausen?"

Johann raised his head—he would stare Dieter in the eye, not bow before him. The end of the pistol dragged over his hairline and ended up pressed against his forehead, the metal potent and menacing.

"You think that the documents I left you have no significance?" Johann said. "They are records, Dieter, proof of the most awful cruelty and inhumanity. You think that by ignoring them or burning them—like the contents of the briefcase—their significance diminishes? That the acts that generated them are undone or forgotten? You will kill me, and I will be one less witness to what your Party did to millions. With me gone, you will be able to deny what you did to my father, but that doesn't diminish your actions."

"You appear to have no sense of your own criminality," Dieter said. "You tried to kill me in the hospital. You were responsible for the deaths of Ostermann and Lehman. Do you think that you are immune from judgment simply because you believe you have a higher calling?"

"I don't have an answer for that," Johann said.

"Ha!" exclaimed Dieter, gesturing around them at the ruins of the city. "I think that you're a little too late for superiority. You too are a killer. Maybe you have found your element. We are standing in the middle of the world's biggest mass grave—and the bodies will be piled ever higher in the next few days."

"You got what you wanted," Johann said. "All of you."

"Our vision would have been possible if we hadn't been undermined by weaklings, cowards, and traitors," Dieter said.

Johann was tired of hearing such nonsense. He just shook his head, worn out by Dieter's maintenance of National Socialist pretense.

"There was something else in the box you must see," Johann said. "I am going to reach into my jacket and pull it out."

He looked up for approval. Dieter nodded, pushing the gun against his half brother's forehead even harder. Johann opened his jacket wide to show Dieter exactly what it was that he was doing.

He slid his hands inside a damp pocket and pulled out a small rectangle bundled in leather and placed it on the ground in front of him. Johann carefully unwrapped the bindings. He unpeeled the soaking layers to reveal a small package of letters and a book.

"These too were in the security box," Johann said. He rummaged through the letters and pulled out a document. Dieter took the paperwork and stepped back to give himself space in case Johann tried to jump him. The object was damp, but still readable.

He scanned the page. It was his birth certificate.

"It's the original," Johann said.

Dieter looked down the page and all appeared to be in order. Then he noticed something different from the version he had seen at the bank—an asterisk against the name of his father, Wilhelm. He cast his eyes to the bottom of the document and, next to the asterisk at the bottom, there was a single word: "Deceased."

"What does this prove?" Dieter asked.

"More than you are able to imagine," Johann replied. "Look at the dates."

Dieter stared at the paper again.

"Can you not count?" Johann declared impatiently. "Wilhelm Schnell died in January 1915, but he had been in a mental institution since September 1914."

"Meaning what?"

"You were born in July 1915."

Johann saw the shock cross Dieter's face. The *Sturmbannführer* sucked in some of the filthy air that whipped around them.

"Mother cannot have gotten pregnant by Wilhelm," Johann said. "Your war hero father wasn't even your father."

Dieter pushed the barrel of the gun across Johann's scalp.

"You lie!" he screamed.

"There is something else," Johann said, handing Dieter another document. "It was also in the security box."

Dieter stepped back again in order to read it. He kept glancing at Johann, but his half brother wasn't moving—he was rapt, wanting only to see Dieter's reaction. Dieter adjusted his position slightly; he found it hard to stand for long periods. The paper had yellowed over the years, its edges close to a golden color. There in black ink, in a tight, old-fashioned German hand, was the date: September 3, 1915. The ink had run slightly from the effects of the water, but the writing was still legible.

Johann watched Dieter as he read. His face remained neutral for a moment, before creasing deeply in disbelief. It was a legal document, a sworn affidavit. He scanned through the legal jargon until he reached a passage that felt like it might make the world stop.

. . . I, Hannah Schnell, being of firm mind and good reputation, declare the biological father of my child Dieter Schnell to be Nicolas Meier, not Wilhelm Schnell, as per the public record. In all civil matters, however, Dieter should continue to be regarded as my deceased husband's child, as knowing that the child was conceived out of wedlock may prejudice society against him. I make this statement under oath with the intention only of protecting Dieter's interests should legal matters arise in which his provenance has bearing upon the outcome . . .

It was signed in what Dieter knew was his mother's hand.

"Nicolas left no riches, Dieter," Johann said. "Just the truth."

Dieter said nothing, although Johann noticed him stagger slightly.

"You had your own father killed," Johann said. "*Our* father."

Dieter pressed the pistol harder, his index finger red from the pressure it exerted on the trigger.

"There is one other item," Johann said. "I was going to keep it for myself, but you should see it."

Johann leaned down and pulled a black book from the leather bindings. Dieter took it and examined the front and back covers. It had absorbed water, but was largely undamaged.

"What's this?" Dieter said.

Johann said nothing, his silence serving to increase Dieter's curiosity. He opened the book and flicked through it, his eyes jumping from the pages back to Johann.

"The other way round," Johann said eventually.

Dieter glanced at him as if he were being tricked. He continued to flick through it. The pages were damp beneath his fingers but flowed relatively freely.

"You open it from the back," Johann said.

Dieter looked at his brother. Why was he handing him this thing—a book in Hebrew?

"There was no necklace, Dieter," Johann said. "Nicolas left us only this."

"I can't read this shit," Dieter said. He moved as if to fling it.

"No!" shouted Johann. His voice echoed across the wasted ground. Dieter paused. "Look inside the cover," Johann continued. "The back cover."

Dieter stepped back farther to protect himself; he would need to use both hands to open the book, meaning that he had to lower his weapon.

"Read it," Johann persisted. Dieter folded back the cover. Inside he saw neat, old-fashioned handwriting.

Dieter read: "To Hannah, with much love, from Mother."

Johann watched Dieter as he fathomed what was before him. His face remained neutral for a moment, before twisting incredulously. He was looking at his grandmother's handwriting. Neither he nor Johann had ever met her, but her words—written to her daughter nearly a half century beforehand—traveled through the decades and landed on him with the power of a collapsing building.

Johann waited until he could bear it no longer.

"How's that feel, *Sturmbannführer?*" he said sourly. "How does that feel? Or should I call you *brother?*"

Dieter's arm fell to his side, the book barely in his grasp. It hung loosely, between his fingertips.

"Too full of hate to feel remorse?" Johann asked. "It was all lies, Dieter, you see. Everything you believed was a lie."

Dieter stared back at Johann darkly, his brows thick with rage. There was no contrition, no remorse, and—Johann realized disconcertingly—there was no doubt. Dieter was angered, not altered, by what he saw.

"Our father died protecting us," Johann said. His tone contained no trace of bitterness; he was trying to communicate with Dieter as a sibling. "When he was packed onto that SA truck he had done everything he could to hide our heritage, to keep us safe from the state, who were hunting for people like us. He was an easy target—a liberal intellectual. But he was also something else—a guardian who kept our secrets at the cost of his own life. Who do you think went and altered the documents in the archive and placed the originals in the bank to protect us? Who held back from telling you that he was your father out of respect for our dead mother's wishes? He hid what might prove fatal to us."

Dieter dropped the book on the ground. As it fell, it opened, so that its pages lay facedown in the dirt. Johann looked at it for a moment. He realized that, for Dieter, nothing had changed. Johann knew that he was the lone custodian of the book. He couldn't bear the thought of it being damaged. He began crawling forward. As he inched toward the object it began to rain. Dieter raised his weapon.

"Stay where you are!" he screamed at Johann, his face purple with exertion.

Johann ignored him. He dragged himself through the brick dust, the powdered mortar, and the grime toward the book. Raindrops collected on the back of his hand as he reached for it.

"Our father saved us both—and you had him killed," Johann said, knowing now that there was no hope for Dieter. There was nothing that Johann could say or do that would change his brother. He was beyond all reason. All hope. All humanity.

"You would tell me lies like this?" Dieter said to Johann. He re-placed the weapon against his brother's head, the barrel trembling again.

"No lies, Dieter, no lies . . . ," Johann said, looking at his brother defiantly.

This was it, he thought. This was it.

He closed his eyes and waited. Other than a few distant shouts the city was quiet.

Johann waited. Still nothing. He opened his eyes. He tried to speak, but words wouldn't form on his lips. Terror had rendered him mute.

His eyes met Dieter's.

"Death is a lonely business," Dieter said quietly.

"Please . . . ," Johann pleaded, trembling. "Please, just . . ."

"I have a better idea, *brother*," Dieter continued. Something had changed in Dieter's demeanor.

"Stand up," he ordered Johann, who followed the instruction. He stood shivering with fear and cold and wiped the grit from his hands on his uniform. A hundred yards away a man was trying to light a fire with pieces of timber he had foraged; the sight of an SS officer holding another at gunpoint held no interest for him.

"Move," Dieter said, waving the gun toward the *Kübelwagen*. "Over there."

Johann stumbled toward the vehicle, his legs weak. His body was failing him now that he had gotten Anja and Nadine out of the city. He had no reserves to tap. He shook his head to clear it and tried to focus on the task in hand. Surely Dieter would drop his guard at some point. Johann leaned, drained, against the car.

"Over there," Dieter said, gesturing to the driver's side while keeping the weapon trained on his brother. Johann got in and looked at the blood smeared on the windshield and elsewhere. He wondered when he had last sat down. Dieter landed beside Johann in the passenger seat, placed the briefcase on the wooden runners beneath his feet, and jammed the pistol into his brother's ribs.

"Drive!" he ordered, and handed Johann the keys.

"Where are we going?" Johann asked.

"What does that matter?" Dieter replied.

Johann turned the engine on and began to maneuver the car away from the station. As they exited Washingtonplatz, he paused to let a young woman with two toddlers, their possessions stacked inside a carriage, pass in front of him.

They moved south toward Potsdamer Platz. Johann gasped at what he saw—it was utterly unrecognizable. He remembered being told as a child that this was where the world's first traffic light had been situated to coordinate the high volume of activity. He had caught streetcars here hundreds of times, yet it was now as unfamiliar to him as a city that he had never visited.

"Where are we going?" Johann asked eventually.

"Turn east," Dieter said. As he spoke a Yakovlev roared over the city, its wings barely clearing the chimney stacks.

"To die in Berlin will be glorious," Dieter said, looking up briefly.

"You call *this* glory?" Johann asked, navigating through the brick-and-mortar carcasses of a once imposing city.

Three other Soviet fighters swept over the east of the city ahead of them. Edgy civilians carrying pathetic bundles crept along the perimeter of buildings ready to scurry to safety at a moment's notice, their progress slow as they navigated the rubble of their homes, schools, and workplaces.

"And what's your glory?" Dieter replied. "Stabbing a man with a syringe? Murder is murder. You can dress it up in other words or explanations but it's always the same. One triumphs. The other ceases to exist. It's the way it is."

Johann thought back to Ostermann and Lehman. He was responsible for their deaths, but no remorse stirred within him. He would kill them both again if he needed to. He wondered what he had become. Had he been sunk so deep in the bloody mire for so long that he had lost all humanity? Were he and Dieter so very different? Their motivations might differ, but their actions were not unrelated. His perspective had changed utterly, but not unaccountably.

"Keep going east," Dieter instructed him, slapping the dashboard with his palm.

Johann slowed. A group of *Volkssturm* had dragged a streetcar into the middle of the road and was filling it with rubble as a makeshift barricade against tanks.

"Put your foot down," Dieter insisted as Johann pulled slowly around the obstacle. One of the old men gestured cordially at the SS car as part of it crept over a heap of brickwork to one side. "Come on," Dieter demanded impatiently.

They encountered a clear stretch of road for the first time. "I told you to put your foot down," Dieter insisted, striking Johann on the head. "Move!"

Johann angrily slammed the accelerator down and quickly ran through the gears from first to fourth. The engine screamed in complaint, racing to keep up with the demands. The jeep was at its outer limits. The vehicle shuddered forward as the needle hovered around seventy-five miles per hour. The passengers were thrown about as the engine reached full capacity and the vehicle hit debris that littered the road.

The road was coming at him too fast—bricks, lengths of wood, pieces of masonry—and Johann swerved to avoid what he could, but he was unable to miss much. He wondered that the tires hadn't yet blown out. The boulevard in front of him had become imperceptible—he was simply too exhausted to be able to focus clearly. Berlin had broken down into a blur of debris.

Then he noticed something more distinct—a break in the roadway marked by a jagged dark line that they rushed toward ominously.

"Forward!" Dieter ordered him. "Forward!"

Johann realized what it was: an antitank ditch that had been dug by the *Volkssturm* to hold up the progress of the Soviets. If it was like the others he had seen, it would be nothing more than a pathetic hole in the ground—but it would be enough to kill them if the *Kübelwagen* tumbled inside.

Johann swerved wildly around the obstacle, dragging the car onto a pile of sand that had been left by the side of the roadway. The car shuddered and tilted at an extreme angle, throwing both Dieter and Johann violently to the left, but somehow the vehicle kept moving, and Johann pulled it back onto the roadway.

"I said forward!" Dieter shouted. "Don't do that again."

Johann was horrified.

He realized, finally, what his brother had in store for them: They would die together in a mangled piece of wreckage.

"Your letters and documents and the microfilm will go up in flames with us!" Dieter shouted at Johann over the noise. "Now drive!"

And, as they rounded a corner, they both saw what might be their destiny: another streetcar that had been left on its side in the middle of the road, like the carcass of an ancient beast. Johann wavered. He couldn't imagine doing what he was being ordered to do.

"Now!" Dieter shrieked, jabbing the pistol into Johann.

Johann stared ahead, wondering whether he could accept that this really might be the end. He considered the streetcar. If he accelerated, he would be dead within a matter of seconds.

The moment of reflection made up his mind for him: If he was dead, Dieter would be too. Johann's final act would be to remove this terrible blight upon humanity. He would take his brother with him.

Johann felt almost manic now, delirious with exhaustion and trauma. Anja and Nadine were safe—he had saved his wife and niece. That was all that mattered, and he had no right to expect more than that when there were so many millions perishing. What gave him a right to live? And if his death brought about the death of the loathsome killer who sat next to him in the jeep, then surely that was an accomplishment. Killing Dieter Schnell—his brother—was a service to all mankind.

Johann pressed the accelerator flat against the floor.

The car growled and lurched forward even faster, gathering speed. Johann thought about Anja and Nadine. He had no idea if they would be safe beyond Berlin, but to not have Dieter pursuing them would remove one more threat upon their lives. Taking Dieter with him would protect them.

The needle on the accelerator topped out again at seventy-five miles per hour. There was nothing Johann could do to increase the speed. The vehicle was not designed to go faster. Berlin flashed past, unrecognizable and unvarying: a ghostly city inhabited by the living dead, a ruined hulk adrift in a lifeless sea. They hurtled wildly toward the streetcar.

Ten seconds until impact.

Johann clung to the shuddering steering wheel and stared forward grimly. He felt grit and detritus of the city striking his skin. He tensed his body, awaiting the impact.

Nine seconds.

He tried to empty his consciousness, to erase all feeling, to flatten his emotions; he knew he had been dead the moment Dieter found him in Lehrter station.

Eight seconds.

No, he was dead before that; the second he had set eyes on Dieter in triage he knew that his hopes of surviving the horror around him were over.

Seven seconds.

Dieter never gave up.

Six seconds.

Dieter was resolute to the end.

Five seconds.

Dieter had won.

Boom!

Johann jumped. He had been expecting impact in a few seconds. What was happening?

There was a thud to his left.

He looked around, and Dieter's head—bloody and lifeless—was slumped on the dashboard.

Three seconds.

Johann slammed his foot on the brake. The tires screeched like injured animals. The stench of burning rubber filled his nostrils. The clamor about him was as if the world had imploded.

Two seconds.

He steeled himself for impact as the streetcar loomed above him.

The hood of the *Kübelwagen* crumpled on contact, with an abrupt earsplitting screech. Johann's body was slammed against the steering wheel, knocking the breath out of him. He felt the cavity where the car's pedals were located fold around his legs. It took him a few moments to rouse himself from a daze, his head whirling with incomprehension.

What just happened?

He had stopped moving. Dieter's body had been thrown forward and was now pressed against the windshield awkwardly. There was a ticking noise, and he realized that the liquid on his face was his brother's blood. He wiped his face with the sleeve of his uniform and tried to move. By twisting his body he was able to lever himself from the seat. Blood was dripping into the bottom of the car, pooling on a rubber mat where Dieter's boots still rested by the briefcase. His dirty blond hair was soaked crimson. His hand clung to the handgun that had been jabbed in Johann's side only seconds ago. Johann prized his brother's fingers away from the handle and put the weapon in his holster. Unbelievable, he thought. Not that he was alive, but that his first act of survival was to take a weapon from his dead brother's hand.

But how had Dieter died? Had he decided to end it all before they hit the streetcar?

He heard a click behind him.

Johann froze.

There was silence. Johann began to look around slowly. There, in the back of the car, his nose streaming with blood, was a familiar face: Lukas.

Johann couldn't believe what he was seeing. The boy was holding a handgun, the same one Johann had returned to him back in the boy's quarters in the carpentry shop.

"Are you all right?" he asked Lukas. The boy nodded. His face was dispassionate. He showed no signs of the ordeal he had just endured other than that he was gingerly dabbing at his bleeding nose.

"I came to the station," he said after a while, unfolding his body from the space behind the seat into which he had fallen. "I saw what happened with your family and then this SS officer led you outside. I knew he was going to kill you. I hid in the car. It took me a while to build the courage to, you know"—he looked at Dieter—"do it."

The two of them leaned back in their seats, exhausted and stunned. Dieter had finally been brought low by someone who had little memory of life before the Nazis.

In the distance—perhaps only five miles away—there was an explosion. Then another, and another . . . and then a deluge; hundreds of shells roared pitilessly down on the city. The Soviets were pulverizing what was left of it before the infantry's advance. The last remnants of the SS were hiding among the ruins ready for the final, unforgiving reckoning.

"We need to get moving," Johann said. To be found in an SS uniform could mean immediate execution. Even the boy might be shot if he was discovered in possession of a weapon. Johann wrenched his way out of the passenger seat and lifted Lukas from the rear of the vehicle. The engine continued to make a ticking noise. Its hood had been crushed beyond recognition. Johann knew the T-34s that would roll down the street in the next few hours would not find it such a formidable object.

The rumble of artillery continued in the distance. Johann wiped the boy's nose.

"It's stopped bleeding already," Johann said. "That's a good sign."

A group of civilians made their way along the street, hurrying away from the rolling thunder of the artillery. Johann reached into the car and pulled the briefcase from below Dieter's feet.

"Come on," he said, moving away from the car. "We need to be quick."

"But where are we going?" asked the boy, trotting to keep up with him.

"Somewhere you will be safe," Johann replied.

"Is that possible?" Lukas said dismissively.

Johann stopped and looked back.

"Yes," he said. "Yes, it is."

Johann did not turn and look back at Dieter's body. For Johann, his brother had long since been dead.

"Not here," the boy said when Johann knocked on the door.

"There's nothing to be scared of," Johann said. "You'll see."

They heard footsteps on the other side. The door swung open and Otto's lumbering bulk filled the doorframe. The men said nothing. They stepped forward and embraced.

"Who is this?" Otto asked, seeing Lukas. He ushered them inside. "Quick, quick . . ."

"This is Lukas," Johann said. "The bravest boy in Berlin."

"Well, that's saying something," Otto replied. "Because I've met an awful lot of brave Berliner boys."

Otto walked them down the corridor.

"Everyone is in the cellar," he said, leading them down a staircase. There were about a dozen people in the dark subterranean room, most of them elderly. Three women played cards by candlelight. Two decrepit men slept on makeshift cots. Johann assumed that they were members of the *Volkssturm,* many of whom had abandoned their positions and sought sanctuary. They wanted nothing to do with what was to come. He looked around.

Someone had propped joists to support the ceiling. There were buckets of water for drinking and to put out fires, and some supplies lined up on a table.

Lukas recognized one of the women—she was the mother of the boy who had been hung from the lamppost.

The woman reached her hand forward and touched the boy's face.

"Come and sit next to me," she said, pulling Lukas to sit on the bench beside her. She examined his face.

"What happened to you?" she asked.

"I was in an accident," Lukas said. Johann noticed a change—a fragment of Lukas's toughness had slipped away. The woman stood up. She found a rag and dipped it in one of the buckets.

"Don't worry," she said. "We don't drink from that one."

She dabbed at the boy's face.

"I know that there's someone else under here," the woman said.

The boy smiled for the first time since Johann had met him. He looked up at Johann.

"I must go," Johann said to him.

The boy stood up, his face once again creased with worry.

"Why? Where are you going? The Soviets will be here soon."

"That's why I can't stay," Johann said. The boy sat down without needing any further explanation. He knew that two able-bodied men of fighting age would only bring trouble to those sheltering in the cellar.

"I'll be upstairs," Johann said. "Frau . . . ?"

"Breinbach," the woman said.

"Frau Breinbach will look after you now."

The boy considered this for a moment before nodding. Johann wanted to think that Lukas had made the decision willingly, but there was an awareness between them that there was no other choice. There was a crash of artillery in the distance. Johann and Otto began to walk back up the stairs to Otto's apartment. Johann turned for a final look at the boy, but Lukas's attention was now fully absorbed by Frau Breinbach.

The two men sat in Otto's living room. Johann was slumped in his coat.

"You need to get rid of that," Otto said to him, meaning the uniform. "I'll get you something."

He went into another room while Johann peeled off the filthy, still-damp uniform. He wanted dearly to bathe, but the fresh clothes that Otto gave him would have to do.

"They were my brother's," Otto said. His brother, a captain in the navy, had been killed in the North Sea in 1942. Otto took the clothes into the backyard, dug a hole, and buried the uniform.

Johann wanted nothing more than to sleep. He closed his eyes, but something was keeping him awake.

"Do you still have the piano in the back room?" he asked Otto.

"Of course," Otto replied.

Johann stood up and walked slowly through the apartment and pushed open the door to what had once been Otto's family's living room. He looked at the photographs on the top of the piano. All those people, all gone. He flipped open the lid and hit middle C. It hadn't been tuned recently, but it was playable. Johann sat down and pulled the stool forward. He reached forward to the keys to see if he was the right distance away. Once he was satisfied, he rested his fingertips on the ivory.

There was a crash of ordnance a few streets away, a percussive blast followed by the sounds of masonry falling.

He began to play, unevenly at first, thinking back to the night in 1934 when he had last felt Bach flow through him. He remembered playing a piece from the *Goldberg Variations* for Nicolas that night, remembered how his father would close his eyes and suck on his pipe, lost in the music. After a couple of minutes, Johann felt himself relaxing; his fingers moved over the keyboard more fluidly as he felt the melody pouring from him. It was as if he had no control over it. He was simply a conduit for the exquisite composition to find its way into the world. At that moment, it was just him and Bach. The Soviets and the Nazis be damned.

Johann finished playing and replaced the lid on the piano.

"I have a surprise for you," Otto said. He left the room and returned with two bottles of pilsner. "I'm not sure what I was saving them for," Otto said, flipping off the bottle tops with a metal opener.

"Thank you," Johann said as Otto handed him the beer.

"Auf uns," Otto said. They clinked the bottles.

Johann couldn't quite believe the deliciousness of the beer. He drank quickly, forcing himself to stop before he finished it all.

"That's the best beer . . . I've ever tasted," Johann said.

"At least that's one thing the Nazis didn't fuck up," Otto replied.

They sat in the house silently. They could hear small-arms fire and the desperate shouts of German soldiers in retreat. Boots thumped along the street. Next there was the growl and the squeaking of the T-34s. The snarling engines sounded amiss in a residential street.

Neither Johann nor Otto commented on what they could hear outside; instead, Johann told his friend about Anja and Nadine.

"They will find you," Otto said confidently. "They know the address of this apartment. They know that you will be in contact with me. Once we have a postal service again, they will write. I know it."

Johann nodded his thanks and took another sip of beer.

"We will just have to wait," he said.

They could both hear the shouts of Russian voices now, the first wave of infantry—the soldiers who had injured the men whom Johann had spent years putting back together again.

"I am so damn tired," Otto said.

"I can't even remember what being rested is like," Johann said. It felt like he'd lost the gear for sleep. He'd forgotten how to do it. When he closed his eyes they felt swollen and ached. There was nothing happening at the front of his mind, but he felt a vigorous hum somewhere in his head at all times that prevented him from sleeping. His entire body hurt.

"I have a little food, if you want to eat," Otto said.

Johann shook his head. Like sleep, he had forgotten what hunger felt like. His being had become about existence. He had no need to thrive. If he was left alone he would continue to exist without the intervention of the outside world. He was peaceful in the chair. He wished only to be left alone. He would be content to remain sitting there for weeks until this whole mess had been sorted out.

Small-arms fire crackled through the air. Moments later they heard the front door of the building being kicked open. Johann and Otto stood up, walked toward the front door, and stood with their hands raised in the air. They could smell cordite.

Johann kicked the briefcase in front of him—the Soviets couldn't miss it. They would trip over it when they entered the room.

The apartment door was kicked down. There was a burst of machine-gun fire.

Then silence.

AFTERWORD

This is a work of fiction, but some of the events in this book are based on fact. The Demolitions on Reich Territory was an executive order passed by Hitler on March 19, 1945, aimed at denying the Allies all German infrastructure. It became known colloquially as the Nero Decree. Acting under this order, the SS flooded Friedrichstraße U-Bahn station on April 25 by planting explosives on the ceiling of the north-south axis. The station was said to be full of injured soldiers and civilians. Due to the chaotic conditions in Berlin at the end of the war, there are no records of how many lives were lost. What is known is that the flooding affected sixty-three kilometers of tunnels and twenty-five stations—one-third of the Berlin U-Bahn system. A 1990 study by the Militärgeschichtliches Forschungsamt (the Armed Forces Military History Research Office) estimated that between 360,000 and 370,000 German civilians were killed by Allied strategic bombing during the Second World War during which sixteen square kilometers of Berlin were reduced to little more than rubble.

ACKNOWLEDGMENTS

Jonny Geller and the team at Curtis Brown for, once again, steering me through choppy waters, the team at Amazon—Andy Bartlett, Terry Goodman, and Alison Dasho—for giving me a shot, and Michael Trudeau for his judicious copyedit. Thanks are also due to the family members, friends, and colleagues who have offered thoughts and observations during the writing of this book.